Traci Harding live  a q
the Hawkesbury
talented husband, Da
year-old daughter, Sarah

After the success of the Ancient Future Trilogy, and
the overwhelming reader demand for more
adventures with Tory Alexander and co., Traci
Harding is currently sitting in her office overlooking
the river and mountains beyond in deep
contemplation of the continuing affairs of the
'Chosen Ones'.

You can write to Traci Harding at the following
email address: hardingd@ozemail.com.au

Or visit her on the worldwide web at the site of
'Artisus': http://www.ozemail.com.au/~hardingd

Masters
of
Reality
the Gathering

Traci Harding

HarperCollinsPublishers

Voyager
An imprint of HarperCollins*Publishers*, Australia

First published in Australia in 1998
Reprinted in 1999 (twice)
by HarperCollins*Publishers* Pty Limited
ACN 009 913 517
A member of the HarperCollins*Publishers* (Australia) Pty Limited Group
http://www.harpercollins.com.au

HarperCollins*Publishers*
25 Ryde Road, Pymble, Sydney NSW 2073, Australia
31 View Road, Glenfield, Auckland 10, New Zealand
77–85 Fulham Palace Road, London W6 8JB, United Kingdom
Hazelton Lanes, 55 Avenue Road, Suite 2900, Toronto, Ontario, M5R 3L2
and 1995 Markham Road, Scarborough, Ontario, M1B 5M8, Canada
10 East 53rd Street, New York NY 10022, USA

National Library of Australia Cataloguing-in-Publication data:

Harding, Traci.
Masters of reality: the gathering.
Bibliography.
ISBN 0 7322 5892 8.
I. Title.
A823.3

Cover illustration by David Harding
Printed in Australia by Griffin Press Pty Ltd on 50gsm Ensobulky

9 8 7 6 5 4 3   99 00 01 02

To David,
for his love,
his art,
his patience,
and belief in me.

Contents

PART iii THE HOLY GHOST

Acknowledgements

Firstly, I would like to thank all those readers who have patiently waited a whole year for this final instalment of 'The Ancient Future' trilogy — your letters and emails have been a great inspiration, bless you all.

A special hunk of gratitude to my husband, David, to whom I dedicate this book. Quite apart from his artwork, fast becoming famous, I wish to acknowledge his creative contribution to this story — I would have had great difficulty plotting industrial espionage without him.

Many thanks to my parents, all my friends, my agent, Selwa Anthony, and my editors, Sue and Stephanie. Their support and guidance has been essential to the completion of this work.

Last, but by no means least, I would like to thank all those at HarperCollins who have worked so hard to make this trilogy a success. A better publishing house I could not want — what a team!

CHARACTERS

The Crew of the *Goddess*, *Merlin I* and *Merlin II*
Tory Alexander (Thurlow)
Miles Thurlow
Rhiannon Thurlow
Brian Alexander
Naomi Alexander
Daniel Alexander
John Pearce
Jenny Pearce
Nicholas Pearce
Teo
Electro-mechanical Design Engineer —
Ray Murdock
Reporter — Noah Purcel
Psychic Diagnostician — Walter Cadfan
Cadfan's Secretary — Mary-Anne
Cadfan's Novice — Patrick Haze
Shaman/Healer — Thomas Mateus
Guardian of Britain — Mryddin
Mryddin's Sister — Aunt Rose

Watarrka
Tory's Son — Rhun
The Hacker (Code Breaker) — Floyd
Park Ranger — Pete Nangina
Japanese Geneticist — Dr Leigh Sukemi

International Crisis Agency
Head of I.C.A. — Doc Alexander
Doc's Secretary — Emma
Head of Doc's security team — Stanley Brennon
Doc's Computer Whiz — Eddie
I.C.A. Space Station — The Brunanburh

US Government
President of the U.S — Robert Langford
Vice President — Maxwell Hagar
Head of Defence Dept — General Berkley

Middle East
The Unken (circle of elders) — Terrorist Group
Leader of the Uken — Lugal/Shamash
The Daughter of Alexander — Neraida
Neraida's Son — Ethan
Neraida's Grandson — Eli

The Dragon's Line

Marduk - Nin Bau

Cunedda Wledig

Einion Yrth

Caswallon Lawhir - Sorcha   **Mryddin**

Caradoc   **Maelgwn - Tory**   **Brian - Naomi**
(Taken by the Otherworld)

Rhun   **Rhiannon**   **Daniel**
(Mysteriously vanished)

Cadwell
(Taken by the Otherworld)

Cadfan
(Mysteriously vanished)

Cadwallon
(Taken by the Otherworld)

Cadwaladr
(Mysteriously vanished)

PART I
THE
FATHER

I

THE PLATO
PROJECT — 2017

The *Goddess* was christened on the 4th of January, 2017. She immediately put to sea for six months of testing.

The bathyscape had submersible capabilities of up to ten thousand feet, and looked more like a spaceship than a sub. The interior was not cluttered and dingy like navy-designed vessels; the *Goddess* could comfortably accommodate thirty people. Combining the latest technology with luxurious living, she was the ultimate observation and research vessel made to date.

Tory Alexander and her brother Brian had commissioned the design and building of the submersible for a specific project they had in mind. It was entirely funded by their father, whom most of the world saw as the aging Professor Renford Alexander — Tory and Brian, who knew him better, named the submersible's two smaller reconnaissance subs after him: *Merlin I* and *Merlin II*. Each vessel had a separate holding bay that also served as a launch pad. They could disembark from the mothership either above or below the waters' surface. If submersed, the containment bays would be flooded, the hatch doors opened and the probe vehicles launched.

As the bathyscape was privately-owned, their project was beholden to no one. This was all-important because Tory had a map in her possession which identified the exact location of the lost continent of Atlantis, and she claimed that it pinpointed the major cities of this fabled landmass. The richest of these had been Chailidocean, Plato's 'City of the Golden Gates' that, according to Tory, was currently residing under ten thousand feet of water off the coast of Spain.

'Deep Sweep', a project based in the Azores and headed up by Dr John Pearce of the Institute of Oceanography, had for many years used navy-owned submersibles to explore the floor of the Atlantic. They had discovered many galleons and warships, but no evidence to support the theory of Atlantis.

John Pearce was an associate of Tory's husband, Miles Thurlow. Miles, Tory and Brian had joined the project early in 2001, intending to prove Tory's map to be correct, but the project had been put on hold around that time. The navy had recalled all their equipment after the Californian quake of 1999 had virtually destroyed an area stretching from Los Angeles to San

Francisco. In the years following, earthquakes and volcanic eruptions kept the Navy occupied with massive rescue and salvage operations, and 'Deep Sweep' was finally cancelled altogether in 2012.

Dr Pearce was somewhat of a sceptic with regard to the lost continent. He'd seen the rocky chasms and miles of vast white sand on the seabed of the Atlantic, but no traces anywhere of a superior culture that might once have existed. Yet Miles Thurlow was a Professor of Archaeology, one of the most highly regarded authorities on antiquity, and also a clever businessman. John knew Miles would never consider going into such a project, that had now been dubbed the Plato Project, if he wasn't at least ninety per cent certain it was a winner. John Pearce and his family were intrigued by the Project and were easily persuaded to join the team in the search for the lost continent.

After running the *Goddess* and her mini-subs through their paces in the shallow waters around the Azores in the first months of 2017, the hush-hush search for the lost city began on the 30th of June.

That day the weather in the North Atlantic was glorious. The sun was shining and the conditions were calm. There seemed no reason not to take advantage of it.

Most of the crew and the dive team were hovering around Sub Bay One as the hatch doors opened to expose *Merlin I* still perched in its cradle.

'*Merlin One*, this is the *Goddess*.' Teo's voice came through the headsets to Brian and Tory, who were already inside the tiny sub. 'Are we comfy?'

'Roger that.' Brian had to smile; compared to the navy submersibles they'd been diving in with 'Deep Sweep', Merlin I was a Rolls-Royce.

'Opening the Lower Sub Bay doors and lowering you down.'

'Lower away, Goddess.'

Divers followed the sub into the water, checking the vessel's descent weights before it could begin its fall into the deepest depths of the north-eastern Atlantic Basin.

'Goddess, I am releasing the safely line on Merlin One, and my blowers are on.' Brian pulled the lever above his head that detached them from the mother craft, and initiated the start-up sequence.

'Ah, roger that, Merlin … the divers tell me you're looking good. You have permission to dive.'

'Yeah!' Brian had been thinking that this day would never come. 'Tell Jenny and Co I'm flooding the ballast tanks and starting down.'

Tory peered out the small porthole just off to her left to see the divers give them the thumbs-up. 'Okay, we're outta here,' Tory informed base.

'You all come back now, you hear?'

Teo gave them leave to depart.

The journey took on a dreamlike quality as they descended at maximum speed into the silence of the blue-green depths; it would take them nearly two hours to reach the ocean floor, some ten thousand feet below.

The journey took on a dreamlike quality as they descended at maximum speed into the silence of the blue-green depths; it would take them nearly two hours to reach the ocean floor, some ten thousand feet below.

'Goddamn it, *Merlin*, come in!' Teo tried for the twentieth time to get a reply.

They had lost visual and voice contact with the sub. The crew in the support vessel on the surface watched their monitors indicating that *Merlin's* oxygen tanks had been damaged and were leaking rapidly. It also had numerous electrical difficulties as a result of a collision.

'They're going to run out of air.' Naomi, Brian's wife, was very close to a fit of hysterics. 'Even if they start their ascent now, they won't make it.'

Miles didn't seem as worried; he knew Tory too well. She always had a trick or two up her sleeve.

'They have stabilised.' Teo threw in glimmer of hope.

'*Goddess*, this is *Merlin*.' Tory's voice came over the intercom, receiving a round of applause, which quickly subsided when they all heard how grave her tone was. 'I have re-initiated the ascent sequence. Situation bad. I shall maintain radio silence to conserve oxygen.'

Teo was aghast, though his personal feelings did not reflect in his voice. 'Roger that. We'll be waiting.'

Naomi grabbed a headset. 'What about Brian?' When there came no response, tears began to well in her large icy-blue eyes, trickling down the small, pointed features of her face. 'Please Tory, talk to me. I just need to know he's okay.'

As Teo had lost his wife twelve years ago, when the volcano on Pico Alto exploded into life and showered the neighbouring island of Faial with debris, he could relate to how Naomi was feeling. Teo removed Naomi's headset and held her at arm's length. 'Wait here,' he advised. She pulled away, preparing to protest, but he didn't give her the opportunity. 'Chances are we're going to have to revive him. I'll let you know when we have.' Naomi gasped in horror and melted into a chair, the mere suggestion of serious injury being more than she could cope with.

'I'll stay with her.' Miles volunteered. It was easy for him to be calm; Tory was in no danger.

Teo gave a nod and made for the Sub Bay.

When *Merlin I* re-surfaced, Brian's son, Daniel, was the first diver in the water; he'd popped the hatch before the rest of the team had even finished securing the support lines. He climbed inside the cabin, fully expecting to find two dead bodies. To his great bewilderment, the submersible was empty.

Daniel was so stunned it took a moment for the discovery to sink in. As he stood staring into space a large droplet splashed against his forehead, startling him. He wiped the drop of moisture from his brow to find that it had stained the back of his hand.

'Blood!'

2

†HE GE∏E

'Taliesin?'

Tory paced up and down inside the large, regal entrance room to the Merlin's Otherworldly abode, her brother's dead body bleeding rivers along the cracks in the stone floor.

'Please be here! Tell me what I'm about to do is what was meant.'

Tory missed Taliesin's counsel after leaving her sixth century life to return to the twentieth century. She had no regrets, but the modern world was a far more frightening place than the Dark Age, especially without the High Merlin's guidance. But then, Tory had her father to turn to in this Age — provided she could find him. Tory could find most people with just a thought, but not Myrddin.

'You know he is not here, child.'

'Father!' Tory flew into his arms upon sighting him. 'Brian is …' She burst into tears.

'So I see.' Myrddin patted her back gently, urging her to calm herself. 'It's alright.' He left her to take a look at his boy.

'I have this potion.' She held out the little bottle that contained the precious brew she'd been saving all these years. 'I never gave it to its intended, because … well, it's a long story. Then Taliesin told me to save it, that it was meant for another. But how do I know Brian is that other? How do I know that he would even want to be immortal? God knows it's not all it's cracked up to be.' She marvelled at all she'd been through since becoming thus, and felt close to tears again. 'Taliesin said I would know who the right recipient was, but I do not.'

Myrddin raised a brow at her predicament. 'Well, I can tell you this much. Immortals are not made, they're born. The thing that sets them apart from normal human beings is the presence of a particular gene. This gene you inherited from your grandfather, my father.'

Tory's interest was engaged. Her father had never discussed her Otherworld grandfather with her. 'Did you know him at all?'

'I *do* know him, yes, but let's not get off the subject.' Myrddin didn't feel Tory was quite ready for that conversation yet. 'Now, if someone is born with this gene, but it is dormant, it would have to be genetically activated as was the case with you. And because the gene was activated before your children were born, as soon as they experience physical death their immortality gene will kick in.'

10

Tory's eyes widened. Now she understood. 'If the ET gene hadn't been activated by my death before I had Rhiannon, the ET gene in her would've been dormant, and she would die a normal death as Brian has.'

'Correct.'

'That means that even if I had given this to Maelgwn, it may not have worked?'

'Correct again. But rest assured, Maelgwn is also of the Serpent's clan via his great-grandfather Cunedda. He is in safe hands.' Myrddin smiled.

'So that only leaves Brian. This must be destined for him.' She breathed a sigh of relief and rushed to administer the life-giving elixir. Tory rested the open end of the little bottle at the side of her brother's mouth. 'Sorry for dragging you into this world of eternal turmoil, but hey … I wasn't given an option either.'

She let the liquid flow.

Everyone aboard the *Goddess* spent that evening trying to explain the unexplainable. Most were completely perplexed, but not Teo, Miles, Rhiannon or Naomi. They knew Tory was capable of physical teleportation; they'd seen her do it. The question for them wasn't *how*, but *why* — and where?

If Brian was still alive, why did Tory not transport him up to the ship for treatment? They had the equipment to cope with nearly any emergency that arose, and Pearce was a fine doctor. If Brian was dead, what was the point in taking him anywhere? His wife and son didn't know what to think, or feel.

'What a bunch of bums you lot turned out to be.' Brian stood in the doorway, hosting a smile that stretched from ear to ear. 'I disappear for five minutes and you all take a holiday.'

'Brian!' Naomi ran into his arms. 'You're okay?' She ran her hands over him just to check.

'Never better,' he assured her, brushing long ash-brown hair back off her face to kiss her forehead.

To those who viewed him, Brian didn't appear any different. Now that he was immortal he could project outwardly any appearance he chose. To Tory, however, he was no longer an aging fifty year old. Brian had returned to his prime, and looked no older than he had at thirty. All the grey in his hair had turned brilliant blond. His piercing blue eyes had come alive with youth and vitality, and the failing muscles of his body were now restored to their former warrior glory.

Daniel braced his father's shoulders, giving him the once-over. 'But how?'

'*Yes!*' Dr Pearce came forward. A logical mind such as his demanded an explanation. 'That's a very good question.'

Tory rolled her eyes, for when John was in one of these moods he was very like his sixth century incarnation, Sir Rhys. Although his dark hair was graying now, and his tall, slender form was rounder and slightly stooped, she could still see the wary knight in the doctor before her.

Brian smiled. 'Well, isn't it obvious?' He looked around, but everyone appeared to be none the wiser. 'It

… hell, I even spent six months in space, working on a tracking station.'

'Great Scott!' Tory backed up, her eyes rolling around as she put two and two together. 'It makes sense.'

'Well, I'm glad it makes sense to somebody.' Ray was still very confused. 'Who are you?' His eyes did another quick check around the piers. 'And don't you have anywhere we can talk that isn't quite so public?'

'Sure.' Tory wandered towards the gangplank to board the *Goddess*.

'You work for your husband then?' Ray collected his bag and followed her on board, admiring the vessel as he went.

'We're partners. He's the professor, my family own the rig.'

'You're shitting me?' The thought brought a smile to Ray's face for the first time in months.

'You ain't seen nothing yet.' Tory motioned him to follow her inside.

Ray got the grand tour of the *Goddess* and he was most impressed.

They were alone on the vessel this morning. The younger members of the crew had taken a small power boat to go snorkelling for the day. Everyone else was out shopping and picking up supplies or equipment parts.

'I can't believe you have a gym on board.' Ray shook his head at the sheer decadence of it while Tory made him a cappuccino.

'Most of us are fitness freaks here, and it helps the

was the Bermuda Triangle. It just sucked us straight out of the sub.'

'Off the coast of Spain? I don't think so.' John wasn't in the mood to play.

'Now, Brian, don't be cruel.' Tory freed herself from Rhiannon and Miles to approach the good doctor. 'The truth is, John, it was extra-terrestrials.'

Tory and Brian burst into laughter, as did everyone else — except John.

'You people are just too weird. I *demand* to know what happened.'

Most of those in the room could barely breathe for their hilarity. To them it didn't matter how Tory and Brian had been spared from the disaster, only that they had been. John couldn't accept that sort of miracle without some explanation; pondering such a paradox would drive him insane and it was already starting to.

'Come on …' John lightened up, thinking now that perhaps they were all playing an elaborate hoax on him. 'How did you do it?'

'It doesn't really matter, does it?' Tory calmed herself enough to place a hand on John's shoulder. 'Because in your reality, the only thing that's going to count is how *you* think we did it.'

Everyone jeered, knowing how Pearce hated being chastised for his scientific mind.

'Yeah, John.' Brain baited the doctor further. 'Let's hear your theory.'

'Oh, stop it.' Jenny hated to have her husband be the odd one out, and so stood up for him. 'He may be a little backward when it comes to the ways of the spirit, but he can't help that.' Everyone burst into laughter at this, and Jenny realised she was being just as cruel as his attackers.

'That's it,' he exploded suddenly. 'I have had it! I can't work in this three-ringed circus.'

Tory stepped forward to pacify him. 'Oh John —'

'Don't!' He held up a finger in warning. 'One of two things is going on here. One, this is a hoax, in which case you jeopardised this project with your fun and games. Or two, something amazing occurred during your dive this morning. Something that, for some reason, you feel I am not fit to be privy to. So which is it?'

My, but he was quick. Tory didn't know what to say, which seemed to anger John all the more.

'Well, somebody had better come up with some answers by tomorrow, or I am taking my family out of here.'

As Pearce headed for the door, his son intercepted. 'But Dad —'

John brushed past Nick without so much as a sideways glance, and stormed out the door.

'I am not going anywhere!' Nicholas announced to everyone in the room, his steely, blue eyes conveying his conviction.

Jenny made a move to pursue John, but Tory knew she was the only one who could really right the situation. 'No, Jenny. Please, let me go.'

Tory dropped by her cabin to pick up a few items which she kept stored in an old sports bag. She was a fool to think John would let a stunt like that pass, but the incident had happened too fast for her to think about how she was going to explain it.

'Tory, I don't want to hear any more of your hocus pocus bullshit,' he warned as she stormed into his cabin and cast down her hand luggage.

'Okay John.' Tory closed and locked the door behind her. 'You want to know what happened today?' She turned to challenge him. 'You're not going to like it. The truth is far more bizarre than our lies.'

'I hardly think so.' John took a seat to listen.

'Well, you'll be surprised,' she announced, flashing a grin.

'You can start with telling me what caused the collision.'

'The unidentified object we spied on sonar, just before we lost contact, was some sort of large deep sea creature.'

'A sea monster?' John scoffed.

'I kid you not,' she assured in all seriousness. 'It was quite docile, so it shouldn't be any further threat to us. I shall try and capture it on ROM for you, if it shows itself again. I also had another episode while we were down there, another vision.' Tory's eyes glazed over a moment, as she recalled the events this vision had foretold. Then, with a blink, she put them to the back of her mind. 'Brian was going to abort the mission to bring me, in my entranced state, back to the surface. But the sound of the ascent pumps must have startled the creature. It turned abruptly, colliding with *Merlin* and sending us into a spin. When I awoke … Brian was dead.'

15

John rolled his eyes in disbelief.

'Don't say a word till I'm finished. About four people in this planet know what I am about to tell you. I'm taking a hell of a risk. The least you can do is listen.'

'Alright, go on. Brian was dead and …?' He motioned her to proceed, obviously still sceptical.

'Look, I'll cut a long story short.' Tory figured she may as well let him have it. 'I brought Brian back to life with an Atlantean potion, which I got from that orichalchum ball you fished out of the ocean twenty years ago. But wait, I have proof.'

'This ought to be a hoot.' He sat, looking most unimpressed, as Tory rummaged through her bag of tricks to find the ancient device she'd used to track down the ball of rare metal.

'Do you recognise this?' She handed it to him and watched the smirk slip from his face.

'It once featured in a nightmare I had after hitting my head against a filing cabinet and knocking myself out cold.'

'No, John, that's just what Miles led you to believe,' she informed him in no uncertain teams. 'You were right. I did vanish with your treasure. I needed it to retrieve the life-giving potion I gave Brian today.'

John sat quietly for a few moments.

'Okay, just say you're telling me the truth. How did you know the potion was there?' he asked.

'The same way I know where to look for Atlantis. I've been there.' She resolved the question as if it were a foregone conclusion. 'Where do you think we got that map from?'

'Tory, I swear to God …' John was about to say something he'd regret.

'What, you don't believe me?'

Her glare was daring him to doubt her when, to John's great horror, she pulled a dagger from her bag and slit her wrist with it.

'*Jesus, woman.* Have you lost your mind?' He dived at her intending to do something to stop the bleeding, but by the time he got there it had already stopped, healed over and disappeared. He raised his eyes to look at Tory, mystified and dazed by what he'd seen.

Tory smiled. 'Do you believe me now?'

3

†HE LOS†

On the second attempt to probe the seabed beneath the north-eastern Atlantic, Project Plato changed its strategy and launched both *Merlin I* and *Merlin II*. If they ran into their monstrous friend again, one sub could be a decoy whilst the other made for the bottom.

Brian was piloting *Merlin I* with his son, Daniel, who was manning the camera. Tory and Rhiannon were in *Merlin II*. These two teams made for both sexual and family rivalry on the hunt. Teo was Tory's base-man up on the *Goddess*, as Naomi had chosen to guide her husband's descent.

It was nice having another sub to accompany you into the dark depths, Tory decided. A switch on the intercom allowed the two submersibles to converse solely with each other, with base, or both. Yet Tory hadn't heard from Brian since the launch; he must be taking this race to the seabed seriously.

'*Merlin Two*, this is the *Goddess*, you're halfway there and looking sweet.' Teo flirted ever so slightly, as neither Tory's brother nor her husband were within earshot.

'Well, thank you so much for noticing.' Tory played along, pausing from her system check to smile at his cheek.

'Don't encourage him.' Rhiannon gave her mother's shoulder a slap.

'Hah!' Tory had to laugh. 'Like you're a perfect angel.'

'I'm not married,' Rhiannon lectured. 'So I may tease men all I like.'

'Just tease?' Tory posed.

Rhiannon shrugged as she melted into a grin. 'Mostly.'

Tory snapped to attention as the sonar sounded its warning. 'It looks as if our big friend is territorial, after all.' They had hoped that he was a deep-sea drifter and so moved on.

'*Merlin Two*, this is the *Goddess*. Life-form reading. Ascending your way. Switch to decoy mode.'

Tory looked to her brother in the sub close by her, returning his wave.

'Copy that.' She veered *Merlin II* off due east, as Brian took *Merlin I* due west.

It was Teo's team that won the toss, and delight was reflected in his voice. '*Goddess* to *Merlin Two*. Brian has become fish bait. You have the all-clear to continue your descent.'

'Well, piss off and leave us then.' Brain grumbled. 'But you two had better come up with the goods, you hear?'

'Don't I always?' Tory was revelling in her good fortune. 'You just worry about yourself, 'cause I'm fresh out of miracles.'

Half an hour later *Merlin II* was stabilising and switching to the propulsion system. This gave Tory more manoeuvrability through the cavernous landscape of the sea floor.

'*Goddess*, this is *Merlin Two*, we are switching to short-range sonar, and diving. Cameras and floodlights are on. Please confirm visual transmission. Over.'

'The *Goddess* is with you, *Merlin Two*. You have permission to proceed.'

The sonar gave a solid echo bearing thirty degrees. According to their ancient map, this rise should prove to be the Mt Dur-an-ki plateau, located in the mountain range to the east of Chailidocean.

'Proceeding to target area,' Tory advised.

If the truth be known, Tory didn't need the sonar, lights or cameras to tell her she was close. This place pulsated with the unmistakable energy of a ley-line crossing — a gateway to the Otherworld.

'Wow!' Rhiannon commented, exhaling heavily.

'You can feel that?'

'Yeah … I can,' she confirmed, thinking it felt rather exhilarating.

Tory was following the contours of the land on the sonar very closely when Rhiannon spied the lip of the plateau through her headset, which was linked to the exterior camera on *Merlin II*.

'Land ahoy at eight o'clock,' Rhiannon informed base, zooming in and enhancing the image.

But as soon as the sub passed over the rim of the plateau, it lost all power and began to drop like a stone.

'Holy moley.' Tory steered hard right. They just managed to clear the ledge; power was restored and she regained control of the vessel.

'*Merlin Two*, this is *Goddess*. What the hell happened?'

'I lost power. I should have known.' Tory breathed a sigh of relief in the wake of a close call. 'Back in Atlantis this place was renowned for its alien frequencies.'

'*Merlin Two*. How do you know you've got the right place?' John had obviously grabbed a headset. 'We haven't *seen* anything yet.'

'Now don't get testy, Doctor. We'll get your pictures.' Tory brought the sub to a standstill and shot a line of cable into the cliff wall for a little extra anchorage.

'How, may I ask, do you expect to do that,' John persisted, 'if none of the electrical equipment will function?'

'John …' Tory was losing patience, 'you figure it out.' She threw down her headset and left the pilot's seat.

Rhiannon disengaged the camera headset. 'How am I supposed to know!' she answered John, who was still firing questions through the com-link. 'I'll call you back.' Rhiannon switched off, wondering why on earth her mother was putting on a wetsuit and flippers.

'Don't look at me like that.' Tory made light of the nightmarish thing she was about to do. 'It can't hurt me.'

'You've never tried something like this before? No one has!' Rhiannon began to fret.

'All the more reason to try it out.' Tory grabbed an underwater flare and a stills camera, hoping that both worked at the depth claimed by their manufacturers. 'It will be a whole new experience for the superconscious of mankind.' Tory vanished without so much as an oxygen tank.

'Hah!' Rhiannon was shaken for a second; her mother had pulled some crazy moves in her time, but this was beyond the beyond. 'And then they wonder why us kids end up so screwed up?'

Though her time exposed to the deep sea depths had felt like wading through icy cold mud, Tory didn't leave the site until she had a firm confirmation that it was the mount she believed it to be. With the aid of the yellow-green light of her hand-held flare, her efforts had proven most fruitful.

Tory had been surprised to find that sections of the site's large, quartz stone circle still remained and, digging a little way under the sand and soil on the ground, she uncovered pieces of the marble base. But the greatest discovery of the day was a solid gold altar box, engraved with the symbol of Caduceus. This was in the shape of a winged rod, with serpents entwining it in opposing directions. The sculpted rod had been the Atlantean symbol of the Lord of Time and Space, and this golden container had once housed the Ark of the

Covenant, though, unfortunately, it did not any longer. Perhaps it was best that such a powerful tool remained hidden from mankind for now.

Naturally, John was over the moon when he viewed the photographs. No other find had ever come close to this. He didn't even want to know how Tory had acquired them; 'whatever' was fast becoming his motto. And on subsequent dives, whilst dodging their large friend, which was identified by those in the know as a Plesiosaur, akin to the fabled monster of Loch Ness, the subs followed the mountain range down into the valley to find an antiquity-seeker's paradise.

The lost city of Atlantis was officially declared found on the 15th of July 2017. *Merlin I* and *II* had photographed several sets of large gates made of solid gold that were half-buried amongst the flattened city ruins. These were dated correctly at over 12,000 years old, which convinced even the greatest sceptics that this was indeed the city Plato had described in *Timaeus and Critias*.

Once again Professor Miles Thurlow and Dr John Pearce found themselves in the spotlight. Every university that taught ancient history, archaeology, or oceanography was inviting them to speak.

The *Goddess* returned to the port of Horta on Faial to meet the press and pick up supplies. Miles and John were embarking on a string of lectures, primarily in Britain and the United States, that were looking like keeping them away for the better part of six months. The remainder of the team would return to sea to continue surveying, and they would feed Miles and John any new photographs or information as it came to hand.

Though Tory knew this was all part of Miles' job, her last vision had foretold disaster, both natural and man-made. She didn't like it that her husband would be travelling throughout the two areas of the planet that were the most likely to be effected.

'Miles, couldn't you just postpone it for awhile?' She watched as her husband fastened his suitcase.

He looked at her as she knelt on their bed, wrapped up in a sheet. 'Tory, you really do make things difficult at times. Look, aren't you the one always telling me to trust in the universe?'

'Well, yes ... but the universe is telling me not to trust in the planet.' She crawled closer to him.

Miles glanced at the clock. 'And it's telling me to go, or I'll miss my connecting flight.' He kissed her to end the debate. He was going and the wrath of God would not stop him. There were still so many great scholars out there who thought, as he once had, that the present was as technologically advanced as mankind had ever been. But the Plato Project was now on the verge of blowing that theory right out of the water. 'Are you sure you'll be alright to handle the press here? I told you *National Geographic* are sending a guy.'

'No,' Tory frowned, 'you didn't.'

'I gave him permission to go to sea with you for a couple of weeks. He's doing a story on the dive sites and the *Goddess* facilities, and possibly our big fish. So make him feel at home. It could mean future projects for us.' Miles ruffled her hair to vex her further.

'Oh, my lord!' Tory suddenly rose and moved to the porthole window.

There was a young man seated on a suitcase on the dock outside, looking kind of lost.

'Could this be him?' she wondered aloud.

Miles looked out the other porthole to see a rather scruffy-looking man, roughly thirty years of age, who could have been mistaken for either a bum or, perhaps, a tortured genius. 'Must be.'

Tory pulled on her jeans and a T-shirt, and moved out onto the pontoon to investigate.

The young man in question had his eyes lowered to the ground as Tory's shadow fell over him.

'Are you lost?'

When he looked up to view Tory, the sun was shining through her long golden hair and shed a halo of light around her. He was so stunned upon seeing her eyes of violet that he fell backwards, taking his suitcase with him. 'I … t …'s you!' he stammered, trying to pull himself out of his embarrassing predicament. 'You actually exist! Jesus, there is a God!'

Even with the bushy growth on his face there was no mistaking Sir Bryce. Tory was certainly curious to hear the story behind this obviously more than chance meeting, and so helped him to his feet.

'Sorry about that. It's just such a shock.' He pushed his glasses back up his nose, and shook her hand firmly. 'The name's Ray Murdock. And ah, who might you be?' he inquired politely.

Tory hesitated to answer. It wasn't that she didn't

trust this stranger, for in reality he was no stranger at all. In the sixth century, this man had been the eldest son of a dear and valued friend. She wanted to get his end of the story clear first. 'Now, Ray. How can you know me, and not know who I am?'

Ray scratched his head through the masses of dark curls, pulled back into a long, ratty ponytail. 'I was kind of hoping you'd be able to tell me that.'

'You're not a reporter?'

'No way.' Ray had a chuckle and then paused to take a deep breath. 'Look, nothing I am about to say is going to make any sense, I'm warning you in advance. But what the hell, here goes. I had a dream about two weeks back —'

'The thirtieth of June?' Tory clarified.

'Yeah.' Ray figured that was about right. 'I was advised to seek you out, and told where you might be found. The voice in my dream told me you could hide me someplace, where no one on Earth would ever find me.'

Ray fell silent as he noticed Miles and John Pearce exiting the *Goddess*.

Miles approached in a rush and kissed Tory goodbye. 'I've got to run.' He regarded her a moment — six months was a long time to be apart. 'You must be from *National Geographic*.' Miles looked to Ray and shook his hand. 'Sorry I can't chat, but Tory will fill you in on everything.'

'Hold on.' Ray was confused. 'Who are you?'

'I'm Professor Thurlow,' Miles informed him, watching the outsider back up a few paces.

'And you two are married, I presume?' He waved a finger from Miles to Tory, wondering why such a raving beauty would marry a graying old professor nearly twice her age.

'Twenty years.' Miles was proud to announce.

How was that possible? This woman must be a lot older than she looked. 'Now listen, God.' Ray walked further away to address the sky. 'You didn't say anything about this *before* you sent me off on this ridiculous quest.'

'I think he's had one too many rough assignments,' Miles whispered sideways to Tory, then made a move to catch Pearce up. 'I'll see you in six months, maybe sooner if I can get away.' He blew her a kiss and gave a final wave.

Ray rubbed his hands briskly. 'Things are looking up.' He cocked an eye to the sky. 'You're off the hook, for the moment.'

'So, Ray.' Tory turned her attention back to him, folding her arms. 'Who's the no one you're hiding from?'

Ray closed the distance between them, seeming reluctant to confide in her. 'The CIA, the ICA, the Defence Department, NASA … you name it.' He stared her straight in the eye but she didn't flinch. She wasn't doubtful, fearful or shocked.

'Why?' Her eyes narrowed. 'What is it you do?'

'I'm an electro-mechanical design engineer cum technician.' His voice had dropped to a whisper, and his eyes did a quick scan of the surrounding area to be sure no one might overhear. 'I've designed all manner of scary shit for various government departments, in the US mainly. Everything from weapons systems to utilities

divers keep in shape.' Tory placed the coffee in front of him on the bar. 'A gym was our first major prerequisite, my bath was the second.'

'You have a bath on a bathyscape?' Ray was overwhelmed.

'Oh yes. It's all enclosed in its own little room, so it doesn't matter if the water splashes about.'

'But the water supply?'

'It has its own tank, and a filtration system to recycle the water.'

'Very clever,' he conceded. 'Completely frivolous, but clever.'

'Hello? Anybody home?'

'Oh shit.' Tory looked to Ray, stunned. 'That will be the reporter from *National Geographic*.'

'What!' His eyes nearly popped out of his head. 'The last thing I need is —'

'Shh,' she insisted. 'I'll handle this.'

'Why me, Lord?' Ray rolled his eyes and collapsed onto the breakfast bar, wrapping his arms around his head to hide.

'In here.' Tory came out from behind the bar to greet their guest when he came through the door.

The reporter struggled in with his bags, equipment, and cameras. His long, fair hair hung over his face, playing havoc with his line of vision. 'Hey there.' He dropped the hand luggage and shoulder bags, leaving only the four cameras that hung about his neck. 'Noah Purcel, *National Geographic*.' He swept the hair from his face to see who he was addressing, and held out his hand to Tory in a friendly fashion.

It took a moment for her to respond. *Selwyn*. Her heart leapt to see yet another ally from her distant past. He was of slight build, as Selwyn had been, and eyes of deep blue were set in a face that was open and full of expression.

She shook his hand. 'I'm Tory, the custodian and part-owner of the *Goddess*. On behalf of Project Plato, welcome aboard.'

'Thanks for having me.' He began turning in circles to check everything out. 'This is quite a rig you got here.' Noah noticed the large fellow slouched at the bar.

'You haven't seen the half of it,' Ray commented, without raising his head.

'This is Ray, our new on-board systems technician.' Ray raised one hand and waved. 'It's his first day, he hasn't quite got his sea legs yet.' Tory steered Noah toward the corridor. 'Allow me to show you to your quarters. Once we offload all this … stuff, I'll show you around.' Tory stood aside and motioned him out the door.

'It was nice not meeting you, Ray. Hope you're feeling better soon.' Noah received another wave from the technician as he left the dining quarters.

'Stay put,' Tory whispered to Ray. 'I'll be back.'

When they'd gone, Ray raised his head and wiped both hands down his face. 'That was … *scary*.' He looked at his reflection in the mirror behind the bar, stroking his long beard. 'Time for a change.'

Tory left Noah to unpack in his cabin. As all the guest quarters were located near one another, Tory decided to hide Ray in her cabin until such time as they could alter his appearance.

As it turned out, the fugitive had no personal effects with him. His suitcase contained books, notes, tools and a personal computer system. Tory rustled him up a pair of crew overalls, a towel, a shaver, and other bits and pieces he might need.

Ray now sat on the bed watching her, unable to really grasp the situation. 'I don't get it? Why would you do this? You know how much shit I'm in. Why risk all this on my account?'

'I'm not risking anything.' She dumped the bundle she'd put together into his arms. 'If they find you, I shall plead ignorance.'

He shook his head. 'You don't know these people.'

'And you don't know me.' Tory grinned.

'But somehow I get the feeling that you know me?' Ray knew he was right. 'And you haven't answered my question?'

'Well, Ray, the truth is, I have a feeling that very soon I'm going to require the services of someone with your technological expertise. You see, I also have had a vision,' she confessed. 'As a matter of fact, it would have been the same day you had yours.'

Ray dared to smile. 'Was I in it?'

'No, but something you might possibly design was,' Tory teased, raising her eyebrows. 'But more about that later. Right now, I'm going to leave you to it.' She motioned to the en suite.

'Yeah, but —'

'Uh!' She held up a finger. 'We can talk tonight,

once you've had time to *change*. Meanwhile, I'd better go show our reporter friend around.'

'Ah … Tory.' Ray detained her a second longer. 'Have I said "thank you" yet?'

She smiled, slowly shaking her head in the negative.

'Thank you,' he stated sincerely. 'This is a real miracle for me.'

'For me too,' she assured him.

4

THE PROPHET AND THE DIPLOMAT

None of the crew doubted Tory's word when she introduced their two newest shipmates ... except for her daughter. Rhiannon could sense her mother's anxiety at having both Ray and Noah in the same room, and as their new systems technician felt wary also, Rhiannon realised that she wasn't getting the entire story. But she knew the protocol, and said nothing to make anyone aware of her suspicions. She would just have to curb her curiosity until she could get her mother alone.

Ray was in Tory's cabin later that night telling her of the events that led to him fleeing the United States in fear of his life. He felt uneasy disclosing the information; if the Agency was prepared to kill one of their top designers because of what he knew, they certainly wouldn't hesitate to kill Tory. What *she* couldn't tell *him* was that she couldn't be killed. So Tory took the line that her Navy connections would protect her.

Ray said he'd always liked his work; it took him to interesting places, and gave him top security clearance in most government departments the world over.

The Californian quake had marked the beginning of a major world emergency, but it also began a shift towards greater global co-operation. The United Nations had set up a special organisation called the ICA (International Crisis Agency). This was headed by a financial whiz cum social strategist named Doc Alexander, who had been recruited from the IFC (International Finance Corporation).

The United Nations couldn't have picked a better man for the job. Doc Alexander was said to be a young, charismatic genius, although he had few close friends. A big supporter of 'global planning', he spoke many languages, and regarded all men and women as equals. He saw no countries, just land and sea; no races, just human beings. 'One world, one team,' was Doc's motto.

The movements of the Earth's surface due to plate-tectonics, the floods caused by the greenhouse effect, pollution, drought, famine, the slow tilt of the world's axis, the shrinking natural forests that would result in the slow suffocation of the planet, the general strain on the economy of dwindling resources; these were all global problems now, and Doc Alexander was aiming for global solutions. He brought together teams of scientists and technologists from all over the world to address the problems facing the planet. This was seen by the world, via the media, as a wonderful sign of lasting international peace and good relations. In its first ten years, the ICA proved to be a great success.

Doc's team working on the Greenhouse Effect, for example, estimated that the water level would continue to rise some twenty metres over the next century before it peaked and began to subside. With this information to hand, the ICA set about designing flood barriers that could act as artificial coastlines for those major cities that the world would not allow to succumb to the sea's will. New York was one such city, and the construction of its breakwater was already well under way.

Needless to say, Doc Alexander was fast becoming a worldwide phenomenon. After he had the logging of the Amazon rainforests banned on the grounds that they were needed to help reduce the amounts of carbon dioxide levels in the atmosphere, even the greenies loved him.

'So what was it you were working on, Ray?' Tory had already gathered he was employed by the ICA.

'I developed a system to monitor a fusion reactor. It warned of impending fluctuations or instabilities in the reactor.'

Tory's eyes widened in anticipation. 'You were successful then?'

'That I was.' Ray seemed kind of proud of himself, despite what he'd been party to. 'It wasn't until I was briefed on my following assignment that I found out the ICA were actually after power of another sort.'

'Yes?' Tory urged; it was like being enthralled by a really good spy thriller.

'Well, well.' Rhiannon entered, closing the door behind her. 'There's a strange man on my mother's bed, and father's not even been gone a day?'

Tory knew the accusation was a joke to make Ray feel uncomfortable. 'I don't recall hearing you knock, sweetheart. You might have interrupted something *important*.'

'Look.' Rhiannon folded her arms. 'I kept my mouth shut in front of everyone else, but I think I deserve to know what's going on. Who are you really?' Her cool glare turned to Ray. 'Who are you hiding from?'

'Jesus.' Ray sat up, amazed as he looked from Tory to Rhiannon and back again. 'She's just like you. A little less subtle, perhaps.'

'Just answer the question.' Rhiannon stared him down with eyes so black, they gave the illusion they were deep purple.

'Down, girl,' Tory intervened. 'It's a very *long* story, which Ray *was* in the process of telling me. If you calm down, you may stay.'

Ray stood. 'I don't think so. She's just a girl.'

'Look Ray,' Tory pushed him back down. 'Rhiannon is telepathic, so she'll find out anyway.'

'Yeah, right,' he scoffed.

Rhiannon gripped hold of his wrist and closed her eyes. 'The last time you got laid was ...?' She smiled. 'Whoohoo, just last night,' she announced, laughing at his dismay.

Ray snatched his arm back. 'You could have guessed that.'

Both women were staring back at him with their eyebrows raised and hands on hips.

'Relax,' Tory advised him. 'She can't read your mind unless she's touching you. Still, between Rhiannon and I, nothing is sacred. If you tell *me* your woes, you tell her.'

Ray calmed down, but was still staring at them as if they were some sort of advanced alien species. 'I think I'm beginning to see why God sent me here.'

The assignment that changed Ray's mind about the ICA was the designing of a special mechanical glitch for each power storage unit on the world fusion grid. He hadn't been told all the details at his first briefing, and Ray guessed the Agency were testing his resolve. He already knew too much about the secret fusion project for the ICA to just let him walk if he decided not to play ball. So, as he had no other option, Ray decided to co-operate. But that night he'd had the vision concerning Tory.

'And, as God is my witness,' Ray swore, 'the next morning I awoke in a field that was miles from the ICA facility where I had gone to sleep. All I had were the clothes on my back, and the stuff in my case. Still, I don't think I was followed.'

'You could have sleepwalked,' Rhiannon put forward.

'Straight through all the Agency's security measures? I think not.' Ray rubbed his weary eyes.

'Well, maybe you have the ability to travel without moving,' Rhiannon began. 'Mum can —'

'Ah!' Tory jumped in before her daughter said too much. 'Ray, you look totally stuffed. Maybe you should get some rest, hey?' She moved to see him out the door. 'We'll have plenty of time to postulate *theories*,' she impressed on Rhiannon, 'once we're out at sea.'

By nightfall of the following day the *Goddess* had made the trip back to the dive site once again.

Noah was eager to have his first ride in a bathyscape, but as he could not drag any of the pilots away from the television set to take him joy-riding he resigned himself to waiting until the scheduled dives the next day.

The television report that had everyone so fascinated was about a psychic diagnostician and healer named Walter Cadfan. Cadfan had risen to fame over the past ten years due to his ability to diagnose people's ailments and advise treatment without ever having to see the patient. But it wasn't the miracles he'd been performing that had the crew of the *Goddess* so engrossed. He, too, had experienced visions on exactly the same dates as Tory and Rhiannon, the last of which was the 30th of June. However, Cadfan was better at predicting the time and place the foreseen events would take place than they were.

'Those who have read my latest predictions will know that …' The middle-aged, slightly balding healer turned his droopy, blue eyes from the interviewer to address the camera directly, 'by the time this interview goes to air, large tremors in Denmark and England will cause large areas of those countries to fall into the North Sea, where a new land is emerging.'

'But dad's in England.' Rhiannon's fearful eyes turned to her mother.

'Is this some kind of joke?' Brian became angered as the station interrupted the program for an emergency news bulletin.

Teo came bursting into the rec-room, looking like he'd seen a ghost. 'There's been a quake in the U.K. The waves will hit us in a little over two hours.'

He didn't have to say any more; everyone was already making for their stations.

'Looks like you'll get your wish after all,' Tory informed Noah.

'Could I dive with you?' he appealed, throwing the straps of numerous bags across his body for easy cartage.

Tory gave a shrug. 'I don't see why not.'

'Bonus.' Noah made after her to Sub Bay Two.

Minutes later the divers were in the water with *Merlin I* and *Merlin II* making sure they were okay to dive. The two mini-subs would guide the mothership down. Once submerged deeply enough inside the Atlantic basin the north-eastern wall would protect their craft and the wave should pass straight over them.

'Hatches are all secure,' Jenny's voice advised through the intercom to those in the *Goddess'* control room. 'We're clear to dive.'

'*Merlin One* and *Two*. I am pleased to advise that the *Goddess* is going down,' Teo broadcast with a chuckle, throwing the switches to flood her tanks.

'Are you alright?' Tory enquired of her mystified passenger, whose eyes were fixed on *Merlin I* which he could see outside the large porthole in front of him.

'What a life,' Noah mumbled. 'There couldn't be a safer place on the planet.'

'Don't let the peace give you a false sense of security. Down here nature rules, and we're the invaders.' Tory gave a thought to the two members of their team that weren't there, and fell silent to continue her system checks.

The headset, the eyes for the exterior camera, captured Noah's interest. 'Is this for stills or film?' He placed it on his head and the lights went out. 'Geez, you can't see much.'

Tory reached over and switched it on. 'It's CD ROM. So you just take the stills from the moving footage.'

Noah was waving his arms around in front of himself, as if trying to swim through the water. 'Holy smoke, I'm out there!'

'You certainly are.' Tory placed one of his roving hands on the control stick, and the other on a set of buttons. 'The movement of your head controls the angle of the camera.'

Noah looked from left to right, getting a feel for it. 'Whoa!'

'The joystick guides the remote when the camera is mobile. The buttons at your left hand are your zoom, wide angle, and filters.'

'This is amazing!' He sounded put out. 'Why did I bother carting all my stuff?'

'*Merlin One*, this is *Merlin Two*. I'm picking up a large life-form reading and that can only mean one thing.' The sonar in front of Tory was pinging and tracking a large shape.

'Roger that, *Merlin One*. I have him too,' Brian answered.

'Me, three,' Teo cut in.

'We'll try to lead him elsewhere.' Tory switched on her propulsion system and took off after Brian, whereupon he veered left and she right.

'Yee-ha.' Noah was still hooked up to the camera. 'This is excellent!'

'I beg to differ.' Tory's eyes did not waver from the controls. 'Our big friend isn't worried about our tiny craft. But I don't know how it will feel about something as large as the *Goddess* invading its territory.'

Noah removed the headset, the information grabbing his attention. 'Danger … good, there must be a story in this.' He grabbed for his folder.

'O-oh.' Tory swung her rig around, almost throwing Noah from his seat as she brought *Merlin II* to a standstill.

'*Merlin One* to *Merlin Two*. He's not taking the bait.' Brian sounded more than a little annoyed. 'I'm heading back.'

'I'm with you, bro.' Tory looked over to Noah, who was madly scribbling notes. 'Make yourself useful. Get that headset back on and keep an eye out for Moby Dick.'

'Aye, aye, captain.' Noah jumped to the call, thrilled by the notion of being part of such a team — if only for an hour or so.

Teo had stabilised at a depth of five thousand feet. Tory had the *Goddess* and *Merlin I* within her sights when Noah cried out.

'Down there!' He blindly pointed off to the right.

Tory swerved to avoid getting in the monster's way. '*Merlin Two* to the *Goddess*. We have visual at four o'clock.'

'I copy *Merlin Two*.' Teo was sounding surprisingly calm. 'Stabilise at a safe distance, and stand by.'

All they could do now was wait and see how the huge beast was going to react.

The creature was drifting slowly towards the mothership.

'This is the most incredible thing I've ever seen.' Noah sat, frozen into stillness.

He could see the picture of the huge ancient creature face to face with the space-age sub plastered across the cover of every major newspaper and magazine in the civilized world. The tip of the beast's great snout eventually touched the bathyscape so gently that those in the *Goddess* didn't even feel the impact.

'I think it's in love.' The scene was so heartwarming that it brought a tear to Tory's eye.

On the bridge at the *Goddess*' controls, Teo and Naomi were looking straight into the eyes of the huge monster.

'Do you think he'd understand if I told him we have a headache?' Naomi attempted humour.

Teo was not happy; a couple of thousand feet lower and he could have shot some support lines into the basin wall. He didn't want to activate anything, to save alarming the beast, so they seemed to be stuck.

'We've got less than an hour till wipe-out.' Naomi updated their state of affairs. 'So we'd better think of something.'

Rhiannon entered the control room at full steam, then slowed as her eyes met with the much larger ones outside the ship.

'What are you doing up here?' Teo quizzed, though there was no response from the girl. She stared at the beast and closed her eyes.

We must go, there is danger for us here. Rhiannon willed the creature to back up.

After a moment, the beast slowly turned out of their path.

Teo frowned, bemused by what he suspected was happening. *Nah,* he decided, it was just a happy coincidence. 'We are clear to continue the descent,' he informed the others.

The *Goddess* surfaced the following day, unscathed. In their watery bed, they'd not even felt the killer waves pass over. Those on the Azore Islands would not have been so fortunate. If this quake had happened one day sooner, when the *Goddess* was in port, most of her crew would be dead.

As far out to sea as they were, the sky was dark with soot and the sun burned red. One would have thought the scenes described in The Book of Revelations had surely come to pass, but they had seen this eerie scene at other times in the last twenty years.

Walter Cadfan's vision proved not to be as destructive as he'd described, though most of the ash and smoke in the air was the result of the new land rising in the North Sea. A volcano had burst through the sea floor spewing lava that solidified in the cool water to form its own small landmass. Denmark and Britain had felt the shock waves of this, but the damage and death toll had been minimal. Still, if one considered the effect of this disaster upon the gradually rising tide levels, most of these two countries would eventually end up underwater as Cadfan foresaw.

News of Miles and John didn't reach their families until the following day. They'd survived the ordeal in Britain and managed to get themselves into the newspapers in the process. The old university hall where they'd been lecturing at the time of the quake had partly collapsed.

The majority of the faculty and staff were seated near the back of the large amphitheatre, and were close to the roof when it fell. Some two hundred students had been trapped. So, as opposed to giving a talk on digging up ruins, Miles and John set about organising an on-the-spot demonstration of how to dig your way out of one.

This story, on top of the publicity they'd already stirred up with the Plato Project, landed Miles and John on the guest list of a United Nations charity ball for the quake victims. This was held at the UN premises in London, two weeks later, after the clean-up was well underway.

As John had disappeared to the bar, Miles planted himself in a quiet corner of the room to read the article *National Geographic* had done on the *Goddess* and the sea monster. The picture of the sub and the plesiosaur was the cover story, and the article featured a beautiful photo of Tory manning *Merlin II* during the event. Miles admired this photo for some time; the three weeks they'd been apart felt more like three years.

'Professor Thurlow, I presume.'

Miles was startled from his fantasy to find a slick young man waiting to present himself. Blond-haired and blue-eyed, this corporate paragon exuded vitality and drive. He was surrounded by an entourage of five or six people, all hovering about him while he awaited the Professor's attention.

'Doc Alexander, ICA.' He held out a hand, his beaming smile exposing a perfect set of brilliant white teeth.

Miles recognised his name from the invitation and closed the magazine. 'I am sorry. It's my wife's rig you know?' Miles flashed the cover as he shook the diplomat's hand.

'I know, I read it … fantastic project, lovely wife.'

Miles felt disturbed — he'd expected someone much older to be in the ICA's top position. 'Thank you. I consider myself very fortunate.'

'She's Professor Renford Alexander's daughter, so I believe?'

The man was only making polite conversation, but for some reason it bothered Miles. 'Do you follow Professor Alexander's work?' he queried.

'I do.' Doc took a very interested stance and folded his arms. 'We're distantly related, so they tell me.' He shrugged it off as hearsay. 'But I *am* fond of British antiquity.'

'Really?' This surprised Miles, as Doc seemed a one hundred percent American kind of guy.

'In fact,' Doc took Miles underarm to walk with him, 'there's a piece in my office upstairs that I bought a few weeks ago … but I have an *awful* feeling I got screwed on the price. Could you take a quick look at it for me? Tell me what you think.'

'Sure.' Miles looked around for John, who was nowhere to be seen.

'This way.' Doc accompanied Miles to the stairs, motioning his own following to stay put.

They entered a spacious office that was dimly lit. The room contained some truly lovely antiques; both its furnishings and works of art were exquisite.

'Why is it,' Miles posed as he observed a beautiful medieval painting on the wall, 'that you look and sound like an American, but have the tastes of an Englishman?'

Doc was taken aback a moment, but smiled resolutely. 'A Briton, you mean.'

'Do I?'

Doc motioned Miles to take a seat. 'I am American by birth. But I was educated here, and my ancestry is here. You see this?' He diverted the professor's attention to a model that was in a glass case by the desk. 'This will be the ICA's first space station. I am naming her the "Brunanburh."

'After the Battle of Brunanburh?' Miles was curious to hear why. Dated at 937 AD, this two-day skirmish had seen the Briton's forced into recognising the Kingdom of England.

'I thought some good should come of it,' was Doc's reply.

'Fair enough.' Miles took a seat, starting to feel a mite uneasy. 'So, which piece do you want me to evaluate?'

Doc's exuberant mood left him as he came to stand over his guest. 'You can drop the front, Professor, I know who and what you are.'

'Sorry?' Miles went to stand, but Doc thrust him back into the seat and held him there, one hand clenched round his throat.

'God, Maelgwn. You really let yourself go to hell.'

'Maelgwn!' Miles swallowed. Who the hell was this guy if he could identify Tory's first husband, who hadn't walked the Earth since 540 A.D.?

'Please don't play dumb, Your Highness. The Goddess who is your other half would never bond with anyone but the Dragon.'

Does he mean Tory? Miles fretted on the quiet.

That I do. Doc took delight in Miles' horror, as the Professor realised his mind was being invaded. 'Or perhaps you're just an incarnation, and not really Maelgwn at all.' Doc glared deep into the Professor's eyes. 'Only one way to find out.'

Noah had enjoyed every minute of his time with Project Plato, and he considered most of her crew good friends.

The *Goddess* was heading for port at the end of the week, and all aboard seemed of the impression that Noah would be disembarking then.

'Can I talk to you?' He cornered Tory in her office amidst a pile of paperwork.

'Ah-ha,' she affirmed, not pausing from her search for a missing invoice. 'I'm listening.'

Noah entered, closing the door. He took a seat and waited until Tory could give him her full attention.

When she realised he wasn't saying much Tory ceased her fruitless activity to oblige her young friend, whose expression seemed rather grave. 'Sorry, Noah. Is something the matter?'

'I want to work for you,' he stated plainly.

This request threw her a moment, though it came as no surprise. 'But what about National —'

'I'm freelance. I have no assignment planned for the near future. Though I can't say I haven't had offers.' He smiled at the acclaim his latest stories had brought him.

Tory rubbed her forehead. Despite the fact that she was fast becoming as fond of Noah as she had been of Selwyn, it was nightmarish trying to maintain Ray's cover with a reporter on board. But a fugitive was not the only secret the *Goddess* was harbouring. If Noah had been anyone but a member of the press, Tory wouldn't have thought twice about taking him on.

'I could do the written and photographic records of the expedition,' he suggested. 'I could even write book!'

'Whoa there!' Tory threw up both hands in defence. 'This may surprise you, Noah, but I don't really want the whole world knowing everything that happens on board this vessel. And just for the record, you didn't ask to use that photograph of me in your article either.'

'But it's a beautiful photograph.' Noah appealed to her vanity. 'You're a beautiful woman.' He curbed his enthusiasm, realising he had overstated his case already.

Tory supported her head, trying not to look amused. 'Flattery will get you nowhere, Purcel, and furthermore, you're missing the point.'

'I know,' he admitted, looking anywhere but at her. 'But you didn't strike me as the kind of woman who —'

'Who *what*?' Tory raised her eyebrows, intrigued to hear his impression of her.

'Who,' he paused, 'who would agree.' Noah shrugged.

'That's not what you were going to say.' Tory could sense that Noah was holding back something, and would have pursued the truth had Ray not entered all in a tizz.

'Tory. Have you seen th—' When Ray spotted Noah present, he took his beef straight to him. 'Rhiannon told me you used this photo of Tory in your article.'

'Yeah, it's a great photo.' Noah stated, on the verge of being irritated.

'A *great photo*! Are you kidding me? The lights all screwy or something.'

'What do you mean?' Noah grabbed the photograph, all offended.

'Pardon my saying so,' Ray glanced at Tory, 'but it makes her look like she's fifty.'

'Ray, I am fifty,' Tory lied. She was, in fact, closer to seventy.

'Yeah, but you hardly look thirty,' he announced.

'Really?' Tory stood up, fascinated by his dilemma. 'Noah, would you excuse us a moment. I'll get back to you on that other matter presently.'

'Sure.' Noah looked a little worried about Ray as he passed by him. Was this guy nuts or what?

Tory closed the door and turned to back to Ray.

'What's wrong with him?' Ray wanted to know. 'Don't you think it was a bad picture?'

This image Ray seemed to have of her had Tory curious. Besides Taliesin, Myrddin and Brian, who were themselves immortal, everyone else on this planet was supposed to see Tory as a fifty year old, for that was how she chose to be seen. 'Would you do me a favour, Ray, and I don't want you to misconstrue this as a come on, but would you describe how I look to you?'

'Ah, look.' Ray backed up. 'You're happily married, as everyone on board has gone to great pains to impress on me. I am also advised that you are a five times black belt in Tae-kwon-do. I think I'll pass.'

'Ray, Ray, Ray.' Tory shook her head, holding out her hands as she approached him. Ray, enchanted to have Tory's undivided attention for a change, let her take hold. 'Just a simple description is all I ask.'

She perceived a great flash of light, and then an image of herself appearing just as she saw herself.

'Hey, hold on.' Ray pulled away, holding a finger up in caution. 'I know what you're doing.'

'Ray, how did I look in your vision?'

'That's kind of personal don't you think, Mrs Thurlow?' Ray got all offended, thinking she was making sport of his feelings.

'Ray?' She smiled. 'I think I may have a clue as to how it was you escaped the ICA without being detected. Now, did this dream of your's in any way involve a fairy wood and a white shimmery dress.'

'It might have.' He scowled, sounding both astounded and annoyed.

'What else?' she hounded him.

'You were surrounded by a very bright light, which brought out the colour in your eyes.' Ray gazed down into them. 'It was windy, you were crying …'

'Maelgwn,' she uttered, her heart pounding in her chest at the mere thought of him. *These are his memories.*

'Who?' Ray frowned, as the phone began to ring.

'Never mind.' She took the call. 'Hello. That's okay, who is it, Jen? The UN!' Tory's eyes shot straight to Ray, who went white. 'What do they want? Well, if they insist, you'd better put them on. Hello. This is she.'

Tory went pale suddenly. 'What kind of tragic occurrence? A heart attack!' Tory sank to a seat on the desk, tears building as her sorrow welled. 'Where is John Pearce? I see. Thank you.' Tory dropped the phone.

'Tory. What's happened?' Ray rushed to support her as he thought she might faint.

'Miles is dead.' Her voice went hoarse. 'Cardiac arrest, they said.'

Ray didn't know what to say as she fell sobbing into his arms. He hadn't known Tory's husband very well, and although to Ray this might seem like a fortunate turn of events, he hated to see her suffer. 'Is there anything I can do?'

Tory drew away from him abruptly, shutting off her emotions just like that. 'Yes, there is something you can do, if you would. Please find Rhiannon and send her to me.'

As soon as Ray opened his mouth to speak, a whimper slipped from Tory's lips. He decided to say nothing and just leave her to grieve in peace.

5

İ SPY

The funeral service was held on the dwindling Isle of Anglesey, at the site of Miles and Tory's last major project, the restored temple of the Goddess.

Miles and Tory's cottage by the seaside on Anglesey had long since been lost to the rising seas. But the mountains around the valley at Lynn Cerrig Bach still protected the sacred site.

From the temple it was a short walk up the mountainside to the cliffs overlooking the sea. Here the Professor's ashes were to be scattered to the four winds, over the submerged land where Miles had been born and raised.

Ray remained on board the *Goddess*, which was moored near the new Menai Bridge, on the Anglesey side.

Everyone else went to the service, including Noah. He was still hanging around as he reckoned he could sense a story in the wind. Noah didn't feel right hassleing Tory about a job, present curcumstances being as they were. Still, until she gave him her final answer, he wasn't going anywhere.

What was planned as a small family affair ended up looking more like a holy pilgrimage. The High Druids, the custodians of the temple, performed a beautiful pagan service. Scholars and students came from all over Britain and England to pay Professor Thurlow homage, along with the two hundred or so students whose lives he'd helped save during the most recent disaster. The UN had representatives from the ICA present. Even Doc Alexander made an appearance to pay his condolences.

Needless to say, Noah got his scoop.

Although the diplomat had been watching Tory from behind his dark sunglasses throughout the service, once it was over, he waited until most of the other mourners had offered Tory their sympathies before he approached her.

'Mrs Thurlow. I'm —'

'I know who you are,' Tory informed him, her bitterness plain in her tone. 'You were the last person to see my husband alive.'

'Yes ma'am.' He removed his sunglasses and bowed his head sorrowfully. 'To my deep regret, that is true. But his last thoughts were of you, and your daughter. If there is anything I can do, I —'

'There is nothing, thank you.' Tory forced a grim smile, and patted his hand. Why should she leave this young man feeling responsible? Miles had been nearly sixty, after all.

Just that brief touch told Doc so much. He replaced his dark glasses to watch Tory depart. 'Well, who would have thought?' he mused. He gave half a laugh, motioning one of his associates to approach.

The real surprise visitor amongst the mourners gathered at the burial site was Walter Cadfan.

He, too, had read the article on 'The *Goddess* and the Sea-monster' that named Mrs Miles Thurlow as Professor Alexander's daughter. He'd finally found her: Tory Alexander. The Goddess of legend, the great mother, warrior, and leader of men.

'Lady.' He reached out of a crowd of people to gently take hold of her arm and gain her attention. 'You don't know me —'

'Of course we do.' Rhiannon was pleased to meet him. 'You are Walter Cadfan. We've been following your work with great interest.'

'Thank you, I've been following your work very closely too,' he told her.

Tory noted that a crowd of calm, smiling people had enclosed them while they were in conversation with the guru, acting as a human shield. Cadfan took hold of Tory's hands, and although Tory had never met the man before, either in this life or in any other, for some reason she felt very comfortable with him. It almost seemed as if he were kindred.

55

'Please do not be alarmed when I tell you what I must.' Cadfan's large soulful eyes of hazel had shifted back to Tory. 'A voice from the spirit-world gave me a message for thee.' He broke into Brythanic to deliver it. 'Do not grieve too much, for thou art well aware thy husband lives on in the body of another, and thou art never far from his thoughts.'

Tory gasped, holding her hands to her face to hide her shock.

'All the eyes of the world art upon thee now, but thee must stay hidden, for the Gathering is not yet nigh. The means to avoid those who would persecute thee lies in the old land, as surely as thee will find sanctuary in the heart of thy homeland.'

Tory looked at him directly. 'Did this spirit have a name?'

Cadfan nodded, 'Surely. The Dragon of the Isle.'

Cadfan did not linger long, though his words most certainly did.

In the cab on the way back to their vessel's mooring, Tory revised what the prophet had said about the Old Land and her homeland. Funnily enough, the land down under had been spared from the natural disasters the Earth was experiencing. In fact, Australia was prospering more than ever before — proving it truly was a lucky country.

Her mind then turned to the Dragon of the Isle, and the day they'd met; Maelgwn had been but a Prince then, wild and charming. She lay her head to rest against the back of the seat, for she felt his essence descend on her in waves. His energy, his scent, was all around her, so Tory closed her eyes to quietly enjoy the calming and arousing effect of his memory.

Her blissful state was short-lived, as her next thought was of the first time she'd met Miles. She really hadn't liked the sceptical young professor very much. But, as Miles and Maelgwn were one and the same soul–mind, Tory couldn't help but fall for him.

The incarnation is gone, but the soul lives on. She sniffled back the tears that were welling for the umpteenth time today. *We'll meet again ... Goddess, make it soon.*

When the funeral party returned to the *Goddess*, they found her abandoned; Ray and his suitcase were gone.

They did an extensive search of the craft, until Teo and Brian started pouring drinks at the bar in the rec-room. Everyone gathered there to ponder what might have become of the missing engineer.

'Do you think *they* caught up with him?' Rhiannon whispered to her mother on the quiet.

Even over the din of speculation already flying around the room, Noah managed to overhear her. 'Who is *they*?' He passed their drinks on from the barman as an excuse to get in on their conversation.

'The ICA,' Tory informed him. It didn't seem to matter if Noah found out now.

'What!' He freaked out. 'You had a fugitive from the ICA on board and I didn't find out about it?'

'Well, it wasn't really something I wanted showing up in *National Geographic*.' Tory had a long gulp of her drink.

'I'm deeply wounded, madam.' He covered his heart with both hands, and staggered back a few paces. 'I would never betray you in such a fashion.'

'And Ray?' Tory put forward.

'Hey, Ray's a little nuts, I'll grant. But I would no sooner betray a friend of yours, than I would you.'

'You really want a job, don't you?' Tory guessed this to be the motivation behind the heartfelt confession.

'Yeah, yeah, yeah.' He played along like an obedient puppy, whimpering and begging for attention.

'Alright,' Tory announced with a smile.

Noah clapped his hands. 'Bonus!'

'Wait … there is a condition.'

The young reporter quietened immediately, brushing his straggly blonde hair behind his ears and giving Tory his complete attention. 'Yes, boss.'

This made Tory smile, and she appreciated it. 'Nothing you see, shoot, read, hear, or record on this vessel is to be repeated in any way, shape, or form without my say-so.'

'Yes, boss.' He rubbed his hands briskly, appearing most pleased with himself. 'So then. Do you think the ICA had a hand in Ray's mysterious disappearance?'

Tory winced as she answered. 'How could they know, or even suspect, where he was? If they'd seen him board, they would have reclaimed him weeks ago.'

'Could your husband have said something?' Noah's naturally curious mind was already hard at work, running through the logical possibilities.

Tory shook her head. 'At the time he left, he thought Ray was you, a reporter.'

58

'Well, some of their agents were at the funeral today.' Noah put forward his second theory. 'Did you say anything around them?'

'Noah, if you haven't found out about Ray and you've been living with us for a month, do you think I'd manage to blow his cover in less than a day?'

'My mistake.' Noah bowed out.

'The only person you even spoke to was that Alexander bloke.' Rhiannon chewed her long thumbnail as she recalled the scene. 'And he was quite a babe, really.' She raised both eyebrows and grinned.

'Well, he gave me the creeps.' Tory shivered. 'Something about the way he was looking at us.'

Her memory of Doc Alexander got Tory to wondering about him. She excused herself from her friends and family on the premise that she needed to rest awhile.

'Mum, are you alright?'

Rhiannon entered Tory's bedchamber only moments after Tory had arrived there herself.

'Mother!' Rhiannon crashed against the door to close it, stunned by the transformation.

'You think it's too much?'

Her mother's eyes had turned a pale-blue colour, like ice, and her skin was the shade of dark copper. Her golden blonde hair had gone snow-white and, although it still fell to her behind, it was shaved on both sides, Mohican style. She wore black leather chaps over jeans, like a cowboy, and steel-capped boots. A black singlet and vest exposed her muscular arms and the silver bands clamped around them. It looked as if her mother was going to a New York gang war.

'You're going after Ray, aren't you?'

'Do you think anyone will recognise me?' Tory perused her dark make-up in the mirror, then placed the silver, gold and orichalchum headband upon her brow.

'I'm coming with you.'

'Baby, I can't transport both you and Ray at the same time.' Tory pulled on her leather gloves.

'But I can transport myself. I've been practising.' Rhiannon was nearly begging now.

'Could you still focus with someone firing bullets at you?' Tory proffered.

'You know I could.' She took a step away. 'And I haven't forgotten how to play dress-up either.' Rhiannon closed her eyes to be creative. Her mother had often played this game with her as a child. Although it had seemed nothing but harmless fun and a big secret at the time, Rhiannon realised later in life that it had been training.

Moments later, Rhiannon was completely bald, bar a long ponytail of bright red that shot from her crown. Her face and most of her body was tattooed with a black Pictish style war-motif. Rhiannon's choice of attire was much like her mother's, only she wore shorts and a red singlet to match her hair.

'Truly gross!' Tory shook her head. What kind of a girl had she raised? 'I think the nose ring is a bit much though.'

'What? You don't like it?' Rhiannon admired her hideous reflection.

'What if somebody rips it out?'

Rhiannon didn't seem to find this notion a very pretty one. 'You're right, it's got to go.'

'*What in hell's name are you two doing?*'

Brian was hoisted into the room by both women, being hushed in the process.

'You're just the person I need to see.' Tory informed him, keeping her voice low.

'Really?' quizzed Brian, frowning. 'Who are you?'

'Very funny.' Tory gave him a whack. 'I'm serious, we're in a spot of bother, I'm afraid.'

Brian cocked an eye. He'd suspected there was more to their fancy dress than some weird mourning ritual. 'You'd best spill it, then.'

Tory levelled with Brian about Ray, about her vision and the part she believed the technologist had to play in it. Then she told of what Walter Cadfan had said.

'The *Goddess* is a grand vessel, and a safe haven. But there are still so many things she can't do. If she had land and air capabilities, as well as a decent cloaking device, then we'd surely be one up on our foe.'

'What foe?' Brian objected. 'If we get involved in this, Tory, we'll be outlaws.'

'Brian, don't you see? If a higher force has sent Ray to me, it's not without good reason. I believe I must take him back to the Old Land, to find a means to protect us all.'

'Protect us from what?' Brian implored her.

'Some foreboding, force, occurrence, being … I don't know, but I feel it in my gut,' Tory stressed her concern.

'Me too.' Rhiannon seconded her mother's view, as she usually did.

'Tory?' Brian plastered his hair back off his brow.

'I know it's a big gamble, Brian, but I have a seriously bad feeling that mainstream society is about to take a dive.'

Brian sighed. 'Alright, I'll head us out to sea tonight.' He was showered with kisses from both women. 'Aw, do me a favour!' He knew he'd been conned, and so brushed them both off in protest. 'You look like a couple of drag queens.'

'Head for deep water and stay submerged.' Tory backed up, Rhiannon with her. 'We shan't be far behind.'

Brian shuddered as he watched them both fade from sight. 'John's right, this family is just *too* weird.'

The thought of Ray found Tory and Rhiannon thirty floors up in the office of a new high-rise building overlooking London.

'The new ICA offices, I presume.' Tory wandered to the door to find a light switch.

The room had yet to be carpeted or painted, but as it turned out there was electricity.

'Sweet Jesus.' Rhiannon spotted her crewmate huddled in a corner, badly beaten. 'Ray?' She rushed to squat beside him, gently turning his swollen face toward her.

'Who, who?' He pushed himself hard into the corner, wondering what horror lay in store for him now.

Rhiannon had completely forgotten about her strange guise. 'It's okay, it's me.' She smiled.

'Who?!' He still hadn't made the connection, as his eyesight wasn't the best. Ray looked harder. 'Rhiannon?' he mouthed the name.

'Hey, babe.' Tory gave him a wave.

'Oh my God,' Ray mumbled. 'You two look awful.'

'Well, you know, Ray, you're not looking that crash hot yourself.' She helped Rhiannon to get Ray to his feet. 'Is anything broken?'

'Ah!' He winced with pain as he was raised up onto his feet. 'I think the question is more, what isn't broken?'

'Let's get you back and have a doctor check you out.'

'Not without my case,' he mumbled, barely conscious.

'My sweet, you're dying,' Tory pointed out. 'Is it really that important?'

'Yes,' he insisted. 'I have to get it back.'

'I'll get it.' Tory rolled her eyes, motioning for him to stay put. 'Do you feel confident to get him back home?'

Rhiannon nodded. 'I have been known to provide men with such a service on occasion.'

'You learn too fast.' Tory gave her a wink before she transformed her appearance.

'No, Lord, I'm not seeing this,' Ray whined in protest.

'What do you think?' Tory asked.

As it was Doc Alexander smiling back at them, Rhiannon replied, 'What a babe!'

'Ray?' Tory looked at him, adding another dimension to her disguise by employing Doc's voice.

The engineer was stunned speechless. His eyes rolled back in his head, and Rhiannon found herself struggling to hold the dead weight of his body up.

Once Tory had seen Rhiannon and Ray safely depart, she focused on finding the suitcase. It was old, and had many a distinguishing sticker and baggage tag.

As the case in question took form before her, Tory didn't make a move for it. The smell of cigar smoke let her know there was someone else present in the room where she'd manifested.

She was in a very large office, exquisitely decorated with fine antiques and artwork. Directly beside her, seated in a chair facing a desk, was a big man in a suit.

Out of the corner of his eye he caught a glimpse of Tory and was startled to his feet. 'Christ, Doc, you scared me. I wasn't expecting you for another hour or so.'

'Is that why you're smoking my cigars?' Tory casually strolled round the back of the desk and took a seat.

'Sorry, I got bored.' He stubbed it out in an ashtray on the desk.

'That's quite alright, uh ...?' Tory clicked her fingers a few times and waited for him to jump in.

'Murray,' he obliged, seeming rather surprised.

'Sorry, my friend, it's been one of those days.' Tory could see a gun in a shoulder holster inside Murray's jacket, yet surely this overweight, middle-aged man could not have taken Ray out on his own — or beaten him so grievously. 'Where are the rest of you?'

'They left early to avoid suspicion, just like you said.'

'Excellent.' She smiled to reassure him. Then, slapping her hands together, Tory rose and looked around to locate the bag. 'So, you got it I see, well done.'

'It was just like you told me, Doc. Murdock was on Thurlow's boat. Who would have thought?'

Who indeed? Tory mused.

'That's some smart rig they've got there. I think you oughta check it out sometime.'

'I'll do that, Murray. But right now,' she glanced at her wristwatch, and attempted to walk him to the door, 'I've got to motor.'

'Wait a minute.' He came to an abrupt halt, and Tory's heart shot into her throat. 'What do you want me to do with the brain … dump him in a river, or what?'

'No, Murray, that's okay.' She patted his shoulder to put him at ease. 'I'll take it from here.'

The thug shrugged, and then hesitated again before departing. 'You seem thinner, or shorter, or somethin' … you should take better care of yourself, Doc.'

'I'll do that.' She shook his hand firmly on his way out. 'You take care yourself, Murray.' She closed the door behind him and gave a sigh of relief.

Her bedchamber on board the *Goddess* took form within the ethers, and slowly materialised around her. She was home, far from the eyes and cameras of would-be voyeurs, so Tory dropped the suitcase and resumed her true form.

'I knew it.'

Tory turned to find Noah seated in a dim corner.

'But I had to see it for myself.' Noah stood in a daze, clutching a pile of papers in his hand.

'See what?' Tory scoffed; maybe she could convince him that he was imagining things; it was rather dark in here.

Noah was so completely mind-blown he didn't know where to start, and so paced a little. He didn't want to offend Tory by jumping to conclusions. He had to stick to the facts. 'I know you think I'm not very observant, what with the Ray thing slipping by me and all.' He stopped still. 'But that's because something else has been preoccupying my brain space.'

'I see.' Tory smiled, taking a seat on the bed to hear him out.

'Wow!' He let loose a burst of enthusiasm as the pieces of the puzzle came together in his mind. 'See, I've been doing a bit of reading whilst I've been on this rig — ancient history and mythology, seeing as that is what your CD ROM library has to offer in the main. And I came across this.' He handed her a copy of the printout.

A short life hast mine been,
wondrous and blithe.
I have learned of many a legend.
But who wast the greatest?
I reply …

It was she who tamed the Dragon.
It was she who united this land.
It was she who shaped my future,
the Goddess' right hand.

The head-wind of a storm, wast she,
with more radiance than the sun.
The heart of a warrior, had she,
who fought until she won.

I am proud to say I knew her,
for she wast my truest friend.
The years we had together,
art the happiest I shall spend.

Departed now, for some future age,
and mourned by all who knew her.
I shall recount her deeds till I draw final breath,
Her name? ... Tory Alexander.

It was a piece of poetry that a young druid of the sixth century had written for her before her departure. Thankfully, it was not dated. She'd had it translated into modern English and put on CD ROM, mainly for Rhiannon's benefit, along with the copy of her legend that had been passed down through time to become part of British mythology.

She smiled as she finished reading it. 'It's a joke. A friend wrote it for me, when he'd read the legend. That's why I had them put on CD together.'

'Now, that's what I thought.' Noah let her know he wasn't buying it. 'But, answer me this, Tory Alexander. We've been out at sea for over an hour, so how can Rhiannon show up with Ray less than fifteen minutes ago?'

Tory opened her mouth to answer, but only gave a huge exhalation. She was tired of trying to hide who she was, and if they were headed for dangerous times those close to her were bound to find out anyway. Unlike most in this day and age, at least Noah was eager to hear the truth.

'Departed now for some future age …' Noah quoted the poem. 'That future age is now, isn't it? You are the immortal, time-shifting warrior from ancient British myth.'

'If you say so.' Tory was not really up for a fight.

'No, hear me out.' Noah was far more excited than she. 'You obviously have certain powers, right? And as Rhiannon inherited them, I can safely assume it's passed on from generation to generation.'

'I'll go with that.' Tory was intrigued to see where all this was heading.

'Well, in myth, the first person to strongly oppose the Goddess … *you*,' he pointed out, then took a moment to get a grip on his thoughts again, 'was Caradoc, which could perhaps be shortened to Doc, and the Alexander part, well …' He shrugged, thinking it was obvious. 'Now, that could be just a coincidence, of course?'

But Tory knew better. There was no such thing as chance. She had killed Caradoc out of mercy with her own hand, but she couldn't rule out the possibility that he might have incarnated. 'That's food for thought.'

'But there's more.' He sat on the bed and spread out a whole lot of papers. 'I traced the Kings down from Maelgwn for five generations, to the Dragon's final male descendant to the throne, Cadwaladr. And you know, every single one of them was reputedly taken by the Otherworld before death, or mysteriously vanished after death. And,' he held up a finger in resolve, 'they were all fabled to return to join the Goddess in battle at the Gathering of Kings. The aforementioned battle is against an evil entity with extensive armies, who, it is said, will bring universal slaughter … do you know anything about that?'

Tory shook her head. She had heard the prophecy before, but even she was none the wiser as to the identity of her foe in the affair.

Noah suspected she was withholding information, but didn't push the issue. 'Anyway,' he grinned, gesturing to the chart he'd made, 'this is the family line …

'Maelgwn — taken by the Otherworld. Rhun — mysteriously vanished. Cadwell — taken by the Otherworld. This one is interesting: *Cadfan*, most cultured and renowned of all British Kings, mysteriously vanished. Cadwallon — taken by the Otherworld. And, the last of his line, the great warrior, Cadwaladr, his body mysteriously vanished after he'd been slain at the battle of Brunanburh. Which, just as a matter of interest, is what Doc Alexander named the ICA's first space station.'

'How long have you been working on this?' Tory could hardly believe what a hive of information he was.

'I haven't really … like I said, I've been reading. It only really came together when Rhiannon showed up with Ray.'

'Well, it seems you've already earned your week's pay.' She could see now why he'd wanted the job in the first place.

'We aim to please,' he advised. 'So let me run this theory by you. You believe in reincarnation, right?'

'Most certainly.' She handed the poem of her deeds back to Noah. 'When one considers that you were the druid who penned this poem for me in 540 A.D.'

'Radical ... a druid, eh!' He was pleased. 'So I was a reporter even then.'

Tory laughed. 'Indeed.'

'Will you tell me your story one day?' He forgot all about his theory, as this was far more interesting.

'One day, perhaps.' She motioned him back to his notes and the matter at hand.

'Right, ah ... yes. It just occurred to me — what if these talents of yours had been passed down through the generations? There could be others like you.'

'Oh shit!' Tory sprang to her feet. She'd never considered this. 'The gene would've had to have been activated before each of them bred, but, *holy Goddess* ... there could be thousands of us!'

'Or, at least, six,' agreed Noah calmly. 'So what if Doc Alexander is one of them?'

Tory gasped. 'If he's telepathic ...!' She paused, too horrified to voice her mind at once. 'When I touched him yesterday, Ray was almost certainly foremost in my mind, knowing he was hiding from the ICA.'

'So, you think we have a case for suspicion?' Noah sought confirmation.

'Aye, I believe we do.'

6

WORLDS APART

The next day, when Ray had recovered a little, all on board the *Goddess* met in the rec-room for a major confessional.

As it turned out, Ray's suitcase held the only record of his work on the super-computer for the ICA's new fusion reactors, and chances were, the ICA would try and retrieve these documents. Not that it would do them any good as Ray planned to erase the relevant information from his computer and burn all his notes pertaining to the project.

John Pearce, at fifty-nine years old, did not feel young enough to be taking on the powers-that-be. Miles' sudden death had him spooked and suspicious. Jenny, although she loved the rig, the project and the company, could not bring herself to endanger the life of her only son. She had to agree with her husband — they must leave. Nicholas, of course, insisted he wasn't going anywhere. Yet he knew, eighteen or not, Tory and Brian would not let him stay without his parents' consent.

Naomi knew the rig rather well these days and, although she was concerned about how the present circumstances might affect her son, she firmly believed there was no safer place for them than on board the *Goddess*. Brian would never leave Tory, and Naomi would not leave Brian; thus, they would stay.

This went double for Teo. Tory, Brian and Teo had been a team since high school, and he wasn't about to change that now.

Ray had little choice in the matter, which left Noah. As he'd only just managed to scam the job, and there was a major story to be had, Noah wasn't going anywhere.

John Pearce and his family parted ways with the *Goddess* and her crew in Horta. After sixteen years of working together as a team, this was not an easy goodbye for any of them.

Nicholas was quietly rebellious, insisting they would all be seeing him again soon. Jenny and Tory could barely look at each other without bursting into tears, which made words a little difficult. They had become firm friends in the twentieth century, just as they had in the sixth. Tory would miss Jenny's company every bit as much as she missed Jenovefa's. They gave up trying to express their farewells in the end, and just said it with a hug.

'Goodbye, John.' Tory shook his hand.

'Your secrets are safe with me,' he assured her.

Tory gave him the old chug on the shoulder. 'Well, who'd believe you, anyway?'

Pearce smiled, and thought how much this strange woman had opened his mind of late. 'Don't go changing.' He winked at her, and followed his family down the pier.

The mighty submersible left port that same day, fully stocked.

John didn't realise it, as he watched her disappear out to sea, but he would never see, nor hear of, the *Goddess* or her crew again.

Tory only slept out of habit, and even then it was more like meditation than sleep. Tonight, she could not relax and concentrate long enough to even do that. She needed to talk with someone — someone old and wise. Naturally, her father was the first person who sprang to mind.

She found the Merlin sitting on a throne-like chair inside his cave at Dinas Emrys, chatting with an old owl friend of his.

'Hello.' Myrddin acknowledged his daughter's entrance. 'Tobias seems to think the world is coming to an end. What do you think?'

'Not if I can help it.' Tory bowed slightly to the owl as she challenged his view.

'Hey-ho, it sounds like she's on another quest.' Her father uttered an aside to the bird. 'And I suppose you're requiring my assistance.' He casually polished his fingernails against his robes.

'I need to know the position of the solar system and planets around the time Absalom was nearing the end of his reign in Atlantis.' She raised her brow hopefully.

'Whatever for?'

Tory rolled her eyes, thinking it obvious. 'So I can go back there, of course.'

'Well, you could just take the chariot, like you did last time.' He motioned in its general direction.

'But I thought I'd destroyed it!' This was good news, indeed.

'So why are you going back to the Old Land?' He turned in his seat to view her. 'Didn't you cause enough trouble last time you were there?' The Merlin chuckled and the owl thought it was rather a hoot, too.

Tory opened the nose cone of the vehicle to check out the inner circuitry, ignoring them both. 'I'm going to make some slight modifications to the *Goddess*.' She peered into the belly of the chariot. 'So I'll need something to barter in exchange for their technology.'

'Don't be silly, of course you won't.' The Merlin waved it off. 'You're a Goddess for heavens' sake! They shall supply you with whatever you need, just as before.'

'And if they don't.'

'They will.' He leant back in his chair. 'The Shu Sar Absalom is a past incarnation of mine, so I shall see to it personally.'

'Dad?' Tory spotted the crystal that was the heart of the time-chariot's drive system. She'd completely shattered this irreplaceable piece after her last journey through time, yet it was now perfectly intact. 'Where did you get the quasi-crystal?'

'I have a supplier in the Fourth Dimension who gets them for me.'

'What?' Tory sat back on her haunches, hands on hips. 'Are you telling me you made me time travel without a vehicle on purpose!'

'Well, I was curious to see if it could be done … and you came out of it alright.'

'Yes, but I could have been caught in a time-warp, or another dimension, or —'

'But you weren't, were you darling?' Myrddin absentmindedly rubbed the bridge of his nose. 'Besides, at the time, I wanted my transport back! Having now done all the exploring I care to at present, you may take it if you wish.'

Tory went quiet and Myrddin knew there was something playing on her mind. 'What is it?'

'The ET gene you spoke of last time we met?'

'What of it?' he urged impatiently.

'Well, I know Rhun inherited it.'

Rhun was Tory's first child, born to Maelgwn in the sixth century. He'd been left to rule Gwynedd when Tory had departed for the twentieth century.

'And the gene was activated before he had his son, Cadwell; therefore, Cadwell must be immortal.' She stood, and slowly began to pace.

'Yes.' The Merlin smiled. 'But, your question?'

'Do you know how many of my descendants inherited this gene in its active state?'

'Well …' His face became long and drawn as he

considered the question. 'I can't say I ever wondered. I never pay a lot of attention to the past or future — they always change so much, according to what inter-dimensional reality one is living in at the time. But I guess it would depend on whether or not, in this particular dimension, Cadwell was killed before or after he had children.'

'Tell me something I don't know.' Tory swept her long fair hair back off her face. 'Okay.' She decided to take another tack. 'If the gene had been passed along, say, for five or six generations, might these other immortals have the same talents as I do?'

'Perhaps ...' He was a little vague at first. 'Psychic ability is as varied as its third plane counterparts — creative talents, great sporting achievements, or unusual mental abilities. Therefore, it depends on what area one has developed and what kind of belief structure one has.' The Merlin sat forward, motioning Tory to come and sit before him. 'With you, movement has been vital, teleportation through time and space ... so you developed psychokinesis, and that is your forte. Along with telepathy which you learnt from Taliesin and myself, and have in turn passed on to Rhiannon. But for other immortals perhaps shape-shifting and shamanism is more what is required to fulfil their role in the scheme of things, or channelling, healing, prophecy, extra-terrestrial communication, and so forth. What any individual is capable of rests entirely upon what he or she believes is possible. Most would not attempt the feats you perform, as they consider such metamorphosis impossible. You, however, do not, as you have seen it done.'

'But what if not all these immortals were using these talents for the common good?'

'Then …' he raised both brows, 'those in question could not have developed beyond the third level of awareness. That is … the realm of psychology and thought. At this early stage of spirituality, one still believes the mind is the supreme device. One can hardly be aided by the higher realms of the super-conscious if one doesn't believe they exist. One's ability could only develop akin to the limitations of third dimensional existence.'

Tory took a deep breath. 'So, beyond what is usually considered as normal human activity, what could such an individual be capable of?'

Her father frowned; he didn't like contemplating such things. 'Telepathy would be possible, but only through touch … possibly even hypnosis and mind manipulation for the purpose of disguise. But not teleportation or time travel, as that requires fourth dimensional intervention. In other words, you'd have to have a being that resides on the fourth dimension or beyond it assisting you, just as Keridwen aids you. However …'

'What?' Tory pleaded for him to share his thought.

'One might be able to view the past through one's numerous incarnations, perhaps even assume wilful control of them for a time. But it would take a very disciplined mind indeed.'

'I see.' Tory committed the information to memory. She had seen Maelgwn execute such a feat once; he'd gained control over Miles' body in the twentieth century, leaving his body in the sixth.

'Tory.' Myrddin was concerned by his daughter's grave expression. 'I feel sure that as long as there were immortals in Gwynedd's royal line, Taliesin would have been there to take them under his wing. The High Merlin would never leave such a powerful force to just wander astray.'

'I suppose.' She hoped he was right.

But what if Taliesin had overlooked a couple somehow? The last of Maelgwn's descendants, Cadwaladr, disappeared somewhere in the middle of the eighth century, but there wasn't any mention in history texts of Taliesin after the sixth.

Upon Tory's return to the *Goddess* she went straight to see Ray. Three o'clock in the morning was an odd hour to be paying a visit, but she'd been seized by a sense of urgency she couldn't shake. Nearing his cabin, she was a little bemused to hear Rhiannon's laughter coming from within. Tory hesitated to disturb them at first, but then gave a timid knock.

'Come in.' Ray didn't bother to inquire as to who it was. But Tory wanted to make sure he knew.

'It's me, Tory.'

'Well, don't be shy.' The door opened and Ray invited her in to join Rhiannon and himself, both still up drinking coffee and chatting. Tory stayed in the doorway. 'Hold on a minute, you didn't think we were ...?' Ray gave half a laugh. 'Jesus, Tory. I'm nearly old enough to be her father.'

'Yes, *really* mother.' Rhiannon raised herself to go to bed. 'I do like my men to at least be in one piece.'

Rhiannon served Ray a sweet grin as she slipped herself between him and her mother.

The engineer cringed as he watched the girl disappear down the corridor. 'I think I might have offended her.'

'I think you might be right. Can we talk?'

'In my room! Do think that's safe?' He grinned, although his facial bruises were still ailing him.

'Perfectly.' She entered.

Ray closed the door behind her.

'How are you feeling?' Tory sat on the only chair in the tiny sleeping quarters, so Ray took a seat opposite her on the bed.

'Pearce patched me up pretty good. Most of the swelling has gone now, so it actually looks worse than it feels.'

'Do you feel up to a little trip?'

'With you?'

Tory nodded.

'Sure.' He shrugged, as if he wasn't at all excited by the notion. 'Where are we going?'

Tory hesitated a moment to evaluate just how much of her plan Ray could cope with at once. 'I want to take you to meet an old friend of mine. I believe he might be able to teach you a thing or two that could be very beneficial to our future protection.'

'In what way?' He was curious, as there were few in his chosen field more scientifically up to date or experienced than himself.

'I want to modify this ship,' she informed him plainly.

Ray shrugged, wearing a confident grin. 'I really don't think I'd need any help to do that. What did you have in mind?'

'I want land and air capabilities, and a complete sight and sound cloaking system.'

Ray nearly choked on his smile. 'Whoa there! In five hundred years, perhaps?'

'See, I told you, you need to meet my friend.' She gave him a slap on the knee in fun.

But Ray did not take it thus. 'If this guy's so smart, why don't you get him to do it?'

'Well, I would. Trouble is, I can neither get the *Goddess* to him, nor he to the *Goddess*.'

'I find that hard to believe. Rhiannon has yet to explain how she got me back to this vessel within minutes, *from London*!' Ray stood, spurred on by other concerns. 'And how did you two alter your appearance just like that ... and don't tell me it was make up.'

Tory opened her mouth to comment, but Ray hadn't finished.

'And it seems that I see you as twenty years younger than everybody else does. Why is that? *Who are you?*'

Tory had hoped that perhaps they could leave for the Old Land at once, but she could not push mortal men in the same fashion she pushed herself. 'Look, you're obviously tired, maybe —'

'Don't give me that.' He was bordering on angry now. 'Are you human at least. Can I know that much?'

Tory stood, finding the tone of his question rather hurtful. 'No Ray, I'm really a little green man, and this is my spaceship.' Tory made for the door, before she said or did something she'd regret.

'I really didn't mean that.' He slammed the door closed, before she'd opened it far enough to escape. 'I'm sorry. Jesus, you'd think I'd be more grateful, after all you've done.'

'Forget it.' She waved it off. 'We'll talk about the details of the trip tomorrow.'

'Stay awhile.' He was having trouble getting her to look him in the eye.

'Ray, you'll never get better if you don't rest.' She tried to shift him away from the door.

'Perhaps comforting is more what I need.' He took hold of her hand, and caressed it between his. 'Perhaps, it's what you need too.'

'Ray, please.' She slowly withdrew from his touch. 'I'm really not up for a seduction right now.' He went to speak, but she hushed him with her fingers. 'Nor will I be in the foreseeable future.'

'Pardon my saying so,' he ventured, lowering her hand from his mouth, 'but it would be a crying shame if you were to just lock it up and throw away the key. But,' he spoke up over her pending protest, 'it wouldn't matter if you did. I am very good at picking locks, especially those that are more complex.' Ray moved away from the door so she could open it. 'I don't mind waiting.'

Tory shook her head, knowing better. 'No mortal man is that patient. You shall fall in love with another, way before I ever come around.'

As she stepped out into the corridor, Ray folded his

arms and leant on one side of the doorway. 'I don't think so.'

She cocked an eye. 'I'll bet you a hundred dollars that I'm right.'

Ray found her wager a rather amusing challenge. 'You're on.'

'Sucker.' Tory walked away a couple of paces, before she turned to suggest. 'And ah, if you want to know more about my history, might I suggest you speak with Noah … he seems to know more about me than I do.' She waved him goodnight.'

I'll certainly do that, Ray decided, fully intent on winning their bet.

The next morning over breakfast Tory was studying her daughter very closely.

It had dawned on Tory that Rhiannon was very similar to someone she had known in the Dark Ages. It was Rhiannon's colouring that had prevented Tory from noticing the resemblance before.

Even though Rhiannon had her head in a magazine, reading the latest on the Green movement, her mother's quiet but persistent attention bothered her. *What is it?*

As they were alone in the rec-room Tory figured it was okay to voice her mind. 'You like him don't you?'

'Who?'

'Ray.'

Rhiannon raised her dark eyes to view her mother. 'Why would you think that?'

Tory noted the spite in her daughter's voice.

'Because I feel an attraction to him, and I don't think it's because I'm attracted to him, if you get my drift.'

'Well, maybe you are … and I'm just picking it up off you.' She went back to her reading matter.

'Would you do something for me?' Tory pushed her luck with Rhiannon's precarious mood.

'What?' She turned the page of her magazine, nearly ripping it out in the process.

'Change your eyes to the colour of acorn blue, and your hair to, say … the colour mine once was.'

'Still is, you mean?' Rhiannon corrected her mother's assessment. 'I see you as you truly are.'

Tory was shocked right off her train of thought. She'd never actually discussed the immortality issue with Rhiannon. 'Do you know why I appear as I do?'

'Yes, thank you … Noah told me.' Rhiannon continued to stare at the magazine, though both of them knew she was no longer reading it.

'Oh, *I see*. It wasn't Ray you were mad at last night. It was me.' Tory had wondered why Rhiannon left in such a hurry.

'Oh, you're quick,' her daughter jeered.

'Well, give me a break here. I've had a few things on my mind.'

'Is that right.' Rhiannon finally looked at Tory. 'And what exactly did you have in mind visiting Ray at three o'clock in the morning? Jesus Christ, Dad's body is not even cold! But then again, I suppose you've learnt to recover from these things quickly.'

'Rhiannon!' Tory came within inches of striking her, which she had never done in anger. Luckily the

83

tears in her daughter's eyes prevented what would have been a regretful act.

'Why didn't you tell me!' Rhiannon begged to know, her resentment waning.

'I meant to, I swear it.' Tory placed an arm about her child, who fell sobbing into the embrace. Tory remembered when Taliesin had informed her of her immortal state, and how overawing and difficult to fathom it had been. 'It's not so bad, truly. There's quite a few of us now.'

'But what if the world were to end tomorrow? We'll just be left on a smouldering boulder of vast nothingness!'

Tory stroked her daughter's long, thick hair, as straight and dark as her father's had been, all the while smiling at the notion. 'But that's why we're here. To prevent that.'

Rhiannon felt more at peace after her explosion. 'I never even suspected immortality was the reason we were a little more psychic than most.'

They both had a bit of a giggle at this.

'And who's this Maelgwn guy I hear about?' Rhiannon teased her mother in a jovial fashion. 'Warrior, King, leader, dragon slayer, legend … he sounds like a bit of a babe.'

'Maelgwn is the perfect incarnation of your father. And he never killed the dragon …' Tory took a graceful pause to build the expectation, 'he tamed it.'

They both released a long, soft sigh of adoration.

'You speak as if he's still alive?'

Tory nodded surely. 'He's out there in the cosmos somewhere, keeping an eye on things down here.' Tory was reeling through a string of wonderful memories, and thought she'd best be out with the whole truth. 'You have a brother you know.'

'Yes.' Rhiannon smiled. 'Rhun. I remember the fairytales you used to tell me when I was young. Yet, I realise now, they weren't fairytales at all, but rather my ancestry. My brother was a British King, my mother — a Goddess, my grandfather — a Merlin, and my great-grandfather … an Otherworldly being! I really was born in the sixth century then?' As her mother nodded to confirm this, Rhiannon grasped hold of her head. 'Hell's bells, that makes me fourteen hundred years old.'

'Time is an illusion. Look at me, I'm a seventy year old, pretending to be fifty, when I'm really perpetually thirty.'

They both burst into laughter again, whereby Tory's blissful gaze wandered to the door. 'Ray!' The women nearly jumped out of their skin. 'How long have you been here?'

'Too long.' He ambled in to join them. 'I was coming to tell you that the reporter you hired is nuts! He was trying to tell me you're some immortal sixth century Goddess, who's been jumping around the time–space continuum for God knows how long!' He looked from Tory to Rhiannon, who were both staring back at him with the most pathetic look on their faces. 'Please, ladies, could we have a reality check here?' He clicked his fingers a few times.

Rhiannon picked up a sharp knife off the table and passed it to her mother. 'I guess Ray wants proof.'

'This is a nightmare, right?' Ray got a little edgy when Tory took the knife in hand. 'What are you going to do with that?'

When Ray had witnessed Tory do the deed, he slumped in a seat and went silent for a time. 'This friend of yours we're going to see,' he spoke finally, 'where is he, *exactly*.'

'When is more the question.' Tory smiled and frowned at once. 'His name is Shar Turan. He was the head of the technologists at the Dur-na-ga temple in Chailidocean. Which is, of course, the ruined city we have been surveying for the past month.' To her surprise Ray did not freak out about the announcement, but rather, he smiled.

'So that's how you found it!' Ray came crashing back to earth. 'How do you plan to get us there? I mean, how many thousands of years ago are we talking here? Ten?'

'Twelve.' Tory thought it best to keep their mode of transport a secret till the last minute. 'You just leave the flight details to me … and I'll have us there, safe and sound, by nightfall.'

'I'll believe it when I see it.'

Tory gave a chuckle, recalling her first glimpse of the city of the golden gates. 'No, you won't.'

7

MADE İN HEAVEN

The sun rose over the three-ringed islands and canals that comprised the city of Chailidocean. The islands were connected by arched, sandstone bridges and at each end of these stood a set of large, golden gates. Breathtaking temples made from all manner of marble lined the gleaming white sandstone streets. Lush, colourful gardens featuring stately statues and glistening crystal fountains lay between nearly every dwelling. Building, road, path and garden alike followed the same flowing circular design.

The sight was like a dream, or something from another planet, or even the distant future, yet recalling the world they'd left behind. Ray couldn't imagine the Earth ever being this pure and fair again.

'You were right, I see it and I still don't believe it.'

Ray stood gazing out of the large, round window of the spacious circular room where Tory had brought them to rest.

Under Tory's navigation, Ray had travelled through the brilliant blue–white light of the ethers. This etheric field had obscured the world around him until, before he'd even realised it, he was somewhere else. This journey had taken them from the *Goddess*, in the north Atlantic, to a cave of treasures — Tory would not tell him where it was. Here he'd been bundled into a vehicle that appeared rather like a large, space-age jet-ski, which had brought them forth to this place.

'Are you feeling okay? You're the first mortal to ever ride in the chariot,' Tory told him, as the bells of the great citadel tolled to call all to the first solar rite of the day.

As Ray was engrossed in watching the people of Chailidocean flood into the streets below with their prayer mats, he was not that fazed by his achievement. 'I feel fine, just fine.' His eyes remained transfixed on the activity below.

'Turan will be pleased.'

Tory could hardly wait to see the Shar for he, too, was an incarnation of Maelgwn, just as Miles had been. Unfortunately, Turan was so accomplished in the ways of the etheric world that he floated around in a spiritual form most of the time, making any intimate relations with him impossible. But it would be grand just to pass some time in his company; there was still much she could learn from him.

'Are you trying to tell me,' Tory's words had finally registered with Ray, 'that this Shar friend of yours, built *that*?' He pointed to the chariot.

'Yes indeed.' Tory grinned at how brilliant Turan was. 'This is his work station.' She motioned to the room around them that was a little more furnished since she'd last seen it.

'Are you kidding me?' Ray was gasping now, and experiencing surges of panic and self-doubt. 'I'll never be able to fathom technology like that! Compared to these people, I'm going to seem like an intellectual retard.'

'No, you won't.' She made light of his fears with a laugh. 'Turan is a very good teacher. He even taught me a thing or two about quantum mechanics.'

'Oh, Tory!' Ray was stressing out and shaking his head, when the door to the room suddenly vanished and two men entered.

One was a dark-eyed, red-skinned warrior with long, straight black hair. He was dressed all in red, and bore a rather striking resemblance to Teo. The other was a seven foot tall, and much younger version of, Miles Thurlow. He was dressed in long flowing robes of white, that were bound with a purple and blue scarf at the waist.

'Turan! Jerram!' Tory bounded towards them.

'Lamamu!' both men cried, ecstatic to see her again.

The shorter of the two rushed to meet Tory halfway, and spun her around in the air.

'I told them you'd be back!' Jerram was pleased to boast, as he came to a stop with her. 'And on today of all days!'

'What do you mean?' she questioned, as excited as he.

'Adelgar and I are to be wed. Not to each other, of course.'

Tory grinned. These matches weren't really that hard to figure. 'The lucky ladies would be Nin Tabitha and Nin Mahala, I presume.'

'Are you very heartbroken?' he teased.

'Excuse I,' Turan cut in, picking Tory up and bringing her comparatively tiny form to stand on a small table so she was more his height.

That's when Tory noticed the Shar wasn't floating. He was standing on his own two feet, his tall, slender body as solid as a rock. 'Hello.' She gazed into his grey-violet eyes, interlocking her hands behind his neck.

'Did you miss me?' Turan smiled as she'd rarely seen him do. His return to a physical form was a most unexpected and pleasant surprise.

'You know I did,' she confessed. 'The more pertinent question would seem to be, did *you* miss me?' The Shar's smile broadened and his cheeks became slightly flushed.

'It would appear so, no?' He motioned to his person with his eyes. 'You left quite a lasting impression on us all, Lamamu.'

Tory was mesmerised by his voice, his gaze. And feeling ever so compelled to kiss him, she slowly closed the distance between her lips and his.

'Ah-hmm!' Ray put an abrupt stop to the cheery reunion, as all eyes looked his way.'

'Zadoc. What are you still doing here?' Turan lifted Tory down from the table. 'I thought you'd left to try that case in Menocea.'

'What?' quizzed Ray, with a frown.

Jerram eyed Ray closely; apart from the strange attire, there appeared to be a few other things amiss with him. 'Zadoc, you've shrunk!' He was now only minimally taller than Jerram, but Zadoc had always been the same height as Turan. 'And what happened to your face?' Jerram referred to his bruises.

'No, no, no.' Tory hit the panel to close the door. 'This is a friend of mine, Ray Murdock. He's from the future, like me.'

'Holy smoke! You brought one of Zadoc's incarnations back into the same time frame as he?' Turan contemplated the repercussions of this, not looking too pleased about it. 'What were you thinking?'

'I had no choice,' Tory justified her actions.

'You mean I'm already here!' Ray demanded of Tory.

'Well, not in the city, no,' Jerram pointed out in Tory's defence. 'Zadoc is in charge of the Courts of Justice. His services are required in a city to the north, and I believe he left this morning.'

Ray wiped a hand down his face. 'This is not happening.'

As the particle manipulation mechanism in the door alerted them to company, Turan and Jerram jumped in front of Tory and Ray to hide them.

'There you are.' Zadoc strolled in, obviously looking for Jerram. 'I'm off now. Sorry I can't be at the wedding.' He shook Jerram's hand. 'Good luck, tonight.'

'No worries.' Jerram tried to sound perfectly calm, despite the fact he'd broken into a sweat. 'I hope your case doesn't drag on too long.'

Zadoc looked over at Turan, who was older than himself. 'It must be about time you found yourself a good woman. I highly recommend it.' Zadoc slapped Turan's shoulder as he backed up. 'I shall see you both when I do.' He gave a wave and strutted away.

'Correction.' Jerram hit the panel to close the door. 'Now he's gone.'

Tory looked to Ray, who'd gone as pale as a sheet. 'Sorry about that.'

'I'm married?' was all he could say.

'Yeah, three hundred years now.' Jerram concurred with a huge smile, wondering why his brother's double didn't look that pleased about it. 'Is something amiss?'

Ray waved Jerram away. 'That's just a little more information than I can readily comprehend at present. I think I need to … sit down.'

He was making his way to collapse on the lounge when the door again opened.

No one was close enough or fast enough to hide Ray this time, though Tory managed to duck behind Turan's desk.

'Sorry to interrupt Shar Turan, Shar Jerram.' Annora bow her head to each.

Tory recognised this lovely young woman from the Dark Age. She was Aella, Sir Bryce's wife. Tory thus concluded that she must be Zadoc's wife here in Atlantis. *O-oh … here's trouble.*

'I was just looking for … Zadoc,' she resolved, spotting Ray. 'I'm so glad I caught you. What on earth are you wearing? And what happened to your face?'

She approached him, concerned, to discover she was taller than he. 'My god!'

'Ah, Annora,' Turan jumped in. 'It's a new reduction device I've been working on. Zadoc volunteered to test it out for me.' As the woman looked as if she might have a fit, he quickly added, 'It's perfectly harmless, I promise.'

'Well, how do you know it won't cause any permanent damage to him, if you haven't tested it before?'

'I didn't say I hadn't tested it, Nin.' Turan employed a condescending tone. 'In fact, I've tested it on nearly everyone … even Jerram here, look at how short he is.' Turan was having difficulty refraining from laughter at this point, and Jerram was also finding it hard to hide his amusement.

Annora knew something strange was going on, but she let it pass. 'Well, alright, if you're sure it's not dangerous? But you know Zadoc is due to leave for —'

'Yes, yes …' Turan put an arm about her to show her out. 'I'll return him to normal and send him on his way.'

'But … I have to get back to my post, there's a baby due,' Annora protested.

'Well, we shouldn't keep you then.' Turan kept her moving.

'Couldn't *I* just kiss my husband goodbye *first*?' Annora came to a halt, not to be budged.

Everyone looked to Ray, who appeared to be completely captivated by her. 'I certainly have no objection.'

Annora freed herself from Turan and ran to Ray.

She was six and half feet of slender, graceful womanhood; eyes of acorn blue, and long blonde hair the like of Tory's. In fact, she looked remarkably like Tory.

'I just wanted to say last night was fabulous. I miss you already,' Annora whispered, before indulging Ray in a long and gentle kiss. 'Goodbye.' She slowly withdrew.

'Bye,' Ray sighed, as Turan closed the door — making sure to lock it this time. 'Wow,' Ray mumbled. 'Three hundred years of that … I never had it so good.'

'Right,' Turan decided. 'Before we create a major disaster, why don't you tell us why you're here.'

Tory produced the blueprints and design maps of the *Goddess*, along with two huge folders on the circuitry. As Turan assessed the vessel's capabilities, Tory explained the reasoning behind their decision to turn the deep sea submersible into an all-round observation vehicle. She spoke of her fears for her twenty-first century homeland, and the more Turan heard the more concerned he became.

'And you don't recognise this diplomat?' The notion confused the Shar. It didn't make sense. 'Surely if he is to play such a major role in your life, good or bad, you must have run into him during the course of your travels. Could he be disguising himself, perhaps?'

'It's possible, especially if he has sprung from my gene-pool.' The idea gave Tory chills.

'And he was the last to see your husband, in other words *me*, alive?' Turan was interested to note.

'That's right.' Tory wondered why the Shar seemed almost pleased to hear it.

'In that case, we should try and identify this fellow, and I might be able to assist you with that.' He gave Tory a slight wink. 'But for the moment, no one must know you're here.'

'But the wedding?' Jerram appealed. 'Lamamu must come.'

'Out of the question,' Turan ruled.

'But Adelgar will freak if we don't tell him of Lamamu's arrival.' Jerram spoke up for his twin brother.

'The more people who know, the bigger the risk. This Alexander fellow could be practically anyone. And if he has contact with his past selves ...? Let us just say it could be very detrimental to Lamamu's mission.'

This was very disappointing. Tory had been so looking forward to seeing everyone.

'Are we agreed then?' Turan pushed for a commitment, and both Jerram and Tory nodded reluctantly. They would inform Ray of their conclusions later, as he was sleeping on the lounge like a baby at present.

'As for your transport's modifications, I think we may be able to accommodate you.' Turan looked back to the plans of the *Goddess* on the table before them. 'Although the technology is primitive, her design is good.'

'So you think you could invent a way to get her airborne. She must be undetectable, you realise?'

'Well, obviously.' Turan exaggerated his understanding. 'And I don't need to invent such devices. We have been utilizing this technology for centuries.'

'But I didn't see any such vehicles last time I was here,' Tory recalled. 'Apart from a few hovercraft on the outermost island.'

'Well, of course you didn't.' Turan laughed, as did Jerram. 'My cloaking device does work, you know.'

Tory smacked herself on the forehead, she'd walked right into that one.

'Flying craft tend to scare some races,' Jerram explained. 'Thus Turan developed a soundproof shield, which keeps everybody happy.'

'So in reality,' Turan summarised, 'all I need to do is modify the systems to suit your craft, and teach Ray how to install them at the other end.' He thought he'd wrapped up the meeting in time for lunch, but Tory had a few questions still milling around in her head.

'Has Nin Sybil become the High Priestess here since Nin Bau's departure?'

'No. She renounced the right when she wed Shar Xavier,' Turan informed her, knowing Tory was the catalyst behind the romance. 'Nin Sybil is second to one called Temperance.'

This threw a spanner in the works. For Tory was hoping to utilize the site on Mt Dur-an-ki, to send all the parts and equipment for the *Goddess'* modifications back to the twenty-first century, but she needed the co-operation of the High Priestess and her Council to do it. 'Temperance … she sounds rather formidable. What's she like?'

'Who knows?' Turan shrugged. 'We've only ever seen her veiled form in the temple on sacred occasions.'

Oh, well. Tory figured Nin Sybil owed her a favour

or two. Perhaps she might be able to sway the High Priestess to favour her cause. This only left the problem of where the hell Tory wanted all the conversion requirements sent.

Cadfan had said Tory would find safety in the heart of her homeland. Was he talking about Uluru in Australia? The middle of a desert seemed a very strange place to be refitting a sub, and Tory was quite sure she didn't know anyone in the Red Centre.

One problem at a time, she told herself. *The universe will provide.*

The sounds of Chailidocean's residents in the throes of a night of wedding revelry echoed up to Tory in the silence of Turan's darkened lab. She stood alone at the window taking in the faint music and fireworks of the celebration. Ray was still snoozing.

'Knock, knock.' Turan's voice came through the intercom, whereupon Tory rushed to unlock to door.

'Thank God. I've been bored out of my mind.' She watched him enter with a large tray of spoils from the feast.

'Sorry.' He placed the platter on his desk, keeping his voice low so as not to wake their sleeping friend. 'I got away as soon as I could.' Turan turned on a small night-light with thought, and wore a grave expression as he took up Tory's hands. 'I have some news for you that may be rather shocking, I'm afraid.'

'What is it?' Tory couldn't imagine; she'd only been here a few hours. Surely she hadn't caused any major catastrophes yet.

'Let's sit down.' The Shar led her to the lounge opposite where Ray slept, and unable to think of any subtle way of telling her what he must, Turan decided to just come out with it. 'Lamamu, your husband was murdered.'

'How do you know?' Tory felt frantic. This was the last thing she expected. 'Why would anyone want to kill Miles?'

'Calm yourself.' Turan placed a hand over her heart, whereby Tory's anxiety subsided. 'I shall tell you all, if given the chance.'

The Shar confessed that since Tory's departure from Atlantis, he'd spent much time in contact with his future selves — Miles and Maelgwn in particular. Through them he could spend time with her.

'I don't understand.' She was deeply touched and her voice wavered as a result. 'Taliesin said that you'd asked him to wipe all intimate memory of me from your mind.'

Turan gave a vague smile. 'I couldn't part with the fondest memories I have …'

His emotions choked him a moment, and tears built in Tory's eyes, recognising the selflessness of his act.

'It just made the situation easier all round if you believed thus.'

He spoke the truth. It had.

'In any case …' Turan shrugged off the past to get back to the present, 'I spent this afternoon in the E-abzu Temple inside a meditation chamber. I joined with your second husband to observe the events just prior to his death.'

'It was Doc Alexander.' Tory guessed the killer's identity. 'But why?'

'Because he mistook your husband for Maelgwn. When the professor died under the pressure of a mind-induced heart attack, your foe figured he had the wrong incarnation.'

'Doc Alexander killed Miles by the power of suggestion. Is that what you're saying?'

Turan nodded.

'He must be of my line,' Tory decided with a heavy heart. 'But then how would he know Maelgwn? Rhun's son was not even born at the time of Maelgwn's departure.'

'Perhaps an enemy of Maelgwn's reincarnated into your descendancy?'

'Caradoc.' Tory's eyes narrowed. Noah had also suggested this connection. Maelgwn's treacherous brother was the same soul—mind as Turan's twin brother here in Atlantis. 'Shar Alaric must *under no circumstances* find out that I am here.'

Turan shook his head. 'This man was not my brother. Even if he'd incarnated I would still recognise him.'

'But what if he was disguising himself, as you suggested earlier?' Tory appealed.

'I think you might be right about Doc manipulating the minds of others.' Ray's voice came out of the darkness, as he propped himself up on his elbows. 'A lot of people radically changed their beliefs after coming into contact with him, me included.'

'And this man is friendly with nearly every political figurehead in the modern world.' Tory thought this was a bit of a worry. 'Well, I can see we shall have to do some serious research into Mr Alexander upon our return.' She knew hatred to be a complete waste of energy, but it was very hard not to despise this man for what he'd done.

'Good luck,' Ray scoffed. 'His personal files will be under tight lock and key.'

'Why Mr Murdock, I thought you said you were good with locks.'

'I just design and build systems,' Ray advised her. 'To acquire that kind of information you need a code breaker. A hacker, I ain't.'

'Then the universe shall have to provide us with one.' She looked to the heavens, hoping they were taking note.

In a little under a week, Turan had modified a hover-system and cloaking device to fit the *Goddess* and her reconnaissance subs, and arranged for the special parts to be made. These new systems would give their craft flight capabilities of up to a mile above ground or sea level, and render them invisible. Since the cloaking device absorbed all sonic, ultrasonic and electromagnetic waves, their craft could not detected by sonar or radar.

Ray adapted these new optional extras so they could be integrated and partly powered from the *Goddess'* existing energy supply. Now he didn't feel as intellectually retarded as he had first imagined. Turan created a crystal generator to give the additional energy required to power the vehicles. This energy source was similar to the one installed in the chariot and, of course, in the everyday hovercraft employed in Atlantis —

except this generator was powered by your average double-terminated quartz wand. Using the crystal generator meant that Ray could design a system to track the craft via its unique energy emission. This energy emission was something their foe would never track, not without sound knowledge of the type of power source. One thing was certain though, these modifications would not happen overnight; there was a couple of years work in the re-routing of the circuitry alone, let alone the installation time.

This came as no surprise to Tory. All she had to do was to decide where they were going to hide out for such a long time span. Turan had arranged an audience with the new High Priestess and Nin Sybil for the morrow, though he hadn't stated his reasons for the meeting to the two women. If they consented to aid her, Tory planned to have all the parts and equipment sent to her father's secret cavern at Dinas Emrys until such time as she had sought out a safe haven where Ray could carry out the operation.

At the appointed hour, Tory manifested in the room that adjoined the High Priestess' council chambers underneath the great temple of Chailidocean. She had arranged to met Turan in this place. Her sudden appearance startled Nin Sybil, who was also awaiting the Shar.

Lamamu? Sybil was thrilled once she'd recognised the intruder. *Surely I am dreaming.*

'No.' Tory took hold of Sybil's outstretched hands, noting she no longer wore a veil. 'It is I, seeking the High Council's aid yet again.'

Well, of course they shall assist in any way they can. We are all much indebted to you for our lives.

Tory laughed at this. 'Not if you consider that I was the reason your lives were under threat in the first place.'

Sybil shook her head at how modest Lamamu was. *But, thanks to you, our nation and the Antillians are at peace. I feel quite sure that the Council will take this into account.*

When Turan made an appearance, Nin Sybil entered the High Priestess' chamber to familiarise the Priestess with the situation before the meeting commenced.

'I know I haven't had much time to spend with you this trip.' Turan made conversation whilst he and Tory waited. 'But I shall miss you when you leave.'

Due to the recent loss of her husband, Turan had kept his distance, knowing that Tory still mourned Miles. Tory, on the other hand, didn't feel it fair to start something she couldn't possibly finish.

'Oh Turan, I am so sorry.' She wanted to confess how badly she felt about the way things never seemed to work out between them, but the Shar wouldn't hear a word of it.

'I understand. Believe me, I do. I've seen what you and I have been up against at various stages of the Earth's history, and I also realise we have the whole of eternity to be together.' Then he smiled. 'Maelgwn is coming for you.'

'What do you know of it?' Tory became most curious.

But Turan clammed up as Sybil opened the door of the council chamber and invited them both to enter.

8

INCONCEIVABLE

The round chamber was dimly lit. The decor, in dusty shades of red, brown, green and blue, gave the large, regal room a rustic quality. In the middle of the chamber the High Priestess sat calmly in her large throne-like chair, which was carved out of timber and lined with fur. Within seconds of setting her eyes upon Tory and Turan, the holy woman's hands were clutching at the ends of her armrests.

What kind of mockery is this? The veiled face of the Priestess gave nothing away.

Forgive me, your reverence. Sybil was stunned by her reaction. *But I do not understand.*

Please, leave us. Temperance instructed Sybil. *If you, too, would be so kind, my Shar.*

Of course. Turan bowed, gripping Tory's hand briefly in encouragement as he followed Nin Sybil from the room.

Once the door was closed, the Priestess looked back to Tory and observed her for a moment in silence. *So, you are the one. The Goddess of love and war, time and space … the famous Lamamu.*

'Yes, highness.' Tory humbled herself, for the holy woman had a very peculiar edge to her tone. 'I am sorry if I have offended you in some way.'

Not offended so much as startled, she clarified, holding a clenched fist to her heart.

'Is your holiness feeling alright?' Tory took a step closer. It was hard to know what to do with that damn veil hiding the woman's facial expression.

Temperance held out a hand to stop Tory in her tracks. *I have been a student of the High Order of Heliona since birth, and in all my four hundred years in this world, I have observed the sacred ways of my order.*

'Yes Nin.' Tory frowned. Why was she telling her this?

In all that time — the Priestess stood up — *no one, not even my parents or peers, have glimpsed the face behind this veil.*

Oh no, here we go again … Tory kept the thought to herself, for this had been the story of Nin Sybil's life before they'd met.

The High Priestess lifted her veil and Tory backed up in fear and astonishment.

'You're me!'

Although she had once had a visit from her future

self, Tory had never before met with a past incarnation —
not a live one in any case.

The Priestess nodded. *And you are the woman Shar
Turan has been pining for this year past.* Temperance
plonked herself back into her seat, exasperated by the
realisation. *I was offered the option to marry before I
decided upon whether or not to take up this position. When
the one man I desired held no interest in marriage, my fate
was decided for me.*

'Turan.' Tory swallowed, realising what she'd done.
'Didn't you show him who you were?'

How? Temperance scowled. *He would not even meet
to discuss the matter, for his heart was lost to another.*

'But that was *me* ... you!' Tory cried.

Was I to know that? She turned her rueful stare from
Tory to the floor, and bowed her head to let her anguish
pass.

'It's not too late ...' Tory appealed, her heart going
out to her.

It is! Temperance curbed her remorse as she recalled
her position. *I wasn't forced to assume this appointment, I
chose it freely ... and I will stand by my decision.*

'Great!' Tory threw her arms in the air, it was just
like her to be so damned righteous. 'So both you and
Turan will live a long life of loneliness and misery,
because you can't admit you might have made a
mistake.'

I made a mistake! Temperance was on her feet,
outraged. *I am not the one who has been playing havoc with
the time continuum. How dare you presume to defy the
Gods!*

'Look, I am only following the orders they give me. I am not afraid to follow my heart, and by doing so I serve and honour the will of the universe. And, I might add,' Tory placed hands on hips, 'if you didn't insist on wearing those *stupid* veils all your lives, Turan would have fallen for you centuries before I even got here.'

You don't know that. Temperance hated to think Tory might be right.

'Are you kidding me?' Tory emphasised her point, motioning to herself. 'You're talking about the man we have loved from one end of eternity to the other.'

The holy woman was bemused, excited and maddened all at once.

'There is no way I'm *not* going to tell him,' Tory informed Temperance, bluntly.

The Priestess was alarmed, then stood tall to look down upon her tiny double. *If you do, I shall withdraw my council's aid to your cause.*

'Goddamn it.' Tory wanted to punch something. 'You're making a huge mistake! Doesn't the very nature of your name tell you that!'

Temperance looked on, unconcerned. *Do we have a deal?*

Tory tamed her frustration, trying to figure the best way to get around herself. 'You have no idea what you're giving up.'

Vow to me your confidence, or find another to aid you. The priestess resumed her seat, appearing very confident of getting her own way.

'Alright then,' Tory was fuming again. 'Die a bitter old woman. See if I care.'

Thank you. I trust your word is as good as my own.
She waited for Tory's answer.

'I shall not tell him.' Tory confirmed their
arrangement.

Then you may go. Temperance lowered her veil. *You
can count on the support of the High Council of
Chailidocean.*

Tory gave a slight bow, turned, and stormed from
the room.

When Tory reached Turan and Sybil in the outer
chamber, she slammed the door behind her and began
to pace.

'Will she not aid you?' Turan enquired, concerned
by her behaviour.

'Oh, she agreed alright.' Tory's words were filled with
contempt. 'She'd cut off her nose to spite her face, too.'

'What is eating you.' Turan pulled her to a
standstill. 'I don't understand?'

Tory took a deep breath, looking at him fondly to
say, 'You will, my sweet. Once I am gone, everything
will make *perfect* sense.'

Ray had almost finished revising the specifications of
Merlin I and *Merlin II* on the psychokinetic computer in
Turan's lab to give them the same new systems that
were planned for the *Goddess*. But cabin fever was
starting to set in. He'd been locked up in this same
room for a week.

When Shar Jerram popped by and offered to take
Ray for a test drive in a hovercraft, he jumped at the
chance to explore the world beyond these walls. Just as

important as installing the systems was knowing how to handle them once they were functional.

Turan had sensed Ray was getting a little restless, and so had given Jerram the all-clear to take him outside for a spell — with the proviso that they kept a low profile.

They clothed Ray in a long white robe with a huge hood to cover his face. This was the normal attire of the Higher Orders of learning here in the golden city so, except for his lack of height, Ray thought he blended in quite well.

With his head constantly swivelling from left to right, and back again, the entire way, Ray ambled along beside Jerram to the fourth and final island ring. The main harbour and the boat docks were located here, and the town's marketplace sprawled along the streets. Ray marvelled at the wild array of people, livestock, and foods on display, and nearly had a heart attack when a tiger just wandered past down the road.

'Shouldn't that be in a cage or on a leash or something?' Ray directed Jerram's attention to the tiger.

Jerram laughed. 'Whatever for?' He stopped to look over the baskets of fruit along the roadside and selected a couple of large, bright blue berries, tossing one to Ray.

'Thanks.' Ray looked it over. It certainly smelt quite palatable. Ray took a bite and was pleasantly surprised. 'Hey, this is *really* good.'

'Aphrodisiac!' Jerram stirred him up with a wink.

'Help! Somebody, please!' Annora spied Shar Jerram as she darted through the crowd, and headed straight for him.

'Speaking of which …' Jerram muttered sideways to his companion.

'Shar Jerram, quick.' She grabbed hold of his arm to hoist him away. 'One of the natives — he's Antillian, I think — is beating a woman. He's going to kill her.'

Both Jerram and Ray leapt into action, racing after her through the multitudes on the docks.

'Good Lord.' Ray spotted the eight foot tall native who was the cause of the dispute, and slowed to a stop. Shar Jerram didn't seem fazed by the giant's size. He stormed up to the irate man, yelling threats up at him in his native dialect. Ray rushed to the battered woman, beside whom Annora crouched. He struggled a little as he took the ailing female native up in his arms. 'Where do you want her?'

'It's you?' Annora spied the face underneath the hood. But, as there were greater concerns at present, she stood to guide him. 'This way, hurry.'

'What are you doing?' Jerram called out, as he watched Ray follow Annora back towards the city. 'I knew I shouldn't have given him that fruit.' Jerram said to himself and set off in pursuit of his charge.

Once they'd delivered the ailing woman to the Temple of Healing, Ray loitered out front in the hope that Annora would be curious enough to come seek him out.

'There you are.' Jerram bounded up the stairs of the Shi-im-ti temple, and took hold of Ray's arm. 'Let's go.'

'Just five minutes,' Ray implored him, not budging an inch.

'Five what?' Jerram didn't really care, they were going.

'Stop right there!' Annora descended the stairs. 'I think I deserve an explanation.' Coming to a stop before the hooded double of Zadoc, she peeked under his disguise to address him. 'You're *not* my husband.'

'Well, not exactly, no,' Ray confessed, controlling his urge to smile. She was so lovely, and so familiar. It wasn't just that Annora resembled Tory; Ray felt that he'd met her somewhere else, but he couldn't place it. 'It was the kiss that gave me away, wasn't it?'

Annora raised both eyebrows with a smile, and gave a nod. ''Twas tamer than I'm used to.' She shrugged. 'But nice all the same.'

As the pair stood staring into each other's eyes, Jerram rolled his. 'Yeah, alright … we've got to go.' The Shar dragged his lovesick captive away.

'Where are you going?' Annora came after them. 'I am at leisure today.'

'That's great news!' Ray nudged Jerram, pleading with his eyes to let her come.

'This is not what I call keeping a low profile … nobody is supposed to know.' Jerram said anxiously.

'I'm very good at keeping secrets,' Annora vowed first to Ray, then looked at Jerram … 'Really. I am.'

'Heaven forbid! Alright, already, she can come.' Jerram caved in.

'Good.' Annora took Ray by the arm. 'Where are we going?'

'To the E-na-mu.' Jerram advised her. This was the 'abode to ascend to the skies' where the hovercraft awaited.

'Flying … excellent.' Annora greatly approved.

In the wake of her dispute with herself, Tory floated away her frustrations in the hot spa pool in Turan's palace chambers. Although Turan communicated with her in English, she was pondering if he also could read the language. *Too risky*, Tory decided. She had to be sure Turan understood her parting message. *I shall leave a mental note in his computer. That's not telling him.* She justified her scheming. *It's more a thought transference, really.* She grinned broadly at her rationalisation.

The sound of the door vanishing warned her that company was arriving. Tory immediately transported herself elsewhere.

'Alaric!' Turan casually arose from his seat, but his eyes jumped from his brother in the doorway to the spa pool behind him. Tory was gone, and he quickly looked back to his visitor. *What can I do for you?*

His brother appeared rather puzzled as he entered. *I could have sworn I saw a woman in your bath.* He approached the pool to take a closer look.

If only. Turan smiled, and steered Alaric in the other direction when he noticed Tory's clothes piled in a corner.

Weird, Alaric mused. *She looked rather like Lamamu I thought.*

Now you're really teasing. He motioned his brother to the lounge. *Please, sit.*

No, no, Alaric declined. *I just wanted to make sure your expenditure details for next semester have been handed in to the council.*

All taken care of, Turan assured him. *En Seba has them.*

111

Very good then. Alaric headed for the door, pausing to look once more at the pool, and then at his brother. *I could have sworn ...* He shook his head with a smile. *Sorry it couldn't be so.*

Not as sorry as I. Turan waited for Alaric to depart before he gathered Tory's gear up in his arms and hurried off to his lab. He knew she would be there.

Ray was reeling from his sightseeing flight over Chailidocean and the surrounding area, and his elation was more intense for having spent the afternoon in Annora's company.

Jerram did not seem to share his good humour. Jerram knew Turan would fry him if he found out what had happened. Still, when they returned to Turan's lab to find Tory wearing nothing more than one of the large sheets used to cover the equipment, Jerram's mood perked up considerably. 'Get that off,' he demanded with a laugh. 'It's filthy.'

'Tell me about it,' she grumbled, clutching it tighter.

'Here you go.' Ray removed his bloodstained disguise and handed it to her.

'Spoilsport.' Jerram folded his arms, amused to see how Tory would go about the change.

'Turn around, please,' she requested politely.

Jerram chuckled at this. 'Not if my life depended on it.'

'It does,' she warned with a sweet grin.

The Shar thought a moment, recalling her prowess in battle. 'Ah,' he waved it off, 'it will be worth it.'

'*Jerram.*' She was getting annoyed.

'Tory!' Turan came racing through the door, whereupon Jerram's hands shot into the air.

'I didn't touch her. She was already like that.'

'Did he see me?' Tory beseeched Turan.

'Long enough to know it was you.' The Shar's huge form came to block her from the view of the other two men, and he handed her the clothes he carried. 'And as he knows about your teleportive abilities, I dare say he might have guessed.'

'Hey, not fair. Why does he get to watch?' Jerram protested, but was ignored.

'How long are those parts going to be?' Tory struggled to put her attire on as quickly as possible, not even looking to catch Turan's reaction.

'A couple of days.'

She didn't have to look, she could hear the smile in his voice. 'Have you got a safer place for us to hide till then?'

'Annora will hide us,' Ray coyly suggested. 'She even said she would.'

'When did she say so?' Tory came out from behind Turan, fully clothed.

Jerram frantically motioned Ray to refrain from further comment.

'This afternoon,' Ray admitted, at which time Jerram started to back out of the room.

'Is that so?' Turan raised a hand in his younger brother's direction, willing him closer. Jerram was hauled back for interrogation through no will of his own.

'I had nothing to do with it.' Jerram washed his hands of the affair.

'You were supposed to be watching him.' Turan was feeling edgy. 'Alright, here's what's going to happen. I'll seek the permission of the High Priestess to hide you in the Temple.'

'She'll never agree to hide a man there,' Jerram pointed out.

'Let Annora hide us.' Ray was more insistent this time.

Tory had to agree with Ray. 'I don't think anyone would think to find me there. Annora and I have never even met.'

'But what if Zadoc returns?' Turan didn't like it one bit, nor did he trust Ray with his brother's wife.

'I doubt he will.' Jerram offered his viewpoint. 'I heard the trial has been suspended while they search for a piece of missing evidence. He could be weeks yet.'

Tory. Turan bethought her only, appealing to her common sense. *You know why I hesitate to condone this arrangement, don't you?*

Yes. She understood his fears. *But I assure you, I have the situation well in hand.*

How can you be so sure? The Shar frowned. There was no controlling the attraction between such obvious soul mates as Zadoc and Annora — or in this case Ray and Annora. But Tory knew something Turan did not, and she was fairly confident she had a deterrent that would keep Ray out of harm's way. *Trust me.*

I just knew you were going to think that. The Shar held his head in his hands.

'Well, don't just stand there staring at each other.' Ray pushed for a decision. 'What's it going to be?'

114

'You win.' Turan answered Ray's question, though his eyes did not move from Tory. *Again*.

Annora had a lovely home on the eastern side of the second island ring, close by the healing temple where she was head of midwifery.

It was far more pleasant staying here, with the lovely garden of fruit-laden trees and flowering foliage. The abode wandered in curves, with no corners to be found anywhere. The furniture, too, was moulded out of the whitewashed interior architecture, giving the place a Mediterranean appearance. The cushions were made of woven fabric featuring earthy designs in rust, brown and black. Large terracotta pots bearing healthy, green-leafed plants brightened the interior.

Tory was soaking up a few rays by the long, narrow pool, perfect for swimming laps, which had been built half inside and half outside the house.

'I must come here more often,' she decided, for it seemed to be the only place in the whole of time and space where she actually had a chance to relax. She heard a splash from inside and Ray swam out to join her.

'Hey, I really have to thank you for bringing me here, Alexander.' He floated on top of the water, next to where Tory lay baking. 'I'm having the time of my life.'

'Yeah, right ... I think you owe me a hundred bucks, Murdock.' She rolled onto her side, supporting her head on one hand.

'She's already married to me, so I don't think it really counts,' Ray ruled, doing a backflip so he didn't have to hear Tory contest the matter.

But as he surfaced Tory grabbed hold of his braid to stop him going under again. 'Doesn't she remind you of someone?'

'Yes.' Ray wiped the water from his eyes. 'You.'

'No.' She hit him on the head playfully. 'Besides me. Come on Ray, think.'

'*I don't know.*' He was immediately exasperated, having been trying to figure it out for days himself.

Tory sighed, disappointed by his lack of vision. 'I'll give you a hint. Imagine Annora was a brunette, with eyes of say, ebony.'

'Jesus.' He thrust backwards through the water as he realised. 'Rhiannon!'

'Very good.' Tory gave him a little clap.

'Oh, my God!' He covered his eyes, seized by panic. 'This is *unbelievable!*' He looked back to Tory, who seemed very calm about the whole affair. 'Aren't you even mildly concerned? She is your daughter after all.'

'Depends on your intentions, and whether or not I get my money.'

Then Ray got wise. 'You knew this was going to happen when you made that bet, didn't you?'

'I suspected,' she granted him, anticipating his next question. 'See, you and I have met before. At first, I didn't recognise Rhiannon as your soul mate —'

'Hold on a minute.' Ray was up in arms about her inference. 'You make it sound like it's inevitable that we'll end up together. She's just a girl!'

'I'm not saying anything … *else.*' Tory stood, ready to go inside. 'I just thought you might want to know. The matter has nothing more to do with me.'

116

'Well, thanks *very much!*' He had never met a woman who could get him so worked up. 'I'm beginning to think I should have taken my chances with the Agency.' He looked up at the cloudless sky as he waded out of the pool: 'As for *you*, there is no God. I am becoming an atheist.'

From that point on Ray couldn't look at Annora without seeing the girl he knew. Tory's promise to Turan was kept.

The arrangements proceeded according to plan and the parts and equipment were delivered to the site on Mt Dur-an-ki.

The other form of Atlantean technology that Tory decided was a must, was a half dozen 'Stormers'. These laser swords could convert into stun-guns, making them a handy item indeed.

Tory had left a message on Turan's computer, advising him as to the secret identity of her Atlantean counterpart. She had only to direct his attention to the information, then hopefully he'd live happily ever after.

As evening approached, the Shar arrived to escort Tory and Ray to Mt Dur-an-ki. Turan had transferred the chariot to the mountain plateau, so that once their cargo had been sent back to Myrddin's cave in Gwynedd, the time travellers could depart without further delay.

Tory and Ray were just saying their goodbyes to Annora, when there came an urgent rapping on her front door.

All four of them stood staring blankly at each other, unsure as to whether or not to be alarmed. As the knock was repeated, Annora ventured to answer it.

'Shar Jerram!' She backed up to let him in.

'Turan.' Jerram bounded through the door, pausing to catch his breath after the sprint he'd just made. 'Alaric is looking everywhere for you. He's requested your presence in father's room of court, right away.'

This was bad timing indeed, still Turan figured he should make haste to avoid suspicion. 'Go on without me, I'll meet you there.' He was out the front door, before Tory had the chance to say anything.

The Shar could not believe the inquisition that awaited him in the palace.

His father — the Shu Sar Absalom — Shar Alaric, and a couple of chief advisers, were seated around the arc-shaped table of court going over expenditure details.

Turan, at last! Absalom rose and motioned his son to take a seat before the council.

Turan did as indicated. *Sorry I proved so hard to find. Can I assist in some way?*

Well, dear boy. We have just been revising your budget requirements for next semester, and quite frankly, Absalom sat back in his seat, *we'd like to know what you're working on that could possibly require so grand an outlay of precious resources?*

Turan had included all the parts of Tory's little bundle in his projection and hadn't thought twice about doing so, as his projections had always been accepted in the past. *Since when am I expected to justify what I need for my research?*

Since now, Alaric told him, bluntly. *It is high time we stopped squandering what wealth we have so that we might save something for a time when things might be not so prosperous.*

But you cannot deny me —

We're not saying you can't have all that you've requested. Alaric cut in on his brother. *We are merely asking that you explain what you need it for. If we think the project worthwhile, your needs will, of course, be met.*

This is unprecedented! Turan stood. *And a giant step backwards for the sciences. Father?* Turan appealed.

Very soon Alaric will be assuming my position, so you may as well get used to dealing with him, Absalom ruled, though he hated to see his sons in disagreement. *I believe these new measures we are introducing at Alaric's suggestion show a fair amount of foresight and are justified. Thus, I expect you to cooperate with these proceedings.*

Really, Turan, I don't see what all the fuss is about. Just tell us what you are designing.

Alaric sat forward in his seat wearing a friendly smile, that seemed to Turan to be mocking him. *I have been commissioned by the High Priestess, therefore I am not at liberty to disclose the details of the project. If you wish to know more, you shall have to take the matter up with the High Orders of Passage.* He moved to take his leave.

Ah, not so fast. Alaric motioned his brother to again be seated, and sent a court official to fetch the High Priestess.

Ray marvelled at the large marble plateau of Mt Dur-an-ki, which was near one hundred and fifty feet around. He closely inspected one of the nine large hunks of polished quartz that were set in a circle around the edge of the Plateau. 'So this is what it looked like in its original form.'

'Indeed.' Tory paced back and forth, not really paying much attention to Ray's awe. She was too busy fretting that she wouldn't get to see Turan before they were obliged to depart.

The Priestess and her council had already sent the materials for the *Goddess'* conversion to twenty-first century Gwynedd without a hitch.

Tory had been disappointed to find that Taliesin was no longer present amongst the holy men. Apparently, shortly after her last visit, the Merlin had decided to return to his rightful home in sixth century Britain. There he would set about re-shaping his homeland's history by bringing Tory into it.

'We should get going while the going is good.' Strangely enough, Ray was anxious to see home.

'Please, just a little longer.' Her eyes were fixed on the doorway leading into the mountain face.

I believe your friend is right. You have no reason to delay. Temperance was also feeling anxious. She had nothing to hold over Tory any more, having fulfilled her end of the bargain.

If she argued the point, Tory felt that the holy woman would surely suspect her motive for delay. So she resigned herself to leaving Turan's destiny in the very capable hands of the universe. If the Shar overlooked or erased her message, then perhaps it really wasn't meant to be.

Nin Temperance. Sybil came racing onto the plateau, stunning everyone. This was hardly fitting behaviour for one of her order. *The Shu Sar Absalom is asking you join him at once in his room of court.*

'Turan.' Tory looked to the veiled woman, fearful for the Shar.

Go, Temperance instructed. *I shall take care of this.*

'But what —'

I am not leaving until I see you gone, the Priestess insisted, forcing Tory to comply.

When Temperance entered the room of court, all stood to honour her presence.

This summons is most unusual, gentlemen, I trust you have good cause. She was seated in the chair Shar Turan had vacated for her, and he stood alongside it.

Our sincere apologies, Nin. Alaric spoke on the council's behalf. *As Turan cannot share with us the nature of your commission, this governing body would ask that you enlighten us as to the intent of his work for you.*

Turan didn't know this Priestess very well, but no holy woman would knowingly lie.

By whose authority, do you ask? The veiled woman sat perfectly poised.

He has my authority in this matter. Absalom advised, knowing full well that his son may just as well try to squeeze water from a stone as get any in the Orders of Passage to disclose their doctrine. But still, it would be a good learning experience for the lad.

But my dear Shu Sar, you know as well as I that my Orders are not answerable to the State.

Well, maybe they should be ... Alaric commented out of turn, and was frowned upon by all present.

If you wish to know the will of the Gods, my Shar, you have only to enter the Order of Helio and all shall be made clear to you. Until such time as you are so spiritually accomplished, however, you shall be kept in the dark. Temperance rose. *Good day, gentlemen. I expect I have heard the last of this matter.*

Thank you. Shu Sar Absalom rose appearing most pleased. The subject was now closed and he hadn't even had to take a side.

And in the future, her veiled face turned to Alaric, *I do not expect to be summoned from my duties to discuss such petty matters. I do not interfere with your charge. Do not interfere with mine.*

She turned to depart, placing a hand upon Turan's shoulder. *The Gods have granted your aspirations.*

Turan bowed in gratitude, breathing a sigh of relief as the Priestess left the gathering.

Alaric was brooding in the wake of his defeat. *Those orders could do anything they chose, and we'd be none the wiser.*

Then join the order, Absalom advised. *You know the rules, as well as I.* He regretted that the breaking-in of his son to the Shu Sar's position looked as if it was going to be a longer process than originally thought.

A couple of days later, when all seemed back to normal, Turan sought an audience with the High Priestess, only to be informed that she was not seeing anyone.

I am sorry, Highness. Sybil pursued the Shar into the High Priestess' Chamber.

Turan pleaded with the Priestess on his own behalf. *I promise not to detain you for long, but I must speak with you.*

Very well, Temperance granted, her voice strained and weak. *Thank you, Sybil. You may leave us.*

As you wish. Sybil bowed out, closing the door behind her.

I want to thank you for vouching for me with the Chailidocean council. Turan got straight to the point.

That is all well and good, Temperance was short with him, *but I did not appreciate being placed in such a position.*

It shan't happen again, he vowed, and added a little shyly, *and I also greatly appreciate your aiding Lamamu. All went well with her departure you said.*

Yes. Temperance became colder still. *You need not worry yourself in that regard.*

And she left no message for me? he coaxed.

Ah … The Priestess rose. *Now we get to the true reason behind your visit.*

Forgive me, Nin, I cannot help it, Turan confessed, coming to kneel at the holy woman's feet. *To love this woman is futile, I know, but it seems I am at a loss to prevent it.*

She said nothing. Temperance was so consumed by her jealousy and hurt that she could barely speak. *Her departure was rather rushed, you understand.*

Turan noticed a teardrop splash to the floor in front of him. *Why are you weeping, Nin?*

Temperance walked quickly across the room, so she did not have to look upon him. *I find your ill-fated match very sad, my Shar.*

Please don't cry for me. Like you, I too am used to being alone. He stood once more, observing the Priestess' movements.

Oneness is a grand thing, she allowed, though her heart was not in the statement and she knew it.

The only problem is, since meeting Lamamu, I no longer feel whole, he confided softly. *That is why I have decided to have my life terminated.*

Temperance spun around to view him. *No, you must not.*

He was adamant, *I cannot live without her. And when I say cannot, I mean that this longing I feel will surely kill me within weeks in any event.*

Then return to your etheric state, but don't surrender your life so rashly.

I don't think you understand. I have no desire to put her behind me. To persist with this incarnation is only to delay our next meeting.

Temperance could not keep silent her anguish, and her hands knotted round each other as she openly began to sob.

Please, Nin. I do not mean to distress you. Turan came near to comfort her. *I am at peace and quite happy to go, I assure you.*

I cannot let you do it. She shook her head to get her wits about her. *Two wrongs will never make a right.*

Pardon? he queried.

Heliona forgive me. She removed the headband and

lifted her veil clean off her head. Then stood, eyes lowered to the ground in fear.

After a seemingly endless silence, Turan placed a finger beneath her chin and raised her head for her to look him in the eye. *You've been here all the time?*

I did propose to you once, she sniffled, forcing a laugh as she shrugged.

That was you? He could have kicked himself. He felt he had no right to ask her to abdicate her position now, and he could not lay claim to her whilst she held it. *If only I'd known!*

Well, now that you do know, know this also. She gazed up at him with a hopeless expression upon her face. *I would sooner give up my life's work than consent to the termination of your life.*

And I would rather live out my days in misery, than force you into that position.

As this was not really the response Temperance had hoped for, she lowered her eyes and moved away from him. *Well then, that would seem to leave us right where we are.*

If that is what you wish. The Shar bowed his head to her.

She turned back to view him, maddened by his stance. Why had it been so easy for him to confess he loved her a moment ago and so difficult now when she so desperately needed to hear it? *What I wish? I would like to know what you wish, Turan.*

The Shar knew what she wanted to hear, yet it was not his place to make this decision for her. *My only desire is for you to be happy. I am entirely at your disposal.*

So I must decide our fate alone then?

No, Temperance. Turan ventured to close the space between them. *You have only to choose your destiny, and mine shall follow accordingly. But, if I could be so bold as to put forward something in my own cause?*

Yes? she appealed, feeling that she would renounce everything at even the slightest hint that he felt as she hoped.

Turan's response was unexpected and convincing. Temperance had never conceived of such emotion as his kiss aroused in her and for a few brief moments she completely lost herself in it.

Yet when Turan realised she had started to weep again, he stepped away. *Forgive me. I have upset you again.*

Not at all, she hugged him, tightly. *These tears are of relief. I was so horrified Lamamu had left without telling you.*

Lamamu knew! Turan was almost enraged to discover this, so Temperance quickly added:

I was afraid of the decision I'd be forced to make, if you discovered Lamamu and I were one and the same.

Turan understood this fear well. It was not so long ago that Lamamu had forced him to make a similar choice. As scary as it had been at the time, resuming his physical form was one of the best decisions he'd ever made.

So she never did tell you then? Temperance was amazed. *Which means, I have brought this on myself.* She seemed pleased about it. *It really was meant.* She gazed up at the Shar, her beaming smile conveying the peace she felt in her soul.

No one knows better than I, he said, *that as surely as you and I are upon this earth, we belong together.*

Then who are we to question the will of the Gods? Her lips lingered only inches from his. *So be it.*

PART II

THE SON

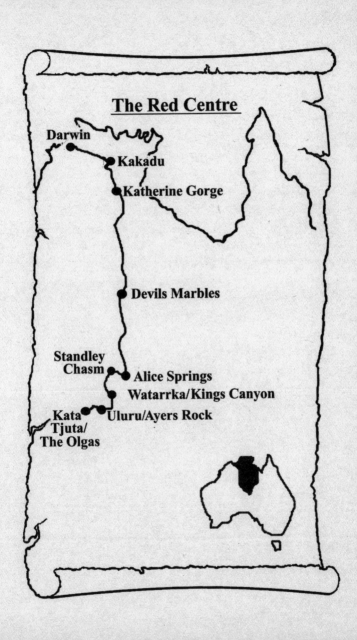

The Red Centre

Darwin

Kakadu

Katherine Gorge

Devils Marbles

Standley
Chasm

Alice Springs

Watarrka/Kings Canyon

Kata
Tjuta/
The Olgas

Uluru/Ayers Rock

9

İП ┼HE BLOOD

Tory and Ray returned to the twenty-first century the day after their departure for Atlantis. The ICA were probably searching for them, and Tory didn't want to risk losing her kin or her craft. Since Myrddin's cave was chock-a-block with the Atlantean spoils for the *Goddess*, she manifested the chariot in the torch-lit earthen corridor that led to the secret cavern of treasures at Dinas Emrys.

'Tory!' Myrddin stepped out from within the piles of equipment, looking rather cranky.

'Yes, father, I know what you're going to say.' She climbed out of her transport, unfazed by his obvious irritation. 'I'll have it all out of your way in a couple of days.'

'Well, why on earth didn't you send it to Taliesin's abode? He's not using it at present.'

'Look, I'm sorry.' Tory was feeling a little tense herself, having left without saying goodbye to Turan and knowing he might be in a bit of a bind. 'I wasn't thinking straight.'

Myrddin rolled his eyes. 'So what else is new?'

While Tory and her father argued, Ray silently crept over to inspect the large metal plates that would house the *Goddess'* hover-systems.

'Tory!' Ray looked at her, aghast. 'He just walked straight through this!'

'Sorry, Ray, you've never met my father, have you?' She casually motioned to the bizarre character dressed in the long flowing robes of a druid.

Myrddin's long, black, wispy hair was streaked with grey. A dash of grey hair began at each side of his mouth, also, and extended to meet in a central point below his chin to form a perfect triangle amidst the dark hair of his beard. The man's eyes were wild, wide and green, like a stormy sea, and those bushy eyebrows made him appear all the more ferocious.

'This is your father?' Ray squeaked, with a gulp. 'I thought Professor Renford Alexander was —?'

Myrddin spun around in a clockwise direction and turned into the aging professor of British history. 'Now you see him …' Renford spun anti-clockwise, 'now you don't.' The Merlin raised his eyebrows a couple of times.

'Ray. I'd like you to met Myrddin.' Tory placed an arm around her awestruck friend as he was looking a little green around the gills again.

'As in King Arthur … Myrddin?' Ray hesitantly extended his hand, and Tory cringed knowing her father wasn't going to appreciate the comparison.

'No, you silly goose.' Myrddin slapped Ray's hand away, angered by the long-standing misconception. 'Arthur never actually existed! He was merely conjured up to account for the feats of a number of great warrior kings. Who, I might add, were robbed of *their* due.' He nodded sagely, leaving through the same wall of metal plates that he had emerged from.

Ray felt a little bemused. 'Am I in the twilight zone, or do I just need to brush up on my history?'

'You'll have to forgive Dad's intolerance. He's more used to the company of trees and animals these days.' Tory took hold of Ray's hand, eager to get back to the rest of her kin.

'Ah-ha,' Ray uttered, bleary-eyed, as the light ethers began to engulf them.

When they appeared back in her quarters on board the *Goddess*, Ray and Tory were unexpectedly thrust off balance and flung to the floor.

'What the hell was that?' Tory struggled against the force of the vessel to raise herself from Ray.

'It felt like we hit something.' He struggled to get them both upright, when the craft suddenly tilted in the opposite direction and they slid to the other side of the cabin. 'You do care …' Ray grinned as Tory again attempted to peel herself off him. 'All bets are still on, you know … one hundred bucks.'

'Murdock! Just get off the door, so we can open it.'

She gripped the handle, and, along with another jolt of the sub, the door swung open. Tory managed to hold fast and grabbed hold of Ray as he was flung past her. 'Where do you think you're going, the control deck is that way.' She gave Ray a great shove and got him moving in the right direction.

They bumped and clawed their way to the central control room. The rest of the crew had huddled behind Teo and Naomi who were busy piloting the vessel.

'What's the story?' Tory stumbled over to join them all.

'It's about time you showed.' Brian gave her a dirty look. 'You were right. We're in deep shit.'

A blast was heard outside the vessel and everyone braced themselves as Teo swerved the *Goddess* away from it. 'Jesus, that was *too* close.'

'Would somebody please tell me what is going on?!' Tory was annoyed to find she'd jumped through time from one traumatic situation into another.

'There's a naval sub on our arse trying to persuade us to surface.' Brian was none too happy to admit it. 'Any bright ideas, Einstein?'

It took a few seconds for the news to sink in. 'How far are we from the dive site for Chailidocean?'

'About three miles, and four thousand feet,' Naomi informed.

'Head for Mount Dur-an-ki,' Tory suggested, 'but, for God's sake, don't pass directly over it.'

'I follow.' Teo grinned, recalling what had happened to *Merlin II* when Tory had attempted to land there.

'We're going to get fried before we even get close,' Brian whispered urgently.

'Yeah, right! And lose all Ray's precious research. I don't think so.' Tory set his mind at ease, knowing it was the risk to his family that was making him so edgy. 'Where's our huge friend when we need him, hey?'

I'd forgotten about him. Rhiannon braced herself as best she could as a plan formulated in her mind. She needed to be able to concentrate.

Teo led their pursuers deeper, planning to do a $180°$ arc around the mount. He hoped he was far enough ahead for the navy to anticipate his course, cut the corner to intercept the *Goddess*, and encounter the strange energy field that emanated from the mountain. 'Tory, you know they won't last five minutes at this depth without power?'

'It's us or them,' she stated coldly.

Ray looked at her, poised like a statue, with no hint of uncertainty. 'Those men are only following orders. They don't know what's really going on.'

'Well, what would you suggest we do? Have you already forgotten that the last lot of men who were following Doc's orders beat you senseless?'

Ray had to think about it a moment. 'It still doesn't make it right though, does it?'

A grim smile crossed Tory's face. 'Once the chief of justice, always the chief of justice, eh Ray?'

The sonar pinged and they could see there was now a third player in their dilemma.

'Animal, vegetable or mineral?' Brian had found his sense of humour, having realised Tory was right; if their pursuers were aiming to harm them they'd be at the bottom of the ocean by now.

'It's the dino-fish, alright.' Naomi confirmed.

Another torpedo exploded nearby. How Noah wished he was on the *Merlin* shooting the entire incident. 'Moby Dick is surely not going to like those guys treating his girlfriend in this fashion.'

'What's lover boy doing?' Tory steadied herself against the back of Teo's seat to view the sonar.

'He's headed for the bogey, and … contact! They seem to have changed their course.' Teo cheered, as did everyone, ecstatic to have them off their tail.

'Best get moving.' Rhiannon snapped out of her daze. 'He'll keep them turning in circles for a while.'

'How do you know?' Tory queried, taking her daughter under her arm.

'Call it intuition.' Rhiannon winked at her mother.

'Where to now then?' Teo turned in his seat to consult Tory and Brian.

Brian was perusing the large screen of the map table, mulling over their options. 'Are we thinking to head for Australia?' He glanced at his sister.

'I'll need a few hours to confirm it, but I believe we are.' She chewed on her lip, frustrated. They were more pushed for time than she'd expected.

'Well, north through the Pole is out. It will be crawling with UN personnel. Doc Alexander dropped another bombshell last night,' he advised Tory and Ray. 'But I'll get to that presently.' Brian looked to the south on his map. 'So, going down around the bottom of Africa would be the ticket, though we'll be damn lucky to make Australia without being spotted.'

'You let me worry about that.' Tory eyed the great distance. 'Tell me about Doc?'

'Come to the rec-room. I recorded it for you.'

At the UN health summit for AIDS, held in Geneva the previous day, the ICA put forward several proposals aimed at controlling the disease. The first of which was compulsory AIDS testing on a world-wide scale. By the year 2020 every man, woman and child on the planet would be carrying a card that stated they'd been examined. This card would be required to gain employment, health care and benefits, travel visas etc.

'ID cards,' Ray was most annoyed. 'They may as well be!'

Doc Alexander gave a very convincing spiel on why this drastic measure was necessary. The rapid spread of the disease, especially in third world countries, would never be contained unless isolated and removed. If this policy was not embraced by every single nation, even this attempt to defuse the situation would prove useless.

A visual presentation on a new clinic incorporating all the most up-to-date medical technology, currently under construction in northern Alaska, was shown. But this was more than just a hospital for AIDS victims. This was a whole city, where everyone who was diagnosed with the disease would be sent.

At first, the assembly was outraged, as this was reminiscent of the old leper colonies. With the announcement that the ICA had discovered a cure, Doc turned the opposition into a standing ovation.

This clinic was the only place where the remedy would be administered, at no cost to the sufferers. Every government who wished to be rid of this threat would contribute to the projects funding. As the antidote was a series of treatments, rather than just one injection, Doc maintained that it was safer to remove the victims from society altogether so there was no risk of them infecting others before they were cured themselves. Once the sufferer had physically and psychologically recovered from the disease, they would be returned home. Or they could choose to stay to help with the rehabilitation of others.

Doc wrapped up his proposition with a quote from The Book of Revelation of St John the Divine: '*And the second Angel poured out his vial upon the sea; and it became as the blood of a dead man: and every living soul in the sea died* ... Esteemed colleagues, ladies and gentlemen, I am offering you the chance to put a stop to this menace, before this is truly the case. The decision is yours.'

Brian let the tape run long enough for Tory to get some idea of how great the applause was, then switched the screen off.

'This is his first step towards controlling a world economy, you just wait!' Ray was fuming. 'Who needs weapons to rule the world?'

'I think he means to find us, the immortals.' Tory looked to Brian. 'Our blood is like no other.'

'Well, how the hell does he even know we exist?' Brian reasoned, becoming agitated again.

'I suspect Doc may be an immortal himself.' Tory restrained Brian to get his full attention. 'He murdered Miles because he mistook him for Maelgwn.'

'Murdered?' Brian's eyes narrowed.

'I don't know how he knows, or why he seeks us. I just know he does.' Tory wished she had more of the puzzle figured, but there were still so many pieces missing.

'Well, why don't we pay Alexander a visit and find out why?' Brian thumped his fist into the palm of his hand, fed up with guesses and hearsay.

'First things first. We have to find a safe haven for the *Goddess*, so Ray can get cracking on her modifications.' Tory headed for the door.

As it seemed she was forever charging off somewhere, leaving him to cope with the flak, Brian pursued her. 'Where are you going now then?'

'To get changed. I'm going to Uluru.'

Brian ceased his chase, realising this was about as much information as he was going to get. 'What is the use of taking a deep sea submersible into the middle of a bloody dessert?' he put to Ray. 'I must be mad to listen to her.'

Ray smiled to disagree. 'Well, that would be the last place I'd be looking. And besides, once I get finished with this vessel, it will be a hell of a lot more than just a bathyscape.'

After a quick shower and change, Tory felt herself ready for her next exploration. She was sensibly attired in jeans, a cool, long sleeved shirt, hiking boots and a wide-brimmed hat. She also decided to carry a jacket with her, as the temperature in the Australian outback was known to plummet come nightfall.

Tory was on the verge of transporting herself to the Red Centre, when Rhiannon arrived. She was of the mind to accompany her mother. As Rhiannon had never been to Australia and was dressed sensibly for the trip, Tory couldn't see any reason why she shouldn't tag along.

Tory had never actually been to Uluru, nor did she know anyone there, but she'd seen so many images of the immense red earth formation that locating it was not difficult, for there was none other like it in the world.

As the image in her mind manifested before her, Tory was rather surprised to find herself standing in a field of lush green bushy scrub. Hundreds and thousands of yellow and pink wildflowers covered the flat red earth leading to the massive rock, their spicy, sweet scent filling the air. The distinctive smell of the Australian flora was so familiar that Tory took a deep whiff and savoured it with a smile. 'Home.'

'Mother, it's lovely.' Rhiannon eyed the terrain before them. 'Though I have to tell you, I was expecting a desert.'

'You're not the only one,' Tory said. 'It looks as if the weather conditions here may have altered somewhat of late.' She was spellbound by the timelessness of the landscape. 'There's more than a few ley lines running through this place. It's literally oozing Otherworldly energy.'

'This is a crossroads of many a dreaming track.'

Tory and Rhiannon spun around to find a tall Aboriginal man of about thirty years of age, wearing the uniform of a park ranger.

'I hope we're not trespassing.' Tory knew there were several Aboriginal sacred sites in the area that were forbidden to foreigners.

He laughed at this. 'Hardly, you're standing in the middle of Uluru National Park.'

'Are you a ranger here?' Tory approached him to introduce herself.

'Nah, I'm just visiting. Just north of here is my territory.' He informed her, a huge smile on his face as he viewed her more closely. 'The name's Pete … Pete Nangina.'

'G'day.' Tory returned the friendly greeting, holding her hand out to shake his. 'I'm —'

'Tory Alexander,' Pete answered for her, his smile broadening as the two women looked absolutely flabbergasted.

'How did you know?' Rhiannon found her voice before her mother did.

They were even more flabbergasted by his reply. 'Well, Rhiannon, a little dragon told me.'

Did he mean Maelgwn? It was Maelgwn who'd instructed Cadfan to direct her here in the first place. Tory cocked an eye and put it to Pete … 'So, am I to assume this dragon sent you to find us?'

'Down to the very square inch of land and moment of your arrival,' he advised her, casting a probing eye across the landscape. 'But if my understanding is correct, you're a little pushed for time … so, if you'll just follow me.' He did an about face and headed off through the scrub.

'Hey Pete, wait up.' Rhiannon bounded off after him, excited by the development. 'Where are we going?'

'Watarrka,' he advised as she caught him up.

Still stunned by these events, Tory was slower off the mark. Did this mean Maelgwn was here? Was this man leading her to him at this very moment? She caught up to him. 'Pete … by any chance, does Watarrka have a European name?'

The tall bushman stopped and turned back to her, still wearing his knowing smile. 'King's Canyon.'

The information sent Tory's heart leaping into her throat.

On this afternoon the temperature in the Centre was a comfortable twenty degrees, though by midnight it could be expected to have dropped to around the five degree mark.

Pete had a four-wheel drive. From what he told them, it seemed that around here just about everyone in-the-know did. Not all of the tracks were sealed, and even parts of the bitumen roads had been coated with dirt during the heavy rains. The many large puddles and mudslides made for a tough ride, and at one point they lost sight of the road altogether.

'Are you sure this is wise?' Rhiannon queried as the wheels spun round in the mud until they found traction, and their vehicle was thrust on its way towards the next deep hole.

'She'll be right, mate,' he winked. 'The conditions are pretty good today.'

Pete got them as close to the canyon as they could get by road. The place was all but deserted.

'This is Watarrka,' Pete announced, throwing some climbing gear over one shoulder. 'I hope you two are fit.'

'We'll try and keep up,' Tory assured him.

Rhiannon and Tory followed him up a track that led them along the northern rim, towards the head of the canyon.

After the initial uphill climb, the rocky red land was reasonably flat, although there were short jumps to be made over wide cracks. This huge monument of nature stretched out towards the horizon on all sides. One couldn't help but feel rather insignificant in comparison. Their trek led them past an area of strange, domed rock formations that were about nine metres high and between ten to fifteen meters in length. These resembled abandoned houses and streets; the site had thus been dubbed by Europeans 'the Lost City'. Passing over a small and rather dicey footbridge that spanned a deep cleft in the rock, the track passed dangerously close to the edge of a sheer cliff top.

'Great views, eh?' Pete slapped Tory's shoulder, nearly startling her out of her wits.

'Well, you've got to give him that.' Rhiannon dared to lean over to view the floor of the canyon about one thousand feet below them. 'The view is spectacular!'

Further on, they came to a deep chasm where they stopped while Pete rigged up a line to take them down into the head of the canyon.

'Are we allowed down there?' Tory wondered; the terrain seemed somewhat precarious.

'Trust me.' Pete motioned her to the rope and harness.

Known as the 'Garden of Eden' the well-watered, sheltered floor of the deep ravine was a regular little oasis with its towering gum trees and abundant low-lying native plants. Wildlife abounded here, and trickling streams led to larger freshwater drinking holes.

It was as Tory approached one of these large pools that she spied something with a metallic shine catch the sun.

'What is it?' Rhiannon spotted it too, and pursued her mother to investigate. 'Why, it's a sword!'

Tory withdrew the blade from the soil, wielding it around herself in a figure of eight motion before eyeing it over with recognition and delight. No doubt about it. This was Maelgwn's weapon, which she'd entrusted to her son when she left ancient Britain for the twentieth century.

'Rhun ...' Tory breathed, sensing his presence close by.

'Hello, Mother.'

Rhun manifested before her, though Tory hardly recognised her boy in his modern attire — a vest and shorts of army green, and a rugged pair of hiking boots. 'Praise the Goddess!' She embraced him in earnest. 'It took you long enough to find us.'

He hugged his mother until she recovered from the shock. 'I've been waiting for you.' Rhun kissed her forehead, then looked to the other beauty Pete had brought down into the canyon. 'Please don't tell me this is my sister.'

Rhiannon was eyeing this warrior-like figure of a man, also wishing this was not the case. His shiny dark hair fell dead straight to his shoulders, and his large dark eyes were akin to her own. 'Looks that way, wouldn't you say.' It was like staring at the male version of herself.

'At long last we meet.' Rhun bowed. 'I bid you welcome, Rhiannon, to your new home.'

She eyed the surrounding area, yet there was no abode within view. 'Home?' Rhiannon quizzed, confused.

'Allow me.' Rhun offered her one of his hands and Tory the other. 'Thanks Pete. I owe you one.'

'Rubbish,' Pete waved it off, then waved goodbye. 'We owe you many.'

As his friend disappeared into the trees Rhun looked at his mother, flashing a cheeky grin. 'You're going to be so proud of me.' He closed his eyes to focus on their destination.

IO

GLIMPSING THE FUTURE

Moments later, Tory and Rhiannon found themselves in a small earthen sleeping cave. It had no windows, and judging by the rough red texture of the walls, Tory imagined they were somewhere underneath the canyon.

'It's a little cosy for all of us, don't you think?' Rhiannon commented shyly, not wanting to offend their charming host.

'This is only my room.' Rhun ruffled her hair. 'I didn't want to overawe you with too much at once.' He backed up towards a heavy timber door. 'Are you ready for this?'

'I think so,' Tory granted, yielding to her son's excitement. 'Impress me.'

'Open,' Rhun instructed, and the door vanished.

'Hey!' Rhiannon neared him, intrigued.

'Particle control.' Rhun shrugged it off as an insignificant detail, motioning with his finger for them to follow.

Stepping onto a solid red earth walkway, both women were struck speechless by the sheer size of the thriving community they beheld. They were not so much under the canyon, as inside its walls. Stairways and pathways lined the huge red earth walls, leading to abodes which looked similar to the one they'd just exited. The floor of the enormous dug-out cavern looked like one big BBQ area, with fires for cooking. The cavern was artificially lit. The lighting became dimmer towards the top of the huge cave, increasing in intensity as it reached the floor.

A thousand questions sprang into Tory's mind. 'Power, water, food? How did you ever get the Aboriginal people to agree to this?'

Rhun looked smug. 'Come on, I'll show you around.'

He guided them down a string of pathways and several sets of spiralling iron stairways to ground level. Rhun greeted and introduced people as they went. Apart from the native Australian's who inhabited the cavern, the remainder of the population were generally scientists or inventors who wished to pursue their projects without any government to misuse their genius.

'A ready-made rebel alliance ... just what you need, yes?' he asked his two honoured guests, already knowing the answer. 'You see, when the time came to hand over the rule of Gwynedd to Cadwell, I decided to do a little time exploration of my own ... well, actually, Taliesin insisted on it. The High Merlin took me shopping in the year 2035 AD, and much of what you see here is a direct result of that journey. This series of caverns, though already naturally existing, were extended, moulded and fortified using a combination of bacterial quarrying and organic cementation, a process that will not be perfected for a least another fifteen years.'

'Wow.' Rhiannon didn't really have a clue what he was on about, but it all sounded very impressive.

Passing through a huge triangular opening in the wall, they followed a wide thoroughfare into a second cavern that was even bigger than the last.

'*Food*,' Rhun announced to answer one of his mother's questions as he escorted them over a large bridge. 'This is the hydroponics and farming centre of our little community.'

The moat that encompassed the circumference of this cavern was sectioned off for the farming of various species of fish and molluscs; large greenhouses were filled with all manner of thriving vegetables and herbs, whilst the exterior gardens, and orchards of fruit, were host to small livestock, such as chickens, ducks and geese.

'To graze cattle or sheep here is out of the question, so we mainly stick to seafood, fruit and vegetables, although we do keep some cows and chickens in the large barn yonder, for dairy goods and eggs. The Aboriginals tend to go their own way with their food, so everyone is also free to cultivate what they please. The more nationalities of people who end up here, the more diverse our diet is becoming.'

Tory was turning circles trying to comprehend everything that was going on around them. People were harvesting, planting, pruning, picking, fishing, feeding, watering and just plain relaxing. 'But how on earth do you generate enough power for all this?'

'Natural gas, or you could say, *shit*,' Rhun informed them simply. 'It's a Sakahauchi methane processor, first developed in America with moon colonisation in mind. This also supplies us with water and fertiliser for agriculture, whilst addressing the sewerage problem at the same time.'

'You are far too clever.' Tory gave him a huge hug as they approached the far end of the farming cavern. 'I am impressed beyond my wildest expectations.'

'Where does this lead?' Rhiannon was poised ready to race off across a bridge that crossed over the moat to yet another thoroughfare through the cavern wall.

'Why don't you find out?' He gave her leave to go on ahead. 'I have a present for you,' he advised, putting his arm around his mother's shoulders.

'Through there?' Her eyes motioned to the tunnel Rhiannon had disappeared into.

'You guessed it.'

'Oh Mother, quickly.' Rhiannon bolted back to wave Tory on. 'Wait until you see this. You won't believe it!'

This final cavern was the largest of the three so far and contained several enormous pools of water. Natural sunlight poured in through a hole in the roof at the far end.

Rhiannon headed towards the boat ramp and a tool shed at the side of the largest body of water.

As Tory stood staring at her saving grace, he leant over her shoulder to whisper, 'The universe always provides.'

She gripped his hand, appreciative of having at least one of her major problems solved. 'Now all I have to do is figure out how to get the *Goddess* here.'

'What do you mean?' He was surprised at her. 'Just will it here.'

Tory burst into laughter. 'Something as complex and huge as our craft? I don't think so.'

Rhun shook his head, emphasising his disappointment. 'You haven't been developing your abilities, have you?' His scolding expression melted into a confident grin. 'Well, it's a good thing for you that I have.'

'What?' Tory thought he was surely joking.

'I can get her here, crew and all.' He shrugged. 'All you need do is take me to her.'

'Well, let's do it!' Tory clutched both his hands.

'Settle down!' Rhun was amused by her eagerness. When he'd last seen her it was he who was the impetuous one, but now it seemed just the reverse was true. 'There is someone you really must meet first.' His mother still seemed a little anxious, until Rhun assured her, 'Your vessel is fine for the moment, so indulge me a while longer.' He offered Tory his arm, which she took with a smile.

On the way back to the cavern of abodes, Rhun told the story of how he and Pete had come to found this colony.

By 2035 the Earth was well and truly feeling the effects of the tilt of its axis. The slow magnetic reversal resulted in a weakening of the Earth's magnetic field, making the planet more vulnerable to strikes by meteorites, comets, and exposure to cosmic rays. A nuclear air blast, triggered by terrorists, ripped a huge hole in the ozone layer in 2020, creating erratic weather conditions which wreaked havoc on the world's food supply.

A huge supernova flare had been predicted for the year 2037. It could increase the already unbearable levels of radiation to the point where the Earth was uninhabitable. Rhun hadn't stuck around long enough to find out whether this came to pass, but by the time he had left, those with the money to pay their way had already started heading for the moon colonies, leaving others to inherit the Earth.

Many years before Rhun departed, the climate in the Red Center had begun to change, returning the desert to the tropical oasis it had been long ago in Gondwanaland. As more and more resorts took advantage of the climate change and sprang up around Uluru, Watarrka and Kata Tjuta (the Olgas), the Aboriginal people were robbed of their tribal lands. Of course, they did not take this lying down and the resultant bloodshed could only be compared to the first white invasion of the territory, way back in the early 1800s.

'But what brought you to Australia?' Tory wondered.

Rhun shrugged. He'd had no option. 'In less than twenty years, Australia will be a major super-power, and some of the most outstanding technology will be designed and produced in this country. This was where I first met Pete Nangina, in the future. A bitter old bastard he was too, resentful and angry at *all* white men for the dwindling numbers of his people. In fact, the only reason he spoke to me at all was because he discovered he couldn't kill me.' This memory made Rhun smile. 'Once I told Pete my history and why I had travelled to his time, and of my plan to return to the late twentieth century, we began to see a way we might be able to save both our peoples from the holocaust ahead. He wrote down an account of the injustices that would befall his people, which I brought back to Pete Nangina in 1999. After the first two of the said disasters came about, I was taken to the tribal elders to put forward my plan for this place.'

This particular site had been selected for several reasons. Watarrka was government land and a tourist attraction, so there was no chance of their little community ever being built out or mined. The majority of the park rangers were native Australians, who could do a fine job keeping people away from the place. But the real deciding factor had been that, during all of the Earth's natural disasters, this part of Australia had remained the least affected area on the planet.

'Since the day our alliance was formed, many of the tragedies that Pete Nangina predicted were, if not avoided altogether, very much delayed and their consequences less harsh,' Rhun was pleased to boast.

'So you and Taliesin have altered the future yet again.' This made Tory uneasy, but who could really say if it would be proven good, bad, or indifferent?

'That we have.' He paused 'For, in an alternative future, you, Taliesin, and father decided it would be best.'

This must have been the same time that Tory's future self had decided to go back to the Dark Age to advise herself to conserve the life-giving potion that had subsequently saved Brian's life. So, if the future was now on a different course, did this mean Tory no longer had to make that journey, because she would still carry it out in some other inter-dimensional reality? She gave up thinking about it. 'Where is Taliesin now?'

Rhun shrugged, resuming their course. 'He returned to Gwynedd years ago to see to the higher education of Cadwell.'

'Speaking of whom?' Tory pulled Rhun up again, hoping to solve another of her life's riddles. 'At what age did Cadwell assume his immortal state?'

Rhun gave a heavy sigh as he recalled the most fearful moment of his parenting life. 'He took a bad fall from a horse at five years of age … luckily, I was the only person present.'

'And your grandson?' Tory urged, as gently as possible.

'Cadfan …' Rhun smiled, proud of him.

'Alias, Walter Cadfan?' Rhiannon finally got a word in.

'The same.'

'I knew it!' both women exclaimed at once.

'So, although I was not in Gwynedd to witness his physical death,' Rhun qualified his next words, 'Cadfan told me, when we bumped into each other here, that he first died in a freak accident, aged twelve and a half.'

'And Taliesin tutored him?' Tory knew this must be so, as Cadfan had seemed an enlightened soul.

'And Cadwallon, after him.'

'What about Cadwaladr?'

Rhun had been wondering the very same thing himself. 'Your guess is as good as mine.'

They scaled the pathways and stairs leading to one of the highest caves in the cavern, and Tory was surprised to hear a favourite song from her youth wafting from their destination. She mouthed the words to the tune a moment to recall the artist. 'My God, you know I haven't heard Pink Floyd in over ten years!'

Rhun laughed. 'You know them? Floyd will be impressed. That's how he got his name, or rather … his handle. Open,' he instructed, and the door vanished to disclose a room full of computer monitors, processors and a vast array of accompanying hardware.

A middle-aged man was slouched in a seat, his crossed feet up on a bench. He was singing along with the stereo as he happily puffed on a very large joint.

'Hey, Floyd!' Rhun yelled for his attention.

'Woe, excuse I.' Floyd turned down the volume, stubbed out the joint, and swivelled around on his chair to make their acquaintance. 'You must be she?' He put on his little, round, wire-framed glasses to get a better look at Tory.

'Must be.' Tory held out her hand to shake his.

She'd been wondering how long it would be before her old champion, Sir Tiernan, showed up in the twentieth century. He had a radically different look now, in his Grateful Dead T-shirt and ratty old jeans. A beard and moustache hid his handsome face and his fine, fair hair fell halfway down his back. Tory imagined that when he wasn't so stoned, his eyes would be the same gentle blue she remembered Tiernan having.

Floyd gently took hold of the legend's hand. 'This is truly an honour. I've heard *so much* about you.' He pointed to Rhun as his source. 'It is wonderful that you are finally here amongst us.' Floyd's attention drifted to Rhiannon. 'That goes for you too, young lady.'

'Well thanks, dude.' She held out her hand to give him some skin and Floyd obliged her, swiping the palm of his hand across hers. 'It's most excellent to be here.'

'Floyd is the eyes and ears of our operation.' Rhun placed a hand on his colleague's shoulder. 'Anything you want to know about anyone on the planet, Floyd is the man to ask.'

This information brought a smile to Tory's face. 'Doc Alexander?'

The computer boffin clapped his hands and laughed. 'One of my favourite case studies.'

'Are you a hacker then?' Rhiannon took a seat on the old, but comfortable sofa.

'Darlin', I have designed encryption codes for the computer systems of some of the world's biggest security agencies. Hacker is such an ugly job description, I prefer to think of myself as a code breaker.'

'And there's not a code in existence that Floyd can't break,' Rhun boasted, and Floyd winked to comfirm the claim.

'You and Ray Murdoch have got to meet,' Tory told him.

'The missing ICA engineer?' Floyd stood, provoked by the possibilities this presented. 'The one who designed the monitoring systems for their new fusion reactors?'

'The very one.' Tory observed Floyd's excitement snowball.

'He hasn't destroyed his research, has he?' He gripped hold of Tory's shoulders in a sudden state of panic.

'No, not yet.'

'Hah-ha!' Floyd threw his baseball cap into the air. 'We can really mess with the big boys now!'

'Well.' Tory was pleased by Floyd's obvious enthusiasm. 'Speaking of the others, shouldn't we go get them?'

'That's probably a good idea,' Rhun considered, 'before the Navy drives them onto dry land.'

Tory freaked. 'I thought you said they were in no danger?!'

'Well, they're not if we leave now.' Rhun held out his hand, very calm about the whole affair.

No sooner had Tory touched her son, than they were gone.

Floyd gave a chuckle, looking at Rhiannon on his sofa. 'The government doesn't stand a chance.'

Back on the control deck of the *Goddess*, Tory and Rhun found the crew in a full state of alert. Three fully-armed navy submersibles were closing in on them from the north, south and west; in ten minutes time they would be forced to surface due to shallow water.

'Shut down all your systems,' Rhun instructed Teo.

Teo glanced back, not recognising the voice. 'Who the hell are you?'

'He's my son,' Tory advised in haste. 'Do as he tells you.'

'But without power, we're stuffed!'

Rhun hoisted Teo from the pilot's seat and took control of the vessel. He placed both hands on the control panel and, seconds later — blackout.

'Jesus.' Naomi gasped, horrified — as were the rest of the crew. Plummeting downwards out of control through the inky blackness was their worst fear come true.

Suddenly, everything in the vessel, including the occupants, took on an eerie blue-white glow that became brighter and brighter. It no longer felt like they were sinking; rather, they drifted, floated, flew even.

When the illumination subsided the natural light from the subterranean cavern poured in through the portholes of their craft. Rhun had brought the *Goddess* to rest on the ramp he'd had built for her.

'That was *incredible*.' Tory kissed her son's cheek; it was obvious she had much work to do on her own psyche.

'Well, holy shit. Will you look at this?' Brian perused the world outside. 'Where the hell are we?' He smiled at Tory and his nephew, most relieved to be wherever he was.

'Welcome to Central Australia, Brockwell.' Rhun, a little drained from his feat, held out a hand to shake his uncle's.

'Brian,' Tory corrected Rhun in a whisper.

'I knew what he meant.' Brian gladly shook his nephew's hand.

Rhun raised himself from the pilot's seat, receiving a round of applause from the very appreciative crew. He cast his eyes over them, unable to believe how many of them he recognised. *Bryce.* He spotted Ray first who in the Dark Ages had been his closest and most trusted friend — for over sixty years. *Selwyn.* His eyes passed by Noah to Daniel — *Cai ... and Queen Katren of Powys.* Rhun's sights came to rest on Naomi in the seat beside him.

'Please,' he gestured for silence. 'I'm so delighted to see you all, the pleasure is all mine, really.'

Tory introduced everyone to him stating their current name and occupation. The one person on board that he didn't recognise interested Rhun greatly. This stocky, middle-aged, red-skinned warrior, who had eyes and hair that were as dark as his own, Rhun guessed to be his mother's childhood sweetheart.

'So, you're the one who had my father green with jealousy,' Rhun commented upon learning Teo's identity.

'Maelgwn, jealous of me.' Teo glanced at Tory. 'Is that a fact?'

'Don't make his ego any bigger than it already is,' Tory advised her boy. 'I've got enough problems, thank you very much.' She left them to show the others around outside.

'She's living in denial, poor woman,' Teo informed Rhun, once she was out of earshot.

'Not for much longer though.' Rhun made a point of clueing Teo in. 'My father will be returning for her soon enough.'

'Come again!' Teo nearly had a fit. 'I thought Maelgwn was dead.'

'Well, then.' Rhun gave him a wink in parting. 'You'd best think again.'

The tour finished in Floyd's observatory room, overlooking the encampment. Here the crew of the *Goddess* were treated to Watarrka home-grown, shots of Jack Daniels, and rock'n'roll from the 70s and 80s.

Ray, Teo and Floyd were seated around the computers devising a means for the ICA to regain possession of Ray's work. The idea was to get the Agency off their backs by giving them what they wanted. For, as Floyd pointed out, it was far better that the ICA utilise a system that they, 'the Rebels', already knew inside and out, than someone else's system. Espionage would be that much more difficult. It was of the utmost importance that the Agency re-acquire the plans for Ray's prototype under circumstances that would not be deemed suspicious.

Noah, in between taking snapshots of the control room with his camera, suggested the airport as a solution. 'Just book Ray on a flight somewhere, preferably to and from destinations as far removed from us as possible. Then all you need do is send a suitcase. The ICA will, *without doubt*, intercept the luggage. Upon finding it unaccompanied, they will simply assume Ray got wind of them and split,' the reporter concluded with a sideways wave of his thumb.

His fellow conspirators were speechless a second.

'We'll have to start calling you the answers man,' Ray commented, amazed at how quickly Noah's mind processed information.

'It's just too simple,' Floyd resolved with a smile,

slapping his hand down on the desktop. 'No wonder I didn't think of it.'

Brian's son, Daniel, meanwhile, had taken a decided interest in the telescope that was in the large adjoining room. Rhun opened the voice-activated porthole in the cavern roof, whereby Daniel was able to sit and observe the clear evening sky through the small, though powerful lens.

Taller than his father, Daniel had the same distinguishing features: his piercing blue eyes, his fair hair, even the dimple on his chin was the same. As the lad fired questions at Rhun, he smiled at Daniel's excitement; it was obvious he had the same thirst for knowledge as Cai had had when Rhun had known him in the Dark Ages.

Rhun left Daniel to his observing. Back in Floyd's control room he began entertaining Brian and Naomi with tales of their adventures together in sixth century Britain, and Rhun's rather zealous account had Rhiannon completely captivated.

Her son had greatly matured during their time apart, and Tory thought him so much more like his father these days. It was his eyes that really got to her though. They were so reminiscent of Maelgwn's it was spooky. *Damn*. Now she'd done it. The memory of her love never failed to leave a deep, empty yearning in Tory's soul, that pained her like no physical ailment ever could.

Rhun excused himself from his audience; even from the other side of the room he picked up on his mother's sorrow. 'Don't be sad.' He came up behind Tory and wrapped his arms about her. 'You know there is no need.'

'He should be here.' Tory resisted the urge to burst into tears as she viewed the gathering of their close freinds and relatives.

'You know he will be as soon as is immortally possible.'

'Do I just?' Tory didn't mean to be negative. But why did Maelgwn send her messages through others? Why couldn't he speak to her directly?

'Because you are too out of touch with the Otherworld, that's why. It's not like he hasn't tried.' Rhun reacted to his mother's thoughts and jumped to his father's defence. 'But if seeing is believing, it might be arranged.'

Tory looked over her shoulder to see if he was serious, and Rhun nodded to substantiate the offer.

'You'll need to do some serious work on your psyche first.'

'Whatever it takes,' Tory stated surely. 'You know I would go to hell and back to be with him.'

'And have done so,' Rhun acknowledged, lightheartedly.

'Tory.' Brian called to her as he crossed the room. 'I've been thinking about how badly the ICA seem to want to find us, and in retrospect, perhaps it wasn't such a good idea to let Pearce go.'

Seeing so many of the Dragon's circle gathered here this day, Tory had also been thinking about Pearce. 'So you think we should find him, and let him know about this place.'

'Well, if what you say is true, and Doc Alexander has killed before … chances are he'll do it again,' Brian openly put forward.

'Who has he killed?' Rhiannon demanded, although in her gut she already knew. Her mother and uncle stared blankly back at her, which she found completely infuriating. 'Goddamn it! I am so sick of you all treating me like a child!' As Tory reached out for her, Rhiannon backed up. 'My father was *murdered*, and you didn't see fit to tell me?' She shook her head in disbelief.

'I —' Tory attempted to explain.

'You were *going* to tell me.' Rhiannon had heard this one before. 'Well, perhaps next time *you're going to tell me something*, you might consider doing so *before* I hear it from somebody else.' Too infuriated to pursue the argument, she waved them all off and left the room.

Rhun found the animosity that Rhiannon felt towards their mother completely overwhelming. Thus, he prevented Tory from going after her and went in her stead.

As suspected, Rhun found his sister leaning over the earthen wall of the walkway outside his abode. 'Couldn't get in, huh?'

She shook her head, her eyes still glued on the large fires that were being lit down below on the cavern floor.

'It's only programmed to respond to my voice.' He leant against the wall beside her.

'I figured,' was all she said.

He didn't want to force her to talk, although he knew she wanted to. After a long silence, Rhun nudged her shoulder with his own. 'You look like you could use a drink.'

'I don't like alcohol,' she informed him, as if it were beneath her.

'Ah, but this is special.' He made the invitation sound more enticing. 'My grandfather's mead.'

'Myrddin?' She queried.

'No, the other grandfather, Caswallon.' He backed up to the door. 'Gwynedd was famous for such brews. Open.' Rhun did the honours, dispensing with the door. 'After you.' He motioned her inside.

Rhun pulled up a couple of chairs, placing a flask and two mugs on the table. 'Please,' he bade her, 'sit.'

'You're going to defend her, aren't you?' Rhiannon slouched into the seat, throwing one leg over the arm of the chair. 'You think I'm being childish and unreasonable.'

'I certainly do not,' he emphasized to the contrary, pouring the mead as he sat down. 'You think I don't know what you're going through?' He had to chuckle, passing a mug to her. 'Still, *you* have not travelled through time as I have. I believe there might be certain things that you have not taken into account when judging our mother.'

'You think?' Rhiannon polished off the contents of her mug in a gulp. 'And what might they be?'

'Well, for starters, the reason she doesn't mourn the death of your father as you do, is because she cannot … she knows he lives on in his immortal self.' As Rhiannon started shaking her head to disagree, Rhun became more insistent. 'Yes, he does —'

'No, I was at the funeral.' Rhiannon poured herself more of the spicy brew. 'I saw his ashes. *My father* is

165

definitely dead. Murdered in fact!' She drank the liquor down.

'Look.' He was becoming kind of exasperated; he had to make her see. 'I was twenty-one years old and about to assume the throne of Gwynedd when I found out mother was pregnant with you. When I discovered Maelgwn had not fathered you, I wanted to kill her, thinking she had been unfaithful to him … which I realise now, she never would be. But I didn't understand, as you do not understand, that your father and my father were one and the same soul–mind.'

'Well, where is this legend you speak of?' She thumped her mug down on the table and folded her arms defiantly. 'If my father were alive and well, he would be here helping us.'

'You found this place didn't you?' Rhun raised both brows to challenge her.

'Well … yes. But that still doesn't answer my question?' She sat forward. 'Where is he?'

Rhun smiled; she spoke to the point, just like their mother. 'Physically, he's thousands of light years away. But ethereally speaking, he's right here, listening to us now, most likely.'

'And how is that possible?' Rhiannon was trying to refrain from a smile that would appear condescending.

Rhun looked her in the eye, feeling her cynicism and almost envying her ignorance. 'Over the next few years I intend to teach you just *how* that is possible. But, in the meantime, I need you to try and have a little more patience with mother.'

Rhiannon rolled her eyes off to one side.

'I'm completely serious. There are enough forces working against her without you adding to her problems.'

'Her problems,' Rhiannon protested. 'What about my problems?'

'You don't even know what a problem *is* … yet. I've been to the future. I know what awaits us there.' Rhun finished his drink and placed his mug aside.

'But I thought you and Taliesin had changed all that?'

'The events of this planet, perhaps? But some … occurrences,' Rhun chose his words carefully, 'are time asymmetrical, and therefore unavoidable.'

He was starting to scare her now. Rhiannon's nightmare of spending the rest of her days on a fiery ball of vast nothingness was seeming closer to the truth than previously imagined. 'If that's the case, what do you expect mother is going to do about it? In fact, why bother with any of this?'

'You really don't have the slightest clue who our mother really is, do you?' Rhun couldn't imagine how anyone in this day and age could be so uninformed. 'Haven't you read any of the ancient texts, or the prophets … or Revelation, at least!'

'That's all a crock of religious propaganda.' She crossed her feet on the table, getting comfortable.

'Well, if you haven't read any of it, how do you know?' He sat forward to advise her to keep an open mind before taking up the flask and pouring more mead for them both. 'I'm afraid if you were familiar with the original Sumerian or Akkadian texts, you might be a little better informed as to who you are, where you came from, and why it is you are here. The prophecies of the ages are telling the story of our lives. For example,' he selected a couple of books from the shelf beside him, and finding his page, read: 'St John the Divine, Revelation ...

And upon her forehead was written,

Mystery, Babylon the Great, the Mother of harlots and abominations of the Earth ...

And the ten horns which thou sawest upon the beast, these shall hate the whore, and shall make her desolate ...

For God hath put in their hearts to fulfil his will, and to agree, and give their kingdom unto the beast, until the words of God shall be fulfilled ...

And the woman which thou sawest is that great city, which reigneth over the kings of the Earth.'

Rhiannon's jaw was dropping. 'Surely you don't think —'

'Wait, I'm not finished. Nostradamus.' He opened another book at a marked page.

She who was dismissed will return to reign,
Her enemies found in conspirators,
More than ever will her time be triumphant,
vast numbers to the death most certainly.

'Mother may be a lot of things, but she is not a murderer.' Rhiannon objected to his inference.

'Where does it say she would kill anyone? It says to the death. All immortals have to die before they can achieve life everlasting.' Rhun straightened out Rhiannon's misconception. 'She is the one who will rally the chosen together, and keep the beast in check.'

'And you think the beast is Doc Alexander,' Rhiannon assumed.

'There are several beasts mentioned in the ancient texts, and interestingly enough the numbers six, six, six translate in Hebrew kabbalist tradition to mean, One who has a divine message. Yet, more often than not, in prophecy the term usually relates to the selfish desires of a material world. Who rules that world is destined to be the beast's advocate.

'The third Antichrist, you mean.' Rhiannon was taking her brother more seriously now.

Rhun nodded. 'Nostrodamus foresaw him too.' He passed the book in his hands to his sister so that she might read the prophecy for herself.

The Antichrist quickly annihilates three,
Twenty-seven years of blood will last his war.
The heretics dead, captive or exiled.
Bloody corpses, water red, covering the Earth.

Rhiannon gazed into space; she didn't want to believe him, nor would she, without doing some serious investigation of her own. 'Well personally, bro, I think you're just paranoid. *But*, as a special favour to you, I promise to go easy on mum.'

'Much appreciated.' He smiled; she would see the truth before long, once she knew the all of it.

II

UΠSEEΠ

The weeks that followed the arrival of the *Goddess* and her crew at Watarrka were eventful to say the least.

Priority number one, to return Ray's research to the ICA without suspicion, was executed without a hitch. Rhun delivered the suitcase to Gatwick airport, England, and saw it placed on the conveyor belt of a flight bound for Mexico City. The luggage was signed in under an old, assumed identity that the ICA had supplied Ray with for a mission some years before. In the guise of an old man, Rhun waited around to witness the pandemonium erupt.

Inside fifteen minutes, two unmarked black limousines sped to a stop in front of the airport. A band of UN officials invaded the management office and control room, flashing identification papers as they demanded that the 2 p.m. flight to Mexico be delayed for reasons of international security.

The suitcase was recovered, yet the Agency representatives seemed none too happy to discover that its owner continued to elude them. Airport security and the local police were called in to assist with the search. Of course, they came up empty-handed.

The plan to make contact with John Pearce and his family proved not so easy.

Tory and Rhiannon decided to locate them via thought projection, only to then manifest themselves in the middle of a forest somewhere in England.

Their first conclusion was that perhaps the Otherworldly energies emanating from the earth around the Watarrka base were playing havoc with their intent. Yet Rhun had experienced no such trouble when willing himself to the airport just one day earlier? Before leaping to any conclusions they waited a couple of days, then attempted contact again. When Rhiannon, Rhun and Tory found themselves again in the forest, they had to figure it was no accident.

'Same place,' Rhun supposed, as he'd not escorted his mother and sister last time out.

'Yep!' Rhiannon was exasperated, pointing to a fallen oak that she recognised.

Rhun placed a hand on the healthy old tree beside him, and began to smile broadly as he discovered their whereabouts. 'Mother, John Pearce was Sir Rhys once — right?'

'You know it.' She thought the question pointless and continued her search of the area.

'Well, Rhys' immortal or "Chosen" incarnation was Robin of Loxley and we're standing in the middle of Sherwood forest!' He gave a chuckle, thinking it ironic.

Tory was not laughing, however. 'How do you know?'

'The tree told me.' He waved a finger in its direction.

'Not where we are!' Tory scolded; he knew well enough what she meant.

'Oh, about Robin you mean?' He was having second thoughts about mentioning it. 'A mutual friend told me.'

Tory's hands were perched on her hips as she considered the response. 'In other words, your father.'

Rhun raised both brows, nodding and shrugging in a non-committal fashion, when, rather fortunately, his mother's attention was diverted to the woodland.

'What was that?' She got them to strain their ears for any sound out of the ordinary. 'John!' she called, suddenly racing off through the trees.

'Did you hear anything?' Rhun inquired of his sister as they set off in pursuit.

'No.' Rhiannon shook her head in the negative. 'You?'

'No,' he stressed, gaining speed to chase after his mother.

'Oh Goddess, please!' Tory wailed, as she fell to her knees in the scrub ahead of them.

'Mother?' Rhiannon screeched to a halt as she spied the blueish hand that sprang from the soil, still wearing the wedding rings belonging to Jennifer Pearce. 'Maybe it's just a ploy to make us think they're dead.' She refused to believe their friends had met with such an end.

'No. There's no mistake.' Tory's mood darkened as she raised herself upright.

'Perhaps it is fate that this should be his final resting place.' Rhun quietly offered his view.

Tory squeezed her eyelids together, her hands clenching into fists. 'I must not hate, I must not hate,' she repeated to instill it in her mind. 'First Miles, and now John, Jenny and Nicholas ... four of the people I hold dearest in this world. Why?'

Rhiannon held her mother as she was reduced to tears, all the while the words of Nostradamus running though her mind. *The Antichrist quickly annihilates three.* Perhaps it had no bearing on this instance, but she couldn't get the damn sentence out of her head. 'We're still not one hundred percent certain what has happened here.'

'Are you suggesting we exhume them?' Tory was completely repulsed by the notion.

'Mother. She's right, we have no choice.' Rhun seconded Rhiannon's view. 'These graves are far too shallow to be restful in any case.' Tory stared back at him, her face drained of colour, and Rhun understood she couldn't cope with taking part in such a task. 'Come on.' He helped Rhiannon support her. 'We'll see you home, then I'll come back later with Brian and Teo.'

Tory looked back to the protruding remains, her jaw tensing as she did. 'Their deaths must not go unanswered.'

'Nor will they.' Rhun's tone suggested that she could leave the matter in his hands.

The dig turned up two bodies, those of John and Jenny. Nicholas was not found with his parents as initially feared, and locating him became the immediate concern.

Rhun left Teo and Brian with the grievous chore of re-burying their good friends, and reported back to those waiting at Watarrka.

The news seemed to energise everybody's drained spirits.

As his mother assumed her outrageous guise to seek out the whereabouts of their lost crewmate, Rhun outwardly changed his appearance to escort her. His long dark hair retracted into his head until it was only one centimetre long, and turned fair. His eyes changed to blue, and his attire was as outrageous as his mother's, so that they might be mistaken for members of the same gang.

Then joining hands, the pair concentrated their energies on finding the lost lad.

Nicholas was seated in the centre of an empty chamber. As his head was bowed low, they could not readily discern whether he was conscious or not. Big steel braces clasped around his chest, stomach, arms and ankles held his form to a bulky metal chair. If he wasn't dead, he certainly wasn't far from it.

'Nicky,' Tory whispered, as she moved to approach.

Upon hearing her voice, Nick's head shot up. Although he could not see her through his swollen eyes, he knew who had come for him. 'No, leave!' he implored her. 'He seeks to test the Goddess, see what she is capable —'

Nicholas' outburst was cut short by an electric current coursing through his body, and he screamed himself to tears enduring the agony.

'That's quite enough from you.' A voice came over the intercom and reverberated around the room. 'I wouldn't,' the voice warned as Tory moved to aid her young friend. 'Go anywhere near him and the next charge will be fatal.'

Tory refrained from movement or speech. Hatred had such a grip on her being, its blinding effects took a moment to abate. *Can you get him out of here from where you are?* she bethought Rhun without so much as a glance in his direction.

No such luck. But if you can get between the camera and Nick, that should hide me from its vision. Then, perhaps I could manifest behind his chair and get him out.

Tory perused the ceiling, spotting the camera in question. 'Are we afraid to make such threats in person?' She approached the camera to try and monopolise their voyeur's attention.

'Regretfully, business prevents me from being present to address you in person.' The voice paused. 'Whoever you are.'

Tory hazarded a glance in Rhun's direction to find him gone. 'I'm your worst nightmare, if you do not desist in your attack on the kin of Tory Alexander. Whoever you are,' she said icily in conclusion.

The camera swung back suddenly to note Rhun's disappearance. The sound of crackling electricity startled Tory into an about-face, where she found an empty chair. She breathed a deep sigh of relief, no longer subject to the whim's of her foe. 'Just what the hell is your problem?'

'No problem, just a few questions … like, how it is that you came to be in an electronically-locked room to which I alone know the entry code? And how would you explain the apparent disappearance of my hostage?' He chuckled like a man well-satisfied. 'No great loss, I'll grant, but you know, I never would have believed it if I hadn't seen it for myself.'

Tory wanted to cringe, recalling what her father had told her.

Most could not perform the feats you do, as they consider such metamorphosis impossible. You, however, do not, as you have seen it done.

Shit. She decided she should get out of there before she made matters worse. 'Look, if you need spiritual counseling, I'd suggest an exorcist.' She made for directly beneath the camera, where she was out of its line of vision.

'Very amusing … I'm sure. Let's see how much of that wit you have left tomorrow.'

She was not even tempted to query his meaning, though his mocking laughter taunted her well into the ethers of her flight.

'That's it!' Tory announced, manifesting in the communications room at Watarrka where the rest of her team were attending to Nick's injuries. 'I've had enough of being on the defensive. Rhiannon.'

Her daughter raised herself from Nicholas' side, wiping the tears of sympathy from her face. 'Yes?'

'I want you to go to Oxfordshire and bring your Aunt Rose here.' Tory placed a hand on her shoulder to give Rhiannon strength. 'We're not leaving anybody in the outside world who can be traced to us.'

Rhiannon seconded her reasoning with a nod, and was gone.

'How is he?' Tory asked, as Naomi cleaned the wounds on her patient's face.

'I'm not qualified for this, Tory. He needs a doctor.'

'No,' Rhun considered, 'he needs a healer. Take him to my mother's chamber. I'll join you there presently.'

'If you're going for Cadfan …' Tory caught him by the arm. 'Tell him nothing. The less he knows —'

'I am with you,' he stated surely.

Sometimes Tory forgot Rhun was not a reckless juvenile any longer. 'I didn't mean —'

'I know.' Rhun cut her short with a wave of his hand. 'Just … stay close to Gawain, your healing energies will keep him alive.' As his mother went to correct him, Rhun added with a grin, 'I mean, Nicholas.'

'Sorry.' She realised she was doing it again. 'You as an adult takes a bit of getting used to.'

'Tell me about it.' He held her gaze until he'd vanished.

Walter Cadfan was leading a large group of people through a guided meditation when Rhun unexpectedly appeared in the corner of the room. Fortunately, the healer was the only person present who had his eyes open. He wound up his calming tuition, and quietly stood to make his way towards his visitor, instructing his class to remain as they were. With the flick of a switch, gentle music began to filter quietly over the gathering and Cadfan motioned Rhun towards the door.

Directly across the hallway was the healer's large office and herbarium, where they would not be disturbed.

'Very impressive.' Rhun followed Cadfan inside, admiring the shelves stocked with medicines, and spying many a long-extinct cure thereon.

'I knew you, of all people, would appreciate my collection, Grandfather.' Walter was most excited by his visit.

'Cadfan, must you call me that when you insist on appearing twice my age?'

'Well, it adds to my crediblity. Besides I am, *well and truly*, twice your age.'

For although Rhun had been time travelling for a couple of hundred years or more, Cadfan had taken the old-fashioned route down through the ages to the twentieth century from his birthplace late in the seventh.

'If only I'd possessed some of your talent,' Walter sighed.

'Well, actually, I'm needing your talents,' Rhun confessed, to Cadfan's obvious delight. 'A dear friend of mine has —'

'No, no, don't tell me.' The healer closed his eyes to concentrate. 'Ah!' He was enlightened as to the requirements for the task, and began scampering around collecting salves and potions to take with them. 'We must hurry.' Cadfan threw a few last bits and pieces into a bag, then held out his hand ready to be transported.

After two hours of a 'hands on' healing session, Nick was massaged with cooling ointment and fed a warm herbal brew to remedy the damage done to him on the inside.

Cadfan did not question how his patient had come to be in such a state, nor did he inquire as to his whereabouts. Perhaps he simply assumed both topics would be taboo, but Tory thought it more likely that he already knew some of the answers.

Walter was very accomplished at his chosen craft. Present immortal company excluded, Tory had never seen such a miraculous recovery. A lot of Nick's swelling and bruising had disappeared within the first half hour of the consultation.

'You'd best beware,' Tory whispered to Cadfan, watching their patient drift off into a peaceful slumber. 'They'll be hailing you as the next Messiah.'

Walter gave a quiet chuckle. 'Don't think they haven't tried.' He placed two bottles on the bedside table for further treatment. 'But I don't go for any of that rot. There is only one God, the creator, and only he can correctly guide the individual along the right path back to him.'

'What about your otherworldly ancestors?' She wondered if he still followed the ancient faith of the Britons.

Walter cocked an eye in her direction. 'Well, the ethers and their occupants are part of God, and can aid humanity via the proper channels ... as with your good self and Keridwen. But one has only to recall what became of Ossa to see how cunning and misleading some entities can be. You must be able to discern the difference between good advice and manipulation. The differing planes of the etheric world are frequented by all manner of spirits, denizens, and extra-terrestrials ... some of which can be very mischievous indeed if the seeker is inexperienced, or calling on their wisdom for reasons of ego and personal gain. Such a person may find themselves led a merry dance, just to be taught a lesson. Such is life.' Cadfan shrugged. 'I never take as fact anything I'm told. I rely on what I feel, for only the God inside can ultimately be trusted.'

Tory thought this was a good philosophy, and reminiscent of her own beliefs. She thanked Cadfan for his views and for coming to the aid of her kinsman. 'If I can ever return the favour ...'

'Nonsense,' Cadfan insisted. 'You are my great-grandmother. Thus I am entirely at your disposal during *this*, your time in exile.'

At this point, Rhun advised his grandson it was high time they got him back to the natural therapy centre where Walter was supposed to be lecturing at present.

Left alone with nothing but her thoughts and their sleeping patient, Tory mused over Cadfan's parting vow. Tory had not considered this predicament in which she found herself so dire as to classify it as 'in exile'. Yet

Cadfan made it sound like the whole nightmare was a foregone conclusion, and had been for some time.

Since her arrival at Watarrka, Tory had done quite a lot of research into the mysterious origins of her family. The various mythologies and histories of the creation of the world that Rhun had given her to resource all cited the same story. Of how the great immortal ancestors (the Gods, the Shining Ones, the Lofty Ones, the Old Ones) had created the world and fashioned mankind — even the Old Testament hinted at this. For Genesis clearly stated, that after Adam and Eve had eaten from the tree of knowledge, the Lord God said: *Obviously in knowing good and evil man has become like one of Us*. It also spoke of how, *the sons of God took notice of the daughters of men, admired their looks and married all those of them they chose*. Was this the explanation behind her grandmother's mysterious pregnancy, the event which had introduced the immortal gene into her family via her father, Myrddin. If so, which one of these infamous Gods had her grandfather been?

Tory stemmed from the lineage of the one the Celts called Bedi, that much Taliesin had told her. This was no great help, however, as Bedi was the King of Heaven. Sumerian texts called him Anu, the Egyptians — Ammon, the Greeks — Zeus, and from him all other immortals had sprung. Her grandfather could be any one of Bedi's wild array of descendants, few of whom she would feel proud to claim as kin, having familiarised herself with some of their appalling escapades. These so-called Gods were exceedingly greedy, underhanded, incestuous, not to mention cruel and unforgiving. If, as the ancient texts claimed, mankind was the result of a genetic fusion between these Gods and the earliest men, it was easy to see which characteristics humans had inherited from their immortal creators.

Still, these conclusions were based on the hearsay of others and their interpretations of the ancient texts, which was exactly what Cadfan had warned Tory against. What she really needed was to get the story straight from the horse's mouth — her grandfather. It all came back to him. Her father had claimed to still be in contact with their closest Otherworldly relative, so surely she could aspire to the same.

One thing is for certain. Tory looked at Nicholas, whom she knew was damn lucky to be alive. *As of tomorrow, I'm back in training … mind, body and spirit.*

Her life with Miles had been a peaceful and idyllic break from Otherworldly affairs and earthly leadership, but, clearly, the holiday was over. Tory refused to let one more soul be tortured or killed on her account. Emotional vampirism, was what it was. Doc had been nowhere near her and still he'd nearly succeeded in draining her of every ounce of energy with his classic intimidatory tactics, and what was worse, she'd let him do it.

Well, no more, no matter what surprises he had in store for her. Today's episode had made her realise that she was nowhere near prepared to confront her foe — not if she expected to outsmart him, anyway.

Now that all her kindred were safe inside these cavern walls, it was imperative that Tory's first priority become herself.

Tory spent most of that night and into the next morning with Floyd, going through what information he'd collected on Doc. This case study went into Doc's schooling and political background, but she failed to find anything that the famous financier wouldn't want them to know.

Floyd explained that gaining access to Doc's personal computer was virtually impossible because he rarely hooked up to the Net. Therefore, the only way they were going to retrieve information from his PC was to somehow download all its files onto hard disk. Doc would almost certainly have his system encrypted, so they needed his password to save time. Floyd had done an asset trace on their subject to investigate his land holdings, bank accounts and so forth in the hope of finding a discrepancy of some kind, but regrettably, all his financial dealings appeared to be as clean as a whistle.

When Nicholas awoke he was physically repaired, and was scoffing down a huge breakfast when Tory arrived to question him about his ordeal. Recounting the events of the past week was not easy for the lad. He'd been knocked out so many times that his moments of consciousness all sort of blurred into each other.

After they'd parted ways with the *Goddess* in Horta, he told her, his family returned to London to find the ICA awaiting their arrival. They were escorted to a black limousine where they were bound and blindfolded at gunpoint. Nicholas thought it rather peculiar that at no stage of their abduction were his parents asked a single question.

This came as no surprise to Tory. In all likelihood, Doc needed to do no more than touch an individual to withdraw whatever information he required. Then again, with so many blank spots in Nicholas' memory, perhaps hypnosis had been used. Both methods would have failed to produce the information Doc sought, as neither John nor his family knew where the *Goddess* and her crew had gone into hiding.

'Mum and Dad were killed, without any of us having the slightest clue as to why.' Nick's eyes filled with tears as he persevered with his explanation. 'When they started to beat me, I fully expected it would be to the death. But no, I was strapped into that chair, and whilst one of the masked attackers gripped both my hands, his buddies all started firing questions at me at once … questions about you.'

'Pertaining to what? My whereabouts?'

'No. They wanted to know about the weird stuff … you know, like extraordinary feats, strange occurrences, shit like that. But I told them *nothing*. In fact, I didn't even think about it. I dwelt instead on all the good times we'd had together, which seemed to piss off the guy holding my hands no end. He kept whacking me around the head and telling me to concentrate, but the more insistent he became, the more obscure the memory I brought to mind.' This made Nick smile, as he was kind of impressed with himself.

'You did good, my friend.' Tory gave him a huge squeeze, wishing she could somehow relieve him of his loss. She'd not seen such bravery in one so young since the Dark Age, where, coincidentally, Sir

184

Gawain had also lost both his parents at roughly the same age.

'I knew you'd find me,' Nick confessed, as though nothing was ever surer. 'Half of me prayed you wouldn't, knowing I was the bait in a trap set for you. But the other half of me knew that, somehow, you'd outsmart the bastards. Which obviously, you did.'

Tory smiled at his reasoning, though she knew different unfortunately — *played right into their hands more like*. Doc Alexander's threat to wipe the smile from her face within twenty-four hours lingered in her brain. His vow toyed with her imagination to conjure all manner of horrifying scenarios, which she did her best to dismiss or ignore. A good workout was what she needed: kata, yoga, meditation. For the day was still young, and she utterly refused to spend it pondering their doom.

It was coming on to evening when Floyd summoned all interested parties to the communications room to view a news report on the disappearance of Dr John Pearce and his family.

The news team, from a reputable British television station, were speaking with people who alleged they were close friends and associates of John Pearce, none of whom Nicholas could say he recognised. They spoke of the differences in opinion that arose between John Pearce and Tory Thurlow after the unexpected death of her husband Professor Miles Thurlow. At this time, it was reported, Tory was knowingly abetting a man wanted for blackmail by more government agencies then they had airtime to list. They claimed John had managed to escape with his family when the *Goddess* docked in Horta for supplies a few weeks back.

'But John still feared for the safety of his family because of what they knew.' A sweet-looking, elderly lady informed the very concerned woman conducting the interview.

'The police have yet to find any trace of the marine archaeologist and his family,' the female reporter turned to camera to advise her viewers. 'Nor have the authorities had any success in locating the luxurious underwater observation vehicle that was once the base for the now famous Project Plato. These people are wanted for questioning in regard to the disappearance.'

They showed a shot of Ray, which came from his ICA file, that made him look like Charles Manson before the haircut. The photo they used of the *Goddess* crew was one Noah had taken at the time he'd done the story on the sea-monster. This particular photo had not been used with the article, but it had been sent to *National Geographic* at the time.

'They're trying to frame us, not only for Pearce's death, but your husband's as well!' Ray was ready to have a complete meltdown.

Tory was contemplating the same, when she noted Teo and Brian didn't appear as perturbed about the news as everyone else.

'Well, good luck making a case,' commented Teo, picking his dinner out of his teeth with the aid of a toothpick. 'Without the bodies they've got no hard evidence to work with … or should I say mess with.'

'They know where the bodies are, they'll only have to dig a little deeper and —' As Teo was slowly shaking his head and sporting that cocky grin of his, Tory queried, 'Why no?'

'Ask Brian, he's the one who heard *the voice*.'

All eyes turned to Brian who went bright red.

'What? So my dead friend spoke to me, big deal! It happens to my Aunt Rose all the time.' He clearly did not want to discuss it.

This was the first sign Brian had ever shown of clairvoyance, apart from a minor past-life flashback he'd had when he'd first met Naomi.

'But, Brian, this is marvellous.' Tory was excited for him.

'I just knew you'd think so.' In Brian's opinion it just meant he was going nuts, like the rest of his family.

'You spoke to my father?'

Nicholas stepped in to be sure he'd heard correctly, and Brian couldn't put him off in the same lighthearted fashion he had the others. 'Yeah Nick, I did.' He took the lad underarm, and escorted him out of the room to have a chat.

'So where are the bodies?' Tory reverted back to Teo for an answer.

'Bloody miles away from where you found them.' He dismissed any chance of anyone ever unearthing them.

'But what if someone saw you?!' Rhiannon stressed out. This would just fuel the Agency's story.

'It was a lousy day,' Teo defended. 'Nobody saw us, believe me! I couldn't even see what we were doing half the time.'

'What about tracks?' Tory was still not convinced.

'We covered our tracks all the way back to the original grave site.' He folded his arms, defiantly. 'So the ICA can kiss my arse, if they think they're going to frame us for this … cause it ain't going to happen.'

As predicted, nothing came of the allegations made against Tory, Ray and co. If the Agency hadn't found the bodies after two weeks of searching, they weren't going to. So, for the crew of the *Goddess*, life took on a less stressful tone. They all found plenty to occupy their time at Watarrka. Some utilised their already developed talents, whilst others discovered a whole new calling.

With conspiracies surfacing left, right and centre, Noah barely left his computer. Day and night he recorded what had unfolded to date, tracing the saga all the way back to its origins in the Dark Age, though he and Tory now strongly suspected it could be traced to the dawn of mankind. Tory had asked Noah why he bothered wasting his time on something no one could ever read. He'd smiled and raised an eyebrow. After the Gathering, which Noah was now fully convinced would come to pass, those left to nurture the new world would want to know the truth. And it was his belief that he was responsible for making sure they got it.

Rhiannon had safely delivered Aunt Rose into the arms of the alliance, unharmed. Rose thought the trauma of being forced to leave her long-time home on the farm in Oxfordshire would prove too much for her old heart to take. Not loneliness, senility, nor the elements had been able to drive her out of her cottage.

But when her friends in the spirit-world had advised Rose it was time to go, she was packed and ready to leave when her brother's grand-daughter arrived to collect her. At nearly eighty years of age, Rose expected her adjustment to a whole new environment and way of life to be a long one. Yet when she arrived at Watarrka's little community, Rose found paradise in the cavern of produce. She'd always had a green thumb, and was thankful to still be able to put it to good use.

Naomi, whose background was in archaeology and restoration, had been at a loss as to what use she could be with the *Goddess* out of action. At Rhun's suggestion, she volunteered her services in the produce laboratories. A Japanese geneticist and cloning expert, Dr Leigh Sukemi, and his family headed up the research department. Like Ray and Floyd, Sukemi was on the run from the authorities because of his work and the foreseen government misuse of it. Although the horticultural side of science didn't interest Naomi greatly, the animal and sea-life breeding programs captured her interest at once. Birthing animals was a far cry from digging relics from the ground, but when one considered Naomi had been head of veterinary science back in Atlantis her natural aptitude in this area was not really so surprising.

Underground, in the desert, one would have thought those who remained of the Plato Project dive team would be like fish out of water — this was not the case, however.

Daniel found a more practical use for his longtime passion for astronomy when Rhun appointed him their official stargazer. Daniel slept most of the day, and spent his nights searching the skies for abnormal activity.

Young Nicholas' near unnatural obsession with the Internet increased tenfold after a couple of days in Floyd's company. The hacker's computer had virtual-reality capabilities, and was hooked up to the virtual-net of the worldwide web instead of the older keyboard-accessed network. In this fabulous cyberspace, a point of your finger would take you anywhere you wanted to go: to a live concert, with the best seats in the house, to a lecture or a forum on just about any subject imaginable. Once you created a cyber-image for yourself (so you could be distinguished from other cyberspace dwellers), you could go to a virtual bar to meet and chat with other cyber junkies from all over the world — BYO of course. Exploring cyberspace and helping Floyd plot industrial espionage served to keep Nick's mind off the recent death of his parents, while also providing him with a non-violent means by which he might avenge their sad fate.

As Teo and Brian were both technically-minded, they volunteered to assist Ray with the nightmarish chore of re-routing their vessel's circuitry — outside of training hours, that is. For as soon as Tory had re-established a regular Tae-kwon-do program in the morning, the rest of the crew had joined her. Teo, who was a Shihan (a nine times black belt) of the art, handled the instruction, which came to a close at around midday. Most then went about working on their other projects, except for the immortals — they had a further three hours of training with Rhun. His subjects included telepathy, psychokinesis, shamanism, clairvoyance, psychic self-defence and all forms of Otherworldly communication and appreciation.

Brian was a little wary of these practices at first, but the female competition served to fuel his ambition. Already he'd nearly mastered the art of altering his appearance, and had learnt to project his physical form over short distances.

As Rhiannon's forte was definitely telepathy, not just with humans but animal and plant life as well, Rhun concentrated on enhancing her ability to read thoughts without contact with her target. At first she was only able to communicate with Rhun and her mother, for they were well practiced in projecting their thoughts. But soon Rhiannon found she could hear the unsaid in everyone, though she did not advise her unsuspecting subjects of this at the time.

As Tory refused to concentrate on any skill that didn't relate to contacting Maelgwn, her son had spent several days assisting her to cleanse her chakras and auric field. When this empowerment was completed, learning to cast a decent psychic shield around herself became the next ability she must master before astral projection could be attempted. She'd been taught this simple skill before, so this was really just a refresher course. With all the training she'd been doing of late, her will was strong and her focus was excellent. Which is why Tory found it rather odd that Rhun made her practise this over and over. Even when she was certain she'd perfected the routine, her son refused to commence tutoring her in astral travel, and it occurred to her that perhaps he was stalling.

Days later, when the two of them were taking a wander along the canyon ridge at sunset, Tory seized the opportunity to confront Rhun about his rather obvious reluctance to allow her contact with his father.

The query brought Rhun to an abrupt halt, and slowly he turned to confess: 'Actually, that's why I coaxed you out here.'

'Well, I really didn't think it was for the romance of it all.' Tory folded her arms. She just knew she was being had.

'Now don't get angry at me, I'm just the messenger,' he appealed, before humbling himself a tad. 'Although I misconstrued the meaning of one of Father's requests.'

'Which one?' She called his attention back to her, as his eyes had drifted to admire the view.

He was reluctant to answer, knowing his mother's reaction was not going to be favourable. 'The one that stated you were to remain hidden. For I have since been informed father wasn't just referring to the physical world, but the etheric world as well.'

'Come again.' She frowned, annoyed. 'Who told you so?'

Rhun winced, as he was just about to make matters worse for himself. 'Cadfan.'

'The day he came to see Nick?'

Rhun nodded.

'But that would imply you've been leading me up the garden path for weeks!'

'I was waiting for you to be at *one* and at *peace* before … before I told you I'd been denied permission to make good my promise.'

'Maelgwn refused me an audience?' It hurt Tory to think this was the case. Did he no longer pine for her as she for him? Perhaps he'd spiritually matured since last they'd met, and was beyond craving the physical love of another.

'Only because he fears for your safety,' Rhun stated, to prevent her from jumping to conclusions.

'Rhun, I'm immortal for God's sake. How can I possibly be in any danger?' She wasn't buying it.

'In this universe there are hazards still completely inconceivable to us. So, unless you are the one all-knowing God, how can you be so sure?' He succeeded in taking away his mother's feeling of rejection, only to replace it with fear. 'I have a message for you,' he resolved, on a more cheery note.

Tory shook her head, confused enough already. 'No more secondhand reports, thanks all the same.'

'No, this one you'll like, I swear!'

Her son's big brown eyes pleaded for her to hear him out. 'Alright.' She caved in, as any mother would. 'Let's have it?'

'Um?' Rhun looked around for a comfortable place to seat her, and motioned Tory to a rock that would suit.

'This can't be as crash hot as you say, if I need to sit down.' Still, she complied; anything to get to the bottom of all this. Rhun came to stand behind her, placing his hands over her eyes, and before Tory had even realised it, her breathing had fallen in time with his. The deep yogic breaths cleared her mind of clutter, so she forgot even the purpose of the exercise.

Tory.

An image of Maelgwn's face and the sweet sound of his voice so clearly resounding in her head startled Tory from her peaceful trance-like state, and they were forced to start over.

'Relax, it's just like a video recording.' Rhun settled her back into position.

'You could have warned me.' She drew a deep breath to open herself to the transference.

Once again Maelgwn's image emerged from the blackness behind her eyes. Faint at first, the clarity of the impression improved until the features of the visitant were unmistakable. *Maelgwn*. Tory's heart leapt and she nearly lost her focus again. But her beloved's expression was so gravely serious, that it captured her attention.

Tory, I beg thee, under no circumstances art thou to attempt contact with me. Conditions are most unstable. To project thy spirit into the Otherworld, be to leave the body open to invasion. An unfortunate situation hast arisen that demands my full attention. All will be made clear upon my return, which I trust will be soon. I long for our reunion, Tory, as thee must, but please believe me when I tell thee to keep thy distance from me at this time. Listen to our son's guidance, keep thine head, and do not lose thine heart. He bowed and faded into the recesses of Tory's mind.

Her eyes opened to behold the brilliant red sun melting into the horizon of the wilderness over which it cast the shadow of night. She looked up to the stars already twinkling in their thousands above her, trying to savour every detail of Maelgwn's image.

'When the great star burns in the sky, so that two suns appear,' Rhun quoted, 'your reunion with father will be nigh.'

'*The supernova.*' Tory swung around to a standing position, recalling the year Rhun had said this would occur. 'Two thousand and thirty seven,' she whined. 'But that's another twenty years from now!' This realisation knocked the wind out of her sails somewhat and she sank back on her rock, disheartened.

'If it makes you feel any better, I too must endure the same wait to be joined with my one true love.'

'Bridgit?' Tory assumed.

'Aye.' Rhun smiled as he reminisced upon his wife, long since departed to the grave. 'And her "Chosen" incarnation will go by another name, but I shall recognise her and she me as surely as day follows night and night follows day. For we are two integral halves of the same perfect whole.'

Tory recalled that Taliesin had claimed that the same was true of Maelgwn and herself. 'Twenty years without sex. Now that's depressing.'

'Granted.' Rhun could sympathise on that point. 'But, then again, it seems a small price to pay in exchange for an eternity of bliss.'

It did indeed, but there was more to this 'Gathering' than just the uniting of lost loves and old comrades. Who were the Evil Ones who were to do battle with the Shining Ones and their Chosen? Tory shrugged, not too worried that the answer eluded her at present. The truth was buried somewhere and she had two whole decades to dig it up.

THE AFFAIRS OF
GODS AND MEN

'Here's a reference.' Noah captured Tory's attention, and read: 'Even now, many Antichrists have arisen, from which we gather certainly that it is the final hour. They went out from us, but they never belonged to us: for if they had been ours, they would have remained with us.'

'Interesting,' she mused. 'Where did you find that?'

'Here, in *The Bible*. The first general epistle of John, Chapter 2, paragraph 18.' He passed it to her across the large study table, strewn with the histories of the ages. Noah and Tory spent most of their evenings here, attempting to learn as much as they could from reported interaction between the ancient ancestors and mankind.

Tory perused the paragraph Noah had highlighted, then referred back to the book she was reading on the beliefs of an old African religion. 'This foretells how the Shining Ones will overcome the Evil Ones, and of the new age that will follow. This clash would be heralded by a *certain star's* appearance in the sky. This will be testament to the Nommo's resurrection, who, like the Christ of the Christian faith, would be sacrificed for the purification of the universe. *He will rise in human form and descend on the Earth in an ark with the ancestors of man* … sound familiar?' Tory handed the book over into Noah's eagerly awaiting hands.

'So you think that, all the way through the ages, man may have been misconstruing these extra-terrestrial ancestors for God, angels and so forth?' He had to admit he'd read many ancient accounts that pointed to ET-immortals as the sculptors of life on this planet; the Lofty Ones who glowed with beams of light. 'The question is, who or what created them? And where does Jesus Christ fit into all this? Had he been one of them?'

'That last question has driven scholars nuts throughout the ages, I'm sure. Who am I to say?' Tory wasn't touching that conundrum with a twenty-foot pole. 'But the certain star of which they speak is the binary star Sirius. Which, back in Atlantis, they referred to as Nibiru, meaning Planet of the Crossing. The theory goes that the star, Sirius A, is circled by a very small white dwarf star, Sirius B. But this circling is not an orbit, for they share the same common centre of gravity.' She circled her two index fingers around each other to demonstrate. 'The two stars constantly revolving around one another have created a vortex in-between, a gateway in and out of a parallel universe, through which the planet, Sirius C, comes and goes into our universe.'

The notion had Noah completely fascinated. 'How is that possible?'

'Reversing a vortex?' Tory shrugged. 'An advanced form of particle manipulation maybe? If these beings can harden the Earth's crust, push back the seas and raise mountains, does inverting a molecular tunnel in deep space seem any less unlikely?'

'Knock, knock.' Ray meandered in through the open door, looking a little uncomfortable about interrupting. 'I was wondering if I might have a private word.' He directed the query at Tory, although aware that this was Noah's abode.

'Sure.' Tory made to rise, but Noah waved her down.

'No, that's okay. I was just thinking we need more tea … I'll go make us a cup.' He picked up the empties and left them to speak.

Hardly anyone had seen Ray since he'd commenced work on the *Goddess*; he only paused from the mammoth task to eat or sleep. 'So, to what do I owe this rare visitation … you haven't hit any snags, have you?'

'No, no, the *Goddess* is coming along fine.' Ray sat down and rocked backwards and forwards in the chair, undecided as to how he was going to air his concern.

From the look on his face, Tory could tell he wasn't a happy camper. 'I'm sorry, I haven't had a chance ask you how you're liking it here? I've just dumped you down there with a pile of work and —'

'That's not it, Tory.' He wanted to make that perfectly clear. 'This place is heaven for me.'

'Then why the gloomy demeanour?'

'I'm not gloomy!' Ray folded his arms, leant back in his chair, and laughed. 'Not at all.'

'Okay, I give up.' She raised her brows. 'What's wrong then?'

'Nothing's wrong,' he said firmly. 'Not with me, anyway.' Ray's frown returned. 'It's … your daughter.'

'Rhiannon isn't bothering you, is she?' Tory realised this question could be taken several ways, but her inference was neither here nor there.

'Not as such.' He stared at the floor, meditative a second. 'Look, I know it's not my place to bring this up, but, are you aware of the major crush she has on your son?'

'Huh! Rhiannon and every other young, unattached female here.' But Tory knew Rhun's interests lay elsewhere, so as far as she was concerned it wasn't an issue. 'Sounds to me like you're jealous, Mr Murdock?'

Ray shook his head, disappointed that she could be so predictable. 'I just knew you were going to say that.'

'And I knew you knew, but I said it anyway.' She grinned.

'Well, you're *wrong*,' he impressed on her, smugly confident that he was right. 'This is more like … a genuine fatherly concern.'

Tory could almost see him turning green, but for reasons of diplomacy refrained from saying so. 'Look Ray, the way I see it, Rhun and Rhiannon have twenty years of catching up to do. It's only natural that they'd want to spend a lot of time in each other's company …

Brian and myself were no different after being separated for a long time.'

'Really?'

'You sound surprised?'

Ray gave a nod and then a shrug. 'I was an only child, so I guess I find it hard to relate.' He raised both brows and rose, seemingly set at ease. 'But if you reckon the situation is normal, hey, who am I to argue? After all, you're the girl's mother — right?'

Ray gave a wave, leaving Tory to ponder the reason for his abrupt change of heart.

Poor guy … she had to smile. Didn't he even realise he was falling in love?

Sunday was still pretty much a day of rest at Watarrka, and as this particular Sunday was Floyd's 50th birthday, 'the gang' hit the booze and dope fairly hard after lunch to help him celebrate.

They retired to Floyd's base in the communications room, and were all suitably intoxicated when Nick started discussing the reasons why he and Floyd had not been able to gain access to private files in Doc Alexander's computer. Somehow they had to get the diplomat's code key.

'I could get the information you need,' Rhiannon boasted. 'Couldn't I?' She put it to her brother, who was the only one who knew the full extent of her psychic talent.

'I'm not so sure that's such a good idea.' Rhun was doubtful. Their mother would freak, yet if anyone could succeed it was Rhiannon.

'I could change my appearance.' She stood to entertain her all-male audience — Tory was down visiting her Aunt Rose, and Naomi was in the lab. 'I could start by, say ... adding ten years.'

To the overwhelming approval of the menfolk, the girl grew into a voluptuous, shapely woman.

Rhiannon accepted their adoration graciously, motioning them to refrain as she wasn't finished. 'And, judging from Mr Alexander's long and esteemed list of lady friends, it is painfully obvious to me that the gentleman prefers blondes.' She turned her back on the enthralled spectators, so they could witness her long, black hair turn golden and kink into wavy curls.

'Whoa ...!'

The men remained moderately hushed as Rhiannon swung her arms wide. 'So now, the eyes are all wrong. Blue would be more the go, I think.' She turned around to face them once more, batting her new baby blues.

Much riotous acclaim ensued, and compliments were forthcoming from all except Ray.

'What's the matter? Don't you approve?' Rhiannon squatted down in front of Ray to focus on his mind.

What was he supposed to say? Here he'd been steering clear of Rhiannon in order to avoid seeing the likeness of the lovely Annora in the girl. Now here she was before him and it was too much to take.

'I've got shit to do.' He rose to leave.

A silence fell over the room, as everyone tried to figure out his reaction.

In Nick's view, Rhiannon looked drop-dead gorgeous as a blonde. 'Shit, you don't think he's gay, do you?'

'No, I don't think that's the problem.' Rhun saw Sir Bryce's wife in his sister, though he would never have guessed were it not for her game.

'Not a chance.' Rhiannon seconded her brother, smiling broadly, for she had perceived the memories of Atlantis whirling through Ray's head.

'So back to our plan.' Floyd had a query. 'How do you intend to get Doc's code key?'

'Telepathy, of course.' Rhiannon was still dwelling on Ray.

'Ah …' Floyd gained her full attention. 'But you can only do that by touch, so what's to stop him from reading your mind, hey? Stalemate.' He thought it was far too risky. If the Agency found out their location, that would be the game over.

Rhiannon gave half a laugh. 'Not if I no longer need to be touching the subject to know their thoughts.'

'What!' Everyone objected rather loudly, except for Rhun, who found their distress rather amusing.

'That's right.' Rhiannon confirmed to their horror. She stood up. 'And I want all of you to know, that I think you're nothing but a bunch of dirty old men.' She resumed her true form in order to pursue Ray, leaving the party laughing in her wake.

By the time Rhiannon had reached the cavern of pools, Ray was already hard at work. From beneath the raised belly of the *Goddess* dangled a jungle of wires, hanging in clusters as they awaited re-direction. Rhiannon made her way between the huge ramps that suspended the vessel while it was in dry dock, to find Ray at the farthest end. He was melting a metal compound onto the tip of his soldering iron and individually joining each wire of a complicated multicore to another huge clump of wires that sprouted from the hull of the bathyscape.

'Can I be of some assistance?' she inquired politely to gain his attention.

Ray paused from his task, though he did not bother raising his eyes. 'Nope. The best thing you can do is leave me be. I need to concentrate.' He put iron to wire and continued his soldering.

This made her smile. 'You, Teo and Brian rave on while you work. You blast music while watching the sport on tele! So, why then, should my company prove such a distraction to you?'

To suppress his annoyance, Ray drew a deep breath and replaced his tool in its stand. 'What do you want, Rhiannon? I'm busy!' He looked at her, finally, and was surprised to find she was still quite cheery, despite his mood.

'I know why you've been avoiding me ever since we got here. I thought it was because you had designs on my mother —'

'That's exactly right.' He stood to interject. 'She can't stay in mourning forever.'

'Oh, man.' Rhiannon felt for him. How could she put this so as not to sound condescending. 'Are you so out of touch with your own emotions?'

'God!' He felt like strangling someone. 'Do not presume to tell me what I feel. Bloody women, they're always doing that.'

'Alright.' Rhiannon allowed that she was out of line by his reckoning. 'Then how about you explain to me where Annora fits in?' Ray went pale and silent, looking as though he'd been betrayed. 'Mother didn't tell me.' Rhiannon read his mind and dismissed his assumption.

'Don't do that!' His natural impulse was to step back from her, but then Ray realised she'd not been touching him in the first place. 'Oh no!'

'I'm afraid so,' she confessed. 'I'm at a loss to prevent it, even if I wanted to.'

'Well, great!' He threw his arms in the air, not even his thoughts were his own any more. 'I've known some sneaky, underhanded women in my time, but baby … you take the cake.'

'Hey.' Rhiannon could feel his rage brewing, and was not yet so accomplished in detachment not to be affected by it. 'At least I'm not lying to myself.'

'No!' He snapped. 'You just lie to everybody else! And, for the record, just because I was attracted to you in one life, doesn't mean I have to be attracted to you in this one. Because I assure you, *I'm not!*'

'Fine! The feeling's mutual.' She was beginning to wonder what she saw in him anyway. 'You just keep having wet dreams about mother and see where it gets you. There's much finer than you to be had.' She turned to storm away.

'Oh yeah?' He wanted to spite her badly. 'You do realise incest is against the law?' He struck a chord.

'Ohhh!' Rhiannon grabbed for the nearest object, a large spanner as chance would have it, and cast it at him. 'You have the mind of a sewer rat!'

He ducked and, when the spanner missed, grinned triumphantly. 'Hey, baby, the truth hurts.'

'It will be a cold day in hell before I'm your baby,' she seethed. 'Call me that again, and you will truly know God.' Her dark eyes stared him down, as she turned and calmly strutted away.

For several weeks Tory had been attempting to get in touch with her father, without success. Still, his evasiveness only served to make her more determined to find out the truth behind her birthright.

Thus, for the umpteenth time, Tory willed herself to her father's cavern of treasures at Dinas Emrys, to find the place devoid of life. As with every visit she'd made there of late, she was certain she could sense Myrddin's presence. 'I know you're here, Dad. You can't hide from me forever! Please talk to me … I need to know who my grandfather was.' The crackling sound of the torches mounted on the wall seemed almost deafening in the silence, and Tory began to despair. 'I have the right to know what you've all got planned for me! I grow tired of guessing.' She slumped into her father's favourite throne, knowing he would not speak. 'Is there no one to advise me then?' Tears of self-pity welled in her eyes; how she missed Taliesin. Why was he never around when she needed his counsel most?

To enlighten you would be detrimental to their cause.

Tory lifted her teary sights and was almost blinded by the lustre of a form that had manifested over one of the piles of precious relics banked up around the walls of the cave. This celestial woman, whose flowing robes left her half naked, was more beautiful to behold than any starlet of the silver screen, and her speech was more eloquent than the finest Shakespearean actor. Milky-white and soft was her skin, like a newborn babe. Her fair, ash-brown hair fell in long, loose locks, and her eyes were the colour of sparkling sapphire jewels.

I shall tell you the truth, little one, she said, *to spite them. For your grandfather killed my love, just as he killed yours.*

'I don't follow?' Tory's heart began to pound in panic. 'Do you mean Miles?'

No. There was pity in her voice. *It was the chosen one I saw destroyed. I tried to prevent it —*

'Don't listen to her, Tory. She lies.'

Myrddin had finally decided to make an appearance, and Tory had never seen her father so infuriated.

'Begone, *foul* whore.' His order thundered throughout the cavern, causing the very walls to tremble.

I am not the abomination here. Her tone became more forceful. *It is you who offend the mighty Anu, not I. And now you would keep your own child in the dark, and lead her to offend her great forefathers as you have done.*

'Father?' Tory became anxious, unable to take her eyes from the mesmerising entity who stood opposing him.

The images you have seen of your husband are merely that of a clone, the beautiful lady insisted. *This was created to keep you believing that you would be reunited*

*with him at the Gathering. But this false hope ... the Dragon
is dead.*

Tory couldn't stop the tears from cascading down
her face. 'But why —' She did not have the chance to
finish her query, as her father's open hand met with her
cheek and she was thrust to the floor.

'Do not heed her, I said. Her words are like poison
to the mind.' He took a stand before the phantasm,
between it and his daughter. 'And *you* ... evil
enchantress of a thousand names, I bid you leave! Lest
my father send you to join your incestuous husband, in
the darkest depths of creation.'

*Your threats don't intimidate me, nor should they you,
little one.* The woman looked to Tory, still cowering on
the floor in shock. *I'm not asking you to believe me. I'm
telling you to believe no one.* She looked back to the
Merlin with a look a defiance, and vanished into the
pile of treasure from which she'd emerged.

'Praise the universe.' Myrddin hurried over to the
spot where the woman had vanished and, digging away
the surrounding artifacts, exposed the ornate golden
device that had been used back in Atlantis to
communicate with Nibiru.

'The Ark!' Tory gasped. 'So this is where it has been
hiding.'

'And little use it is to us now.' He placed his hands
upon the shiny, metallic dome that rose up out of a
square golden base. After a few moments of intense
concentration the dome sank into the substructure,
whereby the Merlin replaced the ornate golden lid that
featured two, long, slender cherubs with their wings

outstretched towards each other. 'They must have figured out a way to tap into our transmissions. This is most inconvenient.'

'Inconvenient! Is that all you've got to say?' Tory raised herself out of the dirt. 'Who was that? Why would she tell me Maelgwn is dead, if he is not?'

'To confuse you into doing something rash … like seeking Maelgwn, when he has forbidden you to do so.'

'But how do I know she's lying about the clone? Maelgwn's message may have been a ploy to stop me from discovering the truth.' She backed up, pondering the possibilities the claim presented.

'See what a few moments in her presence can do? She always brings out the worst in people. Here am I — angered. And *you*, of all people, are fearful … and of me, what's worse!' Myrddin laughed off their visitor's cunning and shook himself, making a strange babbling sound as he did. When he felt he'd sufficiently rid his being of the negative vibrations, he smiled at his bemused daughter. 'I'm sorry I had to strike you … but you were mesmerised. I had to break the hold she had over you.'

'Who was she?' Tory could not part with the fear that seemed to thrive on his every word. 'Who was my grandfather? I want to know where I fit into this little war you all seem to be having behind my back!'

'Alright, you're right.' Myrddin conceded it was time. This incident proved Tory could be got at, despite all their precautions. He took a seat on his throne-like chair, musing over where to begin. 'I would hope you've read the ancient scriptures that tell how man's evolution was purposely sped up.'

As this was just about all she'd read in the past month, Tory urged him to skip over that part. 'Yes, yes … the great immortal ancestors did this so that man might serve them, the Nefilim, in their mining ventures that were based in Africa and the Middle East. The natural resources of their own planet were depleted and they were forced to seek their minerals, gold in particular, elsewhere. Some accounts say it was because they needed it for a special shield that was being designed to help protect their atmosphere from radiation. Others claim it held the key to their immortality.'

'Splendid.' He raised his brows, not wanting to get too far ahead … 'Now, the cultivation and excavation of the Earth was placed in the hands of the two sons of Anu. Enlil, being the first-born, was the commander of the mining projects here. He was known by the Celts as Math, the Lord of Abundance. Ea or Enki, the second-born, was the engineer behind both the Earth's cultivation and the development of humankind … The Egyptian's called him Ptah, the Creator, and to the Celts he was Bedi.'

'Dad, I know all this! Just cut to the chase. Who was my grandfather?'

Unperturbed by Tory's impetuous outburst, Myrddin continued with his full account: 'You, my dear Tory, descend from the line of Enki, or Bedi, who was your great-grandfather and mankind's foremost advocate at the God's council. Mankind was nearly wiped off the face of the Earth during the great deluge, and if it had not been for Enki defying the wish of his immortal colleagues, none of us would be here.'

209

'Not true.' Tory thought she must correct him on that point. 'Nin Bau was transported from Atlantis to the Dark Age *before* the great deluge, so you'd still be here ... thanks to me.'

Myrddin laughed. 'I'm glad you brought that up. The increasing number of unions between the sons of the Nefilim and the daughters of mankind was the very reason that Enlil wanted humankind destroyed. For humans had been deliberately fashioned mortal, so as to die. The last thing the Nefilim wanted was a whole bunch of half-caste human-Gods running about. What if we discovered how to activate the immortal gene passed on to us by our extra-terrestrial forefathers? Mankind might then threaten the authority and interstellar rule of the Nefilim. I believe they felt that, after the deluge, all these discrepancies had been corrected. The one surviving family were pure-bred human beings, the clan of Dwyfan, as the Britons called him, or Noah as he has become known.'

'The Nefilim hadn't counted on man learning the secrets of time travel, hey?' Tory smiled as she considered how far they'd come. 'So the spirit that was here just now was telling the truth. Our family is an offence against the Gods?'

'She twists the truth to suit herself,' he scoffed. 'Only some of the Nefilim think thus, not all. They have been divided over the issue of humankind for as long as we have been in existence.'

'So, my grandfather was one of Enki's sons, but which one?' Tory mulled this over, trying to deduce the answer for herself. As far as she knew Enki had had six pure-bred Nefilim males.

'Before I tell you ...' the Merlin interrupted her contemplation, 'I want you to know that my father did not go around randomly raping young Priestesses for his own personal pleasure. It was all part of a plan devised by he and his father when they became aware of Enlil's growing hatred of the human race. To raise his creation to demigods, without his brother's knowledge, was the only way Enki could conceive of ensuring mankind's ultimate survival.'

'I understand. We're the good guys.' Tory motioned with both her hands for him to be out with it.

'Not by the Bible's reckoning. You see, Enki was the serpent in the Garden of Eden. It was he who made human's self-aware. Before this, humankind only knew enough to follow the orders of their creators. Humans knew nothing of reproduction, having been genetically engineered by the Nefilim. As he had yet to have an original thought, mankind knew nothing of good and evil; he ate and laboured as an animal. But Enki knew we possessed the potential to have great intelligence, and, given some self-respect and encouragement, we could create, achieve, dream, and aspire to be every bit as wondrous as our creators ... perhaps even more so! For humankind had a far greater capacity to love and respect their fellow creatures ... we did once, anyway.'

It was a lovely story, which she had read over and over. 'Dad?' Tory appealed for the one vital piece of information that eluded her.

'The name you seek is that of Enki's first-born, Marduk,' Myrddin admitted finally, with a heavy sigh.

Tory gasped, her eyes boggling in their sockets, as she thought back over her research. 'Ra,' she stated, to be sure she understood correctly.

'That was the Egyptian name for him, but he has had many others.'

Tory had to sit down before she fell down. 'So, who was the woman who was here just now?'

The question brought a frown to Myrddin's face, but he thought it wise to inform Tory of the whore's identities. 'She is the daughter of Enlil's first son, Narnar, who also went by the name of Sin. She has had many names: Irnini, Inanna, Ishtar, Aphrodite, but the Celts called her Arianrod.'

'You stole the chariot from her!' Tory considered it wasn't any wonder that the Goddess and the Merlin didn't get along.

'No, no, no, no, no!' He became disgruntled. 'Throughout the course of the ages, the story got all twisted. It was she who stole the chariot from me! For a short time, anyway.' Myrddin calmed a little. 'In my travels through time, I spent many years in ancient Egypt during the time of the Pyramid wars. Ashtoreth, as she was then known, stole my transport. And although she never discovered its true function was that of a time machine, she used it to transport herself from one destination to another. Of course, she didn't need any technological assistance to do this. But she took pride in hovering over many a battlefield in a chariot belonging to the bastard son of her greatest adversary, Ra.'

As Tory's mind processed all the information, a few more pieces of the puzzle slotted into place. 'So it is

Enki who has been nominating and collecting the Chosen?'

It made perfect sense. Only recruiting those of his line due to their immortal potential he looked for descendants who were born leaders, thinkers and humanitarians. He would then send an instructor, the like of Taliesin or Myrddin, to guide the Chosen One's spiritual, physical and mental development.

'Half of these Chosen ascended into heaven to learn the wonders of space ...' Myrddin filled in the blanks, 'leaving the other half to protect the Earth and his precious mankind, until the day of his return.'

'Great!' Tory grumbled at her lot. 'Why does Maelgwn get all the fun stuff?'

Myrddin shrugged, for he had been given the same fate as his daughter. 'He must help contend with mankind's enemies in space, as we must deal with our enemies here on Earth.'

Like Doc Alexander, Tory thought on the quiet; just how did he fit into all this?

She strongly suspected that he was an incarnate of Caradoc. Perhaps the last of Maelgwn's line, Cadwaladr, who, according to the histories, was utterly barbaric in temperament and behaviour. He was hellbent on destroying the entire English population of Britain, and spared neither woman nor child, condemning them all to horrible deaths with ruthless savagery. He also called himself a Christian, so Tory could only assume this meant Taliesin had not tutored Cadwaladr as he had those before him. But why? Only Taliesin knew.

After speaking with her father Tory returned, the base to research some of the Gods he had mentioned. And just what had been the cause of the contention between Inanna and Marduk? The answer lay in the disappearance of Inanna's husband, Dumuzi, who was Marduk's youngest brother.

Inanna had been rendered infertile by her aunt, Ninharsag, when she had done her aging relative out of her place in the Pantheon of Twelve — the great council of the God's. In her want for children, Inanna had persuaded her husband Dumuzi to rape his sister and then she planned to claim the resulting child as their own. But rape was considered a most grievous offense, and it fell to Marduk to punish Dumuzi for his crime. Marduk stripped Dumuzi of all his kingly possessions and banished him to the wastelands where he would ponder his wrongdoing for a time. When Dumuzi had repented, Marduk planned to allow him to return to his wife and lands. But Dumuzi mysteriously vanished during his time in exile, and Inanna accused Marduk of murdering him. Although Marduk swore he had done naught but carry out Dumuzi's sentence, he was condemned by the Pantheon of Twelve and banished from their midst.

'But what did Marduk have to gain by murdering his brother, of whom the ancient texts claim he was quite fond?' Noah queried Tory, after they had studied the story closely.

Tory shrugged. 'Well, Inanna was of Enlil's flock and therefore opposed to the human race ... whereas my grandfather was of Enki's line who supported the advancement of mankind. Maybe that had something to do with it.'

Noah didn't seem convinced. 'But what of Inanna's brother, Utu-Shamash? It seems to me that he had more cause than anyone to despise Dumuzi.'

'How so?' Tory queried, most interested to hear. Noah knew these ancient texts backwards, having had more time than she to study them.

'Well, before her marriage to Dumuzi, Inanna and her twin brother, Shamash, had been rather close ... too close, if you get my drift.'

'They were lovers?' Tory queried, sounding daunted but not surprised.

Noah nodded. 'Apparently Shamash was rather put out when she wed Dumuzi. So by getting rid of Dumuzi and framing Marduk for the crime, Shamash would have killed two birds with one stone.'

'Interesting,' Tory granted. 'But I am wondering, how does one murder a God?'

'Well,' Noah raised his brows, 'you can't. However, there are several references to Gods being dismembered, and by separating all their body parts they were rendered as good as dead.'

The thought made Tory a little uneasy to say the least. 'To spend eternity fully conscious, incapacitated and alone ... how completely horrendous! However,' she thought again, 'Dumuzi must still be hidden somewhere on this planet.'

'One would think so,' Noah agreed. 'But the heartbroken Inanna searched from one end of the Earth to the other and found no trace of him.'

'And if my grandfather was falsely accused, you can guarantee he would have searched for Dumuzi as well.' Tory sighed, realising that her chances of succeeding where the God's had failed were very slim indeed.

13

TO CATCH A THIEF

When Tory learnt of the plan to send her daughter to obtain Doc's personal code key from him, her first reaction was to volunteer to go in Rhiannon's stead. But Rhun rejected this idea for two very good reasons. One, his father had instructed Tory to stay hidden. And two, Tory lacked the telepathic knowhow for which Rhiannon had been selected in the first place. After much argument Tory finally consented, but she was not about to let her daughter attempt the feat without a safeguard.

Out came the Stormers that Tory had procured from Atlantis during her most recent visit there. She was of the mind to test the stun capabilities on an immortal. The weapon's effect on a normal man could knock him out for up to twenty-four hours — but someone of an eternal disposition? That was quite another matter. As an immortal who had no integral part to play in their current mission, Brian nominated himself as the guinea pig for their target practice. Rhun had a large section of the earthen floor in the cavern of abodes cleared to use as a testing ground for the handheld weapons.

Floyd, Noah, Teo and Nicholas stood at a distance, observing Tory demonstrate how the Stormers were operated.

Brian was taking little notice of what was being said to him. He was busy mucking about with the laser sword capability of his weapon, when he swung around and accidently severed Rhun's left arm at the elbow.

'Fair go!' Rhun looked to his body part, laying in the dirt at his feet. 'I was using that.'

Brian, who had never been confronted by such a scenario before, was unable to see the humour. 'Jesus, Rhun … I don't know what to say.' The sight of all the blood gushing from the stump that was once his nephew's arm, made Brian's stomach turn. 'Will it grow back?'

'I don't think it works that way.' Rhun knelt beside his amputated portion, and took it up with his remaining good hand.

Brian joined him, eager to help if he could. 'Christ, I feel awful.' He stared at the lifeless limb, full of remorse. 'Take one of mine off … I deserve it.' Brian urged his nephew to take the Stormer from him.

But Rhun's hand was occupied with the dead remains of his arm, until the defunct member gripped hold of Brian's throat. 'Thanks, man, if you insist.'

Rhun left his severed body part to strangle his uncle, and took possession of Brian's weapon to do as he'd suggested.

'Aw, shit!' Brian watched one arm go flying off yonder, whilst the other struggled to release the fingers of Rhun's renegade limb from around his neck. 'You complete bastard!' Brian choked out the words, unable to believe Rhun had actually done it.

'I'll take mine back now, if it's all the same to you.' Rhun willed the stray part back to whence it belonged, and it let go of Brian as it was sucked back to join its elbow.

'Thank God,' uttered Brian as he witnessed Rhun wiggling the fingers of his reinstated arm, which had instantly mended as good as new.

As this was threatening to turn into a scene from a Monty Python film, Tory knocked Brian out with a blast from her Stormer to put an end to the shenanigans. 'Great!' She scolded her boy who she considered was acting like one today. 'Now how am I supposed to know if it was the effect of the Stormer that put his lights out, or the shock of being dismembered?'

'I'm sorry, I just couldn't resist.' Rhun supressed his amusement, retrieving Brian's arm and returning it to its rightful socket on his uncle's body. He stood up and tried to appease his mother. 'Look, why don't you test it out on me?' Both hands upturned, Rhun raised his brow to invite her response.

A second later, he joined Brian in an unconscious state.

Around about six hours later Rhun came to, but Brian did not show signs of life until closer to ten hours had elapsed. Either way this proved the Stormers did have some effect on their kind, enough to give Rhiannon ample time to escape Doc should she be forced into such a predicament.

All memory of Watarrka would be erased from Rhiannon's memory. Rhun claimed this was a simple hypnotic procedure. He would plant a new identity in her head, so that not even Rhiannon would doubt the alias she'd assumed. Her mission would be set foremost in her mind, but with any luck the proper clothing would prevent Doc from making skin contact with her. Even if he did, he would be unable to discern for whom she was working. This memory wash would also suspend the recollection of her father's murder at the hands of her target, preventing Rhiannon from any action she might otherwise contemplate upon making Doc's acquaintance.

Rhiannon found the notion of having her mind tampered with in such a manner a little disturbing. But as Rhun would be close by her every step of the way, and as he swore he could restore her memory to its former order within seconds, she agreed to place herself in her brother's hands.

Confirmation of Rhiannon's mission reached Ray through the grapevine on the day scheduled for the attempt. He'd not had the chance to apologise for their little run-in a few days back, and his conscience was starting to get the better of him.

I didn't mean to say that I find her unattractive, he mused as he soldered. *She's just a bit young for me, that's all*. Then Ray realised he'd joined a whole bunch of wires to the wrong multicore. 'Goddamnit!' He attempted to rip the mistake apart with his bare hands, and only partially succeeded, which made him all the more agitated. 'I don't care what I said, or what she thinks of me! Why should I? It's not like she can get killed or anything? I mean, what's the worst thing that could happen?'

Visions of Rhiannon being drugged, tortured and beaten in the same way as he had been made Ray's blood run cold and the hairs of his body stand on end. What if Doc charmed her into doing something against her will, like he did everybody else?

'Don't do this to me, Lord. If I fall for this girl, I'll have to stay fallen, and you know I'm not very good at that.'

He'd often passed his quiet moments thinking about Tory, but lately her image had been replaced by that of the beauty who'd made an appearance on Floyd's birthday.

'I can't hide anything from her.' He gripped his forehead with both hands to endure the thought. 'She knows what I'm thinking all the time, what I'm feeling!'

Yet, having dwelt on this worry a moment, Ray considered that such an ability also added a whole new dimension to the concept of making love.

'Well, when you put it that way.' He pondered the notion with a smile. 'Oh jeez!' It dawned on him that Rhiannon was due to depart for her rendezvous with destiny. He scampered out from underneath the *Goddess* and made haste to Floyd's quarters on the uppermost level of the cavern farthest from him.

Halfway up the stairs in the cavern of abodes, Ray discovered just how unfit he was.

'Hey, Ray.' Rhun gave him a slap on the back on his way past him. 'You really should come to training … do yourself a favour.'

Using the iron railing to launch himself, Ray managed to grab hold of Rhun's shirt. 'Has Rhiannon left yet?' he inquired between gasps for breath.

'No,' Rhun answered. And before he had a chance to say more, Ray had taken off up the stairs ahead of him. *Typical that he'd pick now to figure out he's in love with her.* Rhun chuckled, finding it amusing. *Best be there, then, to explain.* He gave chase, scaling two stairs at a time.

Practically everyone was gathered in Floyd's computer room playing with gadgets and reviewing the details of the plan.

'Rhiannon?' Ray inquired of Nick over the babble.

Nick pointed to the observatory, and Ray was away. 'Oi, you can't go in there.' The protest came too late, and Nick wasn't fast enough to beat Ray to the door.

Rhun prevented Nick from continuing the chase further, motioning him to stay put.

Inside the large, dim chamber Ray's pace slowed. The woman of his dreams was seated with Floyd, listening to last-minute instructions. Ray thought it a sin, the way she filled the white leather catsuit she wore. Her outfit was complete with matching boots and gloves. Her long, fair hair was bound in a loose bun, leaving long, wispy curls to dance round her face. Dark sunglasses shrouded her eyes from view, as her red painted lips sucked on a cigarette.

Hold on. Rhiannon doesn't smoke?

'Out.' Floyd pointed to the door, most annoyed that he'd been interrupted.

'I have to speak with her.' Ray charged forward determined to do exactly that, but Floyd intercepted.

'Not now.'

'Yes, *now*.' Ray tried to barge his way through, but Floyd held him off long enough for Rhun to secure him in a headlock.

'Who is this then?' The golden-haired beauty dipped her sunglasses to inquire.

'Sorry?' Ray stopped struggling against his captor. 'Rhiannon, it's me.'

She looked him up and down, seemingly delighted to make his acquaintance. 'Well, to my deep regret, you must have me confused with somebody else.'

Ray was dumbfounded. It wasn't just Rhiannon's looks that had changed. Her whole demeanour absolutely oozed confidence, money, and sex appeal.

'What have you done to her?' His mood darkened as he turned to Floyd. 'You're not sending her to Doc like that!' Rhun started dragging him toward the door, and Ray went kicking and swearing. 'It'll be like a lamb to the slaughter!'

Rhun gave the order that locked the door between them and the observatory before he let his captive go. 'Chill out will you ... the situation is under control.'

Pulling his shirt into shape and pushing his glasses back up on his nose, Ray turned around to demand some answers. 'Why doesn't she recognise me?'

Rhun was poised, ready to topple Ray, for he looked as if he might explode at any second. 'We found it necessary to erase certain details of her life from her conscious memory, so that Doc cannot acquire knowledge of our whereabouts from her in the same fashion he located you through my mother.'

'You sick bastards! You're no better than the damn CIA!'

He took a swing at Rhun, but a blast from a Stormer stunned him and Rhun caught him up before he hit the floor.

'Might be best for him to sleep through this.' Tory put the weapon down, motioning for Rhun to put Ray on the sofa.

The vague throbbing sensation in his head was gradually broken up by muffled echoes of chattering voices. Hazy shadows formed into people as he dared to open his eyes into a squint. Where was he? *The communications room.* What the hell was he doing here? *Rhiannon!*

Ray found himself seated bolt upright, eyes wide open and head swimming from the sudden movement.

Most of the regular gang were gathered around Floyd's monitors, while Floyd gave instructions into a phone. 'Okay, that's it. Now replace the crystals, just as I showed you.'

Everyone was paused, breathless, waiting for confirmation that the given task had been completed.

'What's happening?' Ray snuck up from behind and gave everyone quite a fright.

'Jesus, Ray.' Tory whacked his shoulder. 'What are you doing awake already?' She knew she should have set the Stormer on a higher amplitude.

'Why was I knocked out in the first place?' He thought this was a more apt question. 'Where is she?'

More interested in the welfare of her children than Ray, Tory hushed him to silence and her eyes returned to the blank monitor screen.

'Good lad.' Floyd gave a sigh of relief, as did everyone. 'You should be right to hook up … I'll advise when we have audiovisual.'

'Tory.' Ray grabbed hold of her wrist and pulled her aside.

'Alright, damn it.' She cursed his persistence in a whisper. 'Doc is on a flight from London to Paris. Rhiannon, who is in first class with him, has a fibre optics microcamera and a minute high-gain microphone built into the watch she is wearing. These are connected to a tiny transmitter hidden in her suit. Right now, Floyd is speaking with Rhun, who is concealed in the nose carriage bay directly beneath her, where the plane's radio and electronics ranks are located. By changing the crystals in the planes third back-up transmitter, he'll —'

'Change the frequency of the transmission.' Ray comprehended their plan. By doing this, not even the pilots of the aircraft would realise someone else was utilising their satellite link-up to communicate. It was just like using a completely different channel.

A cheer drew Tory back to the monitors, where an image of Doc had appeared.

'So, Miss Devereux, what takes you to France?' His voice came through as clear as a bell.

'Business and pleasure,' Rhiannon informed him. 'My father asked me to take a look at an estate down Monaco way, after I visit a friend of mine in Paris who just got engaged.'

'He's found her already.' Nick was most impressed that all was going to plan.

'Like a bee to the honey pot.' Floyd grinned. 'Confirm visual and audio feed … sit tight, I'm out.' Floyd hung up the phone, most annoyed to observe that Doc already had his laptop out and online. He had hoped they'd catch Doc punching his code-key into the computer on film. 'I sure hope Rhiannon psyched the code out of him, because we sure as hell missed it.'

After some polite and rather aimless chitchat, Rhiannon brought the conversation round to his computer. 'That is a rather impressive little PC you've got there. I surf the net myself, though I find the virtual-net far more appealing.'

'Yes, good!' Floyd thought her approach subtle enough to avoid suspicion.

'I'm very glad to hear you say that, since I own shares in Cybercom.' Doc boasted in a shy fashion.

'Really!' She sounded most impressed. 'We must swap addresses then. Perhaps we could arrange to meet in cyber-space somewhere?' She pulled an electronic notebook from her bag that was the size of a make-up compact. With the press of a button, it ejected a card with all her relevant net information on it. Floyd had arranged this data specifically to suit their purpose.

'A handy little gadget.' Doc looked the card over, breaking into a grin of approval. 'The Chameleon, hey?'

'An appropriate handle if I do say so myself.' Rhiannon jested. 'I can never decide on the right cyber-image you see, so I just keep changing it.' Her fingers sat poised ready to type. 'So, by what handle do you travel?'

With a look of regret that he was not so well-equipped as she, Doc reached inside his jacket and produced a card.

'Oh my god!' she announced upon viewing it, overwhelmed and somewhat embarrassed. 'I knew I recognised you … you're Doc Alexander of the International Crisis Agency.' She played up her surprise. 'Please, you must forgive my ignorance, I don't really follow politics. But I know you've helped a great many countries in need.'

He waved off her adulation. 'That's my job, I —'

'Sorry to disturb you, sir …' Doc was interrupted by one of his associates. 'The pilot of the plane is asking to meet you.'

Doc frowned, obviously thinking the request trivial.

'It won't take a second.' His associate insisted rather adamantly.

Doc stood, closing his laptop and placing it in his vacated seat. 'Excuse I.' He headed off towards the cockpit.

His associate retrieved the laptop to take it with them. 'Madam.' He nodded to her and followed his patron up the aisle.

This disturbed Floyd, hence he hit speed dial on the phone to speak with Rhun. 'They're onto us.' He hung up.

'Now what!' Ray began to panic as they lost visuals.

Floyd shrugged. 'We wait.'

Upon entering the compartment that separated first-class from the cockpit, Doc confronted his security team that was stationed there. 'This had better be good.'

His righthand man, Stanley Brennon, closed the door and handed Doc his computer. 'Our scanner tells us that your lady friend is wearing a transmitter.'

'Don't be ridiculous! Where the hell do you think she's hiding it? They don't make transmitters that small.'

'It's been switched off,' the man behind the scanner advised.

'Did you get a chance to track the transmission?' Stan moved to view the screen for himself, but the man shook his head in the negative.

'I told you to hold off.'

Stan looked to Doc. 'Well, I thought we'd best advise our illustrious leader before he gave too much away.'

Doc was pacing now. 'It's impossible! How could she get through airport security?' But no sooner had he asked the question than the thought of Tory popping in and out of ICA headquarters came to mind. 'Shit!' He was annoyed he'd already handed his net information over to her. What did she want with it? 'Hold on,' he advised, cooling his temper dramatically. 'This can be twisted to our advantage.'

'Do you want us to pick her up at the airport for questioning?' Stan wasn't sure he followed what his boss was on about.

'No. But I want pictures of her, before she gets off the plane.' Doc closed his eyes to cast a psychic shield around himself, and his men fell silent.

Whenever their superior found himself in a precarious situation, he always paused thus for several minutes. His men had always assumed he was praying.

With a clap, Doc spurred himself to action. 'Wish me luck, boys … I'm going to make a date.'

The diplomat returned to his seat to find his charming spy had vanished. *Fickle little minx.* He spied her on the far side of the cabin speaking with another man. When Doc caught her eye, she waved him over.

'My friend's fiance.' She motioned to the young man beside her, all excited by the happy coincidence.

'Imagine that.' Doc shook the young man's hand, noting that he wore leather gloves that ruled out the possibility of skin contact.

Seeking another's company was a clever move on her behalf, as it prevented him from getting too close to her.

Must not dwell on such matters now.

If she came from the Goddess or was indeed the Goddess herself, she was almost certainly more proficient at the psychic arts than he. No thought of what he suspected must enter his mind whilst in her company. Only when he could be sure his thoughts were his own would he ponder the events of this day.

Hours later Rhun returned to base, carrying his sister in his arms.

'What went wrong?' Ray went to retrieve Rhiannon from the boy-wonder, wanting to punch Rhun's lights out for escorting her into such a precarious situation in the first place.

'Nothing went wrong!' Rhun sidestepped the crazed engineer, placing his bundle on the sofa. 'As promised, I returned her to her senses before we left the airport ... *a bad move*. As soon as she realised what she'd done, she fainted.'

'Did she get the code-key?' Floyd wanted to know; the whole success of their mission depended on it.

'Is that all you're worried about?' Ray turned to have a go at Floyd instead.

'Ray!' Tory grabbed hold of his collar and guided him to a seat. 'Mellow. Everybody else, out.' She ushered them towards the door. 'You, too.' She pulled her son away from Rhiannon.

'Aren't you staying?' Ray became anxious as he watched Tory follow Rhun toward the door.

'It's okay. Rhiannon will remember everything when she wakes.'

Still, Ray found it rather disconserting that Tory should grant him special consideration in this case. 'Why do I get to stay?'

'You said you had something to say to her, so say it.' Tory sealed the door on the way out.

Great going. Now everybody suspects what you're not even sure about yourself. Ray raised his bones and neared the girl on whose behalf he'd been acting like a complete whacko all day. *Dark eyes, dark hair, young and halfway innocent.* Ray considered that, in retrospect, this was how he preferred her.

'Rhun, is that you?' She stirred.

'No, should I run and fetch him for you?' Ray thought this was the perfect way out of this situation, as Rhiannon would surely be wondering why he alone was there to greet her.

A vague image of Ray storming the observatory made Rhiannon smile, and she grabbed his arm to prevent him going anywhere. 'Not so fast.' She pulled him down to squat beside her. 'Are we alone?'

Although he knew damn well they were, he cast his eyes around the room to forestall the inevitable. Confessing he desired her was easy. It was admitting she'd been right that really hurt. 'Yep … we are definitely *alone*,' Ray confirmed, just knowing the next question would be why?

Rhiannon raised herself to a seated position and slid a hand inside the collar of his shirt. 'I know why?' she whispered, urging him to a kiss he had no wish to avoid.

Although Ray had not expected this, he was grateful she'd found a way to cut through all the bullshit to get straight to the heart of the matter.

'You're welcome.' She melted to a smile as their lips parted. Ray went to speak, but her hand covered his mouth. 'No. Don't say anything.'

'Well, you —'

'No,' she insisted. 'You don't have to explain, apologise, retaliate, object —'

Ray rolled his eyes and kissed her again, so that he

might have a chance to convey that he felt exactly the same way. He didn't want to discuss the issue any more than she did.

'Enough said then.' She spread her legs and slid into his lap. 'When and where?'

Her frankness took Ray a little off guard, although he couldn't begin to fathom why? Any other woman and he would have had her flat on her back and half naked by this time. *God.* He couldn't think, knowing she'd be following his reasoning.

'It's mother, isn't it?'

'Is it?' He hadn't considered that.

Rhiannon nodded. 'You bet her one hundred dollars that you'd get her into bed before you fell for anybody else?'

After a second's thought, Ray laughed. 'You're right, you know. That's exactly it.' He laughed again, then abruptly stopped. 'Was it really a hundred bucks?'

'A small price to pay.' Her lips did a slow dance around his mouth, along his jaw, and down his neck. 'The question is …' She sucked his earlobe in anticipation. 'When?'

'Now is good?' What the hell, he figured, they were already in the mood.

'No, now's no good,' she contradicted.

'Now's no good?' He couldn't see why.

'Company,' she explained in a word.

Before the shock of the announcement had even sunk in, Ray had them up and standing at attention. 'Asap, my place,' he proposed, as the door vanished and the room filled with people.

Ray left Rhiannon to impart the details of her mission to the others, deciding that perhaps he'd better grab a shower as he'd not had one in days.

Rhiannon handed the info-card she'd managed to scam out of Doc over to Floyd. It seemed Mr Alexander had a rather appropriate handle also, as he travelled cyber-space under the assumed identity of the Dragon Slayer. 'We arranged to meet in a VRN bar called the Cauldron.' She shrugged as she referred Floyd to the address she'd typed into her notebook, which like all web-site addresses was a jumble of seemingly random digits.

'I know that place.' The hacker bit his lip, recalling conversations he'd had there. 'I've even spoken with the son-of-a-bitch!' His attention returned to Rhiannon, with a look of desperation on his face. 'But the code-key, did you get it?'

With a cocky grin Rhiannon advised. 'A, R, W, Y, S, T, L, I, break, twenty-six, dash, thirteen, dash, five-nineteen, stop.'

Tory was watching over Floyd's shoulder as he scribbled it down: Arwystli 26–13–519. 'Oh shit, I don't believe it.' She grabbed up the piece of paper, staring intensely at the information. 'It's a date.'

'How can it be a date?' Teo stepped in to calm her down. 'Look, *thirteen* … there's no thirteenth month in the year.'

'Ah!' Noah politely intervened. 'But in the year five nineteen, there was a thirteenth month by the Celtic calendar … Ruis, if memory serves. Yet the twenty-sixth day is not really part of that month, it being one of the five dark days, which stood apart from the rest of the calendar.'

'Sorrowing, they called it. The dead of the year, when time stood still.' Tory faltered, entranced and horrified as she recalled the events of that particular year. 'This date was the day before I died, physically, that's why I recall it so well.' She looked to Noah, who now knew her story better than anyone. 'Caradoc died on this day.'

'Father's bastard brother! Who killed my grandfather whilst trying to steal Gwynedd from beneath us?' Rhun found this an interesting twist. 'You think Cadwaladr is a reincarnation of him, don't you?' This was almost an accusation, as she'd not mentioned this theory to him.

'Who's Cadwaladr again?' Brian wasn't following.

'My great-great-great-grandson.' Tory jogged his memory, as they had discussed this before.

'The one we suspect might be Doc,' Noah added to further clarify the situation.

'Well, it makes little difference.' Floyd thought he'd bring everyone's attention back to the events of the present. 'Because, if Doc hasn't thrown us a bum steer —'

'Oh, I don't believe he was onto us,' Rhiannon advised. 'Or, at least, he wasn't suspicious in my presence. Although he was quite browned off when Rhun turned up.'

'Good.' Floyd retrieved the code from Tory to admire and relish it. 'Then by this time tomorrow no matter who the prick really is, we're going to know him fairly well, I'd say.'

'And you're sure he won't be able to trace your line back to the ranger station at Watarrka?' Tory, who was no computer whiz to be sure, thought that what Floyd had in mind seemed risky.

'There are ways and means.' Floyd grinned. He would have to go through many computers before he could attempt the break-in, but he would see to it that the base was protected. 'Just leave it to me.'

It was Floyd's turn to usher everyone out of his room, except for his prodigy. Nicholas was in for an all-night session — brainstorming the downfall of the Agency, smoking dope, and key crunching with Floyd was Nick's idea of the perfect Saturday night.

In the wee hours, trying to research became a complete farce. No matter how hard Tory tried to concentrate, the intense sexual ecstasy her daughter was feeling proved too great a distraction — even from three caverns away! Seeing no other way to avoid the event, Tory took a seat on her bed to renew the psychic shield around herself. Even when she'd done this, the sensation of love lingered, along with memories of Maelgwn. She wondered about the unfortunate situation mentioned in his message — if, indeed, the message had truly been from him.

'Did the Earth move for you, too?' Rhun entered, unannounced. He could do this, as his voice overrode all the cavern's vocally-activated systems.

'You felt it too, huh?' Tory smiled at their predicament.

Rhun grinned, dropping himself down beside her. 'I don't suppose we can ask them to keep it down.' Rhun nudged his mother's shoulder in fun and so picked up on her plan to make contact with his father. 'No, you must not. It's absolutely out of the question! Forget what Inanna told you. She's a lying whore.'

'I wish I could. But every time I close my eyes, I see macabre visions of Maelgwn being tortured to death.'

'It's just your subconscious playing tricks on you,' Rhun insisted. 'I assure you, Father is very much alive.'

'But how could you tell the difference between your father and an exact clone of him?'

Although Rhun denied the claim, he understood her reservations. 'Fair enough. How do *you* expect to know the difference?'

'I don't know, but I have to try. There are extra precautions I can take when travelling in an astral form, just as you and Maelgwn did during inauguration.'

'And how do you know that, when the inauguration of Kings is strictly forbidden to those of your gender?' Rhun stood, agitated by her lack of respect for an age-old tradition. 'You were spying on me the whole time, not just during my quest.'

Tory sucked in her cheeks, playing innocent, her eyes looking anywhere but at him.

'Then you should also know I have an Otherworld affiliate. A dragon, who guarded the gateway and my physical form, whilst my spirit wandered through its realms.'

'I, too, have such a guardian,' she informed him stubbornly.

'Rubbish!' He objected. 'Who sent it to you?'

'I don't really know.' Tory mused on the possibilities. 'I think it came of its own accord.'

Rhun thought it highly peculiar that any Otherworldly creature would assist someone of the middle kingdoms without being obliged by some higher force to do so. 'Look, I really don't think it works that way. What manner of beast is it?

'Take me to the strongest ley crossing around here, and I'll introduce you,' she teased.

'You're not serious. Not now! What if something goes wrong? Think about the mission tomorrow.' The safety of their whole community was at risk, Rhun felt they both had to be functioning at one hundred per cent.

'What do you take me for? Of course not.' Tory raised herself to give him a shove, and Rhun smiled at underestimating her. 'We shall wait for the full moon.'

By mid-afternoon the conspirators had gathered in Floyd's headquarters, eager to see the hacker's handiwork.

The plan was that Rhiannon would meet Doc at the VRN bar as previously arranged, which ensured that Doc's computer was online. Whilst she was keeping Mr Alexander visually preoccupied, Floyd would hack into Doc's computer using the password they'd procured. Once they had access to their subject's hard-drive, they required a five minute window per fifty gigabytes of information to download; chances were, Doc would catch them in the act and run a trace. Anticipating this, Floyd went via several different websites and a couple of satellites to place the call. So that, even if they were caught copying files, it would take Doc longer to trace them than it would for them to retrieve the information they sought.

Ray and Rhiannon were the last to show for duty, and although neither of them were playing up the fact they'd been shagging all night Rhun couldn't resist having a dig. 'Sleep well, did we?'

Rhiannon gave him a sideways glance, choosing to ignore his inference. 'Very well, thank you.'

'Well, aren't you the lucky one then. I was tossing and turning all night.' Rhun smiled slyly.

It took a moment for their psychic link to occur to her, but when it had, Rhainnon looked from her brother to her mother. 'No.' When Tory nodded to confirm, Rhiannon suppressed a laugh and covered her face to hide her embarrassment.

'What are you saying? That ...' Ray's ego was smiling as he motioned between Rhiannon and himself, though his mind found their scenario decidedly weird.

'I warned you, Ray.' Tory jogged his memory. 'There are no secrets between my children and myself.'

'Wonderful.' Ray was unsure of whether to be annoyed or not. It bothered him to think that another man could experience their extracurricular activities through his lover. Yet, when he considered that Tory had also perceived the act, the smile returned to his face. 'Well, then, it would seem you owe me a hundred bucks,' he put to Tory.

'How do you figure?'

Ray held up both his hands, as if appealing to her sense of justice. 'You play, you pay.'

Tory found his reasoning amusing. 'We'll call it even, shall we?'

Ray was about to contest her ruling, when Floyd interrupted. 'All right, people, let's rock'n'roll.' He clapped his hands together to get them all to their stations.

A slinky lizard woman who changed colour every couple of minutes was the guise under which Rhiannon would travel cyberspace. She'd already learnt how to direct herself around inside the net, and how to utilize a virtual keyboard to communicate with the inhabitants of the VR world. She could also use a direct voice link, but as they didn't want Doc overhearing what was transpiring around Rhiannon, typed dialogue was the preferred option. Nick had linked a voice sample of Rhiannon's to the VR keyboard, which would make it practically impossible for anyone on the net to know the difference. After positioning the VR unit on her head and slipping the gloves onto her hands, Floyd explained how, by pointing to a tiny symbol to Rhiannon's lower left, she could make her chameleon image blend into her surroundings until she was near transparent.

'Nice touch.' Rhiannon greatly approved. Now she could really toy with Alexander. This was going to be fun.

The credit for the chameleon creation went to Nick, who'd spent the entire night making the cyber-image as impressive as possible. He was seated directly beside Rhiannon to follow her movements through cyberspace on one monitor while keeping an eye on the phone-link that Floyd had graphed out on another. If Doc started running a trace, Nick could follow his progress.

Floyd was seated behind another terminal, limbering up his fingers. It was going to get very hairy in here in the next ten minutes or so, and he only had one crack at this. By tomorrow, Doc would have an entirely new code-key and website address. 'Well, Rhiannon, you can shoot through any time you're ready.'

Nick typed frantically on his keypad. 'Sending a message to Doc's e-mail and pager.' With one final keystroke, he gave Rhiannon a nudge for good luck. 'Go get him, tiger ... or should I say, lizard.'

The virtual-world was ablaze with brilliant colour, the circuits and cities reflecting the bizarre creative genius of its contributors and patriots. Each website was akin to a town with its own tourist information office advising what services, recreation, games, entertainment, and so on, were to be found there. Some of these sites had the appearance of sparkling celestial palaces, others looked like Gothic hellholes, or futuristic space stations. They could also be breathtaking landscapes with terrain that was completely true to life — or, alternatively, completely alien. Yet every single one of these individual worlds had thousands of places or rooms to explore, and millions of people and bizarre images to meet.

Rhiannon would not be swayed from her course today. She was headed for a website in England and upon punching the address into her VR keyboard she was sucked into the technicolour circuits and shot forth to her destination. On arrival she could have chosen to cruise around the website and explore, but Rhiannon was not here for the scenic tour. A simple request at Tourist Information landed her in front of the Cauldron Club. As there was no handle on the door, she used the gargoyle knocker. A small panel slid aside and two glowing-green eyes peered out of the dwelling at her.

'What's your business?' said a voice of doom.

'I'm meeting the Dragon Slayer here,' she replied.

'What's the password?'

'Password?' Rhiannon questioned out loud, hoping Floyd would know.

'Just *swear* at him,' the hacker urged.

'Up *yours* arsehole.'

'Close enough,' declared the ghoulish bouncer, and the door vanished.

Rhiannon went into camouflage mode as she moved down the long dark staircase.

My, but they had some wild-looking characters down here. The dingy interior and atmosphere of the place made most horror flicks look like nursery rhymes. The walls oozed luminous green slime while the doors bled all over the floor. There was one creature in a corner whose head kept exploding with graphic detail, before reforming to repeat the exercise. Mutants of all shapes and sizes frequented the pool tables and video games. Others cheered creatures doing battle in a pit, placing their bets at the bar.

All in all, it was a very lively place. The goings-on had Rhiannon so spellbound that she was startled by the sensors in her right glove telling her someone had taken hold of her hand. Turning her head she spied a huge, dark gladiator.

Tory, who was viewing the monitors over Nick's shoulder, gasped, 'It's Caradoc!'

'It's only a cyber-image for Pete's sake,' Teo scoffed.

'A bloody good one, too,' she agreed.

Rhiannon, seeing no further use for her camouflage, switched it off and allowed the large warrior to kiss her hand.

'Miss Chameleon, how lovely you look.' Doc's chosen guise winked at her.

'Why DS ...' She pressed a button on her VR keyboard and the ornately-spiked collar of her character rose up to frame the Chameleon's face — as a frill-necked lizard might when confronted unawares. 'I'm so glad you could make it.'

'I wouldn't have missed it for the world.' The Dragon Slayer motioned her towards a vacated booth. 'Shall we?'

'Floyd!' Tory demanded an update.

'I'm on it,' he assured her.

As the receiver's PC was online, Floyd requested to log-on. The code proved to be correct, and thus Floyd found himself staring at Doc Alexander's personal files — a wealth of information, to be sure.

'We're in,' he told everyone, chuckling as he perused the titles at his disposal. *Now what would we like to know about? Fusion? Yes, indeed. The Space program, certainly. AIDS research … could be interesting. The US senate and agencies.* 'Shit yeah!' Floyd selected all of the above folders, and then a few, mindful of the transfer time. 'Downloading now.'

As the files began to appear on Floyd's screen he opened a couple, only to find they were encrypted. 'Jesus! What the fuck is this?!' Floyd, who prided himself on his code-breaking skills, didn't recognise the code, or in this case, the language.

'It's Brythanic.' Rhun did know and began to scribble down a translation on a piece of paper.

Nick was hesitant to add to their woes at present, but they had to know. 'Doc's started a trace.'

'This is bullshit!' Floyd decided, reading the memo Rhun had translated. 'Are you sure you're reading this right? The file is called "Fusion". This is a recipe for some sort of casserole!'

'What if Doc's been wise to us all along?' Rhun put forward. 'He could be keeping us entertained with bogus files long enough for him to locate us.'

'Then, to ensure we didn't find any files he didn't want us to,' Ray theorised, 'he's probably stored his real files on a removable optical hard-drive. His computer is equipped with one.'

'Ah!' Floyd grabbed up a blank cartridge, and started waving it at Rhun. 'Take this, and teleport yourself to Doc. He'll have one just like it placed on the desk right beside him. It holds a hundred gig's of info, so chances are there will only be one. In the VR unit he'll be oblivious to the room around him, so, as long as you're quiet, he won't even know you've been there.

Go!' Floyd shoved the cartridge into Rhun's hands, and watched him vanish.

'He's halfway home.' Still following the trace, Nick was starting to panic. 'And it's only taken him two minutes.'

'Well, hang up if the information is of no use to us.' Tory couldn't understand why Floyd would persist.

'When Rhun returns.' He seemed very calm about it all. 'A minute is all he'll need.'

Rhun decided that the huge office in which he found himself was of impeccable decor.

The diplomat was seated behind his desk, obviously preoccupied with Rhiannon. Opposite him sat another man, also wearing VR gear, who was most likely running the trace for him. By the window was a third party, gazing outside as he chatted on his moblie-phone.

Duck, Rhun warned himself and narrowly escaped being spotted, as the man by the window turned and glanced around the room.

Once his opposition returned to looking outside, Rhun raised himself and spotted his objective. The cartridge was just where Floyd had said it would be. So, keeping low, Rhun rounded the desk to where Doc resided, and silently executed the swap.

Sweat beads were forming on Nick's brow; Doc was all but two links away from locating them. '*Boss …?*' He made a desperate appeal to Tory as Floyd seemed determined to hold out.

244

'Floyd, shut it off! Rhun can take care of himself.' The hacker sat playing with his bottom lip, as if she hadn't spoke at all, so Tory got rather irate. 'You're playing Russian roulette with other people's lives! Maybe they won't find us, but think of Pete and the other rangers. They'll have to answer to the ICA.'

'Rhun!' Ray was actually glad to see him, though as they were a little pushed for time he grabbed hold of their 'agent' to shake the result of his mission out of him. 'How did you go? Did you get it?'

When Rhun smiled, holding up the cartridge in question, Tory made for Floyd's terminal. 'Good. Then shut down.'

'Too late.' Nick's eyes filled with dread. 'He's pinned us.'

'Why are you smiling?' Rhiannon inquired of her large, muscle-bound cyber-companion.

'I just got some rather good news,' he said.

'Am I so boring that you would read your mail whilst in my company?' The Shift and F-key on her keyboard changed the Chameleon's facial expression to a frown.

'Never.' He reached across the table to place his hand on hers. 'You are the crown jewel of my company. Believe me, only a matter of top international security would drag me from your midst —' But before he'd even finished begging his leave, the lizard-babe vanished.

Ah well. Doc removed the VR unit from his head. 'We'll meet again. And sooner than one might think.'

He smiled. 'Where are they, Eddie?' He asked the man responsible for the trace.

Eddie raised his gear from his face. 'The mountains, in Vermont.'

'I want Agency men there ten minutes ago.' Doc looked to Stanley Brennon as he folded up his mobile-phone and placed it in his pocket.

'It is done.' Stanley advised.

Despite the fact that everyone was screaming and yelling at him, Floyd couldn't seem to contain his amusement.

'I don't see what's so funny.' Brian was on the verge of knocking his block off, they couldn't afford to run the risk of being found with the *Goddess* in dry dock.

'Doc hasn't found us.' Floyd gasped for breath, trying to calm down enough to explain. 'I broke into Cybercom last night, and switched our number and address with several others.' The aging computer whiz removed his glasses to wipe the tears from his eyes, but found himself unable to refrain from collapsing into another flight of hysterics.

His amusement roused a smile from Tory. 'So then, who is Doc raiding at present?'

Floyd had to hold his breath to force the punchline out. 'President Langford's private country abode.'

The rest of the gang, envisioning the scene Floyd's ploy was going to create, couldn't help but laugh along.

'And do you know what's even better?' Floyd put to his company, who couldn't imagine anything better ... 'This afternoon's spot of industrial espionage has all been charged to Langford's bill!'

14

TJUKUBA — THE
DREAMING

There was much cause for celebration at Watarrka
that night. After decoding one of the many
documents that were stored on the hard-drive
Rhun had appropriated from Doc, Floyd decreed the
information to be valid. Nick and he would start
decoding the rest of the data at once, and provided they
didn't hit any snags Floyd would be able to present
everyone with a full report in a week or so.

In the midst of the revelry, Rhun watched Teo
laughing and dancing with his mother. Her Sensei's
obvious adoration was a worry. Perhaps the contact she
meant to make with his father was more important
than Rhun had first realised. Tory still held feelings for

the man in whose arms she was entwined, and Rhun sensed her deep yearning to be assured that she wasn't deluding herself in believing her true love lived. Hence, Rhun's decision to help her became more resolute. He must create the same protective conditions the Druids did at the inauguration of Kings, for only then could he rest assured that his mother's body and spirit would be properly safeguarded throughout their separation. Perhaps this was being overly paranoid, but better that than facing his father's wrath for carelessness.

According to the code of practice of the ancient rite, a sorcerer was the first requirement. Myrddin was out, as he would not support Tory contacting Maelgwn against his specific instructions. Taliesin? Well, only the Goddess knew where he was at present. Cadfan, although he was a fine healer, was not a sorcerer by any stretch of the imagination. It seemed clear to Rhun that it was time to seek the assistance of the local medicine men, those known by the Aboriginal people as the Mekigar, for they were intimate with this adopted homeland of his. As in any native cultural and religious system, the metaphysical topography within the land could be utilised by those who understood it and dared to open themselves to its mysteries.

Early the next morning Tory was peacefully snoozing off the excesses of the night before, when Rhun entered her abode to rouse her to action.

'Mother, come quickly.' He took hold of her hand to urge her along. 'You're not going to believe this.'

'Believe what?' she beseeched him, as she was hauled out into the earthen walkway and hurried up the stairs that led to Floyd's communications room.

'Rhun?' She halted just short of their destination, puzzled by the hurry her son was in.

'Please.' He urged her to keep going. 'Sometimes a picture is worth a thousands words.'

With a deep breath, Tory folded her arms and decided to humour him. She strolled into the communications room, glancing around for the amazing image Rhun spoke of, and it didn't take her long to find it. Floyd was not at his usual station. He was seated on the sofa, speaking with an old friend of hers. 'Jenny?' Tory mumbled, thinking that she must have been viewing a ghost.

'Tory!' Jennifer was overjoyed to see a familiar face and rushed to embrace her.

Upon making contact with a physical form, the shock passed quickly and Tory hugged her for all she was worth. 'Jen, Jen, just look at you!' Tears streamed from her eyes as she pulled back to look over her once-deceased friend. Jenny was young again, and definitely alive. All signs of age were gone, her skin was free of wrinkles and her blue-green eyes sparkled brightly. Jenny's hair hung in thick masses of long blonde curls, just as it had when Tory first met her. 'How can this be?' Tory gave half a laugh, amazed. 'How did you find us?'

Jenny wiped her cheeks in an attempt to stop crying, smiling as she realised that Tory also appeared to have shed twenty years. 'I was hoping you could tell me.'

'She showed up at the ranger station this morning, asking about you.' Rhun attempted to clear up some of the confusion.

'But how did you get there?' Tory led her back to the lounge.

'She doesn't seem to remember.' Floyd was obviously disturbed by the fact. Although he was pleased that his prodigy was not an orphan any longer, Jennifer's presence was as suspicious as it was unbelievable.

'I know it sounds ridiculous …' Jennifer appealed to Floyd, as she was again seated, 'but after the ordeal with the Agency …' she paused, recalling the look on her husband's face when they realised the end had come, 'the next thing I remember I was walking down the road towards the ranger station.'

Tory looked at the clothes Jenny wore, which were not the same ones she'd been buried in.

Jenny slowly shook her head with an apologetic look on her face. 'I wish I could tell you,' she answered before Tory had even asked.

'Well, what's on the agenda for today?' Nick rubbed his hands together as he reported for duty. Then he spotted the woman. He almost didn't recognise his mother, as she was so young and beautiful.

'It's alright.' She held out her hands to him, too emotional to even raise herself.

As Nick rushed to hold her, Tory, Rhun and Floyd let them be awhile.

Jenny was far too shaken to discuss her resurrection at present. Perhaps given a little time she might remember something that would help explain it.

Clearly, she was immortal, yet the crucial gene had not been active at the time of her death. This seemed to suggest that someone had dug the poor woman from her grave a second time, and then activated the gene. But alas, this was only a theory. There were other possibilities that were even less pleasant, like a clone or an impostor, for instance.

'There's only one way to know for sure.' She knew Brian wouldn't be too pleased by her reckoning, for part of the answer lay buried in an unmarked grave in Sherwood forest.

It was yet another beautiful rainy day in England, which didn't aid their task any. The wind whipped through the trees overhead, creating a rather sombre atmosphere by which to work, and although Tory figured it was just the setting that was making her feel ill-at-ease, she couldn't escape the feeling that they were being watched.

'This is sick,' Brian grumbled, as he and Tory began to dig.

'True.' Tory wasn't thrilled about it either. 'If you have another solution I'd be more than glad to take it on board.'

'No.' He resentfully got stuck in to be done with it.

They worked in silence for a time, and the mindless manual labour left their minds free to wander.

'So ...' Brian paused and leant on his shovel, 'if she's not in here, do we assume Jenny is a distant relative of ours?'

Tory had been wondering the same thing herself. 'I really don't know, Brian. From what I've read, the Gods

251

were pretty liberal when it came to bestowing their favours on the daughters of men. There could be other family lines apart from ours that carry the same gene, either dormant or not.' She ploughed on regardless.

Their excavation uncovered only one set of bones, thus a whole new chapter of the age-old mystery was opened.

'So, even well after death the immortal gene can be activated,' Tory assumed from their findings.

'The dead can rise from the grave.' Brian was looking quite pale as he stared into the pit that was filling with water. 'If the immortal gene in Jenny wasn't activated before she died … then who did this?'

Tory eyed the surrounding forest, searching for the mysterious voyeur, whose presence she could still sense. 'A very good question.'

The full moon was but two days away when Rhun brought Pete Nangina to advise his mother. The Aboriginals were not in the habit of assisting the uninitiated to make contact with the spirit world. Still, when Pete and Rhun had outlined Tory's extenuating circumstances and history to the female Mekigar of Pete's tribe, in the interest of good relations the wise old woman agreed to assist. Therefore, it was Pete's job to ready Tory for her inward Dream Journey.

Fortunately for Tory, Rhun had done much work on her subtle body. The coil of power deep in the pit of her stomach, her Miwi as Pete called it — Kundalini as it might otherwise be known — was well extended up through her chakras. A deep meditation was all that would be needed for the Miwi to extend all the way to her third eye which it was required to encompass if Tory wished to attune to the Kurunba — the metaphysical forces that flowed beneath in the landscape.

'Ley-lines,' Tory surmised out loud.

Pete nodded in confirmation. 'What you would call a ley crossing, we call a hot-spot. This subtle energy grid was created by the Sky Heroes during Dreamtime.'

The Sky Heroes? It seemed that here was yet another name for the Shining Ones or the Lofty Ones; their deeds and reputation had been widespread indeed. She was even more interested to learn that an Aboriginal name for the Otherworldly Spirits was Rai.

Pete explained that it was not really the Mekigar's place to decide whether or not Tory was spiritually evolved enough to pass into the realms of the Dreamtime.

'Those who have not reached the proper level of spiritual perception will not see the Rai, because they lack the knowledge to do so … for the Rai only talk with experts.'

He then elaborated on how the sacred topography was translated into art for the ceremony by means of Churingas. These symbolic diagrams were as varied as the Dreamtime sites they represented and had been passed onto the Aboriginal people from the Sky Heroes. Painted in the four sacred colours of red, yellow, white and black, Churingas were used to concentrate a site's Kurunba, or life-essence. Body painting, sand painting, cave frescos and bark paintings were repositories for the symbols that were hidden in secret places about a particular Dreaming site and only produced when a ceremony was being re-enacted.

Tory was instructed to fast these next two days. Tomorrow Pete would accompany her into the desert where she could centre herself in preparation for Tjukuba.

Springtime in the Red Center brought more obliging weather than the violent storms of winter. The earth had begun to dry out and crack once again, so most of the plant life lay dormant in wait of the flash summer rains.

Barefoot, and dressed in white clothes of pure cotton, Tory wandered the dry wasteland between Lake Amadeus and Uluru, alone. Pete was following her movements, though he kept his distance so Tory was not aware of his presence. Maintaining a calm state of repose was a little difficult with the prospect of seeing her love within the next twenty-four hours, but Tory endeavoured to sweep her anticipation aside in favour of thinking nothing at all. She allowed herself to become mesmerised by the landscape, where past, present and future were intrinsically fused.

After many hours in the sun, Tory became numb to the heat and the hot earth beneath her feet. Likewise as the sun began to set, she was not aware of the drop in temperature. Her aimless wandering had brought her into the shadow of the great rock, Uluru, and upon sighting a cave there she felt the urge to stop and kneel. Her mind, blank for hours, turned to the day of Rhun's birth. The memory of holding the tiny newborn in her arms brought tears to her eyes.

'Has your walkabout come to an end, child?'

When Tory looked up to find a tiny, Aboriginal woman elder staring down at her, she was frightened she'd done wrong and so moved to raise herself.

'Uh!' The woman placed a hand on Tory's shoulder, forcing her to stay put.

'I felt an affinity with this place,' Tory explained with honesty.

'Go on.' The woman's eyes, though dark in colour, seemed to beam with light.

She stared through Tory, into her soul, as did the gaze of Taliesin and her father. This was the Mekigar Pete had told her of, Tory was sure of it. Still, she hesitated to voice the rest of her reason as it seemed kind of irrelevant. The Mekigar obviously sensed Tory's reluctance and encouraged her to answer just the same. 'It brings back memories of the birth of my first born.'

'The boy-child I have come to know?'

Tory nodded, shyly, as her response seemed silly.

'This place tells the story of a similar event.' The holy woman motioned Tory to raise herself, and when she had, pointed out the marks on the ground where Tory had kneeled. 'These are the knee-marks of the woman who assisted with the Sky Hero's birth.'

Tory gasped at the news, fearful that she had perhaps defiled the sacred site. 'I apologise. I didn't realise.'

'No you didn't.' The Mekigar placed a palm against Tory's cheek and gave a hearty laugh.

By dusk, Tory and the holy woman were joined by the other female members of the surrounding tribes, some of whom painted Tory's arms and face with sacred Churingas. The rest of the women were seated in two circles, singing chants to sticks rhythmically beaten on the ground. Tory had experienced a similar heady buzz induced by song at an Atlantean ceremony that she'd participated in once. The separation between her physical body and her psyche had begun.

Seated before the mouth of the cave, Tory observed a large quartz crystal wand emerge from the wrist of the Mekigar and slide into the holy woman's hand. So enchanted was Tory by the ritual, that she thought perhaps this phenomenon was imagined, until she was encouraged to lay down and the crystal wand was rested upon her third eye.

'Allow all fear to pass over you and you will never fear again, for beyond the horror lay the Rai you seek. Balga-ma-ni!' the holy woman cried, which meant 'bring all into being'.

In her mind's eye Tory saw the image of Maelgwn bound and beaten as he was dragged before someone. As it was always from the perspective of his persecutor that she witnessed the event, their identity remained a mystery.

'Join us, Dragon.' The unknown entity advised him in a voice that was so distorted to the ear, one could not tell if it was male or female.

Maelgwn, barely able to hold himself upright, shook his head.

'Join us, or die,' his captor clarified.

Tory's love raised his dark eyes to view his tormentor. 'Then I choose death.'

'Stubborn fool!' Energy like lightning shot from the being's fingertips, inflicting Maelgwn with grievous pain.

No, he is not dead. Tory refused to believe it, and breathed deeply until the fear passed. Her faith made her belief strong and she no longer needed to see Maelgwn to confirm what she knew to be true.

Thinking the dream journey was at an end, Tory opened her eyes to find a misty light spewing forth from the mouth of the cave. From within the disturbance her animal guide emerged. The unicorn, white as snow, came to stand over her.

You are free to go ... I shall protect your body from invaders, until your return.

Tory raised herself to find she had left her physical form behind; her eyes were still closed and the crystal remained positioned upon her forehead.

The door of the Earth is open. The unicorn motioned with its head to the misty cave from whence it had come. *Walk the steps of light to where Ra waits to embrace you.*

Tory looked back to the Mekigar, who nodded to confirm that it was safe to proceed. Tory willed her weightless form towards the light source. The cavern itself had taken on a different guise; torches lit the walls that now featured ancient forms of text. As she ventured deeper, a celestial staircase came into view, glimmering with all the lustre of a divine being. She paused before the seemingly endless flight of stairs to admire it a moment, then began the ascent.

Onwards and upwards the stairway led, until it transformed into a tunnel of swirling light matter. Her

257

consciousness was being propelled through the universe at an inconceivable speed, yet it felt like a gentle glide. Then, rather abruptly, everything came to a standstill.

She alighted in a large room filled with stars. Its walls, roof and floor could only be defined by the vague contours of their shape. In the centre of this star chamber, atop a circular staired platform, was a large throne of quartz crystal which rotated one hundred and eighty degrees, so that the host might look down upon his guest.

Lamamu. This is an expected surprise. His voice resounded out from beneath the ornate helmet that encompassed his entire head.

His headgear was akin to that of the pharaohs of ancient Egypt and the high orders of the Atlantean priesthood. The face depicted on her host's mask was not that of a man, but of a falcon, conforming to the ancient depiction of the God. Beyond his facial facade she could see naught but the beautiful light energy of his subtle body. In fact, given the sombre light of the room, his being gave off its own illumination.

Grandfather. Tory bowed her head, ever so slightly. *I have looked forward to our meeting for what seems like an eternity.*

The God raised his magnificent form, as well-developed as any human warrior. He stood at about seven foot. A three-tiered neckband of gold hung around his neck and shoulders, featuring the motif of a serpent sliding over a large circle — the symbol of his sun-god divinity and his father's clan, Tory guessed. Embossed inside the golden circle was the eye of Ra.

But it is not I you seek. He sounded a mite insulted. *You have come in search of your earthly love for fear that I have murdered him.*

It is true. I have perceived images of such a horror. Tory was tactful. *But as the outcome was conveniently left out and the torturer has taken care to remain anonymous, I have seen no evidence that would implicate you as the antagonist in the affair. Nor have I seen any proof that Maelgwn has even been murdered.*

Why are you seeking the Dragon, if you believe he lives? He was again seated, folding his muscular arms.

Am I wrong to believe so? Tory moved closer to hear an answer.

Oh, don't doubt yourself now … you were doing so well, he encouraged. *Despite the visions and all her sweet assurances, Inanna still failed to fool you.* He chuckled again. *She will be most put out.*

Tory had read about the trouble between Inanna and Marduk of which Inanna had been the instigator. But how on earth had Maelgwn and herself got entangled in their differences?

You have something she desires, Marduk advised her.

What could I have that a Goddess would envy? The chariot? she ventured to guess.

This only served to amuse her host. *You are very naive.* He slapped his knee.

Not Maelgwn! The notion was completely devastating. Tory had never had to compete for his favour before. After all, what woman in her right mind would chose to oppose her? But Inanna was a Goddess, a powerful and beautiful one at that.

Come, come. Do you really think that Inanna would have bothered tormenting you, if she had already managed to convert your lover?

No. The realisation drowned her fears. *Nor would she be vexing me if my husband was a corpse.*

To be sure. He thumped his armrest, proud of her. *So now you see why Maelgwn insisted that you not risk leaving your body, for Inanna is eager to claim it. Only through you does she stand a chance of tricking her way into Maelgwn's favour.*

But I have come so far. Please don't say I must return, without so much as a glimpse of him, Tory pleaded. *Have I not adequately protected myself?*

There is no need to convince me. Who do you think arranged all this? He held up both hands and motioned her to be quiet. *I promised the commander a surprise that would spur him through his next mission, and you're going to help me keep that vow.*

Commander! Tory wasn't really that surprised to learn of her husband's new status. *Mission? What mission?*

Marduk stood. *That information is confidential. But if you wish to see the love of your life, you'd best accompany me. Lest the Dragon mistake you for Inanna attempting to fool him yet again.*

An ultra-modern suiting station materialized in place of the Star Chamber. Suits hung in individual lots around the large circular quarters, where a central domed area shed a mauve light over a large round lounge. Here the sole occupant of the room sat in silent contemplation.

What's on your mind commander? As if I couldn't guess.

'My Lord Marduk?' Maelgwn raised himself to greet his superior. 'My apologies, but I had time to spare before the scheduled departure —'

I know your meditative habits, Dragon. But I did promise you a bit of extra incentive to see you on your way this time, did I not?

'My dear friend,' Maelgwn began to decline politely. 'Do try to understand, there is no substitute for Keridwen's chosen match for me. To offer me another in her stead is a fruitless exercise for all involved.'

Yes, you have made that painfully obvious. Marduk gestured towards the entrance, where Tory waited patiently to be acknowledged. *So I brought you the closest thing I could find to your love in the flesh.*

Sure that he would be dissatisfied with whatever semblance of Tory the Nefilim had conjured up to please him, Maelgwn turned in his seat to behold a splendid vision. 'What manner of illusion is this?' He smiled, enchanted.

No illusion, Dragon, she's the genuine article … or rather part thereof.

Maelgwn's delight turned to dread as he turned to Marduk. 'Impossible. I expressly forbade Tory to seek me thus. She would never disregard my wishes so.'

Where does this fanciful recollection of my unquestioning obedience come from? Tory scoffed at his delusion. *Certainly not from the circumstances under which we last parted, surely? Don't you know me better than to think I would obey any order without tangible evidence of the sender?*

'But my messages via Cadfan and Rhun. Did you not get them?'

Such images can be falsified ... I'm sure. Tory glanced around at all the advanced technological expertise that this chamber alone had to offer. *I might be speaking to a clone right now, for all I know. For I note that you converse with me in English, a language Maelgwn never really took to.*

'Clones can be identified using etheric sight, for they have no subtle body. And as I have become far more proficient in the art of telepathy, every tongue is now a second language to me,' Maelgwn informed her, seemingly insulted by her inference. 'But the Nefilim can assume whatsoever form they choose, as we can, so how do I know that you are not another of Inanna's crafty schemes?'

Excuse I. Marduk felt he must intervene at this point. *Maelgwn, I assure you, this is Lamamu. And though ignorance prevents her from knowing she can trust me, I expect a little more from you.*

What is that supposed to mean? Tory wasn't about to let that accusation pass.

Demanding little creature, isn't she? Marduk baited the man who'd married her, completely delighted by her determination.

'You have no idea.' Maelgwn confirmed.

The unicorn ... Marduk gained Tory's attention, before she could scold her husband for agreeing with him, *was handpicked by myself, from the stables of Horus, who is allied to my father.*

As the ancients had believed the horse was sacred to Horus, especially those of the species that were white, Tory was inclined to believe him. It was also true that Horus had sided with Marduk and Enki, having been born into their side of the family. *You've been watching me a long time then.*

Longer than you might think. You're familiar with my aunt, Ninharsag … though Maelgwn here calls her Keridwen.

Good Lord! She looked to Maelgwn, who nodded to confirm the statement.

So then … Marduk assumed he now had the benefit of the doubt. *I do solemnly swear to you both that you are indeed who you say you are. Thus rejoice, children!* He placed a hand on Maelgwn's shoulder. *No harm has been done. I guided Lamamu safely forth, and she is under my protection until she returns.*

'But what if Inanna, or that incestuously jealous brother of hers, had intercepted instead?'

I had no choice but to let her come, Marduk confessed. *Inanna has been taunting Lamamu with visions of your capture.* He hesitated to remind the commander of the ordeal for he knew he'd suffered much.

Maelgwn now understood why Tory had endeavoured to seek him out, and the realisation saddened him deeply.

The images just made the not knowing where you were, or how you fared, so much worse. Tory spoke up for herself, for the purpose of her visit was not to upset him. *But now I have seen that all goes well with you, I shall go, if that's what you wish.*

'Tory,' he pleaded in protest, forestalling her retreat. 'I have willed you to me so often that this situation is probably more my fault than yours.'

As soon as the emotional outpouring started, Marduk made himself scarce.

'I do praise the Goddess that you defied me.' Maelgwn approached her ghostly form that was even more lovely than he remembered. 'There have been moments during our separation when I would have faced the torture of Shamash and Inanna a thousand times over, for just an hour of your company.'

I know what you mean. And I deeply regret that I am not fully equipped to fulfil all your expectations at this time.

It was just like Tory to get a smile out of him in a moment of despair. 'That's something to look forward to then. And right now I must confess that you are a sight for sore eyes.'

As are you. She admired his spectacular form, his dark, silky hair and sweet smiling face. Lamentably, she lacked the density to touch him, but her hands remained paused close to his face in wanting.

The black suits suspended around the chamber were similar to the one Maelgwn wore. It resembled a wetsuit, rather than a spacesuit, and Tory found it most appealing the way the thick, smooth material moulded itself to her husband's athletic build. The symbol of the golden circle, the snake and the all-seeing eye was featured on the lefthand shoulder. All kinds of strange devices were strapped to a belt slung round his hips, metallic bands encompassed both his wrists, and a strange manner of weapon rested in a holster strapped to his thigh. His shin-high boots were crafted from a solid black metal compound, although his ease of movement indicated they were basically weightless. All in all, Maelgwn appeared every bit as handsome and virile as the day Tory had wed him.

'You are my Achilles heel, Tory. I cannot be got at, save for you.' Maelgwn backed up a little and broke the spell. 'Nothing is worth risking your soul for. If Inanna were to gain influence over you, the woman I know and love would be gone forever.'

Tory watched his joy fade to dread once again. He had never been a man who showed his fear, but he was scared now. *What did Inanna do to instil such fear in you?*

He was taken aback by the query. 'Has Inanna not shared with you all the details of my capture?' He'd assumed as much, from what Marduk had told him.

No. I believe all I perceived was the end result, Tory explained, finding his reaction rather puzzling.

'Oh!' He breathed a sigh of relief, though he wanted to cry out in praise to the Goddess. This piece of providence didn't mean that his foe wasn't saving the grisly details to use against him later, but it was liberating and uplifting to know that Tory didn't know the all of it.

I can't bear to think about what you went through, but I will not ask you to relive it to satisfy my morbid curiousity. Just answer me this, Maelgwn. Was it in any way my fault? Did I deliver you into the wrong hands?

Maelgwn was already shaking his head vigorously. 'No, 'twas my own damn fault. Inanna had stolen a prototype of —' he broke off mid-sentence to watch two of his crew enter the suiting room.

'Well, holy sub-space, Grandpa. Who's the lush?'

Tory recognised both these men. The one who'd made the derogatory comment about her, whom

Maelgwn approached to reprimand with a thump, had once been Vortipor. Yet Tory very much doubted that it was the Protector of Dyfed who addressed her at present, for he had known her well.

'Cadwell, that is no way to speak about your Grandmother.' Maelgwn was pleased to have stunned both his comrades with the news.

Tory was amazed to discover this was her grandson, Cadwell, whom she'd not seen since he was a newborn babe. Cadwell, also Vortipor's grandson, had grown to be the perfect incarnation of the great Upsurger himself.

'This is my great-great-grandmother?!' The darker haired of the two stared at her, his jaw dropping.

She identified this character with Ray, Prince Bryce of Powys, and Shar Zadoc, the chief justice of Chailidocean. *Then you must be Cadwallon.* Tory became most delighted at her realisation.

He smiled, gratified that the legend was so eager to make his acquaintance. 'Yes, Nin, that I am.'

Wonderful! I've been wanting to know a few things about your son … was he tutored by Taliesin, as you were?

The ghostly vision overwhelmed him with her forthright manner, and when he'd had a chance to take a breath, he replied, 'No, Nin. Such tuition would have been more than wasted on Cadwaladr — it would have been downright dangerous. Thankfully, he was born before the immortality gene in me became active, and thus perished at the battle of Brunanburh.'

Are you sure? she appealed. It didn't figure.

'Yes, Nin.' He found her plea confusing, and although he didn't mean to sound condescending, half his mouth curved to a smile. 'I think I should know when I was first killed. Taliesin knew this was the case, and after delivering me into the hands of the Nefilim, he departed Gwynedd for some other timezone to pursue the Goddess' work.'

I see.

She forced a smile, but it wasn't fooling Maelgwn. 'Is something amiss?'

Just as you have problems and a mission of your own to worry about, so do I. If you tell me your woes, I'll tell you mine? Tory bargained playfully, knowing full well Maelgwn wouldn't play ball.

'But we ...' Cadwallon glanced to his frustrated commander to include him in the equation, 'we worry about you, Nin. We would like to help if we can.'

But you have helped, Cadwallon, by ruling out a possibility. Perhaps I just concocted a whole silly scenario that wasn't really ever there?

Photographs of the elusive Chameleon were strewn across the diplomat's desk, along with other pictures of the Goddess and her kin taken at Miles Thurlow's funeral.

In the week since Doc had first made the Chameleon's acquaintance, he'd become completely obsessed with her — and was it any wonder? She had played him for the fool *three* times now. Her most recent stunt had nearly cost him the favour of the American president! And still he hadn't the slightest shred of evidence that pointed to her involvement. If it had been she who'd managed to wipe all the files from his hard-drive when it wasn't even in his PC, he could only admire her cunning. Or had she stolen them? Perhaps he'd failed to load the files properly, or the drive could have been faulty? They had, however, tested the cartridge since and experienced no difficulty in storing information.

But who was this beautiful blonde, blue-eyed enchantress? His enemy, the Goddess? He thought not. For the Chameleon seemed to have an entirely different persona to that of the Dragon's concubine. Doc was well aware that physical traits could be altered at will by those of their kind, as he altered his appearance to suit his purpose and position. However, an individual's chemical make-up, the vibrations they gave off or their personal sonic *per se*, could not be disguised so easily. Thus, the basic laws of physics and his gut agreed that he could never lust after his condemner with such fervour. The one-time Queen of Gwynedd was not the lizard then. However, she had gone to great lengths at the funeral to keep him away from her daughter, Rhiannon. Doc strongly suspected she was his mystery girl.

As her mother's daughter, Rhiannon was a guaranteed immortal. Finally, a woman who wouldn't age or die. *Or be killed*. He also considered the downside, in that he might grow tired of her at some distant point of eternity. *There is much she could teach me before then*. The problem was gaining her trust, and that might prove a little difficult since he'd killed her father. This was a misunderstanding really. He had thought the Professor was immortal and was as surprised as the next person when Miles had croaked.

'Goddamn my ignorance.' He stood, sick to death of pondering the dilemma and finding no answers. Curse his forefathers and their wizards, for leaving him blind to their ways and powers.

Cadwaladr had taught himself telepathy, thought projection and simple hypnosis in order to manipulate the minds of others. But how could he hope to compete against an apprentice of the Great Mother herself?

Doc inhaled deeply to subdue this burst of anxiety, when all at once he became quite giddy.

Do not be disheartened, sub-creature. For having been spared from the occult ways of the Dragon's line you have not been party to their offences against the almighty.

Doc's dizziness forced him back into his seat as he shielded his eyes from the light of the being that manifested before him.

The compassion of the Great One has sent me to aid and guide you in the battle against the Serpent and his kin.

In the twelve centuries since his birth, Doc had never seen such a marvel. This was an angel of the Lord, to be sure.

The being shone with the intensity of the midday sun through his full-length robe of pure white, girded at the waist by a band of gold. Hair and skin as white as new-fallen snow, the messenger's eyes were like the flame of fire. A six-pointed star of gold, not unlike the Star of David, hung at his chest.

Doc, although he had once subscribed to the Christian faith, failed to see how the sum deeds of his life made him worthy of divine providence. 'I hate to sound blasphemous, but are you sure you have the right person ... don't you know who I am?'

Yes, Cadwaladr, we know you. We know your trials, your torments and your woes. But your anonymity and isolation has proven fortunate, as it has kept you shielded from your insubordinate forefathers until this, your era, the time of reckoning.

Deep down Doc had always suspected there was some kind of divine purpose behind his loneliness. Now, with divine power on his side, he would punish those who had sentenced him to live through the darkest ages mankind had ever known. His wrath upon the Goddess and her faithful would be absolute. 'But there is one amongst the Dragon's kin who I wish no harm to befall.'

We are mindful of your desires and the girl-child's soul may still be spared from eternal damnation, for we realise she knows no better. Your intervention and the truth can redeem her in the eyes of the Great One.

'What must I do?' Doc thrived on the knowledge that right was on his side, for he felt a certain purity and purpose that he'd never experienced before. 'How am I to convince her of the truth, when I myself am blind to it?'

First we cleanse your spirit to refine the talents that are your birthright and set you apart from your fellow man. Only when you have achieved your full spiritual potential shall we establish your rule, so that you may hold influence over all nations and they may hear and know the way of the righteous.

'But the girl?' Doc entreated, wanting to know how he could bring his wish into reality.

One must learn to crawl before one can run, warrior. At present your association would be like the blind leading the blind. Forget her for the moment, for she is an unnecessary distraction to your spiritual attainment. The will of the almighty must come before your own. Once you are well versed in his way and have earned his favour, your service and faith shall be rewarded.

Doc had never been the type to take anyone at their word, but surely the vow of God could be trusted. 'And you will help me in this?'

The angel smiled. '*I have been watching and guiding you since before you were born, Cadwaladr, for it is the will of the almighty that I lead you to greatness. So give praise for your deliverance from the Darkness, for I am the guardian you seek. Summon me at will from this day forth, and to the name, Utu, I shall answer.*

The diplomat accepted the celestial herald's message as his destiny. 'Then give me your tuition, Utu … and I shall make it my sole purpose to serve the will of God.'

Upon emerging from her dream journey, Tory was amazed to find she'd been returned to her abode at Watarrka.

Four days had elapsed since the ceremony, and Rhun had feared she was never coming back.

'That couldn't be right?' Tory moved to raise herself, but a heavy head dissuaded her. 'I wasn't gone but a few hours, surely?'

Rhun smiled, relieved beyond belief to have her conscious. 'What we seem to be dealing with here is a classic case of outer time-distortion. The astral plane, being comprised mainly of anti-matter, functions free from gravity and space, but the physical plane does not. Therefore, although the time you spent in transit would have been non-existent, the time you spent in father's company must have been distorted, as time functions differently in space.'

'You gave us such a scare.' Rhiannon tried to refrain from tears, as she knelt by the bed and took hold of her mother's hand.

'Oh Rhiannon.' Tory was overwhelmed to see her so upset. 'Couldn't you sense I was in a heavenly place?'

Her daughter nodded. 'So heavenly in fact, that you might never want to return. Especially considering the horrendous scenes previewed in the latest mass vision.'

'Come again?' Tory did manage to hoist herself upright this time, supporting her head that felt as if it were weighted with lead.

'So you didn't perceive it then?' Rhun presumed from her reaction.

Tory wracked her brain a moment, but only recalled the most pleasant of memories. 'I'm afraid not. What did the vision predict?'

'Famine, disease, war ... the usual,' Rhun advised, with a shrug. It was nothing he wasn't already aware of, having been to the future already. 'So, you found Father?' He seated himself before her, wide-eyed and eager to hear.

A smile took possession of her face that all the self-control in the world couldn't have prevented. 'Did I chance to run into your lover, you mean?"

'I didn't know you had a girl.' Rhiannon raised herself from her knees to join her kin on the bed, finding their conversation most interesting. 'You've never mentioned her.'

Tory became a little fearful of where this conversation was heading, for there were parts of the answer Rhiannon wouldn't want to know. 'Baby, I need to speak with Rhun alone.'

'Why?' Rhiannon backed up off the bed, immediately suspicious. 'Is this Dragon character not my father, too?'

'Please understand, my instructions were very specific,' Tory replied calmly, which only seemed to anger her daughter all the more.

'Yeah, right! My own father wants me left in the dark.' Rhiannon took a defiant stance, hands on hips. 'You know what? I think you're both full of shit.' She went to storm from the room, but then realised her voice did not open her mother's chamber door. 'Open it!' She turned back briefly to demand.

'Open.' Both Tory and Rhun complied in a casual fashion. 'Close.' They activated the door after Rhiannon made her hasty retreat.

'Christ, she's such a drama queen.' Tory couldn't see the need for the performance.

'Well, why didn't you let her stay?' Rhun could relate to his sister's view. 'I knew you were lying about your instructions, so Rhiannon most certainly did.'

'Look. I met Ray's perfect incarnation there. He's Cadwallon.' Tory felt stressed.

'So?'

'So! Do you think she's ready to conceive of the fact that Ray's going to perish sometime before Cadwallon returns, for surely he is Rhiannon's other half, so to speak.'

'I'm sure she realises Ray's going to go sometime. After all, he's not immortal.'

'Yes, but some of us here that aren't necessarily of our family line must be. Or perhaps they are of our family line, but more distantly related. Perhaps they were born with the immortality gene still dormant in their DNA.'

'What led you to this conclusion?'

'Well, I met Ione during my dream journey. She is in Maelgwn's service. Only her perfect incarnation wasn't Ione but the warrioress Boadicea. Therefore her other half, Sir Tiernan, must be currently here on Earth.'

'Floyd,' Rhun resolved, well pleased. 'But how?'

'How did Jenny get returned to us?' Tory put forward. 'I don't know, but it makes sense. I was introduced to Robin of Loxley — you were right he is John Pearce.' The memory of their meeting made her smile, briefly. 'Someone activated the immortality gene in Jenny after her death. Who that was, I don't know. Nevertheless, when God starts handing out immortality to a select few amongst us, leaving the others to perish …' She shrugged, concerned.

'I see your point,' Rhun conceded. 'Perhaps such information would be better concealed until such time as it can be a comfort to those of us left behind, rather than burdening them now with the inevitable.'

'Yes,' she agreed, relieved. This was her very thought.

'But keeping the truth from Rhiannon will not be easy, and you know how much she detests being kept in the dark.'

'Well, we've managed thus far.' Tory regretted keeping secrets from her kin, but Rhiannon and Ray had just settled into a romance and she would not burden their happiness with complications that could be decades away.

'So, what of my other half?' Rhun pleaded to be told, using his big, brown puppy dog eyes to aid his cause. 'Did you learn her true identity?'

Fluffing her pillows to get more comfortable, Tory tortured her son with delay. 'Why do you want to know? So you can pop off and see her?' she teased.

'After witnessing the time-dilation that occurred during your little adventure? I think not,' he answered her surely, though he was saddened by the fact. 'I cannot risk being dysfunctional for days or weeks, as the case may be. What would be the point anyway? I wouldn't be able to touch her.'

His words made Tory very curious. She had been wondering about the consequences of teleporting her physical form to Maelgwn's side. 'Why not transport your physical self. Surely it would take no longer?'

Rhun stared back at her, quite frankly surprised by the assumption. 'The travel time might prove no different, I'll grant. But where etheric matter can cheat time on the physical plane, physical matter cannot. Don't forget that we're dealing with a destination that's light-years into deep space, where gravity and time functions differently to here. And as the universe is constantly expanding, how could you be sure just how much time-dilation would occur during the journey? Could be months, years, longer!'

'I see.' Tory tried not to look disappointed. 'That would explain why Maelgwn hasn't attempted such contact.'

'Don't you think I would have tried it by now, if it were at all feasible?' Rhun put forward, appearing as frustrated as Tory felt. 'I just want to know how Bridgit fares, who she is. Please tell me.'

As Tory could plainly see no harm could come of it, she relented. 'I have actually met Bridgit's perfect incarnation before in my travels. She was an Atlantean Priestess and truth-seer, but she is a Star Warrior now.' Rhun moved to query this further but Tory was already aware of his question. 'The name you seek is Sybil.'

15

2020

The environmental problems afflicting the Earth had continued to increase with each passing year. The population of third world countries had grown by more than half in a decade, and continued to grow despite the high fatalities due to disease and famine. The planet's raw materials were strained to the point of being astronomically expensive to buy, especially fossil fuels. Thus, when the ICA put forward their proposal to build a fusion reactor that could cater to the whole world's power needs, the long-term cheaper, cleaner form of energy appeared most attractive to those assembled at the United Nations.

The first question put forward about the scheme was where the ICA planned to locate the power station when the Earth's surface was growing increasingly unstable. Most of the old nuclear reactors worldwide were being decommissioned due to the immense clean-up operations that were required to mop up the mess left behind when these power stations were damaged by earthquakes, or rendered useless by flooding. No country could risk playing host to a new and experimental fusion reactor, despite the obvious political power and financial advantages of volunteering.

Doc Alexander had a very simple solution to this dilemma that, as it turned out, was the only option; the fusion reactor that the ICA had designed would only function in space. For out beyond the Earth's atmosphere, the high vacuum needed to sustain a thermo-nuclear plasma was free. Fusion power, derived from combining two atoms (tritium and deuterium) to form one helium atom with a consequent release of energy, was a process that required temperatures of around one-million degrees Celsius. In the past, the heat factor had hindered the development of fusion power, but in space the extremely cold temperatures meant the reactor could be vacuum-cooled.

This breakthrough, as exciting as it was, raised many other questions, like: could a malfunction in such a reactor inflict serious damage on our atmosphere, or worse, the surrounding solar system? Absolutely not, said Doc. For even if the monitoring computer system failed to shut off the reactor the second a malfunction was detected, it could be powered down manually within seconds.

One of the greatest problems physicists had had to overcome was maintaining the momentum of the fusion reaction, as the energy created by the imploding atoms was dissipated so quickly. But when the reactor chamber was flooded with extremely energetic plasma, a strong magnetic field enabled the energy to be harnessed and beamed to a storage facility on Earth. The power would then be farmed out across a grid. It was proposed that this grid would require seven major stations, excluding the host. These would be located in South America, Europe, Africa, Russia, Asia, India and Australia. These stations would supply ten sub-stations, and these would supply a further ten sub-stations. Only three underwater links would be needed to connect the seven major stations with the host storage facility in North America. This had been provisionally chosen for its central location.

What Doc failed to mention was that America had supplied most of the funding and manpower for the project and intended to go ahead with the reactor regardless of the world view. For indeed, the construction of the host station had already begun just outside of Farwell, New Mexico.

A pipeline across the Pacific would supply Asia, India, and Russia. A second pipeline across the Pacific would provide Australia, New Guinea, New Zealand and the surrounding Islands with power. The third pipeline across the Atlantic would feed Europe, Africa and the Middle East. The remaining stations could be supplied via land-lines. Each country would incur the cost of setting up their part of the grid, and would pay a rent for maintenance of the stations and their pipelines.

The ICA's AIDS facility in Alaska, funded and handled in a similar manner to this current power proposal, had been a great success. Over fifty percent of the world was rid of the disease and in remaining areas the number of AIDS cases diagnosed had dropped dramatically. The media had reported countless numbers of heartwarming stories from people who surely would have perished from the disease were it not for the ICA scheme. Those cured then urged others who had not yet been tested to register at once — the earlier the disease was detected the greater the chance of recovery.

However, not everyone sent to the Alaskan facility returned home, healed, as originally promised. Reports of abuse and favouritism at the clinic began to leak through to the outside population via underground publications and the internet. Doc Alexander publicly denied these claims, dismissing them as terrorist attempts to sabotage the new era of world peace and cooperation.

The nations of the world were slowly coming to rely on the ICA. There was not one country that had not been aided by the organisation in some way. In fact, many of the world's leaders were very wary of defying the United Nations for fear they would lose ICA assistance. These days one could never be sure when the ICA's expertise might be required. It seemed the Agency had managed to bring about a forced world peace. Doc and his multicultural team of scientists, physicists and the like, always came up with the most feasible solutions to the world's ever-increasing problems.

The conversion of the *Goddess* was all but complete, bar a few minor glitches, as was the work on *Merlin I* and *II*. Under Ray's guidance Brian and Tory were running the two smaller craft through a systems check before their first trial run inside the cavern of pools.

The *Goddess* had been backed out of dry dock and was moored on the largest of the three bodies of water. In the control room, the rest of the crew gathered to observe the tests. Teo and Naomi were at their stations ready to monitor and guide the movements of the smaller craft.

Brian was strapped into the pilot's seat of *Merlin I*, familiarising himself with the new additions to its control panel. 'I always wanted to fly,' he commented to Tory in *Merlin II*, which was parked on the embankment alongside him.

'Yeah, well, don't get too over-zealous,' she warned, glancing at her brother as she finished strapping herself in.

'Listen to her, Brian.' Ray's voice came through their headsets. 'The hover-system controls are very sensitive. Bear in mind you haven't got the drag of the water to slow you down. I can only take an educated guess as to what the *Merlins'* top speed might be when airborne.'

'Do share with the other children,' Brian encouraged, raring to go.

'That is not today's objective. Keep it *slow*.' Ray dampened his test pilot's enthusiasm. 'It's taken me three years to get these vessels operational. Let's not destroy them in a day.' Ray handed the headset back to Naomi.

'Bloody engineers,' Brian uttered under his breath. *Who paid for the damn thing?* 'Could we possibly get this show on the road before I fall asleep.'

'Roger that, *Merlin One*,' Naomi gave Brian the go-ahead as Ray nodded to confirm it. 'You may fire up when ready.'

'Hallelujah!' Brian activated the hover system, and grinned with glee as his craft lifted from the ground.

Tory observed *Merlin I* as it rose to hover about 1.5 metres above the embankment. The several sets of advanced hover blasters that rotated in opposing directions beneath the craft shot compressed air downwards to give it levitation. Yet these powerful thrusters hardly stirred the surrounding area during lift off. This was due to the angling of the opposing, rotating blasters that concentrated the airflow against itself, keeping the disturbance to a minimum while maximising the vehicle's performance. When the vessel moved out over the surface of the water the air pressure beneath it became more obvious. Once the cloaking device was activated the reconnaisance sub would be neither seen nor heard. All that would remain for the naked eye to see would be a small, silent whirlpool of wind. *The visual impression just screams UFO.* Tory amused herself with this thought, as Teo instructed her to proceed with her launch.

'Wow, this feels strange,' Tory relayed her observations to those inside the *Goddess*, as she guided *Merlin II* across the pool in pursuit of her brother's craft. Steering the little submersible had never been too difficult, but in hover mode the controls were hypersensitive; the slightest deviation from course would send the vessel off on a completely different tangent. Tory learnt this all too quickly when a sneeze nearly sent her on a collision course with the mother ship.

'Easy,' Ray winced as he observed the movements of the tiny craft from inside the control room. But his quiet smile of satisfaction returned when he observed how quickly Tory recovered from the mishap.

'Clearly,' Rhiannon kissed his cheek, well proud of him, 'the man is a genius.'

'Now, for my next trick.' Ray glanced from his lover to those manning the guidance systems. 'Ask them neutralise.' He looked back out the porthole and waited for the vessels to comply.

'Aw! I was just getting a feel for it,' Brian protested as the instruction reached him via Naomi. Still, he obliged: 'Neutralising now.'

Merlin I settled to a stop, and Tory pulled her craft up close by it. 'Good …' Ray felt as nervous as an expectant father. 'Instruct Brian to activate the cloaking mechanism.' His eyes remained fixed on the pool below as Naomi passed on his request.

Within moments, *Merlin I* vanished. The air from the propulsion system agitating the surface of the water beneath the vessel was the only evidence of its presence. Ray looked to Jenny who was viewing the electromagnetic radar.

'He's gone alright,' she confirmed.

'Activate tracking device.' Naomi instructed Brian to complete the procedure.

All eyes turned to Nick, who was seated before the crystal-emission tracking system that Ray had designed.

'I've got him, dead ahead.' Nick cocked an eye, impressed. 'It works!'

A cheer accompanied loud whistles and applause

from everyone present, acknowledging the engineer's hard work and subsequent triumph.

'Why do you all seem so surprised?' Ray tried to sound like he wasn't. 'Can Tory confirm Brian's position?' He circled round behind Teo, who put the question to Tory.

'Well, Murdock …' Tory's voice came over the intercom, sounding none too enthusiastic. 'It would seem you're not a complete intellectual retard, after all. Congratulations.' Her tone became sincerer. 'All systems are go here.'

Again the congratulations broke out from his friends and associates, but Ray was not prepared to count his chickens before they hatched. He refused Floyd's kind offer of a celebratory beer until they'd tested the cloaking device and tracking system in *Merlin II*. The celebration wasn't postponed long, however, as the second recon sub's systems activated as smoothly as those in *Merlin I*.

The two hovercraft skirted around each other until mission control were satisfied that the day's objectives had been successfully achieved. Brian and Tory were given leave to wrap it up for the day and come join the party.

As all in the control room were distracted proposing a toast to their young Einstein, Brian couldn't resist the urge to experiment further with his transport's new capabilities.

Tory was guiding *Merlin II* over the embankment to land when she spied *Merlin I* on her monitor taking up position under the opening at the far end of the cavern roof. 'Brian!' Tory switched her voice-link to his direct line. 'Don't be daft.'

'Hey, it's not like it's going to kill me now, is it?' he replied, beginning his ascent towards the wide open spaces.

'I'm not worried about you, you moron!' She re-engaged her thrusters to go after him.

Brian chuckled as he noted *Merlin II* change its course to pursue him. 'Catch me if you can.' He switched off his voice-link, opting to listen to some music instead.

'O-oh.' Nick happened to glance at his monitor to see their two recon vehicles heading out of the camp perimeters. When Ray realised what was happening he bolted for a headset, and was infuriated when he realised he must refrain from using it.

'What is it?' Naomi was confused. 'Do you want me to call them back?'

'No, it's too risky,' Ray ran his fingers through his hair to get it out of his face. 'We don't want to be traced.' As he held no authority over Brian, Tory or the hovercraft, Ray realised he had precious little chance of dissuading them from the joyride. 'We'll just have to let them go, and pray to God they bring the vessels back in one piece. Shit!'

After clearing the cavern roof, Brian skirted along the canyon ridge and followed it to down onto the wide, open plains. The exhilaration of flight made his eyes water, and his heart was pounding ten to the dozen as he gained speed and altitude. Brian looked to his monitor to see Tory gaining on him. 'Not bad, for a girl,' he mused as he approached the large body of water that was Lake Amadeus. 'Let's see what this baby is really capable of. Coming, sis?'

The Red Centre had seen quite a bit of rain of late; thus the waterholes were bursting their banks — Lake Amadeus was no exception. When she saw Brian heading for the lake, Tory prayed he was only planning to skim across the surface. This body of water could hardly be compared to the open ocean. It was quite shallow and rocky in places. 'Brian,' she pleaded, though she knew he could not hear her, 'please don't be doing what I think you're doing.'

The submersible employed the same thrusters as the hovercraft. As *Merlin I* descended rapidly over the water, Brian switched off the rotating air blasters and it plunged beneath the surface of the lake.

'Absolutely incredible.' Tory looked to her radar, and was pleased to find *Merlin I* still moving. She descended to ten feet above the water's surface, and tracked the submersible's readout down the lake.

'Ah, home at last,' Brian sighed, as the bubbles cleared to a clear view out in front. With the drag of the water his speed lessened. The light made visibility quite good here near the surface, and he cruised through schools of fish whilst avoiding rock formations and patches of weed.

Once he'd finished his sightseeing tour, Brian headed *Merlin I* towards the surface. About five foot below the waterline, he re-activated his hover systems which immediately shot his craft up out of the lake; the next thing he knew he was racing over the surface with Tory in pursuit.

Half an hour later, when the two craft landed back at base, Brian was overwhelmed by everyone's protests and lectures concerning his misconduct. He'd anticipated this kind of reception, so the reprimands didn't faze him any. 'What are you all whining about? The ship's still in one piece, isn't it? And I've saved us two weeks of prolonged testing.'

'But what if you'd had a system failure?' Ray was feeling stressed 'We could have lost the craft, and it's not like we can just order in spare parts.'

'Look, Ray.' Brian turned to put the engineer in his place, but calmed himself before doing so. 'I know you've worked long and hard on this project. You've done a fine job, and I thank you. But I've been sitting around this place twiddling my thumbs for three years, whilst that bastard at the ICA leads the rest of the world up the garden path. I shall not waste other second dicking around. It's time we started making a difference.'

Nobody argued as Brian took his leave. They were all too stunned.

'Call it cavern fever.' Tory placed a hand on Ray's shoulder to encourage him not to take it personally. 'We all have our bones to pick with Doc, but I didn't realise Brian's resentment still ran so deep.'

'Well, he's not Robinson Crusoe there.' Ray moved to inspect *Merlin I*, pulling the weeds from its chassis and tossing them aside in disgust. 'I'd best get this cleaned up and ready to rock'n'roll then.'

'You're a good egg, Murdock.' Tory smiled at his resolve.

He shrugged. 'We all want to make a difference.'
'You already have,' she assured him.

Walter was seated behind his desk at the far end of the herbarium, gazing across the extensive lawns and gardens of his Healing Centre for the Mind, Body and Spirit. The floor to ceiling windows allowed the afternoon sun to stream in upon him, yet he was numb to the soothing effect of the warm rays. The news of a close friend's death had left him in a complete state of shock. Even after fourteen centuries of life, Walter still hadn't got used to outliving those he cared about.

At age thirty-two, Patrick Haze was too young to be rotting in his grave. Pat held a special place in the old healer's heart, for the young man had more or less adopted Walter as the father he never had. For many years Patrick had frequented the Healing Centre and eventually, after all his years of study, had ended up working for the Institute. Then, a month ago, Patrick had gone for his compulsory AIDS test and had tested HIV positive. He'd been whisked off to Alaska for treatment almost immediately. Patrick was gay — that had been no secret. The insecurity and low self-esteem caused by his homosexuality had been instrumental in leading Patrick to the Healing Centre in the first place. Walter had expected to see Patrick back instructing his courses by now, but the reality was he would never see his talented young novice again. And as Patrick had no living relatives, his body had already been laid to rest in the cemetery not far from the AIDS clinic in Alaska. It was not often Walter became riled, but he could just imagine the kind of burial rites his friend had received. His powers of restraint were further tried when informed he would not be permitted to travel to the grave-site and pay his last repects, as the whole community was off-limits to anyone who was not ICA personnel or a registered patient.

I just don't understand. Why did I not foresee his condition or how rapidly it would deteriorate?

Walter had diagnosed and healed hundreds of strangers, without ever laying eyes on them in some cases, and yet Patrick's disease had simply escaped his attention. It just didn't figure. He'd read various horror stories since the AIDS clinic had opened, printed by the independent publications over the past three years. These reports told of people in the early stages of the disease whose health had rapidly deteriorated after their arrival at the facility. People had been targeted for termination and they were all either drug addicts or homosexuals who had been disowned by their families or had no living kin who would kick up a fuss about their unfortunate plight. Cadfan had previously subscribed to the ICA explanation of terrorists being behind the propaganda, but now he wasn't so sure.

He looked to the intercom system on his desk and hit a key. The small screen lit up, and a soft ambient tune filtered through the speaker while he waited for his secretary to answer her pager.

'Yes, Walter,' Mary-Anne inquired, her calm, smiling face appearing on his monitor.

This was a brave front, for it was obvious to Walter that she'd been weeping just prior to answering his call.

Bless her, he thought. 'I'd like you to arrange for someone to take my classes over the next few days. I'm sure Tom wouldn't mind, if he hasn't got any other commitments. Send him my apologies for the short notice.'

Thomas Mateus was the very best spiritual tutor Cadfan knew. Although Tom's areas of expertise were the Shamanistic Arts, Earth Sciences and Ancient Cultures he was a fine healer as well.

'Are you leaving us?' Mary-Anne appeared concerned for him, until one side of Walter's mouth curved to a smile.

'Yes, my dear. For it would seem I have a quest.'

'I'm sorry, did you say a *quest?*' This was not the response Mary-Anne had expected.

'I did.' Walter's attention had drifted away from the screen as he recalled a prophetic vision he'd had concerning the American president. He had not understood why the universe was granting him this information at the time, but now he realised it might well be ammunition. 'After you call Thomas, see if you can schedule me a meeting with Doc Alexander in the next couple of days.'

'Sure.' Mary-Anne forced a smile. 'After all, he's only the most sought-after man in the world.'

'Oh, he'll see me,' Cadfan stated confidently. Doc Alexander had extended him many invitations in the past, though Walter, wanting to stay out of the political limelight, had always gracefully declined.

It was three months into the World Power Project and the ICA were already copping flack from the Middle

Eastern sector. A group of religious fanatics, who claimed the Fusion Grid was the seven-headed beast of the Apocalypse, stated that they had procured a nuclear warhead. The launch target would be the host storage facility still under construction in New Mexico, unless the Fusion Grid project was abandoned immediately.

Doc was not overly worried. He'd already arranged to meet with the terrorist organisation's representatives, feeling quite sure he would make them see reason.

Yesterday in Washington Doc had persuaded President Langford to let the ICA handle the situation. The US Head of Defence, General Berkley, strongly objected when the President granted Alexander forty-eight hours to defuse the threat. But the President stuck to his decision.

'Congratulations,' said Emma, as Doc passed through her office on the way to his own. She stood and handed him a diskette containing an update of his schedule. 'Walter Cadfan is already waiting for you inside.'

'Excellent.' Doc had been looking forward to this meeting for a very long time. He'd even detoured to London to take the appointment, and would fly on to Baghdad to resolve the threat to the Fusion Grid afterwards.

'No calls, no interruptions, no exceptions.' Doc was adamant, though courteous about his instruction. 'Thanks, Emma.'

Entering his office, Doc found Cadfan staring up at a portrait of King Cadwallon of Gwynedd. Doc had painted the picture in question near the end of the seventeenth century. During that period of history, to be part of high society, one had to be seen as having an active interest in the arts. Even nine hundred years after Cadwallon had vanished from the face of the Earth, the features of his face remained etched firmly enough in Doc's memory to have reproduced a good likeness of his father. He grinned at Cadfan's astonished expression. If Walter was Cadfan of Gwynedd, father of Cadwallon, and thus Doc's own grandfather, how must it feel to see such a vivid image of his son after so many centuries had passed? 'You like?'

Walter was startled by the query. He glanced at his host briefly, then back to the image that had him so enchanted. 'It's a remarkable …' He wanted to say likeness, but refrained. 'work. Must be worth a fortune,' he commented, seriously considering making an offer for the painting if Doc would part with it.

'Not really.' Doc stood beside Walter and looked up at Cadwallon's image, burying his true feelings down deep so that he sounded neither here nor there about it. 'It's by an unknown Baroque artist, who wasn't especially talented.'

'Baroque?' Walter was stunned. Doc had to be wrong. How could some painter in the late seventeenth century have reproduced the likeness of a seventh century King so precisely? 'Are you quite sure?'

'I'm afraid so. I only brought it because he looked such a menacing fellow.'

'Not at all.' Walter couldn't stop the words from shooting out of his mouth. 'For British history tells us,' he attempted to cover the conviction of his first statement, 'that Cadwallon was beloved of his people. He carried victory into the very heart of enemy territory.'

'Where he vanished after the battle of Hexham in six hundred and thirty three,' Doc added. 'King Oswald of Northumbria claimed to have run Cadwallon through, but you know … they never did find his body.'

Cadfan's jaw dropped as he stared at the man beside him. Doc's expression looked malign, until he tore his gaze away from the picture and shrugged.

'If you like it, it's yours.'

'Oh no, I couldn't possibly.' Cadfan was overwhelmed by his generosity.

'Please, I'm not especially fond of it.' Doc placed his PC and briefcase on his desk. 'Art should be where it will be most appreciated.' He smiled in conclusion, motioning for Cadfan to take a seat. 'I'll have Emma arrange to have it sent to you.'

It was not often that Walter found a material possession that he just had to have. This painting had sentimental value beyond anything he already owned, yet he couldn't help but feel that he'd owe Doc if he accepted the present. *Yet,* Cadfan considered a way around the problem, *if I find something suitable to give him in return, that will cancel out any such debt.* 'I fear I may be pushing my luck if I accept your most gracious gift,' Cadfan trod lightly, 'as I am here to seek a favour.'

'Ah, well,' Doc again encouraged Cadfan to be seated, taking a seat himself. 'A favour is quite a different thing to a gift, wouldn't you say? A gift for a gift, a favour for a favour, isn't that how we Britons do things?'

We? Cadfan wondered to himself. 'I'm sorry, I was under the impression you were an American.'

'A common misconception,' was all Doc said. 'Allow me to be frank, Walter. May I call you Walter?'

Cadfan gave him leave with a nod.

'Truth is, a man in my position could really use a little inside information from the spirit world, if you catch my drift.' Walter was looking a tad concerned at this stage — it was obvious he'd not planned to form a friendship here today. 'Your predictions are more precise then any clairvoyant that ever lived. Including Nostradamus,' Doc thought it fair to add. For he'd known the great seer rather well, and his predictions had been much more vague than Cadfan's. 'It would prove much easier to avert these disasters if I knew a little more about them in advance.'

'Well, I post a complete report on the VR-Net after every episode,' advised Walter. 'Beyond that there is no more to tell.'

'I know your bulletin. I follow it very closely,' Doc confessed. 'I'm actually quite a fan. No, what I am asking is that *if* you should happen to see something that might aid or hinder ICA affairs, that you will let me know immediately. Fair enough?'

'All right,' agreed Walter.

'Good.' Doc tried to sound satisfied — given a little more time he would get Cadfan completely on side. 'So now, tell me, Walter, what can I do for you in return?'

Cadfan had been warned of how charismatic Doc Alexander was, but he seemed just a little too charming for his liking. 'I want ICA clearance to visit the AIDS facility in Alaska.'

'May I ask why?' Doc sounded unfazed by the request, just interested.

'A student of mine died there recently.'

'I am sorry. He must have been too far gone.'

'No, I don't believe he was.' Cadfan voiced his professional opinion. 'I would like to visit his grave to pay my last respects, and take a look at his files while I'm there. After all, I was Patrick's personal physician.'

'Patrick?'

Cadfan nodded. 'Patrick Haze.'

Doc jotted down the name. 'I tell you what, Walter. I'll get a copy of Patrick's file to you in the next couple of days — just let Emma know where you want it sent. I'm taking a trip up there myself next week, you're more than welcome to come along.'

'I don't want to be a bother. I'm quite capable —'

'It's no bother at all,' Doc assured him. 'Consider it a done deal.'

In other words, if Cadfan didn't accept the chaperoned arrangement he could forget the idea altogether. 'You're too kind.' Walter stood, deciding to push the issue no further. Doc had more or less granted all his requests, so there seemed little point in creating a drama when he might still achieve what he hoped to without having to play hardball.

'I look forward to it.' Doc moved to show him out. 'Emma will let you know the flight details as they come to hand.'

16

†HE HOLY LAПD

It had been a long time since Tory had awoken drenched in sweat and panicked.

'Another vision', she'd concluded, until she brought the subject up at breakfast and found it to be news to everyone else.

'I slept like a baby,' Rhun informed her.

'I didn't.' Rhiannon glanced at Ray, seated beside her. 'But it wasn't divine prophecy that kept me awake.'

Tory looked towards Brian and then Jenny, who both shrugged, shaking their heads.

'Maybe it was just a bad dream,' Rhun posed.

His mother had gone quite thoughtful, though she shook her head to reject his suggestion. 'Tell me …' Tory turned to Floyd, who was behind the breakfast bar making himself a cappuccino. Now that the *Goddess* was fully operational, her crew had once again taken up residence on the vessel. Floyd, who liked his spacious control centre high above Watarrka's community, just frequented the *Goddess* at meal times.

Tory thought a while before voicing her question, still trying to recollect the fragments of her dream. 'Besides the usual war and political tension, is there anything out of the ordinary going on in the Middle East at present?'

Floyd appeared somewhat aghast at the question, but was not given the chance to answer.

'Are you shitting me!' Noah's head popped up from behind his portable computer, which he'd set up on one of the many benches in the dining quarters. 'Haven't you been watching the news?'

Tory swung round in her seat to view him. 'Noah. Between training, study and test driving *Merlin*, when do I get the time to watch the news? That's what you're here for.'

Noah was gratified. He liked the suggestion that in some small way Tory relied on him. 'A Middle Eastern terrorist group who, reports say, are religiously motivated, claim to have a nuclear warhead aimed at New Mexico.'

'The host station for the grid,' Tory remembered, thinking back to her dreams. 'I seem to recall a huge explosion, but …' she bit down on her lip, perplexed.

'But what?' Noah pressed.

'Never mind.' Tory decided it was irrelevant. 'What action have the Americans taken?'

'None,' Noah said wryly. 'They're still procrastinating.'

'Well, that's not exactly the whole truth,' Floyd intervened. 'When I heard the host station was under threat, I procured for myself a copy of Doc's schedule for this coming week.'

'I was under the impression you couldn't do that,' Tory told him, 'as Doc's PC is not connected to the ICA's main-frame computer.'

'But his secretary's *is*,' Ray deduced, knowing the setup.

'Quite correct,' Floyd confirmed. 'And as Doc is, as we speak, on a charter flight to Baghdad, I'd say the US are sending him in to negotiate, wouldn't you?'

'Well, the fusion grid is his monster, I suppose,' Tory mused aloud. 'But what of these terrorists? What name are they going by? Who is their leader?'

Noah shrugged, as far the media was concerned, this had remained a mystery.

Floyd startled everyone by casually stating: 'They're calling themselves the Unken, and name their leader as one, Lugal-Shamash.'

Noah began madly typing the references into his computer, concluding his labours with a grunt. 'Interesting. Unken is an old Babylonian term meaning 'council of elders' or 'circle of people'. The 'Lugal', or 'great man', was the head of this council. And the name Shamash you already know the history of.'

'Inanna's twin brother.' Tory enlightened everyone, as she pondered the rest of the information. 'Babylon … wasn't that where the Tower of Babel was supposedly built?'

Noah nodded in response, punching up the relevant references on his computer. 'Then the god of gods descended out of the heavens to view the city and the tower that mankind were building, and he said, This is just the beginning of their undertakings; from now on, nothing they scheme to do shall be impossible for them. Come, let us go down and confuse their language. If they cannot understand each other, then work on the tower will cease. Then the Lord scattered mankind across the face of the Earth.'

'That's right.' Teo recalled his time spent, under sufferance, at Sunday school. 'Humans were attempting to build a tower that reached to the heavens. Quite frankly, I always thought the story to be complete bullshit.'

'Indeed.' Noah seemed to share his opinion. 'Ancient texts claim they were building a rocket launcher under the guidance of one Lord Marduk.'

'*Mankind has come full circle from the Tower of Babel.*' Tory uttered her thought aloud.

'I suppose so,' Noah agreed. 'If one considers the level of communication we have sustained via technology, and mankind's advancement into space.'

'No.' Tory corrected his misconception. 'That is not an observation, but rather a message that came through in my dream.'

Brian, who was finishing up his coffee, shrugged. 'Hey guys, I really don't think that events that took place in the Middle East five thousand years ago have anything to do with us.'

'Yes they do!' Both Tory and Noah insisted at once, but it was Tory who pursued the argument.

'It has everything to do with us,' Tory stated, knowing Marduk was their grandfather. Perhaps it had been he who sent the dream.

'Alright. Settle down.' Brian held up both hands in truce, surprised by the conviction behind her words.

'I tell you what.' Floyd grinned. 'I'd sure like to be a fly on the wall at that meeting in Baghdad tonight.'

'Yeah!' Noah stood, rubbing his hands together, to second the motion.

'Let's do it,' Teo encouraged them, eager to see some action.

The others were enthusiastic also, but not Ray.

'*Now hold on*. With all that's going on in the Middle East, you want to take the *Goddess* there? Have you all taken leave of your senses! We could cause a major international incident.'

'And we could also prevent one.' Tory voiced her feelings.

Brian smiled, delighted by the opportunity to settle a few scores with Doc Alexander. 'Well, boys and girls, it looks like we got ourselves a mission.'

Time did not allow for a detailed strategy to be formed, and Ray got his wish. They all decided the *Goddess* was too large and cumbersome to make it to the Middle East in such a short span of time. Although Tory was reminded that Rhun could psychokinetically transport any vehicle to the said location, the task would drain him, and she thought it best to have him fully functional. Thus, it was decided that Rhiannon and Rhun would transport themselves psychokinetically to Baghdad to keep an eye on Doc's movements. Meanwhile, Tory and Brian would pilot *Merlin I* and *II* overland to rendezvous with Rhiannon and Rhun at approximately the same time as the meeting between Doc and the Unken was scheduled to take place. Even though Floyd had a copy of Doc Alexander's itinerary, the details concerning the meeting place for the negotiations had been conveniently left out. The best they could do was wait at the hotel, and trail Doc's party from there.

The four members of their crew going on the mission wore basic combat fatigues simply because army wear had proven to be the most durable and practical form of dress for such occasions. Tory, Brian, Rhun and Rhiannon could make their uniform outwardly appear to be that of any army. They didn't expect to have any trouble blending in. Even their distinctly different racial features could be camouflaged.

The rooftop of the building across the road from Doc's accommodation was where Rhun and Rhiannon would take up position. Should the diplomat manage to elude their ground surveillance team, Tory and Brian could seek out the ICA party from the air in *Merlin I* and *II* — provided, of course, they could make Baghdad before the entire event was over.

Tory made quickly for her transport and was alarmed to find Teo, suited up and awaiting her, alongside *Merlin I*.

'No, Teo,' she stated, firmly. 'Immortals only. It's too dangerous.'

'Look …' He followed her to the ladder that led up to the hatch. 'If you guys are only allowed to transmit in an emergency situation, I'm serving no purpose here. I'll go nuts!'

'Teo.' She turned back to him, one hand gripping the stair rail ready to hoist herself up. 'I'll not risk losing you on a routine surveillance mission.'

'Oh, come on. Our mission objectives are not going to get any easier from here.' He took a step backward, sounding slightly offended. 'Am I then to assume that my services in this regard are redundant? Tory, I'm the best fucking fighter you've got! I realise I do not possess your talents, but it's not like I won't blend in anyway.'

This was quite true, for although his darker skin colour was tinged red, he was also rather tanned at present. His ebony hair and eyes would pretty much guarantee he'd pass unnoticed where they were bound.

'Or perhaps you think I'm getting too old for this sort of thing?' he posed, wryly, folding his arms.

He stunned Tory with the question. Even at fifty years of age, Teo still appeared, and was, a man in his prime. 'Heavens no, that's not it at all.'

'Then let me come.' He gripped hold of her shoulders in exasperation, yet she was still reluctant to agree. 'Tory, you can't keep me sheltered here forever, sooner or later I *am* going to die.'

Tory's eyes darted up to meet his. All her closest kin were immortal like herself. Teo was the only one she stood to lose. Perhaps she was being overprotective of him, and, in all reality, she had no right to be.

'I refuse to go quietly in my sleep, Tory. That's not my style, and you know it.'

She hung her head. Her gut instinct was to forbid him to come, but it was not her decision to make. 'Alright,' she conceded, before gripping hold of his vest. 'But you stay within an arm's length of one of us at all times, understood?'

Teo placed both arms around her, and announced with a grin, 'Perfectly. But just in case something should go wrong.'

The kiss took Tory completely by surprise. It had been so long since she'd been close to a man that she found the experience somewhat arousing. Though it had been some forty-seven years, by Tory's reckoning, since she and Teo had been on intimate terms, his kiss was immediately familiar. And, though Tory struggled to deny it, welcome as well.

'Damn it,' he said softly as they parted. 'I really pick my moments, don't I?'

'You sure do.' Her voice was hoarse with shock and bewilderment. That old spark was still there, and it had only taken that brief caress to ignite it into full flame. Tory turned back to the ladder to resume her course, conjuring an image of Maelgwn when last seen which helped to quell the burning sensation in her chest and stomach.

'Hey, sunshine.' Teo stopped her again. 'I know this is not the time or the place to go into this, but —'

'Exactly. So let's focus on the task at hand. Coming?' She bounded up the ladder before he could reply.

A hot gust of wind hit Doc the second he stepped out of the private jet and onto the tarmac at Baghdad airport.

His discomfort was only momentary, however, as the diplomat climbed straight into a limousine that whisked him away to his hotel.

Twenty years ago this would have been unheard of. Then, even a diplomat of Doc Alexander's status would have been grilled by Iraqi security for hours before entering the city, and would have been observed closely for the entire duration of his visit. The Middle East had known relative peace in the last ten years, however, and their new President was well disposed towards Doc for lending ICA assistance to rebuild his shattered nation. Doc had also organised United Nations support for Iraq and her neighbours during an extremely bad drought that had yet to break.

Baghdad was no longer the exotic ancient city that the name had once conjured to mind. During the strife of the late twentieth century, when the city was under the rulership of Saddam Hussein, many of the great buildings had been periodically levelled by invaders. But, through the combined efforts of the Iraqi government and the ICA, a large slice of Baghdad had since been rebuilt. Towering hotels and modern housing blocks now accommodated the international community that was trading with Iraq.

As this was an unofficial visit, accommodation for Doc Alexander's party had been arranged at a hotel on the outskirts of the city, though it was still luxurious. Doc and his associates had personally overseen the rebuilding of this hotel.

Shortly after their arrival, Doc summoned his team to the hotel's conference room to finalise the agenda for the rest of the day. The meeting had barely commenced when Doc brought the proceedings to an abrupt halt.

He spoke the word — his secret word — that served as a trigger to send his entire staff into a trance state.

Motionless, and unaware of the psychological manipulation taking place, all present awaited his instruction.

'As far as you will all recall,' Doc began, getting more comfortable in his chair, 'the negotiations scheduled to take place this afternoon, were, at the last minute, cancelled. After reviewing the situation and exhausting all possible channels to re-establish contact with the Unken, we were forced to concede that my hope for a peaceful solution to this crisis was unrealistic. Tomorrow I will report to President Langford and convey these views. Until then,' Doc stood to take his leave, 'you will stay here and keep busy. My absence shall not be noted, for I never left the room.'

As the door clicked closed behind Doc, all the chatter and commotion of the meeting resumed.

'They're at the hotel.' Rhun materialised on the *Goddess'* control deck to report.

'Right on schedule,' Floyd grinned, impressed. 'The meeting isn't due to take place for a few hours yet, so you and Rhiannon stay put. Let us know if Doc makes a move before your air support arrives.'

'We picked up the hire car.' Rhun informed the base personnel. 'It's there, waiting, if we need it.'

'Well, with any luck, you won't.' Floyd threw a curious glance toward Jenny and Nick behind the crystal-emission tracking system, where they were following the progress of the two smaller craft.

'They're less than an hour away.' Jenny took an educated guess.

'No worries.' Rhun was closing his eyes to return to the stake-out, when Ray grabbed hold of his wrist. 'Careful, Murdock,' Rhun broke from his concentration to advise, 'you nearly found yourself in Baghdad. What's up?'

'You take care of her.' The way Ray said this made it sound more like a warning than a request.

'Ray, you know as well as I do, no permanent harm can befall Rhiannon.' Rhun reclaimed possession of his arm.

'You don't know Doc Alexander like I do. He has ways and means around everything.'

'So do we,' Rhun stated in a cocky fashion. 'That's why the Agency haven't caught us out yet, and never will.' He closed his eyes and faded from view.

'Be warned,' Ray yelled after him, 'you arrogant little ...'

By the time Rhun arrived back on the rooftop in Baghdad, the hot afternoon breeze had noticeably dropped in temperature — it was only about one hundred degrees now. Rhiannon was still poised behind her binoculars focused on the building across the road. Rhun shook his head at the sight of her, bent over so as to rest both her elbows on the wall and support the weighty glasses. Rhiannon might have been his sister, but that didn't detract from the fact that she had a great backside. 'What's cookin', good lookin'?'

'Fortunately, not a thing.' She didn't budge. 'How much longer will Mother be?'

'About an hour.' Rhun took a seat against the wall beside her, taking advantage of the tiny bit of shade. He pulled the cap off the waterskin he was carrying and took a long swig, wetting his face and neck in the process. 'Tell me something.' His thoughts wandered back to Ray, as he shook off the excess water. 'Have I done something to your boyfriend that I'm not aware of? He sure doesn't seem to like me very much.' This bothered Rhun, as in Ray's past life in Gwynedd they'd been lifelong friends. Three years had passed since they'd met in the twenty-first century, and they hadn't warmed to each other at all.

'I had a crush on you when we first met,' Rhiannon announced casually, forcing her brother to smile.

'Really?' This was news to Rhun. 'I'm flattered.'

'Ray was *so jealous*,' Rhiannon laughed, pausing from her task a moment as she recalled, 'and probably still is. Never mind about the fact that he still has a thing for Mother.' She rolled her eyes, in a mocking fashion.

Rhun was not really surprised to learn this. 'Bryce was infatuated with her too. His whole life in fact.'

Rhiannon's cheer was dampened as she picked up on the wonderful memories that were flitting through her brother's head. 'You miss him,' she stated, feeling the sorrowful yearning that welled deep within him suddenly.

Rhun nodded, then shrugged, trying to suppress the lump that was forming in his throat. She sensed his inner conflict, and tears moistened both their eyes. Rhun so wanted to accept this new circumstance and yet the memories of the good times he and Bryce had once shared were tearing him apart. 'I'm so sorry, Rhun. I didn't even think. I've been so wrapped up in getting what I want, that I didn't even consider that I might be destroying a friendship in the process.'

'No, Rhiannon, don't blame yourself. Things are just different now. Bryce is a whole different person.'

'It doesn't have to be that way.' She decided to try and resolve the conflict she'd started. 'I shall talk to him.' She took up position and went back to her surveillance.

'If you think it will make any difference.' Rhun wondered if it really would.

Rhiannon gave half a chuckle at something she was viewing through the binoculars, then her amusement was cut short. 'Oh shit!'

'What is it?' Rhun stood to look down at the street below.

A large, dark-haired man, dressed as a local but all in black, exited the hotel alone.

'I thought the Dragon Slayer had walked right out of the computer and onto the streets of Baghdad, then I realised what that means.'

'Doc's changed form!' they both concluded at once.

'Good call.' Rhun was amazed she'd picked up on it. 'Can you psych out of him where he's going from this distance?'

Rhiannon was already focused on her target, who was climbing into a car. She was startled when he re-emerged to look around the street. 'O-oh.' She ducked to avoid being spotted, pulling her brother down with her. 'Jesus, Rhun, he sensed me. This is not good.'

With no one tutoring him in the greater mysteries, Rhun could hardly believe Doc had become so accomplished in just three years. 'I'm going after him. You know what to do.'

Rhiannon, still horrified, gave her brother a nod and he vanished. She dared a peek over the wall to the street below, to find Doc's new persona had climbed into the car. She watched as the car pulled out into the street. Rhun's vehicle did likewise and followed Doc.

Satisfied that all was going smoothly, Rhiannon prepared to transport herself back to the *Goddess* to report that *Merlin I* and *II* hadn't made the party on time. Then the rooftop became awhirl with wind that whipped Rhiannon's long dark hair about her face. As the whirlwind died away, Brian's upper body emerged out of thin air about ten feet off the ground.

'Need a lift?'

Rhiannon laughed as she made for the invisible craft, instructing, 'Follow that car.'

Tory didn't enjoy flying *Merlin* through the city. The radical changes in the topography, the buildings and the various forms of transport on the streets, made for a very hairy ride.

Nevertheless, Teo seemed to be revelling in the bumps along the way, as he watched the cars in question through the headset that controlled the camera in *Merlin II*.

As they approached the hire car Rhun drove, Tory sent her son a mental note to advise him of their presence. Rhun gave them the thumbs-up to confirm he'd recieved her message and turned the car around to discontinue his pursuit.

'He's all ours,' Teo informed.

On the ground, one had to pass many Iraqi troops and roadblocks to exit the city. Travelling outside Baghdad still required official permission and, in some cases, an official escort. But, unlike everybody else, Doc seemed to have no trouble obtaining clearance to move on.

They followed Doc's vehicle through the outskirts of the city, past the farmlands that lined the banks of the Tigris and out onto the flat sun-baked plains. Now that they had entered the wide open spaces, Tory gained altitude. There was hardly a soul to been seen way out here, so Doc's vehicle wasn't difficult to keep in sight.

As did central Australia, the barren desert they crossed had a mysterious timeless quality; little of this landscape had changed since the God's had frequented it. But this place lacked the rich warm colours of Uluru, and so appeared harsher and more forebidding. The area pulsated with the energies Tory had come to associate with ley lines, but where Uluru vibrated with positive energy, the eons of war and strife in the Middle East had manifested themselves in the landscape.

'Looks like he's heading for that mountain range yonder.' Teo voiced his observation.

'Fabulous. Mountains,' Tory commented, none too keen on the idea of flying over more unpredictable terrain.

But the road led into a deep chasm between the mountains that, after a mile or so, came to a dead end. The vehicle did a circuit around the dirt clearing surrounded on all sides by towering rocky cliffs. Tory figured Doc was probably checking to ensure no one had followed him. Then, before she had a chance to consider what he might be doing way out here in the middle of nowhere, he drove the car straight into the cavern wall. Doc, and the car, vanished.

'Now, there's something you don't see every day.' Teo disengaged the viewing headset.

'It would seem my father and Taliesin are not the only ones with such retreats.' Tory did a circuit of the clearing, heading back into the chasm with *Merlin I* right behind her. Halfway down the gorge, its rocky walls parted wide, leaving a large clearing on both sides of the road.

Tory settled the craft down to a gentle landing. The sandstorm beside her was visual confirmation that Brian had landed also.

It was coming onto evening by the time Rhun returned the hire car and joined the others in the chasm.

Rhiannon was voicing her observations concerning Doc's astounding leap in psychic expertise, which seemed to have everyone worried.

'Perhaps we should abort.' Tory was clearly ill-at-ease about what she'd learned. 'It's not worth getting caught over. If Doc has become as accomplished as you say, he'll be able to siphon information from us faster than Floyd sucks it from the internet.'

'High risk, high gain.' Rhun added his two cents worth. 'Somebody has to find out what he's up to. If not us, then who?'

Tory could appreciate Rhun's view, but the stakes were too high. 'If you can think of a way to guarantee that we will not give away the location of our base …'

'I have,' he intervened, calmly. 'I'll just wipe all memory of it from your mind, as I did with Rhiannon for her last mission.'

'Who's going to wipe it from your memory?' Teo wondered out loud.

Rhun shrugged, 'Two of us should really stay here and keep an eye on our transport, so I guess I volunteer. I'm not a great pilot, but if worst comes to worst I could psychokinetically transport *Merlin* out of here.' Rhun looked to Teo, believing he should be the other person to stay.

'Aw, bugger.' Teo saw the sense of it. After what he'd just heard about Doc, he conceded he might be a little out of his depth on this one.

Rhun gave Teo a thump on the shoulder for foregoing the adventure. 'Alright, it's settled then.' He sat his mother down in front of him and begin the hypnosis.

Once snapped from her trance, Tory didn't feel any different. Yet it made her tremendously confident to discover that when questioned about the whereabouts of their base she couldn't for the life of her remember. 'That's amazing!' She racked her brain. 'Absolutely nothing.' Tory was even more astounded when she watched the hypnotic procedure performed on Brian. It took all of five minutes to wipe the information clean out of his memory.

It wasn't long before Brian, Tory and Rhiannon found themselves creeping down the dark canyon towards the clearing.

'This places gives me the creeps,' Brian whispered with a shudder. It wasn't that the landscape was threatening, or that it had spooky noises. It just felt ominous.

'It's been empowered by negative energy to be sure.' Tory seconded.

'That foreboding-type vibe is getting stronger the nearer we get to the entrance,' added Rhiannon, relieved that she wasn't the only one who noticed the repelling force.

'Great.' Brian forced a smile, considering he was happier when he'd been blissfully unaware of all Otherworldly phenomena.

Armed with their Stormers, and a roll of gaffer tape, the three of them cautiously approached the spot where Doc's vehicle had vanished. Night had fallen, but the full moon lit the rock face they sought to penetrate. They kept low, hugging the canyon wall, in the hope of avoiding any electronic surveillance.

'Perhaps we should go get *Merlin*, and fly in,' Rhiannon suggested, seeing this as the only way of proceeding without being detected.

'And risk losing one of our craft in an ambush?' Tory shook her head. 'There has to be another way.'

Invisibility was not a talent Tory had mastered, or even considered, but there was a means to achieve such a feat. One of the thirteen treasures of Britain, the Mantle of Gwydion, was capable of providing its wearer with such a service. Tory had used this garment, handcrafted by the Gods, to render herself invisible once before. The siege at Aberffraw that had cost Gwynedd the life of its King, Caswallon, seemed an eternity ago now. Yet the treasure that had kept secret Tory's participation in the battle, remained clearly etched in her memory.

Tory focused on the details of the image in her mind and, holding out her arms before her, closed her eyes to will forth the Mantle of Gwydion from her father's cave at Dinas Emrys.

Brian watched his sister's movements with growing interest, then suddenly Tory announced: 'Ta-da!' She whipped a cloak out of thin air.

'Great, here I am trying to solve our problem, and you're worried about getting cold.' Brian scoffed.

'Take a chill pill, bro.' Tory reversed the cloak inside out, swinging it round her shoulders, whereupon she vanished.

'Ha!' Rhiannon gasped, astounded.

'Tory?' Brian wondered if she was still with them, the fact that he couldn't see her made him uneasy.

'Yeah, what?'

Tory had moved. Brian turned abruptly to face her as she removed the cloak.

'Get the picture?'

He did, and Brian's sudden understanding made him grin.

Shrouded by the mantle, the three of them passed through the cavern wall and into a long, dark, earthen corridor that sloped progressively downward. The tunnel was lit at ten metre intervals by electric lights imbedded in the walls.

'No wonder Doc drove in,' Brian uttered, softly. 'How deep do you think it goes?'

Tory shrugged. 'Let's find out.'

The night sky above the canyon was ablaze with stars, and it seemed to Teo that he'd been staring at them for ages. Rhun was using the only pair of binoculars that was equipped with night vision to keep watch, so there was precious little for Teo to do. He was bored, and when Teo was bored he liked to chat. Trouble was, apart from Rhun trying to ward him off Tory, they never really had very much to say to each other. The silence really started to bug him after a while, and as he'd thought of a question he'd always wanted to ask Rhun, now seemed a good opportunity. 'Have you been shitting me all this time about your father still being alive?'

'If he were dead, Teo, I'd have no reason to lie to you about it. I want to see my mother happy, just as much as you do.' Rhun looked to Teo, who still appeared reluctant to believe him. 'Think back to a few weeks after we procured Doc's hard drive, and mother was mysteriously struck unconscious for four days … remember? Didn't you wonder why?'

'I thought she was just having another cosmic episode. Everyone was a bit vague about it when I asked, so I figured nobody really knew.'

'She was visiting my father.' Rhun levelled with him. 'Well, her astral body was.'

'Visiting him! Visiting him where?'

Rhun pointed to a star twinkling brightly on the horizon in the east. 'There, the Sirius system, approximately eight point seven light-years away.' Rhun inwardly hoped to one day accompany his father there. 'But don't think that means he's not watching … my father's talents far exceed my own.'

Teo sat thoughtful for a time, then dragged himself up to his feet. 'I'm going to make a coffee,' he felt his way towards the invisible ladder of *Merlin II*. 'You want one?'

'No, thanks.'

Making coffee in the dark kept Teo amused for a while. He stirred in an unknown quantity of milk, before wiping the spoon and returning it to the storage hatch provided. 'Ahh, caffeine,' he sighed, planting himself in the co-pilot's seat and raising the brew to his mouth for a sip.

From the darkened valley beyond the large, front porthole of *Merlin II* gunfire lit up the night. Teo splattered boiling coffee all over himself, as bullets ricocheted off the invisible metal body of the craft in which he sat. 'Fu..' he forced himself to silence. He brushed off the boiling liquid as if it were lukewarm, and keeping low, in case the next round of bullets penetrated one of the portholes, repositioned himself where he could view Rhun out front.

Rhun had dropped the binoculars and had his arms raised in surrender. He slowly got to his feet, waiting to be apprehended.

Teo could vaguely make out a lone figure, advancing towards them. Again the darkness lit up as shots were fired. Rhun did not have a chance to flinch from his stance before several bullets ploughed into his torso and blew him right off his feet. 'Jesus Christ almighty,' Teo uttered under his breath, fumbling to pull the Stormer from his belt.

Even as the sniper reached Rhun sprawled on the ground, it was difficult to make him out as he was dressed entirely in black. His eyes were masked by some sort of radical electronic glasses. Of a sleek wrap-around design, these were unlike any eye wear Teo had ever seen. The lenses that sat over both eye sockets gave the gunman damn fine night vision, that much was plainly obvious.

Rhun lay in wait. He allowed his attacker to kick his body a couple of times, before grabbing hold of his legs and toppling him to the ground. The gun was sent flying in the scuffle, and as the gunman booted Rhun away and made a dash for the weapon, a laser bullet slammed into the ground nearby and he froze.

'The next one won't miss.'

The sniper turned to see Teo land on the ground, his cylindrical weapon aimed at him.

'Who are you? What do you want?' Teo inched his way closer to remove the balaclava the gunman wore. Rhun, in the meantime, retrieved the gun and turned on a mini-flashlight to get a look at their attacker's face.

'I have to be sure you are who I believe you are.'

Teo was shocked as he removed the gunman's disguise to discover a woman. Her long, dark curls fell about her shoulders, and her eyes were violet like Tory's, only much paler.

'Who are you?' Rhun repeated the query, coldly aiming her gun at her and cocking it so it was ready to fire.

'I am Neraida, the daughter of Alexander and the humble servant of the serpent, who was the great-grandfather of my tribe.'

'Not Doc Alexander?' Teo hoped.

'I think she means Alexander the Great, Teo.' Rhun deduced this from her colouring, which was as dark as the native Middle Eastern peoples. Teo was speechless as the woman nodded in confirmation of Rhun's comment. Upon closer inspection, Rhun recognised her as a one-time ally of his father's. She was Cara, the wife of Vortipor the Protector of Dyfed, who had become the High King of Britain after Maelgwn had vacated the position. Upon realising this, Rhun felt inclined to give her the benefit of the doubt. 'I am ...'

'King Rhun of Gwynedd,' Neraida stated. 'Son of Maelgwn, the Dragon of the Isle. Your mother is Tory Alexander, the grand-daughter of the Lord Marduk, and therefore my cousin.' The two men were so obviously taken aback by her words that she obliged them with an explanation. 'I recall much of the life and times of my other earthly incarnations, one of which was in Gwynedd, with your father and Tory Alexander.'

'I remember,' Rhun concurred, 'but Lady Cara died when I was only ...' he stopped himself, thinking the comment might be inappropriate or hurtful to her.

'Indeed. The last memory I have of you, you were just a little boy.' Neraida chuckled at how different he appeared now. 'Sorry I had to shoot you but, if you were who I suspected, it wasn't going to do you any permanent damage.'

'And if I wasn't.' Rhun considered Teo's addiction to coffee rather fortunate in this instance.

'Then you were a dead man,' she stated coldly. 'Where is your legendary mother? Her vision was supposed to lead her to Babylon, not Baghdad.'

Rhun urged Teo to be calm, as he was obviously insulted by Neraida's casual disregard for the lives and worth of mortal men. 'We followed Doc Alexander here.'

'Oh, no,' Neraida gasped. 'Please don't tell me she's attempting to penetrate Unken headquarters.'

'If that's where the secret entrance in the clearing up yonder leads, yes she is?' Rhun, knowing the full extent of his mother's talents, wasn't as quick to panic.

'No, no, no, we can't afford to lose her!' Neraida wandered around, anxiously forming a strategy in her mind.

'How do you figure that.' Teo thought she was overreacting. 'Tory is immortal.'

'I'm not worried about her being killed,' Neraida replied and enlightened them. 'I'm worried about her being brainwashed. I've already lost several of my kin trying to penetrate the Unken ranks.'

'Lost,' Rhun frowned. 'How? Were they not skilled in the higher mysteries?'

'Yes, of course.' Her accent became more pronounced as she became angry. 'I'll explain later ...'

'You'll explain now.' Teo aimed his Stormer at her once more. He didn't recall knowing her in a past life and therefore was not as trusting.

Neraida sighed, exasperated, deciding it would be faster to oblige. 'My grandfather's kin, the Nefilim, recently created a device designed to control insubordinate immortals. NERGUZ they called it, meaning, reversing weapon. The module, clamped around the wrist or forehead of the subject, creates a hole in their electromagnetic field and temporarily drains them of all psi ability. Then the executor of the NERGUZ and subject are mentally linked, until all the insubordinate's undesirable thought patterns are reversed. The NERGUZ module can only be removed by the executor, and only he knows the key word he has used to activate the device. This word, and only this word, will deactivate it.'

'I just know you're going to tell me that Doc got his hands on this technology?' Rhun was turning pale.

Neraida nodded. 'The weapon has since been renamed here on Earth the NERGUZ-I-NUEN — reversing weapon of the dark lord.'

'But how?' Rhun was pacing now, not wanting to waste time on acquiring details that he knew were unimportant.

'The prototype of the NERGUZ was stolen by Inanna, and she used it for her own selfish ends for a time. She was eventually persuaded by her brother Utu, or Shamash as you may know him better, to let him have the weapon — just long enough to analyse and reproduce it. When Doc Alexander formed his alliance with Shamash, he passed the intricacies of the NERGUZ onto him.'

'Doc has formed an alliance with Shamash?' Rhun was stunned to learn. 'How do you know?'

'I have connections in high places that keep me well informed.' Neraida raised both brows. 'Besides, I would have thought that was obvious considering that Doc has become somewhat more accomplished in the ancient mysteries of late and is operating under the God's name.'

'So Doc is Lugal Shamash, the leader of the Unken?' Teo lowered his Stormer.

'Just work that out, did you?' Neraida jeered at Teo as she reclaimed her weapon from Rhun. 'Most of my tribe, including those I have lost to Lugal, are over two thousand years old … Tory Alexander, in psychic terms, is a mere novice compared to them. If they couldn't resist the power of the NERGUZ-I-NUEN, how long do you think she's going to last?' Neraida took a few steps backward and began to fade.

'Wait inside *Merlin*.' Rhun captured Neraida's image in his mind, willing himself after her.

A moment later, Teo was alone. 'Hold on, if Doc is Lugal, why is he threatening his own project?' With no one left to answer him, Teo wandered reluctantly back to *Merlin II* to wait the crisis out.

17

THE LORD GIVETH AND THE LORD TAKETH AWAY

The Unken had a nuclear missile alright. In fact they had several ICBMs (Intercontinental Ballistic Missiles), capable of travelling distances of up to 30,000 kilometres. The first of these was to be launched within the next twenty-four hours, though it was not, nor ever was, intended for the host or main fusion station in New Mexico. This missile had a divine purpose. A purpose that, properly disguised, would make Doc Alexander look like a hero in the eyes of the American people. The US government, in return, would see to it that nobody else learned the truth.

Doc was running over details of the missile launch with the Unken squad, when their head of security entered to report to him.

'Forgive the interruption, O Great Lugal. The motion detectors in the tunnel indicate a presence, but our cameras show nothing.' He shook his head, his hands raised in bafflement.

'Really.' Doc was rather delighted. 'How intriguing.' He excused himself from the meeting and followed the young man to his post.

After following the tunnel for a kilometre or so, Brian, Tory and Rhiannon had paused some distance away from a guard post.

Two men kept watch in front of a solid lead wall that entirely blocked off the tunnel. The door was also lead, and the electronic keypad seemed to indicate that they needed to keep one guard conscious to acquire the entry code.

A good opportunity to ambush them did not take long to present itself, as one of the guards headed up the tunnel in their direction. At first they feared he might be wise to them, but when the guard started to unzip the fly of his trousers, they realised this was not the case.

The soldier had paused in the shadowy area between the lights to relieve himself, when a hand seized his throat. Fingers pressed into the pressure points in his neck, so hard that he immediately blanked out.

Tory assumed the guard's image, whilst Brian taped the soldier's feet and hands together. He then taped over their captive's mouth and right round his head to ensure his silence.

The remaining guard, who awaited Tory's approach by the entrance to the fortress, didn't notice that his comrade's form had become slightly smaller. He was lighting a cigarette as Tory reached him, and he offered her one. With a shake of her head she assumed her post.

Moments later, a noise was heard in the tunnel up ahead of them and the guard immediately ditched the cigarette and cocked his weapon ready to fire. Tory motioned for him to investigate, and cautiously he moved to do so. The guard was so focused on seeking the trouble ahead of him that he failed to notice that his comrade had followed him into the shadows.

'Drop it,' Tory advised, the barrel of her gun pressed deep into the back of his neck.

The soldier obliged at once.

Brian, who had assumed the appearance of the guard Tory held captive, came out of nowhere to claim the weapon, and the soldier was speechless upon confronting himself.

Tory spun the guard around and demanded the code to the door.

'I do not know it.' He spotted his real comrade bound, gagged and unconscious on the ground nearby. 'He has it,' the soldier claimed, pointing to his friend.

'Is that right?' Tory gripped hold of his jaw, her eyes glaring deep into his. 'Tell me the code.' As the soldier persisted with his claim not to know it, Tory bethought the code-key from him. She smiled, triumphant, whereby Brian blasted him with his Stormer and the guard dropped to the ground like a stone.

With the second guard bound and gagged, Tory and Brian headed off towards the entrance to the Unken hideout. Rhiannon followed them, still masked by the enchanted mantle.

Tory headed straight for the keypad, but while she was occupied with entering the code, her Stormer was snatched from her belt. She was startled when a laser bullet hit Brian and he slid down the fortress wall to the ground. She was not given the chance to turn and see their attacker, before she had joined her brother in an unconscious state.

Rhiannon held her Stormer poised ready to fire as Doc, in his regular form (blonde, blue-eyed and handsome), checked over his victims. Then, looking to the weapon in his hand, he grinned, impressed. 'Please, don't fire.' He turned to view the empty tunnel, casting aside the weapon he held. 'I haven't harmed your kin, nor do I intend to. I only wish to speak with you.'

Rhiannon bit her lip. She very much wanted to remind him of how he'd brutally killed her father, but she didn't think it wise to confirm her presence in case he was bluffing. Her finger tightened on the trigger of her Stormer, wanting to shoot, but Doc's form seemed to glow like an angel and she couldn't bring herself to do it.

'Come, come, Miss Devereux. I know you're here, I can sense you.' He looked directly at her. 'Or should I say, Rhiannon?'

His words set her back a few paces. How could he know?

'No, don't be frightened,' he urged, dropping to his knees. 'God knows that's the last thing I want to do. I have gone to the same pains to discover your true identity as you have gone to discover mine. I am in love with you, you see ...' He paused, hoping for a reaction.

What? This was the last thing Rhiannon had expected him to say. *Is he kidding me?* 'Cadwaladr was a merciless barbarian, incapable of love.'

'Yes, I was,' he admitted, freely. 'But I have changed since then. I am more enlightened now.'

But his words only served to make Rhiannon's blood boil. 'You are a liar, a murderer and a fraud, Cadwaladr ... tell it to my father's corpse.' She raised the Stormer once more, of the mind to use it.

'Your father lives. You know that as well as I.' Doc sat back on his heels in a casual fashion. 'There has been no true harm done, so please allow me ...'

'What about John Pearce, his wife, and Nicholas ... is torture a pastime of the enlightened these days?' She brushed the mantle back from her shoulders. Her eyes were filled with tears as all the pain and anger accumulated over the last four years engulfed her, causing her to tremble in her stance.

'They are all still living, too, Rhiannon, in one part of the universe or the other. You have lost no one.' He made a strong appeal. 'If you want to know what it is I am doing, I shall show you. You don't have to trail me ... we are kindred after all.'

Rhiannon was openly weeping now, and she felt him penetrating her psychic shield to influence her. *Shoot him*, she ordered herself.

Doc held both hands out towards her, urging her to take them. 'Doesn't everyone deserve at least one chance?'

This was something her mother often said. *No!* she warned herself as she replaced the Stormer on her belt. *Don't trust him.*

'Here, I have a present for you.' He stood and held out a bracelet made of a pinkish-gold metal.

'I don't want anything from you.' She steered clear of him to approach the entrance.

'Well, I'm afraid if you want to come inside, you must wear this. There are nuclear weapons therein, and this band detects and absorbs radiation. Believe me, these will be in great demand soon.'

Doc showed her the one he wore which was larger and more complex than the one he offered her, but it appeared to be based on much the same principle.

'Radiation is of little concern to me,' Rhiannon bluffed.

'Until you experience physical death, my dear, you will suffer the ailments of mortal man.' Doc was firm with her, then his voice softened. 'Please, radiation sickness is not very pleasant, and I have no desire for you to add falling ill to your long list of reasons to despise me.'

'Alright.' Rhiannon held out her left hand, in a huff, wondering how he'd managed to find out so much about her.

'No, right hand,' he advised. 'It's designed —'

'Oh … here.' She switched arms impatiently. 'Ouch!' she cried as the band clamped around her wrist. 'It pricked me.'

Doc uttered something, a word that was unfamiliar to her.

'What did you say?'

'Nothing.' He keyed the code into the keypad and the heavy lead door clicked open. 'Come, my love.' Doc again held his hand out to her and this time Rhiannon took it. 'Mission accomplished.' He guided her inside, and sealed the door closed behind them.

Neraida and Rhun arrived at the Unken's outer defence wall to find Tory and Brian spread-eagled on the ground.

'Oh Jesus.' Rhun scanned the area. 'Where's Rhiannon?'

'Praise the Goddess.' Neraida breathed easier as she finished checking both Tory and Brian's right wrist and forehead.

'What were you looking for?' Rhun wondered aloud.

'The mark of the NERGUZ-I-NUEN. The module has a tiny needle that pierces the skin and leaves a tiny mark, similar to that of an insect bite.' She stood. 'Your kin are clean, however. How long will this coma last?'

'About six or seven hours.' Rhun spied the bodies in the shadows further up the tunnel and ran to investigate.

'Then I should really get them to a safe place to recover.' Neraida knelt between Tory and Brian placing a hand on each of their foreheads.

Upon discovering neither of the bodies was the one he sought, Rhun waved Neraida on. 'I must find my sister. I'll catch you up.'

'Good luck, little dragon.'

This had been Vortipor's pet name for Rhun, and it made him smile to hear it again.

'Beware of the NUEN.' Neraida's expression became more serious, as she disappeared with Tory and Brian.

'Huh!' Rhun scoffed, 'I'm more worried about what Murdock will do to me should I return without his girlfriend.'

Rhun cleared his mind to focus on Rhiannon. With one hand rested on his Stormer, he closed his eyes and prepared for the worst upon joining her.

The one thing Rhun had not planned on was being unable to locate her. He opened his eyes a few moments later to discover he hadn't moved, and cursed what he suspected had come to pass. 'No, damn it. Doc's will is not stronger than mine, how can it be?' He closed his eyes, trying harder this time, but Rhun's efforts only exhausted him. There was one other avenue he could try, so Rhun stood tall to evoke the Goddess and her elements:

> I am the master of my reality,
> and no will be stronger than my own.
> I am your devoted servant, great Goddess,
> the eyes of the Dragon on this Earth.
> Advise the four winds and their elements,
> that are the source of all creation,
> to speed me to my sister's side.
> I ask this in the name of my illustrious forefathers,
> and the great houses, Don and Llyr!

When even the Otherworld failed him, tears of remorse filled his eyes. 'Goddess have mercy.' Rhun fell to his knees in a desperate appeal. 'Do not punish Rhiannon because I got careless.'

'The Goddess you summon has long been banished from this place. She cannot aid you here,' a sinister voice advised. 'Now, leave! Before I have your body dismembered and sent to the four corners of the Earth to be laid to rest in cement.'

Rhun stood in defiance of the threat. 'I will not leave without Rhiannon. What have you done with her?'

'It's what I *plan* to do with her that should concern you more.' The voice was heard to laugh, but there was not much humour in it.

The vicious overtone of the statement made Rhun furious. He knew he was losing control as his own imagination had started working against him.

Leave, now! Rhun fought his desire to retaliate, turning all conscious thought to Neraida.

In the wee hours of the morning, when Teo still hadn't heard from anyone, he started to really worry. What was worse was how wired he'd become due to the numerous cups of coffee he'd consumed to keep himself awake. He couldn't think straight; he was mortal, he needed sleep.

'I'm going in,' he decided firmly, taking his Stormer in hand. Almost immediately he changed his mind and sat down in the pilot's seat. 'Maybe that's the coffee talking?'

He thought about checking in with the base, but that could be dangerous. If Doc had discovered any of the intruders he would now be on the alert. No matter what happened, Watarrka must remain a secret.

'Come on, Teo,' he scolded himself, 'think of something. If Tory was here she'd know what to do.' The thought that she may be caught up in foul play made Teo even more irrational. 'Dear Goddess, if you do exist, please send me a sign,' he begged, feeling stupid in doing so. 'Tell me what I should do.' When no mysterious voice of guidance spoke, Teo collapsed with a sigh onto the control panel.

Then the sound of a car, some distance away and getting closer, urged him to his feet.

Through the front porthole Teo spotted the headlights of a car speeding out of the cavern road.

'Instruction received and understood,' Teo advised the heavens, strapping himself into the pilot seat and firing up the hover blasters on *Merlin II*.

As consciousness beckoned, Tory's head began to throb. 'Ouch ...' she moaned, resisting consciousness.

'Mother ...' Rhun encouraged her to wake up.

'Come on, Tory.' Brian propped her head up. 'Drink this.' He trickled the cool water into her mouth. 'It's the good stuff ... from the fountain of rejuvenation, or some shit like that.'

Brian had awoken with a splitting headache himself, yet after drinking the water supplied by Neraida he felt like a new man.

Tory's being began to tingle, and a second later it felt as if every molecule in her body was bursting with energy. 'Whoa!' She sat upright, raring to go. Tory cast her eyes around the room, thinking perhaps they'd been captured by the Unken. The architecture was very strange; the walls were of a bizarre, black metal. The curved aerodynamic design gave the chamber an unearthly quality, but there wasn't anything of interest to investigate. 'Where on earth are we?'

Rhun's expression was grave, and yet Brian was absolutely bursting with excitement.

'We're inside an honest to God spaceship, Tory!' Brian couldn't hold back.

Tory freaked, shoving him aside to get to her feet. 'How the hell did we end up in space?'

'We're not in space.'

The tone of Rhun's voice cautioned her to calm, and Tory turned to hear him out.

'We're deep underground, somewhere in the vicinity of Babylon. This is where your dream was supposed to lead you. We interpreted it wrong.'

'How do you know that?'

'Hello, Tory.'

Tory spun around to find a woman clad in a tight-fitting black bodysuit that reminded her of Maelgwn's new interstellar attire.

'Cara?' Tory peered hard at her. This could not possibly be her deceased pupil and dear friend, but it was surely Cara's perfect incarnation.

'Neraida these days,' she stated, holding out both hands.

Tory dispensed with the formalities, overwhelming Neraida with a hug. 'How wonderful. I knew you'd show up sooner or later.'

'We're cousins,' Brian informed his sister, as she and Neraida stepped back to hold each other at arm's length.

'Really!' Tory figured their mutual ancestor at once. 'Marduk ...?' Neraida nodded.

'So, that's the good news.' Rhun hated to break up the merry scene, but there wasn't a moment to waste. 'Now you'd best brace yourself for the rest.'

Rhun enlightened his mother as to the power of the NERGUZ-I-NUEN, and Neraida filled Tory in on the weapon's short, but colourful history. The news of Rhiannon's abduction was not as easy to convey.

'Are you telling me that Doc has brainwashed my daughter?' Tory was overcome by the news, and the shock of it forced her to take a seat.

'We don't know that for certain.' Rhun attempted to put forward a positive view, looking to Neraida to break the bad news.

'The NERGUZ-I-NUEN casts a protective barrier automatically, thus isolating the subject from any outside stimuli. This is why I have been unable to rescue my people,' Neraida sorrowfully informed her. 'They are impossible to locate.'

In one sense Rhun thought this good news, as Doc might not have become as psychically powerful as he'd first feared. His mother did not share his optimism, however, and the rage inside her was building rapidly.

'That won't help us,' Rhun said, bluntly. Deep down he knew that his caution would only infuriate his mother more, but perhaps it was better that she release her frustration now.

Tory raised her stormy eyes to her son. 'Leave me,'

she instructed. She looked at Brian and Neraida, indicating with a movement of her head that they should do the same.

As her brother, Brian felt obliged to at least try and console her, 'Now, Tory —'

'Out, Brian,' she barked, staring him down. 'If you know what's good for you.'

Neraida encouraged both men to comply with Tory's wishes. The chamber door slid open as they approached it, closing again in their wake without a spoken command being uttered — psychokinetic control, Tory noted. Neraida then bowed to Tory in the same fashion as she had when Tory was her Sensei and vanished.

Alone now, Tory unleashed her anger by furiously clearing a space in the centre of the chamber. She knelt down and breathed deeply, summoning up all her hatred, all her pain, all her fear. As the dark ball of evil energy massed inside her it caused her to quiver and she struggled to contain it. The room also seemed to shake, though Tory was too distraught to care as she bowed her head to have a few quiet words with the cosmos ...

I thank the universe for allowing me to experience these emotions, but they do not serve my path to righteousness. Therefore, it is by my own will that I release them back to the universe, to be dispersed or re-channelled to serve the greatest good as you see fit.

On the other side of the door Brian and Rhun had heard Tory recklessly rearranging the decor, but now all had gone silent.

'Do you think it's safe to go back in?' Brian asked.

Rhun cocked an eye. 'I fear not.'

A loud cry of anguish was heard from within the chamber. This was immediately followed by a huge explosion, the force of which caused the very walls of the chamber to buckle outwards.

The noise of impacting metal was deafening. Both Brian and Rhun were startled into backing off a few paces, and said nothing as they waited for the rattling and crashing of the interior damage to settle.

Holy shit — Brian could only mouth the words as it seemed he'd lost his voice.

The door to the chamber opened, and as Tory approached she appeared to be at peace, focused and very determined. 'How long have I been out?'

'About seven or eight hours,' Rhun advised.

'Where is Teo?'

'I left him guarding our transport.' With all that had happened, Rhun had forgotten all about him.

'We should get back there immediately,' she instructed.

Rhun and Brian obeyed without hesitation, transporting themselves back to where they'd left *Merlin I* and *II*.

Then, Tory vowed, *I'm coming for you, Cadwaladr.*

Teo trailed Doc back to the hotel, and was flabbergasted when he spied Rhiannon hop out of the same car. The character she accompanied was a huge, brawny, dark-haired fellow. Teo recalled Rhiannon mentioning Doc had taken on a new guise — Teo assumed he was looking at it. What Teo couldn't figure out was what

Rhiannon was doing with him. Perhaps she was working undercover? And yet, she hadn't altered her appearance as she had last time.

Teo had parked on the same rooftop that Rhiannon and Rhun had occupied when they had been on surveillance duty.

'Will somebody please tell me what the hell is going on?' Teo plaintively demanded of empty space, as he watched Doc and Rhiannon enter the hotel.

As Rhiannon didn't appear to be in any danger, Teo thought it wise not to do anything rash. If she was on a mission, he didn't want to be the one to stuff it up. Best to keep trailing her, and wait for word from the others.

At dawn, Doc left the hotel with his entire entourage in tow.

'Aw, wow, this is too weird,' Teo mumbled as he observed the scene below.

Doc had resumed his normal persona, while Rhiannon had switched to her undercover identity. She was attired as one might expect the personal secretary of a prominent diplomat to be dressed, complete with briefcase and computer. Her fair hair was rolled up into a neat bun, and she wore glasses to complete the disguise. Teo almost didn't recognise her as she climbed into the limousine with the other members of Doc's team, for she blended in well amongst them.

The limousines led Teo to the airport, which was not as crowded or as well-guarded as might be expected at a later hour. The vehicles passed straight through the airport security gates that gave direct access to the runway.

Teo parked *Merlin II* in an out of the way corner of

the airstrip and, as he removed his seatbelt, he considered his attire: an unfamiliar army uniform was probably not the best camouflage in this instance. He had a root around in the cabin and, besides a couple of wetsuits that were unsuitable, he found a greasy pair of overalls.

'Perfect.' He pulled them on. 'I'll just look like another technician.'

With his Stormer in his pocket, Teo checked to make sure the coast was clear and then leapt down onto the tarmac.

Nobody gave Teo a second glance as he strolled towards the parked private plane. Everyone's attention was focused on the limousines. For some reason, Doc's party had yet to board the plane. One of his officials was yelling at the ground crew.

'This is a matter of international security. *Do you understand?* If there is something wrong with the plane, you find us another one. *Now!*'

Doc Alexander stepped out of the car. 'Now, Stanley, we have time for a drink. I'm sure these good gentlemen can have a plane ready to depart in twenty minutes.' Doc stared hard at the man in charge, who humbled himself to assure them that it would be done. 'Come, my dear ...' Doc reached into the limousine to assist Rhiannon out, whereby she took his arm and escorted him to the VIP lounge. Doc's security team surrounded the couple at a comfortable distance, and were on the lookout for any signs of trouble as they entered the terminal.

Near the entrance doors, a couple of guards were stopping the service staff to check their identification before allowing them to enter. Teo swiped himself a roll of electrical tape from one of the many tool boxes scattered about underneath the aircraft and headed off towards the staff toilet block to see if he couldn't procure himself an ID card.

He didn't have to wait long for a suitable victim and the knock-out procedure Teo employed was quick and virtually painless. He used the electrical tape to bind the man's feet and hands to the toilet bowl. He then bound the man's mouth with tape to ensure his silence even after he'd regained consciousness.

The ID card featured a small head-only photo. Teo was thankful that it was overexposed. The fellow was middle-aged like himself and the head-shot hid the vast difference between his own athletic build and his victim's rather frail one. He tucked his long, dark ponytail, streaked with grey, down the back of his overalls, pulling the collar up high round his neck. Then, as an afterthought, he pinched the technician's cap which featured an airline logo.

The two guards were engrossed in conversation now, smoking cigarettes and having a laugh. Just ahead of him, a few members of a ground crew strode towards the entrance to the terminal. Teo hastened his steps to situate himself five or so paces behind the group of men. The guards glanced at the crew members as they passed them, checking for the plastic seal of approval pinned to their chests. More interested in their amusing anecdote, they waved the group on, Teo along with them.

Hey, I'm pretty good at this James Bond stuff, he decided on the quiet, spotting the party he sought in the private bar.

Teo huddled up against a large pillar and gave Rhiannon a wave as she glanced in his direction. Her eyes fixed on him, and as Doc turned to see what had captured her attention, Teo ducked behind the pylon.

'Do you know that man?' Doc asked. 'The one hiding behind the pillar.'

Rhiannon nodded, swallowing a mouthful of drink. 'That's Teo, my mother's Sensei.'

'Really.' Doc foresaw an added bonus here. 'And has the location of your base been erased from his memory?'

She shrugged. 'Not to my knowledge.'

'See, Stanley. Let this be a lesson to you. Even delays can prove beneficial,' Doc emphasized with glee. Then he lowered his voice: 'Bring him to me, *alive* ... he is no use to me dead. Understand?'

'No problem,' Stanley acknowledged.

'Watch it,' Rhiannon added. 'Teo is a Shihan of Tae-kwon-do.'

'We're trembling,' Stanley informed her, motioning for some of his team to follow him.

'There's enough black belts among that lot to sink a ship,' Doc explained, 'and they're all considerably younger than your friend.' He clinked his glass against hers. 'This ought to be a pushover.'

Rhiannon grinned. 'Don't count on it.'

As Teo did a quick check on Rhiannon, he was alarmed to find Doc's bodyguards filing out of the bar towards him.

If Doc has become as accomplished as you say, he'll be able to siphon information from us faster than Floyd sucks it from the Internet.

Teo, recalling Tory's fears, began to panic. *You idiot!* He cursed his lack of foresight, as he made a dash down the terminal to escape the ICA personnel.

'Freeze!' One of the security team shouted a warning, and people began to flee the area as he pulled a gun.

Teo halted alongside another of the airport's large support pillars and turned to discover that he now had several guns aimed at him. He quickly darted for cover and pulled the Stormer from his pocket. He fired off two laser blasts and two of his pursuers went down. But there were so many against him, Teo found it impossible to keep track of all their movements.

A gunshot rang out and Teo hit the ground. Numb with shock, he stared at his shattered left kneecap in disbelief. It didn't take long for the pain to start permeating from the wound in short, sharp bursts. *Shit!* He rolled himself over and continued to fire at anyone who tried to approach him. *Conscious or unconscious, if Doc gets his hands on me we can kiss Watarrka goodbye.* Teo fired another laser blast and raised his tally to four.

Airport security had been alerted to the disturbance by this time, and more armed men were converging on the area.

Blood poured from the wound in Teo's leg, creating a huge dark pool on the floor around him. His sight began to blur, and he didn't expect to be able to hold them off much longer. In the back of his mind he started praying for a miracle. Tory had got him out of worse than this before today. *Goddamn it woman, why do you always have to be right … I shouldn't have come*.

'Drop it.' Stanley jumped out to confront the sniper, closely followed by the remainder of his team and several of the airport security guards. 'You can't shoot us all.'

There's only one thing for it, Teo thought, as he placed the weapon aside and slowly raised his hands.

As two of Stanley's men dragged Teo to his feet, their guns resting against his temple on either side, the remainder of the force dispersed.

Brennon retrieved Teo's weapon from the ground, and after briefly looking it over, clicked it onto his belt. 'You're pathetic,' Stanley spat at his captive, angered that he'd taken out so many of his men. He didn't realise they had only been knocked unconscious until after he'd smashed Teo across the face with the butt of his gun.

'Sir, they're all still breathing.' Someone had finally bothered to check.

'Well …' Stanley stood corrected, watching Teo's nose bleed another river onto the floor. 'You're just a damn nuisance then.' He motioned to the two men supporting the captive to follow him back to the bar.

Halfway to their destination, Teo regained some of his wits. With his one good leg, he dug into the floor in front of him and reached up to grab the pistol hand of the man to his right. *Goddess grant me strength*. He squeezed the man's trigger finger.

'No!' Doc jumped from his bar stool and raced into the terminal, just in time to see his bonus prize splatter his brains all over the immediate vicinity. 'Goddamn it!' Doc was furious. 'What did I say?' He confronted the blood-soaked security guard whose gun had served as the suicide weapon.

'I didn't expect …' he looked to the body he'd let drop to the floor, too awestruck to complete his explanation.

'These are radicals for heaven's sake. Just what do you think that means?' Doc began to lecture the guard, when he was unexpectedly besieged by emotion. Feelings that Doc had not experienced for centuries ran rampant through his being and he was powerless to block or even hinder the overwhelming sorrow and … *fear.*

I'm coming for you, Cadwaladr.

Tory Alexander's promise of wrath resounded in Doc's head, and he looked nervously about him.

'Is something wrong?' Stanley ventured to ask.

'It's time to leave.' Doc backed up towards the bar, a creepy expression on his face.

'What about him?' Stanley referred to the casualty.

'Get the local officials to take care of it. We're a little pushed for time.'

Back in the chasm that had led them to the underground base of the Unken, Tory, Brian and Rhun were concerned to discover one of their recon units missing.

Brian pinpointed the whereabouts of *Merlin II* on his vehicle's tracking system. 'According to this, he's at the airport.'

'He must have followed Doc there,' Tory figured, hoping Teo had the good sense to stay out of sight. 'I'll head straight to him. You two take *Merlin I* and meet us there.'

Rhun gripped Tory's wrist to detain her. 'Promise me that you'll stay away from Doc until we get there.' When Rhun saw the look of defiance on his mother's face, his demanding tone changed to a personal appeal. 'Please.'

Tory's mood lightened. Rhun was her voice of reason when she was beyond reason herself. She reached out to rest her hand against her son's cheek. 'I love you,' she said, tears moistening her eyes. 'Fear not, I hear you.'

Rhun smiled, satisfied with that, as she stepped away from him and disappeared.

Tory emerged from the ethers to find herself in one of the airport terminals. Chaos reigned supreme. Armed security guards were everywhere, so Tory willed herself to be seen as wearing their uniform and to appear and sound as a local of the male gender. She looked about expecting to find Teo close by, when she noted the blood and guts splattered all over the floor.

Oh Goddess. Tory said a silent prayer as she barged into the centre of the commotion.

There, in a great pool of his own blood, was a man unrecognisable due to a massive head injury. The sight repulsed Tory and as she did not spy anything that identified the corpse as her dear friend, she turned away to breathe a sigh of relief. But the image of the dead man hung in her mind taunting her with tiny details.

Her stomach turned as she realised that protruding from beneath the legs of the blood-drenched overalls were a pair of army boots like the ones she was wearing. Slowly, Tory turned to take a second look.

'No, please, no.' She fell to her knees beside the body, as she recognised Teo's wedding ring. 'Oh, Goddess, not him.'

'You know this man?'

Tory did not even hear the security guard question her, until he repeated the query. 'Not really,' she lied, suppressing her urge to explode into rage. 'What happened here?'

'The ICA tried to take him into custody, and the poor bastard shot himself.' The man sounded sympathetic.

Tory wept when she heard this, though no one present could see her anguish or the tears that streamed down her face. 'It wasn't suicide then,' she told the man. 'It was … a sort of martyrdom. He died, so that his friends might live.'

The guard crouched beside her, looking the body over. 'How do you know?' He wondered what his fellow worker had espied that he had not.

'It doesn't matter.' Tory took Teo's lifeless hand in hers. 'Creation knows I'm right.'

Her words made the guard very curious though he was not given the chance to question her. She vanished along with the body he was supposed to be guarding.

'Great wonders of Allah!' The guard bowed low to the ground, as did everyone else, believing they had witnessed a miracle.

Teo was not an immortal, Tory knew, as Taliesin was his perfect incarnation. Teo was also most certainly dead, and still Tory would not give up on him. She'd been in exactly the same predicament with Brian once and if she'd conceded defeat then, her brother would be rotting in the ground right now. Tory recalled Brian mumbling something about the fountain of rejuvenation when she regained consciousness earlier in the day. Babylon seemed as good a place as any to seek a means to resurrect her friend, and even if the healing capabilities of the fountain fell short of her hopes, perhaps Neraida's people possessed some advanced technology that would suffice.

Hence, Tory willed herself to Neraida, but as the blue-white ethers of her flight faded away she was left in total blackness.

'Neraida, are you here?' Tory cried out in panic.

'I am.'

Tory looked to the soothing voice that was quite close by. 'I need your help, desperately.'

'So I see.' Neraida lowered her gaze to the body at her feet. 'Here, put these on.' She placed a set of goggles in Tory's hand. 'I've been expecting you.'

'You have?' Tory was relieved to hear this. She placed the support strap around the back of her head and positioned the lenses over her eyes. *Amazing!* It was as if someone had suddenly switched on the lights.

The large circular chamber hosted many large, round mounds, made from the same strange black metal as the recovery room Tory had destroyed earlier. There were several control panels and a couple of large screens in the room. Tory guessed it to be a communications centre, but she was far too concerned about Teo to be interested in it. 'So you can help my friend.' Tory assumed this was why their arrival had been anticipated.

'No, Tory,' Neraida took a step back, 'I'm afraid I cannot. But I can be of aid to you.'

'What about the water of rejuvenation?' Tory stood tall to confront Neraida, her frustration bordering on rage. 'Isn't there something else we could try?'

'Tory,' Neraida urged her to see reason, 'the waters of the sacred fountains will only work on our kind.' She walked over to one of the large control panels, waving her hand over it. 'I am sorry for your loss, but it was his time ... everything happens for a reason.' She motioned Tory to one of the twelve dark mounds before them.

Tory was about to contest her new friend's apparent indifference to the situation, when a bright spherical light erupted above the mound in question. The tube of light extended from the roof to the mound's platform and grew so intense that Tory was forced to remove her eye wear. A figure took form inside the swirling tubular light mass, and once the form appeared solid the room fell back into darkness. Tory quickly replaced her goggles and her knees went weak when she realised it was Teo who had appeared. Frozen speechless, she watched him approach the stairs leading down to where she stood. As he descended, Teo began to change form.

'Sweet mother of mercy,' Tory mumbled, tears of relief tumbling down her cheeks. 'Taliesin!' she cried, bounding towards him and launching herself into his embrace.

'Tory Alexander.' He held her tight, feeling all that she did and more. 'It has been too, too long.'

Doc and his team made a very dramatic entrance into the US President's oval office in Washington. They barged into a closed meeting and immediately began to rearrange the furniture to set up their computer equipment. The President's men were outraged, naturally. But Doc had a few quiet words in Langford's ear, and the President adjourned his meeting and sent for General Berkley.

Rhiannon was introduced as a rebel spy who had defected from the Unken ranks to aid their cause. To prove her worth she had supplied the ICA with the code-key to the Unken's computer system. Doc, knowing Langford was no computer whiz, endeavoured to explain the significance of this.

'So, as the Unken have refused to negotiate, we can use this key-code to hack into their system and disarm their weapons.' Doc smiled in conclusion. 'If they won't consider peace, we shall force it upon them.'

'That's wonderful news.' Langford seemed surprised to be relieved of the pending disaster so quickly. 'I knew I'd made a sound decision sending you, Doc.'

'Mr President.' The General appeared grave as he stormed into the office, slamming the door closed behind him. 'The Unken have launched a missile on New Mexico, estimated time of impact thirty-five minutes.' Berkley turned his dark eyes to Doc, who appeared to have lost some of his cheer.

Eddie, Doc's young computer pro, was madly typing away on his keyboard. 'I'm in,' he announced, as he continued to key-crunch for a moment. Then Eddie looked to Doc, concerned. 'It's true. One of their ICBMs has been fired.'

'Well, of course, it's true.' Berkley blew a fuse. 'What the hell do you think we do here in the Pentagon?'

'Calm down, John,' Langford urged his Head of Defence, looking to Doc for some answers. 'Can we still deactivate it?'

'Impossible!' Berkley interjected, not prepared to waste any more time on diplomacy. 'We must blow it out of the sky while it's still in the boost stage — meaning we have two minutes to decide and counting.'

'And what,' Doc poised. 'Make us look like the bad guys? No, no, no. For although we cannot change the missile's course or shut it down now that it has been launched, we can detonate it. The subsequent explosion will rip a hole in the ozone layer above the Middle East causing massive devastation. It's too late to avoid that now. Still, I'm sure you'll agree Mr President, better there than here. In the world view, it will be the Unken who are to blame for the cock-up. The ICA will clean up as usual, the US will lend massive support, and we all come up smelling like roses,' Doc concluded, looking to Berkley. Even Berkley appeared appeased.

'This never leaves this room.' Langford gave the nod.

'Where are they?' Brian repeated for the fiftieth time since they'd located *Merlin II* at the airstrip. 'Maybe Tory has gone after Doc?'

'She wouldn't,' Rhun insisted, sick of watching his uncle pace, 'not after she promised me.'

'Where the hell are they then?'

'*I don't know!*' Rhun finally lost his cool. The stifling heat certainly wasn't aiding his patience. 'Look, she said she'd meet us here, so this is where we stay.'

Brian didn't respond, his eyes had become fixed on the horizon. 'This is very bad.'

Rhun looked to the sky to see a fiery trail being blazed across it.

'Either the Iraqi's are launching a space mission, or that's a missile.' Brian boggled at the sight a moment.

'It couldn't be bound for New Mexico, surely.' Rhun was baffled by this development.

'That's it. We gotta make a move.' Brian assumed control of the situation. 'You transport *Merlin One* and *Two* back to base. I'm going after Tory.'

'Hold on,' Rhun objected.

'Don't argue with me, boy. I'm still your uncle, no matter how long you've been kicking around, and I'll whip your butt without hesitation, so don't test me.'

Rhun backed away, half a grin on his face. 'That's debatable,' he challenged. 'And just for the record, I wasn't going to contest you. I was merely going to suggest that I restore the information I wiped from your memory earlier. It might prove a little difficult to find your way home, if you don't know where it is.'

When Brian was snapped out of his trance, Rhun showed him how to restore Tory's recollections of Watarrka so that she, too, could find her way home. Rhun then knelt between the invisible vessels, placing a hand upon each of them. 'When you find the others, for heaven's sake, report back to base. If I don't hear from you within twenty-four hours, I'll assume the worst.'

Brian looked to the rocket charging across the sky. 'How much worse can it get?' By the time he looked back to his nephew, Rhun had gone.

From above there came a huge explosion and a great yellow shock wave burst forth from the missile in all directions. Brian closed his eyes, straining to concentrate on Tory and ignore the ruinous mass bearing down on him.

Sometime later, when Brian opened his eyes to find only blackness, he had to wonder if he'd died. 'Tory?' he whispered timidly.

'Brian.' She startled the wits out of him, having snuck up from behind.

'Stop doing that?' He took a swing at her in the dark and missed. 'Will you turn the lights on, please?'

'Here you go.' Tory pulled a set of goggles down over his eyes.

'Wicked!' Brian smiled as he saw the light, waving his hands in front of the lenses to compare the eye wear to normal vision. 'Not bad at all. Hey, Neraida.' He waved to her now that he could see her. 'Teo, where have you been, man, we've been looking everywhere for you?'

'I had a bit of an accident,' Taliesin explained.

'But we fixed him,' Tory stepped into the conversation to add. 'He's immortal now, just like us.'

'Excellent, bro.' Brian gave Taliesin a high five. 'Together, forever, the world's famous ...'

'*Supreme team,*' they both responded at once, slapping each other's palms in a secret sequence of ways that only they knew.

This made Tory chuckle, as she saw Taliesin in his Merlin's guise. Brian, on the other hand, perceived him as the warrior who was his best and dearest friend. It was better this way, Tory thought. Brian never need know of Teo's bloody transition.

'If you girls are quite finished,' Tory placed a hand on her brother's shoulder, 'we do have things to do. Brian, I need you to go and tell the others we're alright.'

That's what Tory said. In reality, she was buying time to see Teo put to rest, before Brian explored too far and discovered his corpse.

'But I …'

'Please don't argue, Brian, I've had a hell of a day.' Tory looked to the large doors of the chamber as they parted, and a young man, of the same race as Neraida, entered. 'I have grave news.' He stopped before Neraida to report. 'A nuclear missile has exploded over Baghdad.'

Neraida was taken aback by the announcement.

'That's what I've been trying to tell you.' Brian finally got a word in. 'I saw it go up, and as Doc is Lugal I didn't think it was bound for New Mexico. This must have been what he had planned all along, but why here?'

'*So that the road of Kings can be prepared,*' said Taliesin, quoting Revelations. 'We'd best get to the surface.' He took hold of Neraida's hand, sending her calming energy to help soothe her shock. *You knew this had to happen*, he bethought her, and she nodded, sad to concede that he was right.

From Babylon, some ninety kilometres south of Baghdad, the view north had altered dramatically. The clear, blue sky had been replaced by a black cloud of fire and soot, whilst the scorching gale-force winds whipped the desert sands into a deadly frenzy.

'I don't understand.' Brian yelled over the howling winds to make himself heard. 'If Doc really wanted to destroy Baghdad, why did he wait until the missile was way out in the atmosphere before he detonated it?'

'The radioactive effects of a ground blast of that magnitude would possibly mend in twenty years,' Neraida explained. 'This air blast, however, will leave a gap in the ozone layer and subject the lands from here to the Persian Gulf to radiation from the sun for centuries!'

Now Tory had a clearer vision of Doc's motivation. 'That will leave this whole Middle Eastern sector uninhabitable to mortals.'

'Exactly.' Taliesin noted that Tory was as perceptive as ever. 'The waters of the great river Euphrates will dry up.' The Merlin's gaze shifted back to the devastation on the horizon, and he a took a few steps towards it. 'Because there exist spirits of devils that do miracles. They go out to the kings of the whole world to muster them for the war of the sovereign.'

Brian looked to Teo, marveling at his words. 'Are you feeling okay?'

Tory moved Brian aside, also curious about Taliesin's statement. 'The Gathering, you mean? This is where it will take place?'

Taliesin nodded to confirm this, spreading his arms wide to include the apocalyptic scene before them. 'And behold, they assembled to do battle in the place which in Hebrew is called Harmagedon.'

Ray did not take the news of Rhiannon's abduction well. His fist sent Rhun hurtling across Floyd's communications room to land on the couch, his nose bloodied from the punch. Nick, Noah and Daniel all jumped on Ray to stop him from pursuing the fight.

'You wouldn't listen, would you?' Ray snarled, trying to break free.

Rhun staggered back to his feet, his broken nose reforming as good as new. 'I wasn't the one who feared this … you were!' Rhun was incensed. He took advantage of the fact that Ray was restrained and returned the punch with gusto.

'Rhun!' Floyd was forced to join the scuffle, taking the lad in a headlock to lead him away. 'That's enough!' He thrust Rhun back onto the lounge. In a fury, Floyd grabbed Ray and cast him into a seat also. 'Millions of people have just been killed and millions more are going to perish! We are the only ones who know the truth. Divide and conquer, gentlemen. You're playing straight into Doc's hands!' Floyd took a few deep breaths to steady himself, having stunned all those present with his outburst.

Rhun was having a flashback to Gwynedd, to the one and only fist fight he and Bryce had ever had. Coincidentally, the reasons for the clash had been very similar and it had been Sir Tiernan (now Floyd) who had broken up that dispute, too.

Ray was just amazed to see Floyd lose his temper. He was usually too stoned to be that energetic.

'I hate violence.' Floyd was annoyed with himself. 'It's a waste of energy on all levels. We have to be smarter than that.' He looked back to the several television screens all running different news bulletins about the crisis in the Middle East. The whole world had come to a standstill to mourn humanity's loss.

Silence fell over the control room as everyone quietly brooded upon the next move.

'So you made contact with another underground rebel group, you said.' Noah looked at Rhun, encouraging him to expand on the statement.

'Forget that,' Ray cut in. 'How are we going to get Rhiannon away from that, that …' He stood, suddenly infuriated again. 'I can't believe you let him take her!' Ray didn't notice Brian materialise behind him. As Ray moved to launch himself at Rhun, he found himself gripped around the collar and shoved back in his seat.

'Rhun wasn't even there,' Brian informed him. 'Tory and I were with Rhiannon at the time. So if you want to take out your frustration on someone, take your best shot and be done with it. Tory is upset enough about what's happened, without you rubbing her face in it.' Brian backed off when he was sure Ray would refrain from violent action.

'Dad. Are you alright?' Daniel approached to check his father over, as Brian had obviously been through a war zone.

'I'm fine,' Brian assured his son with a pat on the cheek.

'Did you find my mother and Teo? Are they alright?' Rhun braved Ray's anger, changing the subject from his sister for a moment. 'Did you remember to restore her knowledge of Watarrka?'

'I did, they are, and I did.' Brian, filthy from standing out in the desert storms, took a seat beside Rhun in a puff of dust. 'But Teo had an accident. He's an immortal now, like us.'

'But that's impossible,' Rhun objected.

Brian was still caught up in his own train of thought, however. 'It's strange, really. He's got all this knowledge all of a sudden,' he commented, wondering why he hadn't been enlightened with wisdom at the time he'd become immortal.

'But Teo's perfect incarnation is …' Rhun broke into a huge smile as he suddenly felt much better. *Taliesin Pen Beirdd.*

The tidal wave of 2017 in the Atlantic had wiped out most towns on the islands of the Azores. But Horta, on Faial, had already re-established itself as a significant port of call, as it had been for centuries.

The old church and cemetery above the town, having been dug out from under a thick coating of mud, now appeared virtually undisturbed by the disaster.

Taliesin accompanied Tory to the island where they laid Teo's body to rest next to his wife. Neraida's people had embalmed and anointed the corpse, which made the burial less gruelling.

Tory knew the soul for whom she wept was still very much alive in the being beside her, and still she couldn't contain her tears.

'Oh come, come.' Taliesin placed an arm about her shoulder, to lead her away from the grave as it was refilled. 'I am much happier this way. We've been through all this before.'

'No.' Tory pulled away from him, not ready to give up her grief. 'You've been through all this before. I just got here.'

'You're worried about Rhiannon.' He cut through all her other feelings of woe to get straight to the heart of the matter.

'Yes, I am.'

'Don't be. For I have been to the future several times and I can assure you, Doc will not harm her.'

'How can you say that. He's brainwashed her for christ's sake!' Not wanting to take her frustrations out on her old friend, Tory walked away to regain her perspective.

After giving her a moment to brood, Taliesin spoke. 'A long time ago,' he said, 'before Rhiannon was even born, I told you she'd have a special role to play in the Gathering. Do you remember?'

Tory turned abruptly to look at him, confirming that she did remember. She said nothing, however, unsure if she wanted to pursue the conversation.

'Right now I'll grant that, yes, Rhiannon is being manipulated. But Cadwaladr —'

'So you know about the connection between Doc, Caradoc and Cadwaladr?'

Taliesin raised both brows in remorse. 'My greatest mistake, it would seem.'

'But how …' Tory beseeched him, 'how was his immortality overlooked?'

'That, my dear, remains a mystery.' The Merlin gave a heavy sigh. 'This apparent paradox has been left in Maelgwn's capable hands. Hopefully, he and Cadwallon will come up with some answers.' Tory's face had lit up at the mention of her beloved's name. 'But, let's not get off the subject. Cadwaladr has become obsessed with your daughter. Pretty soon, when he is confident that Rhiannon's loyalty to him has been well established in her mind he will remove her restraint. Firstly, because he desires to know that she loves him of her own free will. And, secondly, because she is too powerful an ally to keep restrained. Once the NERGUZ-I-NUEN module is unfastened from her wrist, Rhiannon's abilities and sensibilities will return to her, given time. When they do, she will find herself in the very powerful position of Cadwaladr's most trusted adviser.' Taliesin took a step closer, to emphasise the importance of this. 'Rhiannon is the greatest hope we have of freeing the countless number of immortals who have fallen under the influence of the NERGUZ-I-NUEN.'

'Sorry.' Tory had to interrupt at this point, 'What immortals? Are you talking about Neraida's people?'

'Haven't you worked it out yet?' Taliesin looked a tad surprised. 'The ICA clinic in Alaska isn't just for curing AIDS. It's for finding immortals. Half the people who disappear into that facility never even had the disease.'

'Oh dear Lord, he's building an army.' Tory's eyes bulged in their sockets. 'But the immortal gene could not be active in many of them, surely? What use are these pending demigods, unless Doc has discovered how to activate the gene?' To Tory's further bewilderment, Taliesin nodded.

'No, please, he hasn't,' she begged.

'Fear not,' he encouraged. 'I, too, have acquired a large vial of the formula that transformed both you and your brother.'

'Acquired from where?' She started to wonder what her time-travelling friend had been up to since last they'd met.

'From the same place En Darius got it … the Nefilim.' He smiled, knowing this would confuse her. 'Not even Darius knew the truth of the potion's true origins. The Nefilim, or more specifically, your great-grandfather, wanted none to know.'

'But you know,' Tory prompted, intrigued to learn the truth herself.

'Originally the formula came from the biological laboratories of Ninharsag,' he advised.

'Keridwen.' Tory referred to the Goddess by her Celtic name. 'But how did Cadwaladr get hold of it?'

'Shamash.' They both responded at once and Tory threw her hands in the air, frustrated.

'But there is one big difference between Shamash's potion and Keridwen's. You see, being of Enlil's flock, Shamash is not well disposed towards the human race. The last thing he wants is a whole army of everlasting Homo sapiens running amok beyond the time of reckoning. Therefore, he altered Keridwen's original formula so that its effects were only temporary. How temporary, I do not know.'

'We must stop him.' Tory stated, adamantly.

'There is no stopping him.' Taliesin stated bluntly. 'I have already tried several times, and unfortunately this has proved to be one of those asymmetrical events in time that is irreversible.' He paused a moment, as sorry about the fact as Tory was. 'Therefore, it falls to us to find, identify and activate the immortal gene in as many people left on this planet as we possibly can, before Doc finds them.'

'But hasn't Doc found them all with his compulsory testing?'

'Heaven's no!' Taliesin laughed at this. 'There are many underground tribes — like your own and Neraida's — the world over. And I intend to seek out each and every one of them.'

'So it was you who returned Jenny to us,' Tory deduced.

'Aye, as it was I, Teo, who assisted Brian to bury her.' This explained how Taliesin knew of Jenny's fate and where to find her.

'And what of Rhiannon?' It seemed to Tory that they'd passed right over that subject. 'Surely you don't expect me to leave her to Doc's discretion.'

'What choice do you have?' Taliesin decided to fill her in on a few simple facts. 'If you steal her back, she becomes a security risk, as she will still be loyal to your foe. Even if you manage to remove the NERGUZ-I-NUEN, Rhiannon may not be herself for weeks. Plus, it will take time for her to then re-establish her own psychic shield, making her fair game for anyone with psychokinetic ability — which, by the way, Doc now has. The strength of your psychic shield, and those of your kin whom Rhun has so carefully trained, is the only thing that prevents Doc from finding you at will.'

Tory took a deep breath, already considering another way round the problem. 'The NERGUZ ... tell me, who designed the damn thing? Perhaps they could tell us a way of re-programming the module without the activation word?'

'Gibal, Enki's chief technologist and son, was the creator of the NERGUZ. He disappeared shortly after Inanna stole the prototype.' Taliesin regretfully squelched yet another glimmer of hope. 'Maelgwn is attempting to rescue Gibal from Shamash and his sister as we speak. His first attempt was unsuccessful, I'm sorry to say.'

'I know he was captured and tortured.' Tory relieved the Merlin of having to break the news.

'Maelgwn told you about it?' Taliesin seemed astonished.

'Not exactly.' She found the Merlin's reaction off-putting. 'I saw the end result of Inanna's torment in a dream I had. I didn't feel right asking Maelgwn to recount the events of the nightmare he'd been through.' Her eyes narrowed as she folded her arms. 'What do you know of it?'

'Only what I heard through the grapevine really ...' Taliesin adopted a more official tone of voice, 'which was that Maelgwn was very ... disturbed at the time of his rescue. But his condition has completely righted itself since then. He would not have been reassigned the task of rescuing Gibal were that not the case.'

Although Tory knew there was something the Merlin wasn't telling her, she had enough to worry about at present and so let it pass. 'Okay then, if Gibal is not the answer we shall think of another.'

'Tory, please.' Taliesin was exasperated by her insistence. 'I have thought —'

'... this thing well through!' Tory finished the sentence for him, having heard it a hundred times in the past. 'Well, think again. This is not the Dark Ages, my friend. Gone are the days of sacrificing one's children for the greater cause of king and country. I am not prepared to waste one second of my daughter's happiness on some intergalactic war! Be damned if I will leave Rhiannon's fate in the lap of the Gods.'

Taliesin watched Tory depart down the hill towards town and she vanished before she'd gone ten paces. 'Ah Tory. One fine day you're going realise we're on the same side. And then maybe, just maybe, you'll learn to trust me.'

18

†HE FALSE PROPHE†

Walter received Patrick's files, as promised, and after sifting carefully through the reports could find nothing suspicious, apart from the apparent speed of his friend's decline in health. True, it was not unknown for AIDS to take its toll swiftly, yet Cadfan still felt that something wasn't quite right.

Doc Alexander sent a limousine to take Walter to the airport. It surprised Walter that Doc hadn't postponed their trip to Alaska. He thought the crisis situation in the Middle East would be keeping Doc very busy. Apparently not.

Cadfan had foreseen this explosion over the Middle East in a vision and had publicly pinpointed two thousand and twenty as the year. *How many times must I be proven right before the higher authorities sit up and take notice? Or even better, take steps to avoid the disasters in the first place!*

But, perhaps Doc Alexander had noticed? And this was why the prominent diplomat was going out of his way to befriend him. After all, Doc had been working towards a peaceful resolution to the terrorist threats. Perhaps Doc was frustrated with the politicians also and was letting Walter know the ICA was on his side.

Walter shook his head as he read a newspaper article about the huge number of fatalities that Iraq had sustained, and it was estimated that the initial death toll would be doubled in coming years due to radioactive fallout. The terrorist outfit who had, albeit unwittingly, instigated their homeland's destruction, were named in the press as the Unken. Cadfan hoped that, if the terrorist group had survived, they would not seek vengeance for failing in their attempt to hit an American target.

Walter noted that the Iraqi President and many of his top officials had been in Geneva at the time of the holocaust. The Iraqi President had expressed grievous disappointment that terrorism was still resorted to by fanatics in this day and age — a time of international peace — and he urged the culprits to cease their activities and surrender themselves before any more damage was done. The Iraqi officials then immediately set about rallying support for their cause from within the United Nations.

'How very fortunate they were there.' Walter wondered if the press were getting the full story, and decided that he must be cautious about trusting Doc. He also decided that if an association with Doc could help to avert any more loss of life, he would not close his mind to the possibility of working with the ICA.

Cadfan's vehicle was granted access to the runway and drove up to stop alongside a large, and rather luxurious, private jet. ICA officials guided him between transports, explaining that Doc Alexander had been delayed and would join him presently.

'I do understand that Mr Alexander might have a lot on his plate this morning,' Cadfan assured them as he climbed the stairs to the cabin where the hostess escorted him to a seat.

Thirty minutes later, another limousine pulled up beside the jet, and Doc and his entourage filed out onto the tarmac. The young woman who accompanied Doc Alexander up the stairs seemed rather familiar to Walter, though he didn't place her until they'd been introduced.

'Walter Cadfan, I'd like you to meet Rhiannon Thurlow.' Doc did the honours, having apologised for their tardiness.

'We've met.' Rhiannon took hold of Cadfan's outstretched hand. 'At my father's funeral,' she reminded him as he appeared disbelieving.

'Yes, I remember.' Walter wondered what she was doing in Doc Alexander's company. 'It's wonderful to see you again, my dear.' He covered his concern in case the girl was on some important errand for her mother.

'You know each other. Splendid!' Doc kissed Rhiannon's cheek. 'You must excuse me, I have a few calls I need to make.' Doc headed further down the plane to conduct his business.

'So what takes you to Alaska?' Cadfan seated himself once more, and Rhiannon took a seat alongside him.

'Oh, my interest is strictly personal,' she grinned.

'Mine too. Do you know one of the patients there?'

This made Rhiannon giggle. 'No. I meant, where Doc goes, I go. I love him enough to take an interest in his work, and be of help where I can.'

Love! The word resounded in Cadfan's brain. 'Forgive me, I didn't realise.'

'It all happened rather suddenly,' she assured him, patting the healer's hand. 'We only really met a few days ago, but we hit it off immediately … sometimes love is like that.' She winked at him, and Cadfan took this to mean that all was not as she was telling him, but he couldn't be completely sure.

As their conversation progressed he noticed something lacking in the girl's demeanour — Rhiannon smiled and addressed him politely, yet she'd lost all her spark, and from the sound of it, her individuality as well. Rhiannon seemed content to be a mere extension of her new boyfriend when Cadfan knew damn well that the daughter of Tory Alexander would never be so complacent. He had to figure that this obvious flaw in her character was intended to get him thinking — which it certainly had. Rhiannon's aura was perfectly intact, though perhaps dulled slightly, but this could have been due to the stress of her mission. 'Well, as long as you're happy, that's all that counts,' he told her. 'How does your mother feel about your new romance?'

'Does it matter?'

She was quite short with him, and Walter guessed that Rhiannon didn't want her mother mentioned amongst present company. 'Forgive me —' he began sincerely.

'No, forgive me,' she cut in, 'but that's a touchy subject at present, so please let's just change it. Tell me about you, Walter.' Rhiannon took hold of Cadfan's hand with both her own, and he noticed the mark on her inner right wrist.

'Oh, don't worry. I'm not a junkie,' she hastened to tell him. 'I just scratched the top off a mosquito bite. It's nothing,' she smiled, clutching his hand tighter as if in anticipation. 'Please can we talk about your work, it's so much more interesting.'

Back on the *Goddess* at Watarrka, Tory was greeted warmly by her kin. She was offered food and drink in the wake of her ordeal, but declined.

'What I desire most of all is some time to think,' and she urged them all to go about their normal routine — except Ray. 'Can we talk?' Tory held out her hand to him, which he accepted after a moment's hesitation.

Next thing Ray knew, he was standing on the highest ridge of King's Canyon, overlooking the plains, now blooming where once had been the scrub of the red centre. It was late in the evening and all the tourists had departed.

'We have a very difficult decision to make,' Tory said, a deep, uneasy breath making the unstable state of her emotions obvious. 'But there is much to consider, so I hope that you will hear me out —'

'This concerns Rhiannon, I presume.' Ray couldn't see how there could be any doubt as to what they must do.

'It concerns the whole of humanity,' she told him gravely. 'Please, Ray. You are my only hope of rescuing her without condemning everyone else in the process.'

Her words, so passionate and heartfelt, subdued his anger. 'What is it you need me to do?'

Tory told him of the army of immortals that Doc was secretly amassing at the ICA clinic in Alaska and of the NERGUZ-I-NUEN that was being used to control the will of these soldiers, including Rhiannon.

Once he was made aware of how Doc's brainwashing device operated, Ray conceded that it would be difficult to rescue his love — if indeed Rhiannon still had any recollection of their relationship. He had always thought the Agency was capable of just about anything, but Ray had not imagined in his wildest dreams the full extent of Doc's connections and aspirations.

'So, let me see if I have this straight … you expect me to design and build a device to remove a brainwashing weapon invented by some advanced alien civilisation?' Ray appeared to be a mite daunted. 'The amount of faith you have in me is scary.'

'We're all frightened, Ray.' Tory approached him to cup her hand over the swelling on his cheekbone. 'Even Rhun.'

'We had a fight.' Ray gently pulled away, ashamed of the fact in retrospect. 'But I guess you know that.'

Tory nodded to confirm that she did. 'Rhun is on your side, Ray. He always was, and always will be. He could be your greatest ally if you'd only let him.'

Ray raised a hand to his wounded jaw, seeming a little doubtful about that.

'You don't believe me?' That much was plainly obvious. 'Well, allow me to enlighten you as to why I can be so sure. My son was King of Gwynedd for half a century and for forty-five of those years you were his champion and chief adviser. All in all, your friendship spanned some sixty-six years.' Tory gave half a laugh as she recalled Bryce and Rhun as youngsters. 'The two of you were joined at the hip, sworn blood brothers. Before Rhun had even begun his reign, the two of you had saved the fate of Britain several times over.'

'I'm sorry …' He found the tale hard to swallow. 'But are you sure you've got the right guy? I mean, a knight in shining armour, Tory, is really not me.'

'Oh, you don't think so?' Tory knew he was severely underestimating his abilities, and that had to stop. 'Well, how about I let you judge for yourself?'

'What do you mean?' He became rather anxious as he watched her take up a position behind him.

'Relax, Ray, I'm not taking you anywhere. Not physically anyway.' She placed the palms of her hands against his temples. 'I'm just going to give you a glimpse of the *you* that I have come to know.'

Her mind wandered back to the very first time she'd met Bryce. He'd been all of five years old then, and just another orphan aimlessly roaming the village at

Aberffraw. *I am going to be a knight,* he'd told her with zeal, and the recollection still brought a smile to her face.

Over the twenty years that she trained Bryce and Rhun, there was many a memory of their steadfast friendship, their combined triumphs and the punishments they'd endured together for their mischief.

The second great battle of Arwystli was still clear in her memory — Tory and Bryce had fought off Saxon and demon that dark day. But of the many private moments she and Bryce had shared over the years, none was so dear to Tory as the day they had parted. This was the only time Tory had ever seen Bryce weep. Down on one knee before her, he'd begged her not to go. *I cannot stand that I shall not see thee again.*

But Bryce, thee will, she had vowed. *I shall go on and on, and thee shall incarnate. And even though thee may not recognise me, I shall know thee ... and I will find thee again, I swear it.*

The young knight had startled her with a parting kiss.

Tears were streaming down Ray's face as his eyes opened. It felt as if Tory had reached into the deepest recesses of his mind where sleep-time visions are stored and never consciously recalled. He had seen these images interwoven in his dreams, and had thought them nothing more than flights of fancy.

After giving him a moment to recover, Tory said, 'You asked me that first day we met on Faial why I was helping you ... well, now you know.'

Ray sniffled, wiping away the tears that had formed around the rim of his glasses. 'I must be a great disappointment to you this time round.'

'Hardly … you just fight with your intellect these days, rather than your fists. A fortunate thing in this instance, wouldn't you say?'

Ray exhaled heavily with what might have been a laugh. If only he could feel as confident in his abilities as Tory obviously was! 'So, I gather you've got hold of one of these modules?'

Tory winced. 'Not as yet. But, I thought perhaps we should take another look at the information on the hard-drive we stole from Doc. It might give us some clue as to where the manufacture is taking place.'

'Well, if this is our only means to get Rhiannon back, let's get on with it.' Ray grabbed Tory's hand and caught a ride back to base.

Even when decoded, a lot of the information on Doc's hard drive hadn't made sense to Floyd, though he'd learned that Ray's monitoring system for the fusion reactor was in use. He'd also discovered the nature of the glitch that the ICA had wanted Ray to design into the storage units on the power grid — it was a shutdown and/or self-destruct option that, if installed, could have been triggered from the host station in New Mexico, or alternatively, from the reactor station in space. Still, there were many fine details that continued to elude them, because code words were used for any subject Doc wished to keep secret and these were the key to unlocking the layers.

The events of the last few days, however, had provided a few clues as to the true meaning of Doc's perplexing codes.

'Aha!' Floyd was suddenly enlightened, smiling as he slowly shook his head. 'It's so obvious now.'

'What is?' Rhun returned from fetching himself a glass of water and a coffee for Floyd.

'Radiation detectors,' he explained, and then read a quote from the screen: 'To be worn on the wrist or forehead.' He slapped his knee with the back of his hand. 'Sounds an awful lot like your NERGUZ-I-NUEN, no?'

'That's it, Floyd! You've cracked one of the key words.' Rhun sat down where he could view the screen. 'What else does the document have to say about the module?'

'Not much. This is just a memo to his accountant, justifying the outlay of funds to the manufacturer, one Radtec Trading Company. Still, I can probably track down their whereabouts via Doc's financial records.'

Floyd set about digging deeper, but could find no mention of Radtec Trading among Doc's accounts. 'Either Radtec is a pseudo name, or it's been replaced by a dummy company in his books.'

As the pages of Doc's financial records flipped past on the screen, Rhun noticed a peculiarity. 'Stop!' he requested. 'Go back a couple of screens.'

Floyd complied. 'What is it you're after?' he asked, as the page Rhun wanted appeared on the screen.

'What's that icon there?' Rhun pointed to a yellow, smiley face. The tiny symbol was set at the end of a record detailing payment to a company with an Asian name that Rhun couldn't pronounce.

'Ah yes,' Floyd said warily. 'Doc has these icons scattered throughout his files, but they're booby-trapped.' He double clicked on the symbol and then pressed the control–shift keys to show Rhun what he meant.

The smiley face grew to encompass the whole screen. 'Enter password,' it said. 'But beware ... three wrong guesses and I self-destruct.' The icon chuckled away madly and then fell silent.

'The programming files are protected by the same self-destruct mechanism, so I can't access code words from there either.' Floyd shrugged, 'I haven't messed with any of them yet for fear of losing everything on the hard drive. Mind you, I have taken copies of all the data that is readily accessible. It's all the rigged files, like this one, that we stand to lose. You can guarantee they'd make the most interesting reading.'

'I thought you said you could crack any code,' Rhun jeered.

'Ah, but I never said how long it would take,' he pointed out in his defence. 'Doc Alexander is a smart young pup. I've never encountered an encrypted system with a self-destruct mechanism. Most large organisations that require code protection would lose information to hackers and risk sabotage rather than wipe out their whole system.'

'Well,' Rhun rubbed his hands together. 'I'm game, if you are.'

'It's your call.' Floyd shifted the responsibility,

although he was every bit as eager to gain access to the protected files as Rhun was.

Rhun scribbled down some possibilities, trying to decide which words might be the most suitable, and then eliminated the ones that were more unlikely. In the end, he got the list of possible passwords down to five: NERGUZ, Radtec Trading Company, Unken, LugalShamash, Utu.

'But we only have three guesses.' Floyd eyed the list over.

'They're in my order of preference,' Rhun said, 'so if you agree, feel free.' He motioned to the keypad.

'Alright, here goes nothing.' Floyd typed NERGUZ into the computer and pressed Enter. The smiley face stuck out its tongue at them.

'Two to go before I blow,' it announced with mirth.

'Next,' Floyd droned, typing in Radtec Trading Company and pressing the Enter key.

'Twice wrong, say, so long.' The computer was heard to laugh which set both Rhun and Floyd on edge.

'Damn it. I was sure that one would work,' Rhun grumbled.

'Shall we quit while we're ahead?' Floyd didn't feel so confident about any of the remaining words.

'Try ...' Rhun hesitated, then decided he should follow his gut instinct, 'try just Radtec.'

'I don't know, Rhun ...' Floyd smiled as the same thought had just occurred to him.

The two of them stared at each other a moment, their smiles growing as they encouraged each other to make a decision.

'Stuff it,' Floyd finally announced, typing in the word and hitting the Enter key, before they lost face.

'Live to play another day.' The smiley face dissolved to reveal a detailed account of Radtec Trading's financial affairs.

'My main man.' Rhun gave Floyd a high-five, then looked to the screen in search of an address. 'That figures,' Rhun commented as he spotted it. 'Like everything else, the NERGUZ-I-NUEN is made in Taiwan.'

A few hours into their flight, Walter became drowsy and fell asleep. Rhiannon slipped away to the back of the aircraft and waited while Doc dismissed his staff in order to speak with her alone.

'Anything to report?' Doc fastened the NERGUZ-I-NUEN firmly around her right wrist, uttering the word that activated the control mechanism.

He had discovered that even an individual with the strongest will needed days to recover from the module's brainwashing influence, yet the subject's psychic abilities were restored as soon as the restraint was removed. This allowed him to utilize Rhiannon's talents without risk of losing her to her own sense of reason.

'Cadfan *is* keeping something from you,' she told him, 'but you're not going to like it.'

'Don't tease me, girl,' he warned her playfully.

She smiled at this, getting more comfortable in her seat. 'Your dear friend, President Langford, has AIDS.'

'What?'

'Not only that,' she told him calmly, as if enjoying

his dismay. 'He caught it from an underage male prostitute, so he's a pedophile as well.'

'Shit!' If there was one thing Cadwaladr couldn't abide, it was homosexuals. His project in Alaska had quietly disposed of many of them, and those that had proven themselves to be immortals had been brainwashed out of their chosen sexual preferences. Patrick Haze had turned out to be one such individual, which was why Doc had no intention of ever allowing Cadfan admittance to the AIDS facility. He had far greater plans for the healer.

'Hey, Doc.' Stanley Brennon stuck his head around the curtains to speak with him. 'I think you'd better have a look at this.'

Walter Cadfan had gone as stiff as a board in his seat. His head was thrown back, and his eyes, though wide open, had rolled back so far into his head that only the whites could be seen.

'A vision?' Doc asked Rhiannon, who was quite bewildered. She had never witnessed this phenomenon before — she had always been part of it. Still, Rhiannon had heard descriptions from those observing her in a trance state and this was exactly as they'd described.

'Yes,' she confirmed, a tear trickling down her cheek as she began to tremble.

'Yet, you are not perceiving it,' Doc noted aloud, finding this most intriguing. 'The clan of the Serpent have rejected you, it would seem.'

The comment sent a dagger through her heart, and Rhiannon didn't even know why. She glared at Doc a moment, before heading to the back of the plane and taking a seat on her own.

'Get Vice-president Hagar on the phone, and make sure the line is secure,' Doc instructed Stanley.

As he waited for his instruction to be carried out, Doc observed Rhiannon. Her will was strong, and she was very talented. He had only removed her restraint for a few short hours, and yet his hold over her had lessened considerably. He found that the added element of danger involved in setting her free was deeply arousing. Rhiannon was so much more feisty, clever and fun to be with when he wasn't controlling her. *Heaven help me if I ever slacken her leash too much.*

'Hagar,' Stanley confirmed, handing the phone to Doc.

'Maxwell.' Doc put on his cheery voice. 'I've got a prediction for you … I see you being sworn in as President of the United States within the next few days.' Doc paused to catch his reaction. 'I'm deadly serious, my friend. I've been chatting with Walter Cadfan … yes, the psychic. We need to talk.'

It was dinner time at Watarrka, and the crew of the *Goddess* were in the rec-room, plotting their excursion to Taiwan.

Ray and Rhun were sitting next to each other going over the blueprints of Radtec Trading's manufacturing plant, which Floyd had pinched from the local Taiwanese council's mainframe computer.

As down as Tory felt, it made her smile to see the lads getting along. It felt like old times watching them pay out on each other without any malicious intent. Ray had been stoked to learn that Rhun and Floyd had found the manufacturer's address before they'd even had to ask for it. Judging from the way they were getting along now, Ray had perhaps realised that Rhun might be his greatest ally after all.

'Have something to eat.' Jenny placed a plate of food in front of Tory, who screwed up her nose.

'I'll stick to tea, thanks.' But she only took a couple of sips. Tory's stomach couldn't cope with the thought of anything. She was sick with worry for her child.

'Tory, honey.' Naomi sat down beside her to help aid Jenny's cause. 'Worrying is not going to get her back, nor is starving yourself.'

'I don't need it.' Tory resisted strongly.

'I know that, but you'll feel stronger and more alert if you force yourself to eat.'

'Please …' Tory held her head. The thought of food made her feel giddy and nauseous.

'Tory?'

Naomi's face became a blur.

Seconds later, all the immortals started dropping like flies: first Tory, then Rhun, and Brian. Jenny was the last to go.

Nobody had to ask what was happening. They had all witnessed this phenomenon before and knew the drill. They quietly went about laying out those afflicted flat on the ground, where they could see out their trauma with as much comfort as possible.

Three hours passed. But for those who awaited the prophecy of their unconscious crew members, it seemed like three days.

Tory was the first to stir. With her eyes closed, she began to mumble deliriously. 'Ice … fire … blood!' Noah and Ray went down on their knees on either side of her, helping her to sit upright and encouraging her to awake by means of gentle slaps about the face.

'Tory, it's Ray.'

Her eyes shot open and she gripped hold of the neck of his shirt. 'Langford's going to suicide.' She closed her eyes to recall what else she'd seen that made sense. 'And Cadfan —'

'Yes, what about Cadfan,' Noah coaxed.

'Someone is going to have him assassinated!' In a panic, she attempted to raise herself, only to collapse back into Noah and Ray's arms.

'Calm down,' Ray urged her. 'Think now, was there anything else you remember?'

'A new religious leader.' The voice turned everyone's attention to Rhun, who had found his own way to a seated position.

Rhun continued: 'A Messiah … I didn't see his face, but the man will have one hell of a following.'

'Yes.' Tory remembered seeing this also. 'So many, many people.'

'I saw a couple of explosions …' Brian rolled over on one side, propping his head on his hand.

'Me too.' Rhun seconded his statement.

'Me three,' Tory waved at them. 'So I guess we'd better get in and out of Radtec Trading quick smart, just in case it's one of the targets.'

Everyone agreed. Rhiannon's rescue was still their top priority.

An hour away from the AIDS facility in Alaska, Cadfan began to come round. His eyelids fluttered closed as his body relaxed into his seat. 'I'm not a saviour,' he muttered in protest.

'Yeah,' Doc had to smile, 'but you'll do.' He slapped the healer gently around the face to bring him to consciousness. 'Been speaking with God again, have we?' Cadfan was startled awake and Doc offered him some water. 'I assume you know the plan then?'

'Cadwaladr,' Cadfan named Doc, overawed by his newly-acquired knowledge.

'Grandfather,' Doc acknowledged in return, placing the water aside.

'Yes. I have been made aware of your intentions, Cadwaladr.' The healer finally answered the question, looking out the window over a snow-drenched countryside. 'So where are you taking me, really?'

'Just where I said,' Doc assured him, pointing to a place on the distant horizon. 'We're only about an hour away from the facility. So relax, you'll get where you're going soon enough.'

It was a beautiful day outside, though at this time of the year it was pretty much day all the time in Alaska. It had obviously been snowing outside, but the storm had passed completely, leaving a clear view of the serene white countryside that lay before them.

A flare of light erupted from the very spot where Doc had directed Cadfan's attention.

'What the ...?' Stanley Brennon was on the phone at once. But the aircraft was hit by a shock wave, and he was knocked off-balance before he could interrogate whoever was on the receiving end of his call.

Due to the shock wave generated by the distant blast, the plane lost power and the engines died. Knowing something of the effect an EMP wave could have on the plane's electrical systems, the pilot was quick to shut down and re-boot his computers. The engines roared to life once again, and the aircraft was back on course in a matter of minutes.

'Is everyone okay?' Doc received garbled responses from his team. 'Good ... because it would seem the Unken have retaliated, ladies and gents. Therefore we have a whole lot more work to do.' Doc clicked his fingers to draw Stanley's attention away from searching for his phone. 'Get me to Washington.'

'No!' Cadfan suddenly remembered his most recent vision. 'He's not in control of his own faculties, you have to stop him.'

Doc grabbed the Stormer off Brennon's belt and blasted Cadfan with it. 'We really must look into manufacturing those things.' He passed the weapon back to Stanley. 'It shuts them up for a while, at least.'

Doc arranged a closed meeting with Langford. From the airport the ICA party were flown to the White House by helicopter, and were given a clear run all the way through to the oval office. Doc entered alone.

Langford confirmed that the total destruction of the ICA's AIDS clinic in Alaska had been an act of Unken retaliation for their own fallen nation. 'They claim full responsibility ... what a mess.' Langford rubbed his weary brow, starting to sweat under the pressure. If anyone ever found out that the Unken had not been responsible for the disaster in the Middle East his life wouldn't be worth living.

'Well, here.' Doc passed the President a NERGUZ bracelet. 'This is a little something my scientists have been working on. I hoped we'd never need them, but the way things are going we'll have to make the damn devices compulsory.'

Langford picked up the strange, pinkish metallic band, looking it over with a perplexed expression.

'It's a radiation detector. It also absorbs excess radiation,' Doc explained. 'It's designed to be worn on the right wrist.'

The President tried to look appreciative as he snapped the metal band on. 'Ouch ...' He felt something bite him, and tried to dig under the secured band looking for bugs. 'I beg your pardon?' Langford queried. Doc had uttered something but he didn't quite catch it.

'Enough of the pleasantries,' Doc changed the subject, though Langford wouldn't have known. 'Another urgent matter has come to my attention, Bob, and I'd like to run the scenario by you so we can decide on the appropriate action.'

'Shoot,' Langford bade him, though the last thing he needed was another problem. As his esteemed colleague outlined the cause of his concern, Langford's other woes suddenly paled by comparison. His life was already not worth living.

'Now, I know you keep a pistol in the top drawer of your desk, Bob.' Doc planted the seed before departing. 'I'm going to leave you to mull things over for a while.'

The outer office was filled with the President's staff, all anxiously awaiting an audience. When Doc emerged he was swamped with questions, but he called everyone to silence and addressed Langford's personal assistant. 'The President could use some tea,' he told her, before turning to address the rest of the crowd, 'and a few quiet moments to collect his thoughts wouldn't go astray either.'

The garbled protests were silenced by the gunshot. Seconds later the oval office was flooded with witnesses to the President's suicide — nobody could dispute the fact.

Doc was one of the first through the door, and while others were taken aback by the gruesome sight, he made straight for Langford to check his vital signs. 'I knew he was feeling a little stressed, but this?' While Doc was playing the saint, he managed to retrieve the NERGUZ module without anyone noticing.

'Don't touch anything.' A security man pulled the diplomat aside, and the paramedics moved in.

'What did you say to him?' General Berkley took hold of Doc by his jacket lapels.

'I think what we were discussing is fairly obvious, John.' Doc brushed away the General's hold on him. 'He just couldn't handle the pressure ... can you?'

Doc walked away, leaving the General to stew over what he knew. On the outside, Doc was weeping for the loss of his dear friend for whom there was barely a dry eye in the room. He paused at the doorway, looking back at the paramedics who were unable to help their fallen leader. *But all the King's horses and all the King's men, couldn't put Langford together again.* On the inside, Cadwaladr smiled broadly.

Tory, Brian and Rhun had already left for Taiwan when the news about the Alaskan bombing and the President's subsequent suicide was announced on the television.

Those left in Floyd's control room at Watarrka sat gaping with awe as their crewmates' prophecies manifested before their eyes.

'I saw this,' Jenny gasped, and then burst into tears.

'It's okay, Mum.' Nick placed a comforting arm around her, believing it was what had come to pass that had upset her. In reality, it was what had yet to happen that she feared.

As was to be expected, the ICA were the centre of media attention. The news broadcast crossed to a live press conference Doc had called in Washington.

'There's Rhiannon.' Ray noticed her standing on the sidelines with the rest of Doc's team. She didn't look like she was under restraint. On the contrary, she appeared to be fitting right in. 'There it is …' He spotted the bracelet she wore on her right wrist and got up out of his seat to see if he could get a closer look. There were protests from the others for Ray to stop blocking the screen. 'Hey, isn't that Walter Cadfan?' He pointed to the gentleman standing beside Rhiannon.

'If you'd kindly get out of the way, I'll tell you,' Noah jeered and Ray moved. 'Yes, it is Cadfan,' the reporter was surprised to note. 'What is he doing there?'

They did not have to wait long for an answer. After Doc had said his piece in regard to the Unken retaliation and the suicide of his dear friend, President Langford, he invited Cadfan up on stage. The diplomat stated how Walter had foreseen the disastrous events that had unfolded in the past few days, and he proposed that the world might do well to pay heed to what Cadfan had to say from here on in.

The renowned healer and prophet took the stage, and as he raised his right hand to wave to the television cameras Ray freaked.

'Cadfan's wearing a module too!'

'Shit!' Noah sprang from his seat to join Ray, hovering close to the picture. 'He's right. It's identical to the modules that Doc's team are wearing.'

Jenny started to whimper again, and trembled as she stared at the screen in horror. 'I saw this …' she managed to stammer once more before Floyd realised what had Jen so distressed.

'They're going to assassinate Walter Cadfan.' Floyd remembered what Tory had said.

'But he's one of the Chosen, isn't he?' Ray queried, hesitant to consider what Doc's plan might be for the well-respected psychic.

'Exactly!' Noah sprang up, consumed by an unexpected insight. 'And what do you get when you mortally wound a man on national television and he comes back to life?'

'A Messiah!' They all guessed the punch line. 'And Doc's controlling him.' The notion was not an attractive one.

'There must be something we can do?' Naomi urged them all to think harder, though with their main task force absent their options were limited.

The sniper's bullet startled them, as every person in the room had been anticipating the sound. The close-range shot split Cadfan's skull, taking the top of his head clean off. They watched in horror as his body crumpled to the floor. There was no question that the strike had not been fatal.

'I can't believe they're still transmitting.' Naomi felt as if she might be sick, but was too distraught to move.

'Doc would have arranged it that way,' Ray said softly. 'He'll want the whole world to witness the resurrection of his new and greatest puppet.'

Thrown into complete disarray, the members of the press suddenly hushed and were shown to be looking in amazement at the stage.

'Oh god, they're sick.' Naomi turned away as the camera came to focus on Walter's mutilated remains.

'No, Naomi, look!' Noah urged, riveted to the transmission. 'He's reconstituting.'

It was true. The splattered pieces of Cadfan's head were slowly sliding their way back to rejoin the rest of his form. No sooner had his splintered skull repaired itself than veins, nerves, muscles and skin enfolded it. When every fragment of his person was restored not one drop of Cadfan's blood remained on the stage. As his eyes opened, all those who witnessed the miracle were frozen to the spot in complete astonishment and disbelief. The fallen prophet raised himself up to a seated position, still dazed by his ordeal, when the crowd broke into a round of applause. In a heartbeat, Cadfan was surrounded by reporters firing questions at him. Was he an alien? A vampire?

'Are you the Messiah?' One reporter cut right to the chase.

Cadfan shrank away from the crowd, unable to respond. Doc barged into the middle of the scuffle to retrieve his grandfather.

'For heavens' sakes, man.' Doc wrenched the reporter who'd asked the pertinent question out of the way. 'After what we all just witnessed, do you really need to ask?' The diplomat guided Walter Cadfan away from the commotion with the aid of his security team.

The media went into a frenzy. Journalists started madly whipping mobile phones out of pockets and bags and dialling their editors. Many rushed off to meet deadlines.

With a box full of NERGUZ modules for Ray to dissect, Tory, Rhun and Brian returned home in good spirits. They had also succeeded in releasing a nasty virus into Radtec Trading's mainframe computer. This would slow production of the modules, for a while at least. They could have destroyed the plant, but they knew Doc would only relocate the enterprise elsewhere and would probably capitalise on the propaganda value. And there seemed little point in defeating their enemy if it meant using the same assault tactics they were supposedly rebelling against. An eye for an eye didn't figure in Tory's book, but neither did turn the other cheek. Cadwaladr had lessons to learn in this life, too, and she was just the person to teach them to him. Tory had decided this before she'd even returned to Watarrka, and at that stage she didn't know the half of what he'd done.

In the few short hours they'd been in Asia, it seemed as if the whole world had gone mad. 'So now we've lost Cadfan. And he is to become what he feared and despised most — an idol.' Tory wanted to cry, but knew there was little point. 'It's down to you, my friend.' Tory passed their bounty to Ray. 'I'm fresh out of ideas.'

Ray had already whipped a module from the box and was examining it closely. 'I'll get on it right now.' He wandered off to his tool shed with the box under arm.

'I'll give you a hand.' Rhun went after him.

Brian looked across to his sister. He had to admit that he was exhausted from all the action they'd seen in the past few days, but Tory appeared far more jaded than he. She might have been immortal, but at present she looked more like a walking corpse. 'You, my girl, are going straight to a hot bath.' He grabbed hold of her to escort her there.

Tory wanted to protest, but the thought of a hot bath was far too wonderful. 'Brilliant idea.' She loosened his grip, patting his hand to assure him she would follow his instruction.

Brian felt powerless to help her as he watched Tory trudge out the door. It seemed so unfair that she always came through for everyone else, yet who was there who could possibly return the favour?

'Dad,' he stated resolutely.

19

DWELLERS OF THE UNDERGROUND

As Tory soaked in the tub she was mulling over the conversation she'd had with Taliesin on Faial. He had made it sound as though any attempt to rescue Rhiannon would prove futile, and he'd certainly not offered any suggestions to aid the cause. Nor, in their infinite wisdoms, had the High Merlin or her father gone out of their way to prevent Cadfan's sad plight. This lack of action led Tory to wonder if Doc was truly infallible, or if, for reasons yet unknown to her, the Gods actually wanted this 'end of the world' scenario to be played out.

'I am sick to death of graciously succumbing to the higher agenda.' She raised herself from her watery resting place and stepped out of the bath cubicle to retrieve a towel from the bed. 'I mean, give me one reason why I should even give a shit?'

Tory Alexander. You raise my expectations.

Startled by the comment, she covered herself with the towel before turning to see Maelgwn's free-floating etheric form at the other end of her quarters. She didn't dare move, fearing she was dreaming and would wake. 'My god, is that really you?'

Not God, but close, he granted. *I am your husband, remember?*

'Oh, aye!' She was overwhelmed by his presence and wanted so desperately to run and embrace him, but refrained knowing she could not.

Please, carry on, he smiled. *My memory no longer does your naked form any justice.*

'It is you.' She returned the smile, allowing her towel to drop to the floor.

Even before they'd married, Maelgwn had always had a sixth sense when it came to Tory's bath time and he enjoyed nothing more than catching her in the act.

'Your timing is still impeccable, I see.'

So it would seem. Maelgwn was mesmerised as he watched her approach. He reached out to touch her cheek.

Tory's eyes closed in anticipation, and she released a soft sigh of delight as his fingertips made contact.

You can feel that? He hadn't really expected that she would.

'Aye, it tingles,' she advised.

Interesting, Maelgwn thought, immediately pushing the observation aside. There was a reason behind his visit, and he felt he should deliver his report before he got sidetracked. *Tory, I know how Cadwaladr was overlooked as an immortal.*

'Oh, my love. How romantic!' Tory moved to dress herself. He was obviously here on official business and was bound to act accordingly.

Listen to me. He delayed her. *Cadwallon has been doing some regression therapy, and he discovered that he was not first slain at the battle of Hexham, but in his crib, soon after birth.*

'So Cadwallon's immortal gene was activated when Cadwaladr was conceived. I was right.' Tory took a seat on the bed, still in her naked state. 'But how did the heir to the throne of Gwynedd manage to die without one of his nursemaids finding out about it?'

His mother, Cadfan's good Queen, had a difficult time with birthing. The staff were well occupied trying to save her life at the time her newborn babe was being murdered.

'So you think it was purposeful, then?' Tory was intrigued.

We know it was, and with the very intention of keeping Cadwallon's son's immortality a secret from the family guardian.

'Taliesin,' Tory concluded. 'And who had such incredible foresight? Shamash.'

Correct. But he did have some help from —

'Inanna.' Tory guessed the other half of the equation, before Maelgwn had the chance to deliver it.

Correct again. He was astonished by what she'd

managed to figure out on her own. *Under hypnosis, Cadwallon recounted the whole affair.*

'So it is the entity in whom Cadwaladr has placed his trust who is ultimately to blame for him being overlooked, not Taliesin.' Tory shook her head, thinking it ironic.

Yes, as usual, Taliesin is blameless. Maelgwn still felt guilty about banishing the Merlin from his kingdom all those years ago, and he'd never really had the chance to say sorry since. *You know I regret accusing you both as I did.*

'Maelgwn, you were ill,' Tory stated frankly to induce him to lose the guilt. 'Everyone knew that, including Taliesin, so forget it. Tell me instead of your second attempt to rescue my great-grandfather's technologist, Gibal. Did you succeed?' She lay across the bed to listen.

He was about to ask her how she knew the details of his last mission, but the sight of her laid out before him caused Maelgwn to wonder instead how he'd ever run a kingdom with Tory around to distract him.

I rescued parts of Gibal, he told her, *but as Inanna has hidden the rest of him all over the galaxy, the all-important head is proving a little hard to find.*

'She dismembered him!' Tory sat back up.

Aye, a vengeful gesture. Inanna believes Marduk dismembered her lover, Dumuzi.

'But Dumuzi was my grandfather's youngest brother. Why would Marduk want to dismember him?'

Marduk swears it was not he who murdered his brother, but as the pieces of Dumuzi have never been found, he cannot prove his innocence.

Maelgwn floated down to lay beside her on the bed, and Tory wondered if he knew of their daughter's predicament — or if, indeed, he knew of their daughter at all. 'Have you done much regression work, Maelgwn? Do you remember your past lives as Turan and Miles?'

Of course I do. They are my link to new experiences of you … Turan, Miles, and all the others, they keep me sane.

All the others? She wondered at this, but let it pass. 'You know of our daughter then?'

Rhiannon.

He stated it as plainly as Miles himself would, which was a great relief to Tory. She didn't want to have to go into a long explanation. 'Cadwaladr is holding her captive with a NERGUZ module.'

What! Maelgwn's form went shooting backwards into the middle of the room. *Why was I not told?*

'Well, the impression I got from Taliesin was that the powers that be want her left were she is, as some sort of spy,' she explained. 'Her boyfriend, who just happens to be an electromechanical design engineer, is trying to figure a way around the voice command mechanism on the NERGUZ module. Rhun is helping him,' Tory added in an attempt to ease Maelgwn's distress.

His son's name brought the smile back to Maelgwn's face, but the news that the NERGUZ had reached his home planet saddened Maelgwn greatly. *What are you planning to do?*

Tory slid off the bed to dress herself, knowing a good-sense lecture was forthcoming. 'I'll wait and see what Ray comes up with, before I decide.'

Although he admired her guts, Maelgwn couldn't allow her to risk being captured. *Tory please —*

'Don't Tory please me. I know what you're going to say.' She pulled her singlet on over her underwear with such force she almost tore it. 'I am not going to leave our daughter at that bastard's discretion. You do know who he is, don't you?'

Maelgwn was puzzled by the question. *Aye, Cadwaladr.*

Tory shook her head. 'He's Caradoc, incarnate.'

My brother, Caradoc?

'None other.'

That explains how Doc recognised Miles as me, the day he killed him.

'You relived Miles' murder?' Tory assumed this was the case, as Turan had made the same observation.

Aye, and I wondered how Cadwaladr came to know me by sight. Obviously he has been doing some past-life regression work himself. The thought of Caradoc controlling Rhiannon was both shocking and sickening. Maelgwn knew how it felt to be under the restraint of a NERGUZ module, for he'd been amongst the first of its victims. *I have obviously not been told the half of what is really going on.*

'Ha! Join the club.' Tory pulled on her jeans and zipped them up.

Tory, Maelgwn appealed. *If neither one of us is being told all the facts, then perhaps between us we can piece the truth together.*

'Well, I'm all for that.'

Maelgwn gathered as much. *But if you are captured by Cadwaladr, that would seem to ruin our chances of doing so.*

Though Tory appreciated the subtlety of his approach, she folded her arms in defiance. 'It's alright for you to take the same risks ...'

I have lots of aid.

'So do I.'

Ah ... but I have allies on various levels of the etheric world. He knew he had her on this point. *Whereas you have let your ties with the denizens of the Otherworld lapse.*

'Well, I've been a trifle busy!' Tory found herself wishing he was physically present, so she could thump him. 'Look, if you're not going to be part of the solution, Maelgwn, then you're part of my problem. Nothing you can say or do is going to stop me from trying to free our daughter, and you know me well enough to realise I'm not lying.'

Yes, I do, Maelgwn conceded in a huff. *Then, at least promise me that you shall consult Taliesin before making any such attempt.*

'I already told you. Taliesin doesn't want me to liberate her.'

Then change his mind! Maelgwn remonstrated. *Goddess knows you have an extraordinary talent for getting your own way.*

'That's because I'm always right.' She pushed her luck, grinning broadly.

This was Tory's way of saying she agreed with his caution, so Maelgwn resolved with a smile: *I cannot argue with that. I can only hope that it will always be thus.*

Tory gave him a wink to assure him he could count on it.

Maelgwn did not linger long, though he did promise to contact Tory as often as he could. He feared, however, that his visits would not be as often as he'd like. What with all that was going on in the universe, leisure time was a rarity.

'War,' Tory uttered when she found herself alone, shaking her head as she considered how futile it was. If the Nefilim were so all-powerful and all-knowing, then why were they causing such havoc? 'The trouble is, I have been in awe of these beings … the whole human race has since the day they fused the genes of an ape-man with their own and created us.' Tory began to pace, her trust in herself being fueled by her words. 'But they were not the very essence of our creation. The Nefilim may be a part of God's universe, but the one divine source of all there is? They most certainly are not!'

In her view, humanity's immortal forefathers had really done no more than to be the parents. They had overseen mankind's development until such time as we were able to cope on our own. Granted, human beings had made quite a mess of their planet. Instead of the temple the Nefilim had left behind, the Earth now looked more like a university student's apartment. Yet much of humanity's destructive tendency may have been avoided had the Nefilim not confused our beliefs and principles through all the ages, just as some parents feel the need to strike the fear of God into their children to keep them under control.

'Well, there comes a time in the life of every child when they become the teacher and the parent becomes the pupil. For the Nefilim, that time is now.'

Feeling, for the first time in a long time, that she truly knew her own mind, Tory headed down to see if Ray and Rhun had any initial observations for her. She did realise Ray's task was going to take some time, if indeed he managed to figure out the NERGUZ at all.

Tory was still of a mind to visit Rhiannon; as long as she could persuade Taliesin to aid her, there was a means by which she could seek her daughter without the risk of being trapped. She had already requested a copy of Doc's itinerary for the coming weeks from Floyd, figuring the diplomat would be keeping Rhiannon close by him. In the light of information concerning Cadwallon's murder at the hands of Inanna and Shamash, Tory also had a few ideas to run by Taliesin pertaining to how Doc might be eradicated from history altogether.

Rhun and Ray had already disassembled several of the NERGUZ modules. Ray was half falling asleep as he inspected the circuitry of one through a strong magnifying glass.

'The good news is, these actually are radiation detectors.' He pushed his glasses back up his nose as he looked at Tory. 'Only this tiny area here,' and he motioned to the part of the armband that rested against the inner wrist, 'is of concern to us. Come here.' He motioned Tory round behind him, from where she could view the processor magnified.

Once detached from the metal casing, the tiny processor chip resembled a hexagonal ball that had a minute spike at one end. It was simply beautiful to look at, like a fine jewel that glistened with a myriad of colours.

'I don't suppose you've ever seen anything like this before?' Tory inquired, sounding hopeful, as she certainly hadn't.

Ray shook his head. 'Turan may have, but not I. Still, commonsense tells us that this wee spike here is integral to the control mechanism's function. Therefore, if we were to create a device that would sever it from the processor, it may well deactivate it.'

'If, of course, it doesn't give the wearer a severe psychotic breakdown in the process,' Rhun added.

'Or explode, etcetera,' Ray finished. 'The trouble is, we can't seem to find anything that will even scratch the surface of the damn thing, let alone cut it.'

'Well, keep trying. You're doing good.' She rubbed both their necks in gratitude, and feeling how tense Ray was she turned all her attention to him. 'You should get some rest, my friend.'

'Who can sleep!' he scoffed.

'You would, if you'd just put your head down for five minutes! See to it that he does,' she instructed Rhun as she kissed his forehead on her way out.

'Are you off somewhere?' Rhun inquired, sensing that she was.

'Don't worry, I'll stay out of trouble.'

His mother vanished before she reached the door. Rhun pondered what she might be up to, then, with a shrug, looked back at Ray and the challenge at hand. 'Remind me, in a couple of hours, that I need to check up on her.'

'Bloody parents, eh?' Ray commented. 'You can't let them out of your sight for a second.'

When Tory materialised from the ethers, expecting to confront Taliesin, she again found herself in complete darkness. She could only assume that this meant the Merlin was still in the company of Neraida's clan. This time, however, the room she'd manifested into did not feel entirely stable — in fact, it felt mobile. She was about to call to Taliesin, when the floor underneath her feet tilted abruptly and she was cast off-balance and sent hurtling into a wall. 'Holy Moses!' she muttered, sliding down to the floor where she stood a better chance of keeping her bearings.

'Tory?' She was wrenched from the ground and thrust into a seat. 'Dear me. Are you alright?'

'Taliesin! What's happening? Is it an earthquake?' she questioned anxiously as she felt him strap her securely into the seat.

'No, not quite.'

He placed a pair of goggles in her hands, which she immediately placed over her eyes to discover her surroundings. 'No wonder,' she mumbled.

They were in some kind of flying craft that was heading at an inconceivable speed through a large subterranean tunnel. The dark, rocky cavern through which they moved was so deep that Tory could only barely make out the river of red molten lava that flowed miles beneath them.

'We're underground.' She had deduced that much. 'But —' Tory was too overwhelmed to decide whether she should ask why, where, or how.

Knowing her mind, Taliesin filled her in on the details. 'Why? Because I have identified all the immortals in Neraida's tribe, so I am moving on to the next underground clan in this area. Where? In the vicinity of Mt Ararat. As for how, Eli here,' he motioned to the man piloting their craft, 'is Neraida's grandson. He knows his way through the fault chasms in this Middle Eastern sector better than anyone.'

'Are you saying we're flying in between the tectonic plates in the Earth's crust!'

'We're below all that,' Eli informed her with a wave to acknowledge his new passenger. 'My tribe has been getting around this way for eons.'

'You see,' Taliesin began his lecture, 'fault lines run along a grid where the electromagnetic energy is strongest. And as this craft is powered by electromagnetic propulsion, fault chasms form the perfect highway.'

'Electromagnetic propulsion,' she echoed, knowing this type of travel had yet to be perfected by those living on the surface of the planet.

'This transit system was left here by the Nefilim,' the Merlin explained, 'though they themselves have now discovered far more advanced forms of propulsion that do not rely on such tracks.'

'And you've been getting around this way for eons, did you say?' Tory directed the question to Eli, who nodded, indicating she'd got it right.

'Puts a whole new slant on the UFO conspiracy, doesn't it?'

'I'll say.' Tory pondered this a second. 'So, am I to assume, then, that the Nefilim left this kind of underground base all over the world?'

'You guessed it,' Eli confirmed.

Tory took a deep breath. 'That would certainly seem to explain the connection between UFO sightings, fault lines and the ley-line grid.'

'Indeed.' Taliesin smiled, feeling Tory's curiosity had been satisfied for the moment. 'So, to what do we owe this visit?'

Tory looked at him surprised. 'What, you're actually asking me?'

'Well I know how you detest me jumping the gun,' Taliesin said dryly, 'but I can just give you a straight answer up front, if you'd prefer?'

'As I believe time is of the essence ...' she invited his view.

'The answer is no.'

The Merlin's blunt refusal got Tory's back up. 'No, I cannot time travel back to prevent Inanna and Shamash from murdering Cadwallon in his cradle? Or, no, you will not assist me to rescue my daughter?'

Taliesin took a deep breath, knowing how Tory hated taking his word for anything. 'I have seen the present day in a reality when Cadwaladr was *not* Caradoc's reincarnation ... it was a disaster.'

'You mean the world would be a worse place without Doc Alexander?' The Merlin nodded, and Tory paused before arguing with him to consider all that the diplomat had done for the nations of the world and the planet itself.

'Understand that, as spiteful and manipulative as he has been throughout the centuries, Cadwaladr has also had his quiet moments of victory and achievement.'

Taliesin's glimpse of the alternative future had made that plainly obvious. 'I also know that, deep inside, you know there is good in Doc. Just as you knew there was good in Caradoc, which is why you wouldn't allow Maelgwn to feed him to the Dragon.'

Tory looked at him, realising that ultimately she had brought this upon herself; had she not been so merciful, Caradoc's soul would have been wiped from existence and Cadwaladr would have been someone entirely different!

'Ah, but would he have been a better man? Ask yourself that,' suggested Taliesin, who was following her train of thought. 'For in the reality I saw, I assure you, he was not.'

'Shit,' she conceded finally. Tory hadn't considered she might actually make things worse. 'Just how much time-hopping have you done in the chariot?' Now that they were on the subject, she was rather curious to know.

'In the chariot ... hardly any. I returned it to your father's cave ages ago for you to find.' He thought he'd avoided that question rather well. 'And you?' he inquired, politely.

'I have to free my daughter,' Tory insisted, to avoid the small talk.

'You can't,' Taliesin said. 'You have no means.'

'Then I have to see her, at least! If I astrally project myself to her, I cannot be restrained —'

'To what end, Tory? Are you forgetting that Rhiannon has been drained of all her psi ability. She won't see you, or hear you.' Taliesin hated to be so harsh on her, but she simply wasn't thinking straight. 'And quite apart from that, Inanna is after your personage, or have you forgotten?'

'No, I haven't forgotten. Why do you think I let Maelgwn talk me into seeking your assistance.' The frustration brought tears to her eyes. She couldn't think of a practical reason to take the risk, only a personal one. 'I have to see her, Taliesin. I have to see for myself how she fares. If you really are my friend, as you have so often claimed, and you are not beyond questioning the Nefilim's motives and orders, you will aid me in this.'

The Merlin seemed puzzled by her words, perhaps even a little bewildered. 'This has very little to do with the Nefilim's will, I assure you,' he declared, before sighing deeply. 'But I can see I shall have no peace if I do not agree —'

'Oh, thank you.' Tory grabbed hold of him to kiss his cheek.

'There is a condition, however.' He spoke up before she got too excited.

'Anything, what is it?'

'You will wait a month before making contact, no questions asked.'

'But why?' She couldn't help herself.

'I have my reasons.' His expression gave nothing away. 'Are we agreed?'

Tory hesitated. She knew what Taliesin was like. There was very little point in hounding him about his motives if he was of the mind to keep them secret. 'No deal, I'll do it on my own.'

'And risk never being able to touch your love again?' The Merlin tormented her. 'If Inanna claims your physical self you shall be stranded in the ethers until such time as she is bored with you ... and from what I hear of her designs on your husband, that may not be for some time.'

'Alright, already.' Tory didn't like putting her own selfish desires before the welfare of her child, but the notion of Maelgwn being deceived into an affair with that evil enchantress was enough to make her accept Taliesin's terms. She slouched in her chair, all huffy once more.

'Good, it's settled.' Taliesin pretended not to notice her resentment. 'Meanwhile, I shall visit Watarrka to seek out those in your camp who are Chosen.'

Tory wasn't sure she liked the sound of this. Certainly she was happy for those who would be liberated from their mortal bodies, but what of the others?

'I shall be very discreet,' he assured before she objected. 'How does two days from now sound?'

'Fine, I guess,' she grumbled. Why did he have to be so damn secretive all the time? She was tired of trusting in the universe, as it certainly didn't seem to be doing her any favours of late.

'It's all in the way you look at it really,' Taliesin advised her. 'Why do you have so much trouble believing that every adversity can be turned to one's advantage? The trouble with you is, you have lost your blind faith. You spend too much time trying to figure out the details of your problems and not enough time focusing on a positive outcome.'

'I know what I want, High Merlin, make no mistake about that.'

Taliesin gave a slight nod to grant that this might be true. 'But you can't make wishes for someone else Tory, only for you.'

'Then the universe obviously isn't going to be of much help in this instance, is it?' she concluded dryly, and having no desire to be lectured further she willed herself home.

Brian wasn't making any headway with their father, either; Myrddin seemed to think everything was going according to plan.

News that the Middle East and a large portion of Alaska had been destroyed failed to raise little more than a blank look from the Merlin. Brian ran by him the news of Cadfan's assassination and pending Son of God status, at which time Myrddin nodded as if it were expected and stood poised to learn what had Brian so riled.

'What about Rhiannon's kidnapping?' Brian made a desperate attempt to get some sign of emotion out of his father, to ensure he hadn't turned into a zombie. 'Surely you're concerned about that. She is your grand-daughter, after all!'

'Why concerned?' he queried. 'All is going splendidly.'

'Splendidly!' Brian barked 'If this is what you call splendid, I'd sure hate to see your idea of shithouse. Tory is out of her mind with worry. Can't you do anything to help her get Rhiannon back?'

'I'm no authority on the NERGUZ-I-NUEN, Brian,' Myrddin advised. 'Tory has Ray Murdock looking at the module, and he is far more qualified than I. She is also seeking Taliesin's aid —'

'Taliesin?' Brian frowned. Tory hadn't mentioned the High Merlin's return to the present.

'Teo, then,' Myrddin clarified. 'You know what I mean?'

'No, Dad, I don't.' Brian folded his arms.

'Oops.' Myrddin shrank back, realising that Tory obviously hadn't told her brother of Teo's passing.

'Tell me about "oops",' Brian hounded his father, as he began to walk away.

'I'd love to Brian, but I have to fly.'

'Is there a connection between Teo and Taliesin?' His question tapered off as his father disappeared into the wall of the cave and Brian found himself addressing a rock face. 'Damn it, Dad!' He thumped the solid obstruction that prevented him from pursuing his father.

Upon her return to Watarrka, Tory found the camp in an uproar.

A huge falcon, the size of a man, had flown into their base through an opening in the roof of the cavern of pools. It had perched itself high up in the cavern of abodes and was observing everything from there.

Some of the Aboriginals were of a mind to kill the huge bird for a feast, but Tory rushed down the stairs to the cavern floor to prevent it.

'No don't!' She threw herself at the man who was about to launch a spear at the creature, tackling him to the ground. 'He's a friend,' she explained, setting her startled victim free and getting to her feet. 'Thais?' She looked to the huge winged beast. 'It is I, Lamamu.'

The falcon let loose an almighty screech as it took flight.

Rhun was making his way into the cavern of abodes when he spied the enormous bird, circling its way down to land before his mother. 'What the devil?' He ran against the general flow of people who were fleeing the cavern. But as he got closer to Tory the beast confronting her began to transform. At first Rhun thought it was reconstituting into a human being, and thus he suspected a Shaman in their midst. By the time Rhun reached his mother's side, however, it was rather apparent that this was no ordinary shape-shifting individual. For although it had the head, arms and torso of a strong, healthy human male, it had the hindquarters and four legs of a fine black stallion. 'Mother, is this what I think it is?' Rhun asked, watching the animal prance about as it got the feel of its new form.

'Thais is a centaur, if that's what you mean.' Tory smiled, delighted to see her old friend again. 'Don't look so worried. We go way back.'

'Pleased to hear it,' Rhun muttered, as the beast came to a stand still before them, towering over both.

'Lamamu, Shar Xavier.' Thais bowed, graciously. 'What a pleasure it is to see you both.'

'The pleasure is all ours,' Tory assured him, before motioning to Rhun to correct her friend's misconception. 'This is my son, Rhun.'

'Of course,' Thais realised his error. 'Prince of Gwynedd some sixty years. I'm so pleased to make your acquaintance.'

The centaur gave him a firm handshake. Rhun could only stand there in amazed silence.

'So what drags you from your island home in the Azores, Thais?' Tory began to walk with the creature, ignoring the staring masses who were keeping their distance. 'Or should I call you Thomas?' This was the name Thais went by when in human form, Thomas Mateus.

'Whatever you prefer, Nin. To me, it matters not.' His smile transformed into a frown. 'I am a close friend of Walter Cadfan. I teach classes for him from time to time. You know what has happened I presume.'

'I do, and I have an electronics whiz, Ray, working on a way to get around the NERGUZ-I-NUEN module that Doc is using to control Cadfan … and others.'

'You are well informed.' Thais considered this unusual for an immortal of so few years and experience. Thais had lost track of how many thousands of years he'd seen, and still this young amateur was one step ahead of him.

'Actually, you may be able to help Ray with a few problems he's having.'

'I'd be more than happy to assist.' Thais jumped at the opportunity. 'I was secretly hoping you'd have a plan.'

'Excellent. But, ah … you might want to consider a human form. Ray is rather easily spooked,' she explained.

Thais raised both eyebrows, flashing a cheeky grin. 'You might want to consider finding me some clothes then.'

Tory was pleased to have Thais on the team. He had many talents her kin had yet to master, and a greater knowledge of history than every university, college and institute put together.

As she waited outside the little abode where Thais was changing, Tory thought back to the last time they had met, and quite frankly, the memory made her cringe. 'I'm sorry I was so rude to you that day on Pico. You were right about everything, Thais. I should have listened.'

'I notice you still made it all work out in the end, nevertheless.'

'Ah, I had lots of help.' She waved it off, declining all credit.

Thais emerged from the abode dressed in a pair of jeans and a shirt that had once belonged to her husband. In human form, Thais stood well over six foot tall. Miles was the only male Tory knew who was close to Thais' size and height. Apart from the bronze colour of his skin, Thais had the same colouring and build as her son: dark eyes, dark hair; slender and fighting fit.

'Tell me something, how did you find us?' It was not that Tory was suspicious of Thais. She wasn't. She was more concerned that her psychic shield might be failing her.

'No need for alarm, Nin. I was with Cadfan the day of your husband's funeral, I heard him tell you where you'd be safest. So I came to the heart of your homeland and took in a few of the sights, before I spotted the hole in the cavern roof and flew in here.'

'Tory!' Brian called to her, as he ran down the cavern stairs. 'We have to talk.'

'Look who's here.' Tory motioned to Thais, who waved.

'If it isn't the birdman himself.' Brian strode towards them. 'How's it going, Tom?' Brian inquired, pulling Tory aside. 'I've just been to see Dad. We need to talk.'

'Okay. Just let me take Thais down to Ray and —'

'No, right now.' He grabbed hold of Tory's arm and began to walk off with her.

'Brian!' Tory wrenched herself away from him. 'What's come over you?'

'Mum, it's cool,' Rhun called, having noticed her dilemma in passing. 'I'm heading that way myself. I can take Thais through.' He gestured for their newest arrival to follow him.

Once Brian had dragged his sister into the abode Thais had just exited, he activated the door and locked it.

'Tell me about Teo's accident.' His intense blue eyes turned her way.

'I don't understand,' she frowned. 'Why do you —'

'There's something you're not telling me, Tory. You know I can always tell.'

Tears began to fill her eyes, and she experienced pangs of guilt for withholding the secret. 'I can't tell you, Brian. I'm afraid you'll do something rash.'

'I'll do something rash if you don't,' he vowed,

taking her in hand. 'What's the connection between Teo and Taliesin?'

Tory gasped at how much Brian knew already. 'What did Dad say to you?'

'Never mind what he said, just answer the question?' Brian attempted to shake a response out of her. Tory gripped hold of his hand, and within seconds the ethers enfolded them both.

At the graveside of their dear friend, Tory told her brother about the events that had led to Teo's death and Taliesin's return. She advised of the High Merlin's mission and that he would be visiting Watarrka very soon.

'So Naomi may be an immortal too!' Brian's spirits lifted.

'No, Brian, that's impossible I'm afraid.' Though Tory was sorry to crush his hopes, she was over deciding what others should or shouldn't know. 'Naomi's perfect incarnation is with Maelgwn, and will return here when he does, at the time of the Gathering. Still, Daniel, as your son, is sure to be one of us.'

Though Brian smiled at that consolation, his heart was breaking as he stared at the tombstone that bore Teo's name. 'How did you cope with this alone, along with everything else that's gone down?'

'Severe shock has a dampening effect,' Tory shrugged. 'I had a premonition before we left. I tried to convince him to stay behind, but you know what Teo's like once he has made up his mind.'

'I'm glad he went out in a blaze of glory.' Brian's voice went hoarse with regret and he hung his head to suppress his tears. 'This world won't be the same without you, Teo. A truer friend I'll never know.'

'He's still here, Brian.' Tory placed a hand on her brother's shoulder. 'He's just smarter now, and much more infuriating.'

Brian had met Taliesin once, but couldn't recall the Merlin bearing any notable resemblance to his dear, departed friend. He knew appearances could be altered, so just because he'd seen Taliesin as Teo at Neraida's base didn't necessarily mean Taliesin was indeed his old friend. Only after some careful scrutiny, would he truly believe Teo lived.

As arranged, Taliesin arrived two days later.

To most of those staying at Watarrka he appeared as Teo and thus avoided drawing attention to himself. Only Tory, Rhun and Brian saw him in his Merlin's guise — and Thais, who remembered Taliesin from Atlantis and so insisted on calling him En Razu. Everyone was already used to Thais getting names wrong so none were any the wiser.

With Brian trailing behind them everywhere they went, Tory finished Taliesin's guided tour of Watarrka in the genetics lab. Here she introduced him to Dr Leigh Sukemi — their head geneticist.

When advised that Taliesin needed a work space and access to equipment for some research he was doing, the doctor said he could arrange a small but private lab that he hoped would be suitable.

'That's most kind.' Taliesin bowed in the Japanese fashion. 'I'll be happy anywhere you see fit to put me.'

'I'll leave you to it then.' Tory backed up. 'Catch you at dinner.' She thought Brian might leave with her, but as it turned out he was far too fascinated with Taliesin.

'So, do you intend to be of some assistance, or are you just going to stare at me all day?' Tory heard the Merlin say on her way out the door, and she paused to catch Brian's response.

'You don't speak much like Teo, or act like him for that matter.'

'I see.'

Tory peeked around the door to see Taliesin scratch his brow.

'Brian, you can't hold my death against me. All through the ages I've been dying, and more often than not, it really isn't my fault.' Taliesin began to follow the doctor who was already halfway up the path of the huge greenhouse. 'So I appear different, and have acquired a few manners and pearls of wisdom in my travels. But my essence is still the same. I forget nothing.'

'Alright, throw a few names and dates at me then.'

Tory watched Brian pursue the Merlin, who started reciting important historical events and figures, just to annoy him. 'Yeah,' she grinned. 'Teo's in there alright.'

20

UNTIL EVENTS DO US PART

At dinner that evening, Tory noticed they were a crew member short. 'Where's Noah?

'Working,' Jenny replied.

'You're kidding … but it's his birthday!' Tory stood, not about to let him spend the evening in front of a computer.

'Hey,' Daniel forewarned her, 'he's really not into a celebration right now. He's started writing *the book*,' he explained.

'Say no more.' Tory went to sit down, when suddenly her smile broadened and she looked at Taliesin. 'Come with me.' She took the Merlin by the hand and led him off.

Taliesin got wind of her thoughts on the way out of the rec-room. 'Selwyn is here?' he questioned, so delighted he near choked on his words. For the lad had been a prize pupil of his, and he had gone on to become a fine Bard and High Druid in his own right.

Tory nodded to confirm. 'He's Noah Purcell now, a journalist turned novelist. The poor fellow has it in his head to write my whole family history … thus you and he simply have to talk.'

'The pleasure will be all mine,' Taliesin assured her.

She gave the hatch door a thump, before entering the tiny quarters. 'Hey Noah.' She sought to interrupt him, though his attention remained firmly focused on his typing. 'I've brought you a birthday present.'

Noah finished clicking out a sentence on the keyboard, then swung his chair around to address Tory. 'Sorry boss, I don't mean to be rude. Hi, Teo,' he waved to Taliesin, who appeared kind of mystified.

'It's been so long,' the Merlin uttered, teary-eyed. He had not encountered Selwyn's soul mind since he'd resided over his burial fire, early in the seventh century.

'Yeah, it has been awhile.' Noah nodded in accord. 'How goes all in the Middle East?'

'It's seen better days,' said Taliesin.

Noah gave half a laugh at this, turning his attention Tory's way to look her over. 'So where's my present?'

'Right there.' She motioned to Taliesin.

'Aw!' Noah was clearly disappointed. 'No offence, Teo, but I really didn't miss you that much.'

'No, no. Teo is just the packaging. It's who is underneath that is the surprise.' Tory raised her brow a couple of times to heighten the mystery.

Noah looked from Tory to Teo, thinking they were pulling his leg.

'Look closer,' Tory advised, and Noah did so just to humour her.

When Teo began to transform, Noah jumped right out of his seat, unsure if he wanted to hide or grab his camera. But then he froze, seeing the shining man with silvery hair and flowing robes who'd manifested in Teo's stead.

'Noah Purcell meet Taliesin Pen Beirdd.'

'Oh, my God.' Noah ventured to hold out his hand, and as Taliesin took hold and shook it firmly, the lad calmed a little. 'This is such an honour. I've read so much about you.'

'Much of which you originally wrote, no doubt,' Taliesin smiled. 'For indeed, you were a fine scholar yourself.'

'You don't say.' Noah suddenly snapped back to reality, pulling up a chair for the Merlin to sit on. 'There's so many things I want to ask you, I hardly know where to start.'

'He hasn't changed much.' Taliesin winked at Tory, who agreed.

'Well have fun, guys.'

'Aren't you staying?' Noah was unsure whether he wanted her to or not.

'Are you kidding?' Tory headed for the door. 'I wouldn't get a word in edgeways.'

Both sides of Noah's mouth turned down as he considered she was probably right. And with a decisive nod, he closed the hatch door.

Late that night, and throughout the two nights following, Tory and Rhun went about collecting the blood samples Taliesin needed to run his tests. The advanced gadget used to extract the blood also stored each sample in its own vial. The Merlin wouldn't say where he'd acquired his devices and methods, but Tory had seen the like of them back in Atlantis. Her guess was that they were a gift from the Goddess, Keridwen.

This blood extraction process was so quick and painless it didn't even cause a stir in their sleeping subjects. Not one person was overlooked, as the immortal strand ran through all the tribes of the Earth. Rhun made a special trip outside the base to test Pete Nangina, the other rangers, and their families.

Brian let Tory know when the results were in, and she rushed to the lab to discover who amongst them were Chosen. 'Do you know?' she drilled Brian as he kept pace with her.

'He's been pretty tight-lipped.'

They arrived to find Rhun was also present.

'You don't miss much, do you?' Tory commented, and her son bowed his head graciously. 'So what's the verdict?'

'Are you sure you want to know?' Taliesin teased, and three expectant looks were the only response he got. 'In that case, the two most expected results were

UNTIL EVENTS DO US PART

Daniel and young Nicholas. There were some surprises though. Pete Nangina and several members of his family are carrying the gene, as well as Floyd, Noah and your Aunt Rose.'

As the news sunk in everyone fell silent, feeling a mixed bag of emotions: happy for those who were named, mournful for those who weren't.

'We shall all be united one day,' Taliesin reminded them, 'one day soon.'

'So what happens now?' Tory queried. 'If they're all suddenly transformed to their prime, isn't everyone going to get a tad suspicious? Aunt Rose and Pete are proficient at the physic arts but Floyd, Noah and the boys are going to take some time to train.'

Taliesin shook his head. 'We administer Keridwen's elixir to those concerned, but their immortality gene will not kick in until they experience physical death.' He passed Tory a tray containing several small vials, and a device to administer each dose.

Tory placed the kit aside as Taliesin began packing the rest of his apparatus into a bag. 'So that's it. You're leaving?'

'Well, I do have many other tribes to seek out.' He closed his bag and it vanished. 'You will return my device when you're finished with it, won't you?'

'But you said you'd help me visit with Rhiannon?' Tory jogged his memory before he disappeared on her.

'Has a month passed already?' he queried.

Tory wanted to say yes, on the off chance the Merlin really wasn't keeping track of time, but chances were he was testing her. 'No.'

417

'Well then, I'll be back when it has. Toodles.' He waved and was gone.

That month seemed to last an eternity. Tory was forced to sit and watch the outside world slip further into chaos and ruin.

Its protective shield lost, the Middle East turned into a festering sore on the face of the planet. Her parched ground began to crack and her mighty rivers, the Tigris and Euphrates, were in danger of disappearing; needless to say, the water was polluted beyond repair from the blast anyway. Radioactive rainfall fell over the bottom of Africa and, powered across the Atlantic by the south-easterly trade winds, the poisonous storms reached as far as the coast of Brazil. Strange weather patterns the world over started threatening agriculture, livestock, and so, too, the food supply.

Cadfan had become a mega-star, idol, and guru overnight. The room where the miraculous resurrection had taken place was fast becoming a shrine. People travelled from all over the globe to visit the site in the hope of finding the Messiah who could heal them of their illnesses, or shield them from the holocaust that had seemingly besieged the planet. But their efforts were in vain. Doc was keeping the prophet well hidden at present.

Rhiannon was also becoming a regular feature in the news as the girlfriend of the most sought-after man alive. Through the eyes of the media's cameras the couple appeared fabulously happy, and all at Watarrka were furious that they could do nothing but watch the lie unfold.

It was also made public that the *Goddess* had been found residing at the bottom of the Atlantic Ocean — there had been no survivors and there would be no salvage attempt. Earlier reports that foul play may have befallen Dr John Pearce and family were quashed by Rhiannon, who maintained that there was never any ill-will between John Pearce and her mother. She also advised that the Pearce's were on board the *Goddess* the last time the submersible had left port, which seemed to account for their mysterious disappearance. Rhiannon said she had left the service of the vessel to pursue private studies, and thus had not been on board to perish with the rest of her kin. The yarn was very neat indeed, as the bodies of Dr Pearce and his family were never found, and the *Goddess* had failed to dock anywhere in over three years.

At first Tory couldn't figure why Doc had let them off the hook. But a few days before she planned to visit her daughter the diplomat's reasons became all too clear when he announced his plan to wed Rhiannon. It was apparent that Tory's acquittal in the Pearce affair was so Doc had all loose ends tied up before he married her daughter.

Ray was not present to witness the news bulletin. He was on the isle of Pico in the Azores with Thais, chasing up some orichalchum from inside a cavern on a cliff face there. It was the strongest substance known to exist and he and Ray hoped to fashion their anti-NERGUZ device from the tough, rare metal. The same evening of Rhiannon's wedding announcement, Thais returned to base briefly to advise that the cavern had partially collapsed during the eruption of Pico Alto in 2005. It could take them quite a few days to break through to the chamber of orichalchum, if they managed to do so at all.

Their delay proved fortunate for Tory as Thais would keep Ray out of the way and occupied until such time as she could speak with Rhiannon.

Late in the day that marked the passing of the month, Tory anxiously awaited the arrival of the High Merlin, praying to the Goddess he hadn't forgotten their arrangement.

Floyd was still appropriating copies of Doc's itinerary from the diplomat's secretary on a regular basis. He had found out that Doc was leaving Rhiannon for a week at his estate in England to see to their wedding arrangements, while he attended a conference in Geneva to discuss the Middle Eastern crisis.

This is the best chance I'm going to get, Tory decided, anxiously eyeballing the cavern of abodes from a great height. Maybe that was why Taliesin insisted she wait until now, knowing that the perfect situation would arise?

Tory was slowly coming to the conclusion that she should just go find the Merlin, when a tiny blue ball of light came sweeping through from the cavern of produce, with several children running after it. The children ceased their pursuit and watched with awe when the glowing ball went spiralling up towards Tory.

'I've seen you before,' she smiled, closing her eyes to receive its message.

Meet me at Lynn Cerrig Bach, Taliesin's voice advised as the ball of light penetrated her forehead. *Midnight tonight, Gwynedd time*.

As Tory's eyes parted, all her anxiety had left her. 'I'll be there.'

The restored temple of the Goddess was a sight to behold at night, with inner torches lighting the four cardinal points of north, south, east and west. Tory scaled the stairs to the inner sanctum where the statues of nine comely muses watched over the altar stone. Once inside this dwelling she entered a circle of protection, cast by and fortified with Taliesin's energies. She found it strange therefore that she should feel chilly and ill at ease as she approached the heart of the temple.

The Merlin was standing beside the large altar stone that bore the Celtic cross. 'Let us proceed,' and he motioned Tory to lay upon the sacred rock.

She complied at once, eager to see her daughter. But before Tory lay down, she felt an urge to question. 'Are you annoyed with me, Taliesin?'

'Not at all. Why do you ask?'

'I don't know, you just seem kind of abrupt, or distant or something?' Tory couldn't quite peg what it was.

'I know you are anxious to see your child, that is all.' He placed both hands upon her shoulders and encouraged her to lay back.

'It's a pity you weren't so sympathetic a month ago,' Tory jeered, deciding she never would understand him.

'Shh,' he instructed placing one hand at each side of her head. 'Relax now, concentrate.'

Tory closed her eyes to find her centre, but the Merlin's touch was as cold as ice, and she could not focus. A bad feeling was brewing inside her, as if her own will was rebelling and imploring her not to proceed. Tory sat up abruptly, shrinking from the Merlin's icy touch. 'I've changed my mind,' she was saying, when she spied Taliesin standing at the entrance to the temple. He seemed to be yelling at her very loudly, though she could not hear a word. Her horrified eyes turned back to the head of the altar stone where Taliesin also stood.

'It's a trick,' he told her. 'Shamash is trying to prevent you from making contact with Rhiannon. Quickly, we must hurry.'

Tory moved to comply, yet her instinct again told her no.

'Nay, don't listen to her!' Taliesin yelled from the entrance stairs, unable to penetrate the shield Inanna had cast around the site. He could see the corpse that was residing over the proceedings. The evil enchantress must have killed the security guard in order to utilise his body until Tory's became free. No doubt Tory saw this stand-in as himself, and she obviously couldn't hear anything beyond what Inanna wanted her to hear.

'Could we just take five for a second.' Tory's sudden suspicions urged her to back up. She managed to get clear of the altar, and then a few paces, before her whole body seized up.

'No, Tory,' the Merlin told her, 'we must act now.'

The more Tory resisted his will, the clearer her situation became. The image of the Merlin peeled away to reveal the face of a dead man. She pushed against the stone altar to resist the corpse who was willing her closer, and stared beyond his physical body to glimpse Inanna. *I'm in deep.* Tory had entered the circle voluntarily and in all probability was no psychic match for the age-old Goddess. The Law of Rebound — that a superior force will always defeat a lesser power — stated as much. Whatever Tory projected in Inanna's direction would rebound on her tenfold; not threats, nor spite, nor force could free her now.

You can't hope to defy me child. The Goddess spoke in her own alluring and soothing voice. *Don't force me to hurt you.*

Still firmly gripping the edge of the stone, Tory closed her eyes and thought of her daughter. As she felt her whole being fill with love, the Goddess' hold on her weakened and she was able to back up several feet.

The Goddess laughed at her attempt to escape. *Oh yes, so full of love and compassion is our Lamamu … let us see how forgiving you really are.* Inanna waved her hand about the altar stone and manifested a tiny ball of light which she cast at Tory, and the impact knocked her off her feet.

'Nay!' Taliesin watched in horror, as Tory lay motionless on the stoney ground perceiving the sinister tidings the Goddess had sent her.

Maelgwn is already mine, Inanna told her, as Tory

beheld a clear image of her husband making love to the Goddess.

'It is a lie.' Tory shook herself free of the nightmare, though tears of hurt were streaming down her face.

Ask yourself then why it is you are crying, Lamamu? Deep down, you know I speak the truth.

Tory bowed her head, tempted to admit Inanna was right. 'No, no fear.' She launched herself further towards the exit of the temple. 'Maelgwn despises you,' Tory told Inanna adamantly, dragging herself towards the wide open spaces.

Well, naturally he'd tell you that to hide his guilt and true feelings for me.

Tory held her breath, struggling not to take her comments to heart, but when she came sliding back across the temple floor, she realised she wasn't disputing Inanna's claims hard enough.

'If … what … you … say … is … true,' Tory squeezed out, wrenching herself forward with every word — there was only a couple of meters between Taliesin and herself now — 'then why do you still want my body so badly?' The notion gave Tory the strength to cast herself far enough towards the circle's circumference that her hand penetrated it and Taliesin grabbed hold.

'Good girl.' The Merlin dragged her clear and held her trembling form tightly.

'Oh my God!' Tory blubbered, the image of Maelgwn making love to Inanna recurring in her head, again and again.

'It's over,' Taliesin assured her, calming her with his healing energies.

'But I nearly …'

'But you didn't,' the Merlin stopped her from dwelling on what might have happened.

She looked towards the inner temple in the wake of her ordeal. The dead security guard was slumped over the altar stone. Inanna had gone.

Taliesin went about putting out the torches Inanna had ignited, and so dispersed her energies from the site. 'Come.' Taliesin held a hand out to Tory. 'I have a safer place in mind.'

Even though Tory knew this was the real Taliesin Pen Beirdd who addressed her now, she was still hesitant to join him.

'We could forget all about it, if you like,' he suggested, which served to spur her to certainty quick-smart.

In the great entrance hall to Taliesin's labyrinth there was another huge stone carving of the Celtic cross. Around this Taliesin lay a large unbroken circle of sand, and marked out the four cardinal points by setting a candle at north, south, east and west.

This time, as Tory lay her body down inside the protected area, she did not feel uneasy and found it simple to focus.

'Pray I make contact, old friend,' Tory uttered, before she drifted off.

'I will, thy will.' She saw the Merlin say this to her as she drifted above them both, observing her motionless form as she ascended higher and higher above it. Then Taliesin looked up at her, apparently aware of her departure.

425

'Go in peace,' he said.

Tory turned to move on, and found herself gliding through a beautiful old mansion. Though it was night and the house was softly lit she had no trouble seeing her way as she was exuding her own light. She scaled the grand staircase, passing a housemaid making her way downstairs with a tray of empty dishes. No sooner had Tory wondered if the maid would see her than the woman screamed, threw the tray into the air and went racing back up the staircase. *I guess so.* Tory amused herself, following the terrified maid into the upstairs hallway.

'What is it, Francesca?' Rhiannon emerged from her bedroom to see what all the ruckus was about. The petrified maid could only point, whereby Rhiannon looked to find the phantasm making its way down the hall towards them. 'Mother,' Rhiannon uttered, quietly delighted to see her.

'But your mother is de—' The woman's eyes rolled back in her head, and she fainted.

Thinking this was for the best, Rhiannon looked back to her visitor. 'Please, come in. I've been expecting you.'

Tory followed her daughter into the bedroom, curious to hear her say so.

'A smart move to come in etheric form,' Rhiannon commented, 'however unnecessary.' She closed the door behind them and headed for her seat by the fire.

You think so? Tory bethought her, noting her daughter no longer wore the restraining band around her wrist. *And what do you mean, you've been expecting me?*

'That's why Doc agreed to leave me alone this week. I told him you'd come, if you knew I'd be by myself.'

And why would Doc want to allow me to speak with you alone?

'Because I asked,' Rhiannon explained simply. 'And look,' she held up her bare right wrist, 'no restraints.'

I noticed.

'Please mother, don't be suspicious, at least until you hear what I have to say.'

I'm listening.

Her daughter outlined how Doc had been removing her restraint in order to utilise her abilities, for both professional and personal purposes. But one night, after making love to her, Doc had drifted off to sleep before he'd replaced the module on Rhiannon's wrist. This had been all the time she'd needed to get a grip on her situation. After hanging out with Ray for three years, Rhiannon managed to figure out how to remove the module's control mechanism. Doc continued replacing the band, unaware that it had been tampered with. A week lapsed before Rhiannon enlightened Doc to this oversight. In the interim, she hadn't managed to catch the word that he used to activate the devices — not that it would have done her or her kin any good, as she discovered that the command had to be uttered by the man himself to have any effect. Once Doc realised he no longer needed to restrain Rhiannon to keep her by him, he was immensely happy as he'd wanted nothing more. Able to perceive each other's thoughts, Rhiannon and Doc knew that they weren't lying about their feelings for each other. 'So I haven't been under his control for weeks.'

Then come home, baby, please! Tory pleaded. *If he has indeed set you free, then get out now, while you still have the chance.*

'I'm afraid I can't do that,' Rhiannon announced. 'I made him a deal, you see.'

What kind of a deal?

'I vowed,' Rhiannon stood to advise her mother of the details, 'that I would stay with him, so long as he forgot about my kin and let them be.'

Baby, no, I can't allow you —

'It is not your decision to make,' Rhiannon told her mother, rather forcefully, 'and should you try to remove me by force, I shall return to him given the first opportunity, I swear it. Now, Doc is prepared to do as I have asked, which is why we concocted the story about the *Goddess*. In the eyes of the world, all of you no longer exist.'

Tory shook her head, not wanting to believe her ears. Surely Rhiannon was still somehow being manipulated by Doc's will. *You don't have any idea what he's really up to, Rhiannon —*

'Of course I do! It is impossible for us to keep secrets from each other. I know about the army he is building, and of his so-called guardian angel, Shamash. Which is exactly the reason I want to stay with Doc. I am the only hope those souls, including Doc, have of escaping Shamash's evil influence. Who else can keep an eye on his movements, and warn of pending disaster, if not I? Don't you see, mother, this is my destiny. Doc will listen to me. I have made him see reason several times already.'

And who is going to save you if Shamash discovers you are influencing his Chosen one, hmm?

'I, too, have a guardian,' Rhiannon whispered. 'An old friend of yours, so I believe.'

Tory knew at once to whom she referred. *You have seen Keridwen?*

'Rhiannon nodded. 'And if you think I might have been deceived, ask Taliesin of our meeting, for it was he who brought her to me.'

Oh dear lord. Tory began to float to and fro, as if she were pacing. *And what do I tell Ray?* she implored of Rhiannon. *Have you got any idea what he's going through right now, have you even thought?*

The question seemed to take a bit of the wind out of Rhiannon's sails. She turned away to consider her response, fiddling with the large diamond engagement ring on her wedding finger. 'Ray is a sweetie, mother … I do miss him, and I'm sorry if the decision I have made will cause him pain. I'm a big girl now. I realise the welfare of the many must come before the welfare of just one man. But quite apart from all that, I love Doc.'

Tory looked at her daughter, infuriated to hear her say so. *Do you speak of the man Doc appears to be, or of the barbarian he truly is?*

'Perhaps I should have said, Cadwaladr,' Rhiannon specified, not much liking her mother's train of thought. 'He reminds me of father and Rhun, and he is not at all the monster you have made him out to be.'

He murdered your father, raped you, and despises your kin. I can guarantee, he is nothing like either of them.

'Father's death was a mistake.'

A mistake!

'Yes,' Rhiannon stressed, 'and you know as well as I, father isn't really dead. Now is he?' Rhiannon posed, knowing her mother couldn't argue the point. 'Doc no longer despises you. I explained to him that you didn't know that the immortal gene would be passed on to so many generations, and that Taliesin hadn't tutored him because he was completely unaware that Cadwaladr had inherited the immortal gene in its active state.'

How do you know about that? As soon as she'd asked the question, she knew the answer. *Taliesin told you, of course. But did you tell Doc who was really to blame?*

Rhiannon shook her head. 'But I will, when the time is right.'

And how do you plan to keep such a secret until then?

'After Taliesin and Keridwen had explained all to me, they wiped certain details from my memory and will restore them as required. So please, do not even think of that which I do not know, because then I shall, and that would be dangerous.'

Tory was confused now, and angered that Taliesin had been scheming behind her back. *And what of Cadfan? Have you all decided that being a mindless puppet cum Messiah is his destiny too?*

'No, mother.' Rhiannon's tone softened, sensing Tory's feelings of betrayal. 'That shall be my first priority. Doc knows I do not like what he is putting his grandfather through and that I shall quietly do all I can to put a stop to it. Like I said, we have no secrets. I respect his view, and he respects mine. He is in love with the real me, you see, not the zombie I was when I was under his control. That being the case, our love is completely unconditional, because it has to be. I'm not asking you to like what I am trying to do, I only ask that you respect my decision.'

Tory went quiet as she considered that had Rhiannon been anyone but her daughter, she would have respected and admired her determination. 'I'm just so afraid of losing you.'

'That will never, ever happen.' Rhiannon closed the space between them. 'Despite how it may appear at times, I assure you nothing anyone could say or do would ever demote you in my eyes. You're my hero, mother, and more importantly, my dearest friend. Know that you have taught me well and set me free to do what I must.'

Tory was deeply touched by her daughter's words, for Rhiannon had not spoken of her thus since she was a teenager. *I have taught you well, Rhiannon. There is good in Doc. I too have seen it ... so somewhere, down deep, your resolve makes me very proud.*

'So I have your blessing?'

Though it pained Tory to commit herself, it was far better to be supportive than to oppose her daughter and be cut out of her life altogether. *If you're sure this is what you want?*

Rhiannon nodded. 'Until events do us part, it is.'

Upon returning to her body, Tory awoke. Taliesin gave her a few moments to get her bearings, before he asked, 'Should I run for cover?'

'No need,' Tory told him, as she got to her feet.

'Oh please, Tory, don't look at me like that.'

'Like what?' Tory queried, her voice more sorrowful than wrathful. 'Like you have betrayed me, lied to me, conscripted yet another member of my family into your damn ancestral war.'

'I can explain —'

'No, don't bother,' Tory uttered, bewildered, 'I couldn't believe a word of it anyway.' A single tear rolled down her cheek, as she looked away and faded from his presence.

For several weeks Tory and Ray were a miserable pair. They spent quite a bit of time in each other's company, trying to ease the hurt they shared.

Not surprisingly, Ray lost all enthusiasm for constructing the anti-NERGUZ device. Thais and he had managed to dig out a few large chunks of orichalchum to use in the construction of their prototype, but Thais didn't have Ray's engineering background — he had no chance of developing the device alone. So, in the end, determined to rescue Cadfan, it was Thais who dragged Ray out of his deep pit of despair. Thais was an accomplished spiritual tutor and motivator, so even someone as pessimistic as Ray didn't stand a chance of escaping his positive influence and reinforcement.

Alone, Tory walked the canyon ridge every evening. She felt closer to Maelgwn here; she could see the star system where he resided. She had recovered from her shock at her daughter's decision as much as she was ever going to. But she could not bring herself to forgive the hand Taliesin had played in Rhiannon's decision — no matter how many times she tried to reassure herself he had acted on behalf of the greater good.

'Hey, sunshine.' Teo sat himself beside her to look out over the darkening landscape.

The sight of her old friend startled Tory at first, then quietly angered her. 'Coward,' she called the Merlin. 'How dare you use the open, honest relationship we once had to try and appease your treachery of late.'

'Where is the treachery?' he asked. 'I told you months ago what was going to happen. You refused to listen.'

'Do you really think Rhiannon would have stayed with Doc if you and Keridwen hadn't filled her head with visions of grandeur?' Tory stood, of the mind to walk off her frustration and escape this conversation.

'Tory, I didn't put a spell on her to make her agree, you know.' Taliesin raised Teo's form to pursue her. 'Nor did I give her any mysterious love potion to make her fall in love with Doc. Just because it isn't your ideal scenario for your daughter, doesn't mean it isn't the right thing for her to do.'

'But Doc is not Rhiannon's true soul mate. Ray is.'

'Actually,' Taliesin corrected, 'Cadwallon is her true soul mate. But Doc is evolved from the same soul mind as the rest of us, and is thus a kindred spirit to Rhiannon. I was not your true soul mate either, but that didn't stop you from falling in love with me, did it?'

Tory stopped in her tracks, and turned to confront Teo. 'That was long before I ever met Maelgwn,' she defended.

'And before we left on my last mission, what was that?'

'You kissed me!' Tory insisted.

'You kissed me back,' he was quick to retort. 'I've often wondered what would have become of us had I returned from that tour of duty.'

'Nothing would have happened,' Tory was right up on her high horse now.

He smiled. 'But we'll never really know and it matters not.' He spoke up to prevent her further protest. 'The point is that it would have been your decision to make. We all have things to learn in this world. You cannot learn Rhiannon's lessons for her. And before you start ramming my words down my throat, I ask that you consider this … where would we be now if your father had prevented you from going back to the Dark Age? And don't tell me this is different because Maelgwn turned out to be your true love. The effect your decisions and bravery had on this planet is every bit as beneficial as the effect your daughter will have in the future.'

'Have you lived through this instance in time before?'

'This particular instance, no.'

'Than how can you be so sure of the outcome?' Tory hated feeling torn. She very much wanted to trust him and to know that it would all turn out for the best, but lately the hurdles the universe expected her to jump seemed far too high.

The Merlin went very quiet for a time to allow Tory to reflect a little, before he confessed: 'As I cannot stand the thought of spending the next seventeen years without your friendship, I can see I have no choice but to tell you everything.'

Tory turned her gaze upon him, hesitant to believe he was on the level. 'Do you promise to tell the whole truth and nothing but the truth?'

'I do.' Half his mouth curved to a smile. 'If *you* promise to believe and trust in me as much as you once did. And if you allow me to complete your tuition in the higher mysteries, so you, in turn, can instruct your kin.'

As she felt the torment in her heart cease, Tory ventured a smile. 'I will.'

She embraced him to seal the deal, and the Merlin breathed a great sigh of relief. 'The future is looking brighter already.'

21

REMEMBER?

By the year 2023 many religious wars had broken out, as the various hierarchies argued for or against Cadfan as the long-prophesied Messiah.

Fortunately for Doc, the prophet had already made many forecasts about the future, some of which the diplomat played up to confirm his colleague's divinity. Doc later had Cadfan twist other predictions, concerning Doc's own underlying interests, to mean something entirely different.

Working closely with Cadfan and taking his prognosis with regard to the planet's health seriously, the ICA set about enforcing preventive measures, be it evacuation, shelters, water breaks or whatever. One by one the disasters came to pass, and whether or not people believed in Cadfan's predictions they were at least prepared for the ill-fated occurrences. People knew what to do because Cadfan's publicity machine had made them aware. Needless to say, Doc and Walter were fast reaching hero status in the eyes of the world. What they had to offer transcended race, creed, culture, even religion; people could sleep at night, knowing someone was watching out for them.

Cadfan's teachings, which had once encouraged self-development and the individual's pursuit of spiritual perfection, were shifted away from the ideal to focus on the idol, thanks to the media. Walter said what Doc wanted him to say, and he was so busy touring and doing interviews that there was hardly time for performing miracles. Doc knew that as long as he kept Cadfan under the control of the module, Rhiannon had no chance of stealing the prophet away. The problem was that Cadfan could not predict any more, nor could he heal his faithful followers. But they could only sustain the mirage based on Walter's past glories for so long. Sooner or later Doc was going to have to set Cadfan free to do what he was most renowned for.

'Noah, I'm leaving now.' Tory distracted him from his essay. 'Do you still want to come?'

'I sure do.' He finished off his sentence and scrambled from his seat to grab a jacket.

'How's the writing coming?' Tory wandered over to read off the screen, whereby Noah hit the shut down key.

'Really well,' he replied, 'I'm up to chapter twenty-one of the third volume.'

'Well, when do I get to read this masterpiece?'

'Sometime after 2037, when it has an ending.' He motioned her to the door so they could get on with creating the next chapter.

After having spoken with Taliesin at length, Noah was now eager to see the Merlin's abode. Tory had described the labyrinthine dwelling to him and it sounded too fantastic to conceive of all at once.

Tory was heading to Lynn Cerrig Bach with Ray, so she offered to prove her claims about the place and Noah simply couldn't resist.

Ray and Thais finally had a working model of their prototype, which they dubbed the ENZU-GUZ: 'the wise one's weapon'. This was why Ray was accompanying Tory to Lynn Cerrig Bach. She had not told him where they were going, only that she wanted him to demonstrate his creation for someone.

Tory had become far more proficient in the art of psychokinetic teleportation of late. Even so, Rhun offered his services to transport either Ray or Noah to save unnecessary drain on Tory's energy. They were forced to be aware of such things these days. Any weakening of their psychic defences might lead the enemy straight to them. Of course, the enemy must first know what you look like, which meant most at Watarrka would not be hunted. Rhiannon may have persuaded Doc to let her kin be, but Tory didn't trust Doc as far as she could throw him.

The four arrived in the huge, grand entrance foyer to find Taliesin and Myrddin speaking with Rhiannon.

My god! Tory's first reaction was shock at seeing the two High Merlin's in each other's company. The age-old prophecy was coming to life. The Gathering was truly nigh.

Oh no, thought Tory next, looking around to catch Ray's reaction. He'd taken a few steps backwards and stood staring at Rhiannon, with mixed emotions.

'Hey, good lookin'.' Rhun bounded over to give his sister a hug. They held each other a good while before Rhiannon turned to address Ray. She didn't have to say a word. Her joy became shrouded in feelings of woe; every psychic in the room felt it.

'Delighted you could all pop in.' Taliesin decided to ease the tension by clearing the room. 'Come, let us find some place more comfortable to talk.'

Everyone eagerly followed the Merlin's lead — everyone but Rhiannon and Ray. They remained as they were, eyeballing each other from a distance, neither of them speaking until the doors closed and they were alone.

'If you had to choose between love and destiny, which would you pick?' Rhiannon posed.

'Destiny.' Ray didn't hesitate. 'At least I know what that is.'

'Exactly,' she agreed. 'I was dying at Watarrka, Ray … I served no true purpose —'

'I wasn't enough for you?' Ray interjected, harshly.

'No, Ray, I wasn't enough for myself,' she replied.

He gave a heavy sigh, knowing where she was coming from, though he still didn't agree with her assessment. 'I realise you think you're serving the greater good where you are, but you can't tell me you couldn't have found a way to do that at Watarrka!'

'Get real, Ray ... who needs me when Tory Alexander is around!' Rhiannon played up Tory's capabilities, then calmed and smiled warmly. 'I love my mother, dearly, don't get me wrong. Who can blame her for being so perfect and talented. But there is one task she could never bring herself to do, and that, my friend, is why I took the assignment upon myself. No one else could have pulled it off, not even mother.'

Ray couldn't dispute this, and it slowly dawned on him that perhaps their break-up had been nothing more than the wrong place at the wrong time. 'Do you love him?' He could have hit himself for asking.

Rhiannon shook her head slowly, 'I don't think so. It's more the challenge he represents.'

Ego appeased, slightly, Ray's mood lightened. 'I knew I shouldn't have made it so easy for you.'

'But that's what I loved about us — that it *was* so easy, so comfortable, so relaxed.' Rhiannon paused, thinking she needed her head read for choosing such an exhausting relationship over the bliss she'd known with Ray. 'For Doc, love is a battle of wits, a game!'

'I thought so, too,' Ray said softly, 'before I met you.'

The tenderness of the statement brought tears to her eyes and a lump to her throat. 'I miss you,' Rhiannon confessed, her voice hoarse from emotion.

Not half as much as I miss you, is what he wanted to say, but instead Ray just held his arms wide.

She ran and embraced him, crying her heart out as

he squeezed her tight. 'I understand, Rhiannon ... really, I do. And I bear you no malice.'

He truly meant what he said, she could feel it, which only served to fuel her tears of suppressed guilt. 'Oh Ray,' she raised her tear-stained face and kissed his cheek. 'I do love you ... but the Goddess inside, I love her more.' She pulled away, her chest aching from the conflict raging inside her. 'I must follow her lead ... I must.' As her tears welled for a second coming, Rhiannon covered her face with her hands and vanished.

Ray stood staring into space for the longest time. He was so bewildered by his own behaviour. He had spent a lot of time over the last few years thinking about what he would say to Rhiannon if he ever chanced across her again. He'd imagined fury, a lot of anger and spiteful words. Yet, it hadn't been like that at all. And as a result, he felt calm and at peace. Still a little hurt perhaps, but better for the knowledge that they had parted as friends.

Could it be that we are growing up? Ray's eyes darted about the room, and for the first time he noticed its grand and peculiar nature. 'Where on earth am I?'

On cue, the double doors that led into the maze opened wide and Taliesin entered to collect Ray.

'Hey Teo.' Ray made his way towards him. 'Is this your place?'

'Ah, yeah,' Taliesin answered. 'This is where I hide out.'

Ray was amazed to hear Teo say this — surely the antiques around him were priceless. 'Did you win the Lotto or something?'

Taliesin chuckled at the question. 'You could say I fall under the "or something" catagory.' He slapped a hand upon Ray's shoulder to guide him along. 'Come, let me show you around.'

Rhiannon made a brief appearance in the room where Taliesin had left her mother, brother, grandfather, and Noah.

'Rhiannon, are you alright?' Tory moved to comfort her, but Rhiannon backed up towards Rhun.

'Wipe all memory of this meeting from my mind.' She prevailed upon her brother to make haste about it, too.

'Alright.' He raised his finger for her to focus upon, and began the procedure without question. Once she was under his control, he instructed: 'When I click my fingers, you will project yourself back from whence you came, to awake with no recollection of ever having left there.' Rhun clicked his fingers, and Rhiannon faded from their midst.

'He's very talented.' Myrddin boasted about his grandson to Noah, who appeared to be astonished.

'That's frightening,' Noah decided.

Rhun waved it off. 'I have a way with women.'

'It isn't any wonder,' Noah said flippantly.

'Do you think she's okay?' Tory asked the others.

'She's doing just fine,' Myrddin told her, slightly annoyed, but then his voice regained a tone of pride. 'She brought us word that Doc has released Cadfan from the module's influence, so he should be nearly back to his old self. Apparently, Doc is planning some big shindig for his disciples, the venue for which should be announced in the next few days.'

'We have to get Walter out,' Tory insisted.

'Yes, we do,' Myrddin settled the matter once and for all, 'but if we steal him away, he will be assumed to be missing, and all those followers of his will ceaselessly look for him.'

'Good luck to them ...' Rhun scoffed at anybody's chances of finding Cadfan once the Watarrka community had him.

Myrddin raised his brows at Rhun's certainty. 'Still, why take the risk, when we can make it look like —'

'... he ascended!' Tory cut in to raise a strong objection to Myrddin's plot. 'No way, no day! Then we'd be reinforcing the damn delusion.'

'Well, the world already knows he can't die, so what else are you going to do?'

Tory opened her mouth to argue her father's point, and then closed it again when nothing immediately sprang to mind.

'Mother, if everyone is happy, what difference does it make?' Rhun intervened, taking his grandfather's side. 'The most important thing is that we get Cadfan out of there.'

'And the gang's all here ...' Taliesin and Ray entered the room. Taliesin rubbed his hands together mischievously. 'Let's plot then, shall we?'

Rhiannon's short rest left her feeling emotionally and physically drained. Yet when she tried to recall what she'd dreamt, she came up with naught.

Downstairs she found Doc and his henchmen giving Cadfan a hard time. It seemed his faculties weren't returning quite as fast as anticipated.

'You can't bluff me, old man,' Doc told him, whereby Cadfan appeared all the more puzzled.

'I'm very sorry, but I have no idea what you mean?' the healer said.

'Yes, you do!' Doc insisted, at which time Rhiannon placed a hand on his shoulder to calm him.

'There's no need to squander your energy in this fashion.'

Doc turned his frustration Rhiannon's way. But she beckoned him with one finger into the adjoining room, an alluring smile upon her face encouraging her husband to calm down and follow.

In the privacy of Doc's study, Rhiannon appeased him with a kiss and bethought the solution.

'Patrick Haze,' he uttered as they parted, 'of course.' Doc had forgotten all about Cadfan's young apprentice, who was still hidden among the Unken ranks. 'Brilliant!'

'Did you expect anything less?' Rhiannon took a seat on his desk, crossing her legs in a provocative fashion. She procured herself a cigarette from the case beside her, and held it up awaiting a light.

Doc did the honours, quietly pondering her motives for jogging his memory. 'Why are helping me, when I know for a fact you want Cadfan freed?'

'But not yet.' Rhiannon inhaled the smoke from the cigarette, and exhaled it again before expanding on the statement. 'The fusion project is still a year from completion. After that, you won't need Cadfan to control the masses.' She gave a slight shrug, 'I can wait.'

'That's very obliging of you,' Doc took hold of her knees, and parting her legs wide pulled her close.

'Well, we aim to please,' she advised in a sultry whisper, his hand guiding hers to stub the cigarette out.

'Your aim is true,' Doc assured, his kiss obliging her to assume a horizontal position.

Confronted by Patrick Haze, Cadfan found his memory. His initial shock turned to delight, which faded when he noticed the metallic band clamped around Patrick's right wrist. The lad spoke as if he remembered Walter, yet he seemed a completely different character to the Patrick he'd known. He had lost all his spark and individuality; all that remained was a walking, talking, empty shell of a man.

This has been me for the last three and a half years, thought Walter, regretting that he could recall every tormenting second of his confinement.

'And it will be you for the rest of eternity if you don't co-operate,' Doc advised.

Cadfan's horror doubled as he realised Doc no longer needed to be touching an individual to know their thoughts.

'You had best believe it,' Doc confirmed his grandfather's observation.

Walter turned to Rhiannon, assuming it was she who'd been tutoring him. 'Your mother must be proud.'

The healer's eyes were filled with forgiveness and pity, which, under normal circumstances, might have made Rhiannon feel ashamed. But she had the part of 'the Chameleon' perfected these days. She could camouflage her true feelings so well that not even she knew they were there. 'You can't please all of the people all of the time, Walter.' She approached Patrick Haze and wrenched him from his seat by his hair. 'But I can promise you this … if you don't co-operate with my husband, I am going to beat the life out of your friend here. And you, my dear Walter, shall get to witness every breaking bone. How does that grab you?'

Cadfan didn't know that Patrick was an immortal, and that he was in no real danger. 'Are you possessed, child? What has happened to you?' he wondered aloud, noting she did not wear a module that might have been obliging her to act as she was.

'Not the response we were looking for.' Rhiannon didn't hesitate, she broke Patrick's nose with her elbow and then snapped a couple of his ribs with her knee.

'No, stop!' Cadfan begged her. He knew that although Patrick's spirit was too repressed to cry out in pain, he would still be feeling everything. 'I'll do whatever you want.' Walter's head bowed low in defeat.

Death Valley had been chosen as the location where Cadfan was to meet the people, as this area had remained untouched by disaster. This travesty was to take the form of a healing festival, and the masses had already started to gather.

The evening prior to leaving Britain for Cadfan's big engagement in the US, Doc summoned his guardian to report.

Such meetings took place inside a small circular temple that the diplomat had had erected amidst the extensive gardens of his estate. Inside the sanctuary, torches burnt at the four cardinal points. The walls were perfectly plain, free of incriminating motif or symbol. Long-stemmed flowers adorned long, golden vases situated beneath each of the torches. A large, glass dome featured in the ceiling overhead, exposing the heavens and, at present, the evening stars. The polished marble floor stepped down to a central circular area, where Doc knelt on one knee to address his instructor. With the point of his sword to the ground, he gripped the hilt with both hands, his head bowed low in concentration. Doc gathered his will to invoke Utu; sometimes his guardian would appear. At other times he would simply bethink Doc.

Today, Utu chose to manifest. When informed how Cadfan had been persuaded to co-operate fully the celestial being appeared dubious.

And it was the Dragon's daughter who conceived of this means? the glowing presence inquired.

'Yes, my lord, it was. I believe this is a firm sign of her loyalty to us.'

Utu did not seem as convinced. *I cannot believe, after so many centuries of life, Cadwaladr, that you could still be so blind to the nature of women. Females of any breed are remarkably resourceful and clever. The moment you trust her fully, she shall betray you.*

'I will be cautious.' Doc heeded the warning, all the while trying to conceal the fact that he disagreed.

That is the trouble with human beings, Utu shook his head in sympathy, *always seeing what they want to see, not what is truly there.*

'I'm sorry, my lord, but what would you have me do?'

Replace the NERGUZ on your wife's wrist for the duration of the healing festival.

'But I cannot betray her loyalty thus.' Doc thought of what this would do to the mutual trust he and Rhiannon had built up during their time together.

Cannot, or will not? Shamash challenged. *Mark my words, warrior … she is out to deceive you. Leaving her to roam free is a mistake.*

'How can you be so sure?' Doc questioned defiantly, as he always did. They'd been over this a hundred times already.

Because I know for certain that you are not her true love.

'What!' Doc stood, enraged by the suggestion; this claim had never been raised before. 'Name the man she has deceived me with?' He raised his sword in challenge.

Rhiannon's twin-soul is Cadwallon, though she is not yet aware of his existence.

'Father.' Doc's eyes narrowed, and he began wielding his sword about him. 'He shall never have her. Nor will Rhiannon ever find out about him, is that understood?'

Doc looked to his guardian for confirmation, his sword held poised in challenge once again.

Cadwaladr. Utu appeared surprised at him. *As long as you follow my instructions, she never need know.*

The contempt returned to Doc's face. 'Are you trying to blackmail me, my lord?'

Succeeding, I would say. Don't forget you need me to remove from your memory that which you have just learnt. Otherwise your wife might perceive the fact of Cadwallon from your good self, and we wouldn't want that, would we?

Doc lowered his sword. He could not expect to outwit such a being, and in all honesty, he'd never expected that he might have to.

Restrain your wife, Utu concluded bluntly, before his image shrank into an angry ball of light. The bright manifestation then rammed Doc's head and, by sweeping through his memory of the previous conversation, it neatly edited out the details of their disagreement. All Doc was left with was the overwhelming urge to keep Rhiannon restrained.

The plan was a fairly straightforward one.

A swirling, cosmic cloud mass, disguising their recovery craft, would be orchestrated from deep within Taliesin's maze of a house. Herein was the room of hexagons; technology procured from the Merlin's future travels. He had a device to monitor and manipulate weather patterns within a twenty mile radius of a targeted area. Although this technology could not aid the world's erratic weather problems, it would serve their purpose. Noah had been instructed and briefed on manning the controls, which freed Taliesin to assist Myrddin with the other visuals that would make Cadfan's ascension a realistic and memorable event.

The Merlins planned to conceal themselves in the crowd to carry out their part in the rescue. They were responsible for Cadfan's ascent into the clouds, where his escape vehicle would be awaiting him. Then they were to keep the mystified onlookers entertained long enough for the *Goddess* to get well clear of the area. Tory and Rhun would transport Cadfan to the entrance hall of Taliesin's labyrinth. There they would be joined by other immortals, who would form a protective shield around Cadfan until such time as his own spiritual defences were fully restored. As this process was expected to take weeks, Taliesin had rallied immortals from all the underground tribes to join in the vigil of protection, and he felt quite sure that they would not lack for volunteers.

Being the best pilot, Brian assumed this role and Tory was taking the co-pilot's seat. She was of the mind to record the event on CD-ROM, just in case she should ever wish to expose their hoax. Naomi, as per usual, was navigating and her son, Daniel, was present as a backup in case they needed to launch one of the smaller reconnaisance units. Nicholas was keeping a watchful eye on radar and sonar, and Jenny was his backup should *Merlin I* or *II* be needed. Ray was, of course, overseeing the electronic systems and Rhun was in attendance as all-round trouble shooter. Only two members of the usual team were absent: Noah, who was doing his part from the room of hexagons, and Floyd, who stayed at base to record the media reaction.

Taliesin and Myrddin caught a ride on the *Goddess* to their destination and both were impressed with her performance on her maiden air voyage.

'This is simply splendid, Tory,' her father told her, as he reclined in a luxurious chair, sipping tea. 'I very much approve of my investment.'

'Well, we did invite you to the launch, Dad,' Tory commented, leaving the co-pilot's seat to join her father in the lounge area, located at the rear of the control room. 'But as usual, you didn't listen to me when I told you that she was something extraordinary.'

'For this day and age, anyway,' the Merlin quite agreed.

'Hey, Taliesin,' Brian called back to him from the pilot's seat. 'It's time.'

Ray looked over at Teo after he'd responded to Brian's cue. 'Why does he keep calling you that?'

'It's a nickname,' the Merlin told him. 'You see, Taliesin was a very, very, very wise man, like Einstein.' He was forced to end his explanation there, as Tory and Myrddin burst into laughter.

'So, what's so funny?' Ray's smile wavered, feeling that maybe the joke was on him. Teo raised his brows in disgust, shrugged and disappeared.

'Taliesin was also renowned for his modesty,' Tory explained, spurring on their laughing fit.

'I still don't get it?' Ray looked to Rhun, whose smile indicated he was in on the joke.

'You know my family.' He slapped Ray's shoulder to encourage him to ignore them. 'They're all nuts.'

As Noah eagerly awaited Taliesin's arrival in the room of hexagons, he scribbled down notes for his book. 'All these computers and I don't know how to access a simple word processing program?' He shook his hand, which was beginning to cramp, thinking his situation ironic.

'You were always more partial to the written word anyway.'

Taliesin startled him with the comment, and Noah dropped everything. 'Is it time?'

The Merlin found the lad's reaction amusing.

'You are the very image of an animal stunned by the headlights of an oncoming truck,' he explained.

'That's exactly how I feel,' Noah realised, reaching for his folder to make a note of it.

Once the startup sequence had been initiated, Taliesin was to leave Noah to execute the other functions as taught. But before departing he approached a small control panel that stood facing the largest hexagon in the room. The panel board consisted of nothing, bar a large mottled crystal ball that lit up when Taliesin passed his hand over it.

Noah was so mesmerized by the Merlin's actions that he didn't notice the full-colour holograph taking form inside the large hexagon. Taliesin had to direct his attention to it. 'Holy smoke!' Noah raced over to view the tiny, technicolor landscape more closely.

'Death valley,' the Merlin stated. 'You see that wee cloud forming at your eye level?'

Noah raised his eyes and nodded when he spied the cloud mass erupting in the middle of nowhere.

'That's your cloud.'

'*Wow*,' was all Noah could say — the technology was mind-blowing.

'You know what to do if the ICA put any helicopters in the air.'

A little fearful of the prospect, Noah nodded to confirm.

'It's only to scare them off, my friend. If they don't get too close, they won't be harmed.'

'I understand,' Noah stated surely. 'I'll do my best.'

22

ASCENSION

It was clear skies as they flew in over the crumbling western coastline of the US. The good weather would make it easier to spot Noah's cloud, which Brian estimated would be in sight within half an hour.

The two Merlins departed before the *Goddess* took up station over the target area. Cadfan had been healing people and prescribing natural cures since sunrise; hence you couldn't get within a mile of his healing platform because of all his adoring disciples. Further away, where the masses had spread out and were seated absorbed in their prayers, suited Taliesin and Myrddin better. Here the earth inclined gradually upward, awarding a fine view of the stage in the distance and the cloud mass above it. The temperature in the valley was quite bearable as the climate in this region of the world had also taken a severe turn. It was the weird vibrations emanating from the healing festival itself that were unbearable — both Taliesin and Myrddin felt it — for although people were singing, chanting, and giving praise, their motivation sprang from wantonness and fear, not joy and love.

'I feel this afternoon is going to be a real eye-opener for many of these folks,' Taliesin commented in an aside to Myrddin, who quite agreed.

'That is, of course, if any of them still think for themselves.' Myrddin rolled his eyes and sat himself down. 'I am sorry,' he apologised, as soon as Taliesin had joined him crossed-legged on the ground. 'That was most unnecessary. The vibrations here today are really very unsettling.' He shook off the negative energy.

'Let us hope the elementals are not feeling it as strongly.'

Taliesin hadn't called upon the nature spirits of late. Most had retreated to the fourth dimension, where time does not exist, and from there accessed other ages when the Earth was more hospitable. Those that did remain in the present concerned themselves only with tending the planet. Understandably, they were not well-disposed towards the human race of the twenty-first century; all the ruptures in the Earth's surface were evidence of their discontent. Myrddin had stayed in closer contact with the deva kingdom, mainly those beings who frequented the woodland areas of Britain. So, although desert spirits weren't really his area of expertise, he offered to try and make contact with the elementals in the region — just to make sure all this pandemonium wasn't bothering them too much. Taliesin agreed this was a good idea, so Myrddin disappeared under the hood of his robe to meditate on the task.

He emerged from his private pow-wow about ten minutes later, appearing rather pale. 'We must get these people out of here,' he said.

'That has always been the plan,' Taliesin assured him, noticing the turbulence in the cloud above.

Myrddin shook his head slowly. 'I don't think you understand. I mean this whole valley is very unstable.'

Taliesin knew exactly what he meant, but the plan remained the same and they needed to get on with it. 'I have faith in you. Are you ready?'

Slightly perturbed about the role he had to play in this affair, Myrddin nodded. 'Let us begin.'

It didn't take long for the masses to notice the unnatural movement and glow of the huge cloud above. The anomaly was pointed out to the security guards who lined the front and back of the stage. They also thought it unusual and stood staring up at it just as everybody else did. They certainly didn't expect it was going to steal their charge away, or they surely would have made for Cadfan sooner. Doc would have suspected at once. But, unfortunately, he was having lunch with his associates in a large marquee that had been pitched in the VIP area backstage.

Brian was lining up the *Goddess* to be directly above Cadfan, while beside him Tory watched a live broadcast of the event. The television cameras had switched to a long shot to film the glowing cloud mass expanding above the stage.

'Hey, the searchlights are really effective with all the turbulence the thrusters are creating,' Tory commented.

'I'm pretty sure we're directly over him.' Brian locked into hover mode. 'Hit the searchlight.' They had positioned this earlier, it was aimed directly down.

Tory flicked the switch, her eyes glued to the television broadcast. The cloud had created a shadow over the stage area, and their light beam could be clearly seen as it landed right on Cadfan. 'Direct hit!' Tory squealed with delight, giving her brother a high five.

The light came streaming down upon him. Cadfan raised his eyes from his patient and smiled as his feet left the ground. 'Grandfather,' he uttered, relieved, knowing his kin had finally come for him.

After getting over their initial reaction of awe, the security guards converged on the prophet as he rose into the air. They were not nearly fast enough to catch him however.

Cadfan laughed freely as he ascended, throwing his arms up in adulation. 'Freedom', he cried, tears moistening his eyes at the notion. 'At long last!'

Rhun was there to aid Cadfan as he floated in through the lower doors of Sub Bay One. 'How's it going, Cadfan.' He reached out a hand to assist his grandson onto the platform.

'Are you kidding,' Walter chuckled. 'I'm in heaven.' He got a foothold and then embraced his grandfather, expressing his heartfelt thanks and gratitude.

'You're most welcome,' Rhun assured him, turning to speak into the intercom beside them. 'Close lower sub bay doors. I have him.'

Doc made it outside just in time to see Cadfan disappearing into the clouds. 'Holy shit,' he muttered, quietly fuming as he turned to Stanley Brennon. 'Get those choppers in the air. If we don't prove this is a hoax, we're finished.'

'What if it isn't a hoax?' Brennon posed.

Doc's face was filled with wrath as he pulled the Stormer from Stanley's belt. Brennon decided to acquiesce without further question, rallying his team to the call. Then, as Doc noted some of the press heading their way, he looked at Rhiannon and placed the Stormer in her hand. 'Keep an eye on the fruit,' he ordered, referring to Patrick. 'If anyone comes near him, blast them. Understood?' She gave but a slight nod; as Rhiannon was restrained by the module, he had no doubt that she would do as she was told.

Once he'd learnt that Cadfan had been delivered safely into the arms of his kindred, Taliesin's role was done and he handed the proceedings over to Myrddin.

The Merlin glanced around at the masses, most of whom had fallen to their knees in worship, and a look of disappointment swept his face. Myrddin closed his eyes and again disappeared under his hood.

At a cry of wonderment from the crowd, Taliesin looked to the sky. The cloud had begun pulsing with colour, boiling and billowing more violently than before.

Then, just as suddenly, it settled into another clear form, glowing white in colour. Taliesin saw the symbol of Caduceus, which to him signified striving for higher spiritual awareness, but the people surrounding him had different views: some saw a cross, others the star of David, the face of Jesus, Buddha, or Cadfan. Then a voice was heard, and despite the vastly different languages of the audience everyone understood perfectly.

'Mankind, why do you bow down in awe of your brother? To hope to find spiritual salvation through another's understanding is a farce ... for the path to true enlightenment, happiness and health is inside *you*. The lesson here is one of absolute honesty. Consider, examine, and question everything that is presented to you, even this vision ... for how else shall you ever be granted freedom from delusion. Know yourself, love and manifest the divine in yourself by yourself. For the true name of God is, Taliesin Pen Beirdd.'

What? thought Taliesin, horrified by the announcement. But then he realised that everyone present had heard their own name, and were all just as perplexed by the turn of events.

'Thus, have the courage to take responsibility for your own words, thoughts, acts, beliefs, well-being ... your own life! Leave this place, and in so doing, follow your own path to the divine. For you have only to find the courage to listen and follow your own heart, and you shall be set free.'

Noah was seated beside the large hexagon, madly scribbling notes about the scene unfolding behind the glass screens. He, too, saw the cloud mass take on a clear form, though the image Noah perceived was that of a piece of parchment and a quill. As he completed recording the observation he looked to the holograph for further inspiration, and spotted what he thought were a couple of loose bugs flying around in the device. Upon closer inspection, he realised different. 'Choppers, shit!' He dropped everything and made for the climate controls.

Noah quickly typed in a command and hit the execute key, whereby the beautiful vision of the cloud transformed into a fierce electrical storm.

'You'll stay away if you know what's good for you,' he warned, rushing back to check on the helicopter's movements. Not surprisingly, they had done an about face.

The storm erupted overhead, filling Taliesin's heart with joy as he gazed over the humbled masses before him.

One by one the people rose from their knees to begin their walk out of the valley. It was only a few at first, but then they began rising in droves. Some die-hards, whose religious roots proved stronger than their desire to believe in themselves, continued to weep, believing their God had abandoned them or that the voice in the sky was surely the devil at play.

'It's working,' Taliesin uttered quietly to his accomplice, who was recouping his strength.

The really heartwarming part was that those who had responded did not fall into a line to form a general flow of traffic out of Death Valley. Instead, each person headed off in their own direction.

The television broadcast finally crossed backstage to get Doc Alexander's reaction.

'Will you be leaving the festival now,' one reporter asked.

'If this proves to be a real phenomenon, I most certainly will,' he replied.

'Are you suggesting that what we've just witnessed could be an elaborate hoax, Mr Alexander?'

'You know it is, don't you, arsehole?' Ray jeered, as he viewed the interview over Tory's shoulder.

'You heard the voice,' Doc responded with a grin. 'Question everything.'

As Doc waved off any further questions and headed for the ICA security truck, Ray spotted Rhiannon standing close to a large marquee in the background. 'What gives? She's wearing the module again.'

But before Tory had a chance to confirm this for herself, the station cut to another shot.

'We've got a slight hitch,' Rhun announced, as he arrived on the control deck of the *Goddess* with Cadfan.

'It's more of a request really,' Cadfan explained. 'Doc is holding Patrick, a young novice of mine, captive and will surely take out my disappearance on him.'

'I'll go,' Rhun stated, knowing there was no time to waste. The *Goddess* was well away from the festival site by this time, but they needed to get Cadfan under protection before Doc tried to locate him psychokinetically.

As Taliesin and Myrddin manifested, Tory gave her son the nod to go after Patrick. The two Merlins were powerful enough to shield Cadfan for a time.

'What does Patrick look like?' Rhun questioned, placing his palm to Cadfan's forehead to bethink an image of him.

While everyone was fussing over the prophet, Ray snuck around to retrieve the prototype of the ENZU-GUZ from his work station.

'Don't fear.' Rhun placed a hand upon Cadfan's shoulder in parting.

Ray waited until Rhun had stepped away from Walter and had closed his eyes to focus on Patrick before he grabbed hold of Rhun's arm and vanished along with him.

The large marquee materialised around them, and Rhun was furious when he found Ray had come along for the ride. 'Have you lost your mind? I'm taking you back.' Rhun grabbed for him, but Ray was already halfway to the tent's entrance.

'Take him.' He motioned to Patrick, who was too stunned by their sudden appearance to move. 'Come back for me. I have to free Rhiannon from the NERGUZ.' Ray held up his prototype.

'But she'll kill you,' Rhun began, then decided it would be faster to do as Ray suggested than argue.

Patrick was unarmed, and though there were security men surrounding the tent, there were none inside the marquee. Rhun reached out and grabbed hold of the lad, who appeared terrified beyond reason. 'It's okay, Patrick.' Rhun kept his voice low so as not to alert the guards. 'I'm taking you home.'

'Home?' he queried, as if he'd never before considered the prospect.

'Shh,' Rhun advised with a nod, and the blue white ethers engulfed them.

Ray was creeping towards the open flaps at the end of the marquee when Rhiannon unexpectedly entered alone. Upon sighting him she pulled the Stormer from her belt and, finding her captive missing, aimed the weapon at the intruder. 'Where is he?'

With the banquet table between them, Ray had no chance of grabbing the weapon from her. He wouldn't have tried, in any case, as she was a far better fighter than he. 'I can see you are in no mood for questions.' He tiptoed around her fury. 'You wouldn't, perchance, remember me?'

'Should I?'

Her dark eyes stared him down. Yet, they were glazed — as if only her body was confronting him and her soul had taken flight elsewhere.

'Where is he?' She moved round to confront Ray on his side of the table, and the force of her steps urged him to back up.

'Who? There's nobody here,' Ray pointed out the obvious, 'and I'm certainly not hiding anybody.'

'Why are you here?'

'I have a gift for you.' He held up the device that looked about as exciting as a dentist's tool.

'Not interested,' she decided at a glance, taking aim.

'I'll take that …' Rhun knocked the weapon from her hands and into Ray's, then wrestled Rhiannon into a controllable position. 'Ray.' Rhun motioned for him to do the honours.

It wasn't easy to sever the control mechanism with

Rhiannon doing her best to punch Ray every time he got the ENZU-GUZ into position.

'Rhiannon,' Rhun whispered into her ear, his hand clamped hard over her mouth. 'You have to leave here. There's going to be an earthquake, a big one!'

His words managed to keep Rhiannon still long enough for Ray to complete the procedure. 'Done,' he advised Rhun, so that he could let her go.

When Doc entered the marquee to see Ray Murdock with his wife, it brought the conversation he'd had with Utu about Cadwallon flooding back. 'You'll not have her!' He pulled his pistol from its holster and fired it several times.

Rhun dived too late to block the bullets, but he cast himself over Ray's body to return him to the *Goddess*.

'Are you alright?' Doc raced over to Rhiannon.

She spotted the strange device Ray had offered her still lying on the ground, and hid it under her foot. 'I'm fine … now,' she replied.

'Where is Haze?' Doc's mood turned stormy. Utu's suggestion of betrayal was playing on his mind, and a sudden surge of anger prompted him to lash out.

Rhiannon was fast enough to block the back-handed strike, and gripped Doc's wrist firmly. 'The queer disappeared. I don't know where he went.' She tossed his arm away from her. 'If you think about it a moment, you'll realise I'm telling you the truth.'

She was brutally honest when restrained, and what's more she was right; with the module still firmly in place it was impossible for her to lie. 'You're right. I'll just have to find him myself.' Doc resolved to be more civil. 'I apologise for my outburst.'

'That's alright,' Rhiannon stated dryly. 'No great threat.'

'Jesus Christ! What happened?' Tory rushed to Ray's side, realising he'd been injured. 'You fool, Murdock.' Tears welled when she discovered just how serious his wounds were.

'I got shot,' he informed her, looking down at his holey excuse for a body as if it belonged to someone else.

'Shh.' Tory gently urged his head back as Jenny placed a pillow underneath it. 'Cadfan.' Tory looked to the healer.

Walter knelt down to examine Ray, though he knew at a glance he could do little for him. The bullets had punctured vital organs. Cadfan was a fine herbalist, but a surgeon he was not.

'Who did this?' Tory looked to Rhun for the answer. He'd taken a few steps away, but his eyes were still fixed on Ray.

'The wounds,' he mumbled softly, 'they are the same.'

Tory didn't have to ask what he meant. She perceived the image of Sir Bryce that filled Rhun's mind. The knight was sprawled amongst the dead on a bloody battlefield, and his war wounds matched those on Ray's body to the letter. 'No, it doesn't have to be.' She turned back to Ray, realising she was losing him. 'Stay with us.' She gripped hold of his hand. 'We need you, Ray, please.'

A peaceful smile graced his face as reached up to touch her cheek. 'You don't need anyone, Tory Alexander,' he uttered as his hand went heavy in hers, and his body fell limp to the floor with the departure of his spirit.

'Tory.' Her father placed both hands on her shoulders. 'I am sorry, child, but you have to come with us now.'

'Give me a minute,' she protested, wrenching herself from Myrddin's grasp to hug Ray's lifeless form.

'Tory.' Naomi gently encouraged her to let go. 'We shall tend to Ray.'

Had anyone else tried to move her, Tory would have resisted. But in the face of her sister-in-law, Tory saw Katren — her dearest friend in the Dark Ages, and Bryce's adopted mother. Tory had always recognised Naomi as Katren, but her past-life connection with Ray had not occurred to Tory before now. It was as if Katren had come to collect her son.

'Don't worry,' Naomi urged, easing her away, 'just go.'

Tory looked down at Ray and tenderly kissed his cheek. She then rose to accompany Taliesin, Myrddin, Rhun, Cadfan and Patrick, all standing in a circle. They joined hands, and promptly disappeared.

In the room of hexagons, Noah was revising his notes while he waited for someone to come and collect him. Taliesin had warned of the dangers of wandering off into the labyrinth alone. He still wasn't quite sure if he believed that there were bizarre creatures and unearthly spirits inhabiting some of rooms herein, but Noah respected the High Merlin enough to abide by his wishes and stay put.

You could find your way around this maze blindfold.

'What?' Noah looked up from his notes, expecting to find someone, but there was no-one present.

You need the library.

Noah ceased his search of the room when he realised the voice was coming from inside his own head. It occurred to him that this might be one of those unearthly spirits Taliesin had warned him about. Noah's heart starting pumping so fiercely the beat resounded in his ears. 'Who … who … who are you?'

I am you … or rather I am one of the many yous you have been.

'Selwyn!'

Capital guess.

'W … w … why are you here?'

Please calm down, the voice was heard to chuckle. *I'm here to help you. Has the great Queen of Gwynedd never mentioned me?*

'Yes.' Noah relaxed, having figured out that Tory was the great Queen to whom Selwyn referred. 'She has spoken of you often. She claimed I was you, you were me … whatever.'

And that is the plain truth of it, Selwyn assured Noah. *I am here to help you remember all that you have known, so that you can become all that you are capable of being. Which brings us back to my original request for you to go the library.*

'I'm not going exploring in here!'

I know the way, Selwyn insisted, *and Taliesin won't mind so long as I am guiding you*. Noah was still hesitant, so Selwyn added: *My entire life's work is contained therein*.

Noah had read various interpretations of the Merlin's work — the few rare extracts that still survived in the twenty-first century. But to read the renowned Druid's complete works could only be compared to finding the Dead Sea Scrolls.

'Everything you ever wrote?' Noah nibbled at the bait.

Not only my histories, but Taliesin's as well.

Noah needed no more coaxing. He retrieved his folder and pen and was out the door.

At the end of the corridor he came to one of the main hallways. To the left, this went into a maze of corridors and doors; to the right it led to a similar architectural jungle of stairs and doors. Selwyn directed Noah towards some nearby stairs.

Up, Noah was told, as he contemplated the nightmarish feat of engineering. He ignored the instruction momentarily and leaned out over the polished timber railing to discover that the maze of stairs, doorways, archways, open chambers, walkways and hallways twisted to infinity both above and below. 'My God, are you sure you know where you're taking me?'

As surely as I know that you shall be the eyes, ears, and memory of a whole new generation of thinkers.

'Is that supposed to reassure me?' Noah thought the claim ridiculous, especially since Tory had forbidden him to ever publish the story that was based on her adventures and family tree.

Again Selwyn was amused by Noah's reckoning. *You know the clan of the Dragon are capable of such feats, so why not you? After all, you are one of them.*

'In an honorary sense, perhaps.' Noah released a heavy sigh. He felt so inadequate next to his crewmates who, literally, were changing the world. All he could do was record their acts, and hope that he lived long enough to finish the story.

No, Selwyn replied. *You are related in an actual sense, Noah — a distant descendant of the Dragon's line. The blood of the serpent pumps in your veins. Thus you have also inherited the vital gene that sets you apart as one of the Chosen.*

Noah's legs went from beneath him and he found himself on the floor. Here he was being told that his greatest hope had come to pass. Could he dare to believe it was true? 'You're toying with me,' he decided. If this spirit was in his head, then surely it knew his desires and was using them to manipulate him.

Oh dear, Selwyn sighed, sounding most disappointed. *Are you so afraid to believe that you are powerful beyond measure? Or is it that you will fantasise about greatness, but when it comes down to it, you'd prefer to leave the real achieving to others?*

'That certainly is not it!' Noah got to his feet, insulted. 'Even if you are lying about the immortality thing, I will still do all I can to aid the Dragon's cause.'

Then do it by going up the stairs and to your left.

At the top Noah passed through an ornate gazebo, and then down another set of stairs to a mahogany timber archway. This adorned the entrance to a circular, domed room of pure white marble. The fountain that sprang from the floor in the centre of the foyer had been sculpted in the form of a cauldron — the cauldron of knowledge. Scented water sprouted from the top of several large chunks of quartz crystal that formed the central feature of the fountain over which the water flowed.

Wash your hands and forehead, Selwyn instructed.

'They're not dirty,' Naoh insisted, having looked his hands over.

Physically, no. But spiritually and mentally, yes, you need cleansing.

'Alright … if you say so.' Noah gave in easily, eager to touch the inviting piece of art.

The pool was bathed in a white light, which seemingly emanated from the crystals in the centre. Cool and smooth to the touch, the quartz pulsated with energy. The sweet, silky water flowing over this formation was so soothing to Noah's hands and head that he considered tossing his whole body in. 'Wow.' He sniffed at himself, having shaken off the excess water. 'What's that smell? It's so … invigorating!'

Bergamot — the scholar's scent. Now you are ready for the library …

The huge, twin doors parted before Noah, who was far too curious to fear the force that was opening the way for him. All he could see were the miles of book-crammed shelves that lay within the room, and the desks piled high with parchments and scrolls.

'Paradise,' uttered the writer, as the doors closed behind him.

There was a small desk amidst the larger tables that drew Noah's attention at once. It had several jars of coloured ink on it, all lined up, with quills of matching colour. He reached for the parchment on the desk, and was disappointed to find he could not read a word of it.

Fear not, Selwyn offered. *I shall translate. It reads:*

This be the last will and testament of Selwyn, Chief Bard to the Court and the Kings of Powys. I have placed all my writings in the safe keeping of Taliesin Pen Beirdd, High Merlin of Britain, in the hope that he will see my work into the hands of my Chosen incarnation for completion at the time of the Gathering. I trust that this shall be to my liking, Sincerely thine, Thy sixth century incarnation, Selwyn.

Noah's eyes filled with tears. He no longer doubted the veracity of this spirit anymore, nor his translation of the ancient script. 'You truly are me. I would have done exactly the same thing!' He gave half a laugh at how ingenious he, *they*, were.

Noah, my good lad, you don't even know the half of it.

As hard as Doc concentrated on willing himself to Cadfan and Haze, his efforts proved fruitless. It was as if the men he sought had vanished from creation, along with the rest of Rhiannon's kindred.

'This is useless.' He gave up after hours of trying. 'Your friends must be shielding them.'

Rhiannon only shrugged, as she certainly knew nothing about it.

'Well, say something!' Doc was being demanding, as they were alone in the marquee.

'I say we leave,' she stated bluntly. 'There's going to be an earthquake.'

'How the hell do you know that?'

Rhiannon uncrossed her legs and removed them from the banquet table. 'One of my attackers told me, and the way I see it, he had no reason to lie.'

'Are you daft? Of course he wants us to leave, then it will look as if we're going along with this outrageous scenario they've created.'

'Oh, give it up, Doc!' Rhiannon lectured him. 'Is it any more outrageous than the Messiah you created? What do you care if Cadfan's gone. You don't need him any more. You *have* to tell the people remaining here to leave — they'll listen to you.'

'I will do no such thing. What if you're wrong about the earthquake? Then I'll look a fool.'

Rhiannon grabbed hold of her husband's arm on his way out of the marquee. 'But if they're telling the truth, these people will have you to thank for their lives.' Rhiannon expanded on her theme: 'Say Cadfan has spoken with you, and issued you a warning. I mean, Jesus kept in contact with his disciples, so why not Cadfan?'

'Indeed, two can play at this game.' Doc smiled as he suddenly realised how easily this disaster might be twisted to his advantage. He didn't have to worry about containing the prophet any more, and Cadfan wouldn't dare show up in public, so there was no chance of him refuting any of the propaganda they chose to create in his wake. 'If I could only be sure your friend was telling the truth.'

'Trust me,' Rhiannon insisted, knowing the informant was her brother. 'He was telling the truth.'

A helicopter was standing by to whisk them away after Doc made the announcement. But no sooner had he said his piece, than the Earth began to tremble. In the midst of the turmoil of panicked people, and the commotion caused by the stage scaffold collapsing, Doc's security team still managed to have their boss and his wife in the air within minutes.

From their bird's-eye view, the extent of the quake was much more obvious. The mountains had become walls of tumbling rock, while the barren floor of the valley was cracking and falling away, claiming many souls in the process.

'More of your kin's handiwork?' Doc sneered. 'That would seem to explain why they were so certain the disaster would come to pass.'

'It is more likely they had a vision,' Rhiannon retorted, feeling sure her mother would never knowingly kill so many people.

'Then Cadfan would have had the premonition, too. Am I right?' Doc was following her train of thought, and felt it naive. 'Rhiannon, your mother was hailed as a warrior where I come from — just how do you think she got such a title? It wasn't for being compassionate, I can tell you. So don't kid yourself. Tory Alexander has killed for the Dragon's cause before.'

'My kindred do not have the means to cause a disaster like this! Lights in the sky is one thing; movement in the Earth's crust is something else again.'

Doc shook his head, unable to believe how misinformed she was. 'Taliesin Pen Beirdd can incite nature spirits to war on his behalf! I have seen it! He has friends in realms beyond our wildest imagination. Something like this,' Doc motioned to the devastation below them, 'would be no more difficult for the Merlin than a walk in the park, if he, or those he serves, wanted the problem ended.'

There was no point in arguing with him, Rhiannon realised. Doc's tone said it all. 'You still despise them don't you?'

'Yes, I despise them,' he agreed. 'This is not the first time I have seen their indifferent form of malice.' Doc's mood darkened. His time as Cadwaladr often came back to taunt him. 'I am remembered as the King who lost half of Britain, and why? Because I didn't have any assistance — no mystical adviser to guide my way through all the treachery to greatness. Maelgwn, Rhun, Cadwell, Cadfan, Cadwallon, oh yes, they were legendary. But not I. Oh no, I was left to take the rap for one of the bloodiest massacres the motherland has ever seen.'

'But they didn't know that,' Rhiannon appealed.

'They didn't care,' he snapped. Doc's tolerance for the subject was at an end.

Rhiannon knew that, deep down, it was the fact of being thwarted that was really angering Doc and not the loss of human life that they'd just witnessed. But she also knew he was convinced that her kin were responsible for all the day's events, giving him all the more reason to hate them. It had been foolish of her to believe she had smoothed over the feud with a few well-chosen words. His resentment of them ran deeper than his love for her, and Rhiannon realised that nothing she could say or do was going to change his view of the past.

At the vigil around Cadfan, the atmosphere stripped away Tory's grief and threw her headlong into a state of complete ecstasy.

This mini-gathering of the tribe of immortals was the single greatest multicultural event Tory had ever experienced. Black, white, red, yellow, whatever — all mingled together in perfect harmony like the designs of the Aboriginal people's sacred Churingas.

No one had any problems communicating via telepathy. Tory sang and danced to the chants of every native tongue of the Earth, and understood the significance of every word and movement.

There was a constant circle of twenty-four people around Walter and Patrick, and there was no shortage of reserves to step into their place. The guests spilled over into the first adjoining hallway of Taliesin's maze, inhabiting certain rooms which the Merlin had opened up to accommodate them throughout their stay. The whole affair was reminiscent of an indigenous indoor Woodstock, where the chance to mingle was as exciting as participating in the event itself.

Upon completion of a six-hour shift in the inner circle, Tory and Rhun meandered down the hallway from the vigil room in search of refreshment. Their path was strewn with the bodies of other guests who cheered the pair for their stamina.

'I sure hope that's water,' Tory muttered as she spied Taliesin approaching with a pitcher and two large goblets.

'What a vast improvement,' he commented to Tory, as he watched her swallow the water down. 'You are positively radiant.'

Tory winked at him as she passed the empty goblet back. 'I haven't experienced a natural buzz of this magnitude since the day I wed Maelgwn. Hell, I feel like nothing could ever bring me down again.'

'Unconditional giving is a marvellous thing,' the Merlin said. 'When you expect nothing in return for your efforts, anything you receive is a bonus.'

'Hey, how's it going guys?' Noah wandered out of the depths of the labyrinth and into the festivities, gripping an old scroll in one hand.

'Noah!' Tory could have hit herself. 'I'm so sorry. Did nobody come to fetch you?'

'No apologies necessary,' he assured her. 'Taliesin came and found me in the library, where I was going through my old writings. Selwyn says hi, by the way.' Without further explanation Noah turned his attention to Taliesin, unrolling the scroll in his hand. 'This must be one of yours. Selwyn doesn't understand the language.'

'Well, that isn't any wonder, because it's Atlantean,' the Merlin explained. 'We'll have to get you in touch with your past incarnation Seth, as this is one of the works he left for you.'

'Excellent.' Noah was again stoked by his own foresight. 'Selwyn was right. I don't know the half of it.'

'You will. By the time of the Gathering, you will understand everything.'

Noah was gratified to know that he'd certainly be there, and with this thought he turned to Tory to offer his condolences. 'I was sorry to hear about Ray. Taliesin told me what happened. He'll be sorely missed.'

'Yes, he will,' Tory confirmed, 'till next we meet.'

'Hear, hear ...' Taliesin materialised a pitcher of mead and two more goblets, so that they might toast this sentiment.

While Taliesin filled the goblets, Tory looked from him to Noah to Rhun. The four of them had quite a history together. 'This scene is awfully familiar. It seems the four of us are always left guarding the fort.'

'And, as always, we shall do a fine job of it, until the reinforcements arrive,' Rhun announced with cheer, having regained a little of his cocky attitude.

'To the Gathering then,' Taliesin announced, raising his goblet in the air.

'The Gathering!'

Their goblets met in a clash of metal and they drank to the future — to the loves, friends and adventures that awaited them there.

PART iii

THE HOLY GHOST

CHARACTER HISTORY

The Chosen	the Dark Age	Atlantis
Tory Alexander (Thurlow)	Tory/Sorcha	Temperance
Maelgwn/ Miles Thurlow	Maelgwn	Turan
Brian Alexander	Brockwell	Adelgar
Candace/ Naomi Alexander	Katren	Tabitha
Floyd	Tiernan	Durand
Boadicea	Ione	Lilith
Robin of Loxley/ John Pearce	Rhys	Darius
Jenny Pearce	Jenovefa	Anthea
Neraida	Cara	
Cadwell	Vortipor/Cadwell	
Ethan	Angus	
Talynn	Alma	
Rhun	Rhun	Xavier
Sybil	Bridgit	Sybil
Rhiannon Thurlow	Aella	Annora
Cadwallon/ Ray Murdock	Bryce	Zadoc
Cadwaladr/ Doc Alexander	Caradoc	Alaric
Vanora	Vanora	Antonia
Noah Purcel	Selwyn	Seth
Pocahontas/Rebecca		

Nicholas Pearce	Gawain	Gaspard
Helen of Sparta		
Daniel Alexander	Cai	Lazarus
Cleopatra		
Aunt Rose	Lady Gladys	Nin Bau
Taliesin/Teo	Taliesin	Jerram
Seshut/Donna		Mahala
Mryddin/		
Renford Alexander	Mryddin	Absalom
Vivian/		
Helen Alexander	Vivian	Melcah
Walter Cadfan	Cadfan	
Queen Hatshepsut		
Thomas Mateus		Thais
Hero		
Patrick Haze		
Season		

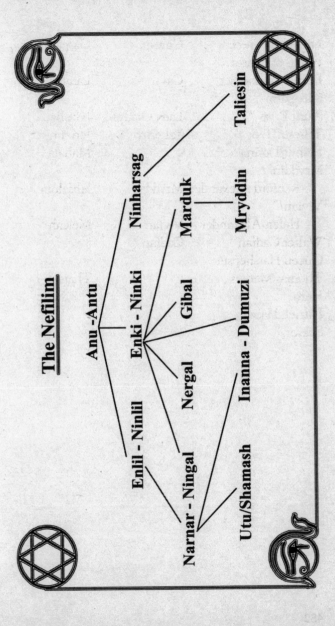

The Nefilim

Anu -Antu

Enlil - Ninlil   Enki - Ninki   Ninharsag

Narnar - Ningal   Nergal   Gibal   Marduk

Utu/Shamash   Inanna - Dumuzi   Mryddin   Taliesin

23

PASSING TIME

After Cadfan's deliverance from the ICA and his recovery from the effects of his zombie state, the volunteers from the underground tribes returned to their individual bases to await the time of the Gathering — some fourteen years away.

Although there were still many immortals trapped by the NERGUZ-I-NUEN, Taliesin advised that it would be wise to wait until the Gathering was nearly upon them before attempting another rescue. If the ICA were left alone they would perhaps be lulled into a false sense of security. The less their abilities were tested, the more lax they would become.

By the same token, Taliesin didn't want Tory stirring up any more trouble either. He reminded her of Maelgwn's request that she stay hidden, then asked her to consider all that had happened since she'd chosen to ignore the warning. How much of it could have been avoided if she'd taken that advice; was the world really a better place for her defiance?

Tory mulled over his supposition carefully. She had saved lives, true, but no one that she wouldn't have been reunited with eventually. She had not prevented the gaping hole in the ozone layer over the Middle East, or the abduction and murder of innocent people in Alaska. Nor, with Ray's death, would they be able to prevent the implementation of the Fusion project. Tory had, however, lost her daughter through their involvement in ICA affairs and this most certainly would not have happened had she heeded Maelgwn's warning. So, in the end, Tory persuaded herself to see reason and vowed to Taliesin that she would leave Doc be.

Although Taliesin wholeheartedly wanted to take Tory at her word, he couldn't help but caution her. One of the trials in these times of tribulation, he said, was to resist wasting their resources on little individual battles. For only then would the Chosen stand a chance of winning the war.

Walter Cadfan and Patrick Haze had no problems fitting in at Watarrka, and before long had set up their own healing practice and a thriving herbarium. With the procession of the years, however, their powers of healing were tested more and more. For, with the weakening of the Earth's magnetic field due to its axis shift the planet was bombarded with radiation from space. The levels of poisonous toxins in the air increased to an unbearable high and with this came a plague of respiratory, digestive, skin and mind diseases, usually fatal.

The human race was driven to seek refuge in the few large bodies of forest the planet had left to offer; for only the trees had the ability to transform the poisonous gasses into fresh breathable air.

Biodcmes were no longer just scientific experiments for collecting data on the biosphere and its ecosystems. They had become an integral part of the future of life on Earth and life in space. Underground, under the sea, on the moon and on the Earth's surface whole cities with carefully monitored environments were constructed. Clean, healthy surroundings became a luxury that only the rich could afford to enjoy every day, though the middle classes could vacation in the Biodome once they'd saved enough money to afford the entry fee. The best bet for the average Joe Blow in the street to be granted residency was to land a job with a major corporation who operated from within one of the Biodomes. The remaining population, though promised residency in paradise when enough Biodomes had been constructed, was continually misinformed about the damaged environment to prevent panic. In their ignorance, a large majority of Earth dwellers were at the mercy of cosmic radiation and its slow but inexorable toll.

The large opening in the roof of the cavern of pools was closed over to protect Watarrka's community from harmful radiation. Under Rhun's guidance, the immortals pooled their telekinetic know-how to help achieve an amazing feat of organic cementation. But, unlike a Biodome, Watarrka was still not completely isolated from the outside world, for their water supply was fed from external sources. The water trickled in through various rocky crevices in the canyon floor, far too many to hope to find and block them all. As a further means of prevention, they planted as many trees and shrubs around the outside pools as possible. They also boiled and filtered all water for consumption. In the end, though, they could only hope to delay the slow poisoning of their people.

These measures kept the health problems of the outside world at bay for many years, but by the year 2028 the mortals at Watarrka starting showing the first symptoms of radiation-induced illnesses.

Due to her age, Aunt Rose was the first to fall ill. As she was an immortal, however, Tory arranged for a fatal injection to be administered to her aunt in her sleep. Rose awoke the following day to find her health and youth restored. Returned to the fair and supple beauty Rose had been in her prime, Tory recognised her as Nin Bau, once the High Priestess of Chailidocean and the lover of the Lord Marduk.

Tory also arranged to have Noah, Nicholas, Daniel, Floyd, Pete Nangina, and his family, put out of their misery before it began. One simple injection whilst they slept and it was done. Floyd was the only one who even wised up to the transition straight away, as he was noticeably more youthful and now sported a full head of hair.

There was one amongst them whose suffering Tory could not prevent.

Brian lost his beloved wife, Naomi, to cancer during the Winter of '29. In the end she went willingly, trusting Tory's word that her immortal self was making her way back to them as they spoke. Since they had met some thirty-three years before, Brian had loved Naomi faithfully. Needless to say he was not the same man for many years after her death.

Having dedicated many years to gazing at the stars, Daniel Alexander finally made a significant discovery.

At approximately midnight on the 16th December, 2036, Dan was making a routine check of the constellation of Taurus when he chanced to witness a new light appear in the night sky. This twinkle, he immediately concluded, had to be a comet.

These great lumps of dust and ice often appeared without warning as they travelled into the inner reaches of the solar system from the Oort Cloud far beyond the reaches of the planets. Comets only became visible once the sun's heat had evaporated some of their ice mass. This thawing released dust from the comet's surface creating a vapour cloud that reflected sunlight and made the comet visible from Earth.

By breakfast time the following day, Daniel was still checking the orbit paths of all the known periodical and non-periodical comets. There was really no need to do this, as Daniel knew them all by heart. Still, he had to be sure. Perhaps there was one obscure comet in history he'd not studied, or that he'd forgotten. When nothing matched up, however, Daniel was forced to concede that he must have discovered an entirely new comet.

By this stage of the century only the immortals inhabited the underground base at Watarrka and the *Goddess* easily accommodated them all. They had reversed the cementation job done on the roof of the cavern of pools as their isolation no longer served any purpose. They took *Merlin I* and *II* on regular runs to scout for any stray immortals who might still be wandering the vast wastelands of the Earth. This gave them something constructive to do apart from their studies. The only terrorist activity they'd participated in of late was their monthly raid on Biodome food stocks. Watarrka's once-thriving cavern of produce had died along with the mortal inhabitants.

Daniel raced through the dark middle cavern that had been powered down long ago to conserve energy for Floyd's computers. This cavern gave Dan the creeps these days — there were far too many ghosts haunting the shadows therein. His pace slowed when he entered the partially-sunlit cavern of pools, where the *Goddess* was docked. Daniel guessed everyone would be at breakfast in the rec room, and ran up the gangway eager to tell his news.

Daniel raved on for a good ten minutes about celestial latitude (declination), longitude (right ascension), and other data he'd been filling his brain with most of the night.

It was Noah who was the first to pick up on where Daniel's spiel was leading. 'Ah, you would be referring to the comet the Anglo-Australian Observatory claimed the discovery of early this morning.'

'That's bullshit, man,' Daniel insisted. 'What was their official time of discovery?'

'One-fourteen this morning.'

Daniel let loose a screech that might have been a laugh were he not so frustrated. 'I discovered it nearly an hour before them.'

Brian gave his son a chug on the shoulder for his achievement, even though they both knew he could not publicly state his claim. 'Well, at least we know it's "Alexander's comet", no matter what the experts decide to name it.'

'Too right.' Noah seconded Brian's view. 'I'll make note of it in my scripts. Perhaps, with the passing of time, the oversight will be corrected.'

'Thanks, guys.' Daniel collapsed into a seat, seeing his chances as grim.

'Oh, come on.' Tory attempted to snap him out of his sudden melancholy. 'You haven't been studying the stars all these years for the glory. Discovery and observation is what it's all about, and that's exactly what you're doing ... so, be glad. I feel quite sure the universe threw that comet into your line of vision for good reason, so you'd best figure out what that is.'

'You think?' he responded more positively.

'Don't you?' She threw the ball back in his court.

'Perhaps you're right.' Daniel reached for the breakfast cereal, his enthusiasm in the new comet rekindled.

'But don't go neglecting the other regions of space,' Rhun warned.

'I know,' Daniel said in a bored fashion. '*Especially* Sirius.'

Rose wandered in half asleep, an absolute knockout in a pair of cut-off jeans and a midriff top. She wasn't even given the chance to wish all of them a good morning before every male in the room broke into loud whistles.

'Looking good, Aunt Rose.' Even after eight years, Rose's transformation still amazed Brian. He just couldn't get used to the fact that this dark-haired, green-eyed babe was his old aunt.

'Thank you, pumpkin.' She tweaked his cheek as if he were a child.

'Ah, you're an awful tease, Rose,' Rhun accused her playfully, as he gave her a squeeze.

Rose giggled, lapping up the attention. 'If you've got it, flaunt it, I say.'

'Here, here,' all the men agreed.

Floyd strutted into the rec-room, his long fair hair flying in the back draft. 'Morning all.' He sounded disturbed, but he kept his beef to himself, strolling straight up to the breakfast bar.

'The usual?' Patrick placed the strong Irish coffee in front of Floyd. 'It's got a little extra kick this morning,' he winked.

Patrick took care of all the catering arrangements these days, and having proven himself a talented telepathist, he prided himself on knowing what people wanted before they asked.

'Cheers.' Floyd sipped on the brew, and finding it a pleasant temperature, drank the whole mug down.

'Jeez, what's eating you?' Patrick immediately replaced the empty with another he'd already prepared.

'Mongolia,' commented Floyd, taking the mug in hand.

'That would have been my next guess!' Patrick appeared a tad concerned for the man's well-being.

'Well,' Floyd threw an arm in the air, 'after blatantly refusing the ICA's request to do some surveying in their region, the Mongolian Government have now had an abrupt change of heart.'

'God, that shits me.' Patrick played along.

'So what's that now?' Noah counted scenarios in his mind. 'Five countries the ICA has blackmailed their way around thanks to the fusion grid.'

'You would think they'd all wise up,' Rose scoffed.

'They probably have,' Tory rose to clear her dishes, 'only now it's too late to do anything about it. Besides, anyone who's *someone* is tucked up safely in the cosy atmosphere of their little domed paradise. And as long as the ICA keep pumping the power their way, they don't give a damn what happens to the world outside.'

'Sounds a bit like us,' Brian grumbled, voicing the restlessness they all felt.

'Don't start with me, Brian,' Tory warned, and he dropped the subject.

'What do you think their interest in Mongolia is, anyhow?' Rhun posed in a general fashion. It was his mother who answered him.

'We don't know, and we don't care,' she stated forcefully. 'Subject closed.'

'Besides …' Patrick reverted back to his original question, and passed Floyd his third refill, 'I don't think that's what's really bothering you.'

'Hey,' Floyd took a swipe at Pat, who jumped back out of harms way, 'don't be getting into my head this early in the morning.'

'Touchy.' Pat provoked him further. 'I was only going to ask her name?'

'I don't know! Okay?'

Tory, who'd finished rinsing her dishes, overheard the comment and was too curious not to inquire: 'To what *her* are you both referring?'

'I just got through telling him, I don't know. I just had a couple of dreams, that's all. More like wishful thinking, than anything else,' Floyd mumbled in conclusion, and was about to walk off in a huff, when Tory glimpsed his mind and a vision of the beauty who was haunting him.

'I know her name,' she announced boldly, and waited for Floyd to do an about-face. 'I even have a couple of photos. Want to see?'

Though Floyd couldn't imagine in his wildest dreams how this could be possible, he knew better than to doubt Tory's claims. He gave a vague nod and followed her to the CD-ROM library.

'I know they're in here somewhere.' Tory glanced through the titles on the computer screen. 'I had a whole bunch of photos from my travels scanned onto a CD for safekeeping. Gwynedd,' she announced. 'Here it is.' She double-clicked on the file, and the computer searched, selected and loaded the CD in question from amid the hundreds it held in its stacker.

A slide show of photographs appeared one by one on the screen.

'Is that your wedding?' Floyd was gaping at the shots, which looked rather like the stills from a grand period movie.

Tory nodded, feasting her eyes on the fleeting image of her love. 'Happiest day of my life,' she told Floyd with certainty. The next picture that faded in was of all twelve of the original members of the Dragon's circle who had served as guardians of Britain during Maelgwn's rule. 'There she is.' Tory froze the screen, selecting only the figures of Ione and Sir Tiernan to blow up and enhance.

'It is her … and me!' he realised, having taken a closer look. 'Rhun told me about my life in Gwynedd as the champion of King Caswallon and then King Maelgwn after him.' Floyd lowered himself into a chair, believing that if he didn't sit down he'd fall down. 'But I always assumed he was either exaggerating or pulling my leg.'

'Don't look so worried,' she chuckled. 'Your dreams are just your past life memories bleeding through. We've all experienced this to differing degrees. The training Rhun and myself have been putting you through is designed to encourage such experiences.'

'So, let me get this straight.' Floyd's new understanding made him smile. 'Are you saying I was involved with *this* woman?'

Tory rolled her eyes at his choice of words. 'God, Floyd, you're such a damn bachelor sometimes. Marriage is not a dirty word you know?'

'*She married me!* Why?'

'She was your wife in two different lifetimes that I know of,' Tory stated. 'Why should this be so surprising to you?'

Now Floyd was laughing. 'Because she has the makings of a super model, or a Goddess even. What the hell would she see in me?'

'The makings of a champion, a genius, or a King, perhaps?' Her response seemed to floor him, and he went quiet for a moment.

'So what is the point of me remembering her? Is this some sort of cosmic torture?'

'Hardly. I'd say she wants to make sure that you'll recognise her when she returns here with Maelgwn and the others next year.'

'Next year!' This piece of information certainly rattled Floyd somewhat as he looked down at his youthful, though undeveloped, body. 'Jesus! If she's expecting a champion, I sure have some work to do.'

'That might be wise.' Tory thought she'd give him a little extra incentive. 'Ione's perfect incarnation was none other than the great warrior, Boadicea — Queen of the Iceni people in the east of Britain. She was an ally of the Romans until she saw her people overtaxed, her husband slaughtered and her daughters raped. In 61 AD she led what became an almighty massacre against the Romans, and burned London and St Albans to the ground.'

496

'So you think I might have been her husband then?' Floyd theorised, fascinated by the tale.

'Almost certainly,' Tory advised, 'though only you can really confirm this for sure by endeavouring to get in touch with your incarnation at that time.'

'Well, I just might do that.' He arose, inspired. 'Thanks for the insight.'

'Any time,' she smiled. Floyd made haste from the room to reach his computers and do a bit of research himself.

24

SUPERNOVA

As 2036 gave way to 2037, the night sky played host to some very unusual activity.

The first episode of note occurred on a moonless night towards the end of January. Daniel was plotting his comet's course across the heavens when a few portions of it were seen to split away from the main body and take off on their own course. The comet itself was entering our solar system, its trajectory against the general orbit of the planets, but the splintered fragments it shed headed off in the same orbit as the rest of the system.

'This just doesn't happen,' Dan explained to his colleagues over breakfast. 'If some force had caused the comet to shatter or explode, then it would have been dispersed in all directions ... the bulk just couldn't maintain its original course.'

'Are you quite sure about what you saw?' Noah looked up from sourcing information on his portable computer. 'You weren't smoking any of Floyd's pot at the time perchance?'

'What kind of an idiot do you take me for, Purcell?' Daniel took great offence at the suggestion. 'I'll have you know I take my work very seriously.'

'Hey.' Noah held up his hands in truce. 'Look, if something of such astronomic importance occurred last night, I'm just wondering why one of the major observatories hasn't reported it?'

'They haven't?' Daniel was stunned. Noah shook his head. 'I have photographic documentation of the event. They must have seen it.'

'If you're right,' Floyd spoke up, 'the only person who could force a conspiracy of silence of that magnitude is Doc Alexander.'

'Why would he care about the movements of some comet?' Rose queried.

'He wouldn't,' Tory cut in. 'Unless, of course, Dan's comet is not a comet, but say, a space station.'

'A space station!' echoed everyone in the room in disbelief.

'Now hear me out.' Tory stood and paced — this helped her to think. 'Tell me, Dan, could any other heavenly body that you know of split apart in the manner your so-called comet did last night?'

'It's hard to say.' He avoided giving a direct answer. 'There is still so much in the universe we don't understand, that —'

'I said, that you know of.' Tory pushed for an answer,

not wanting to get caught up in the 'what ifs' of a left-brain thinker.

'No,' he conceded finally.

'But … a station could maintain course whilst launching a couple of large, deep-space vessels off in another direction. If I'm not mistaken, this manoeuvre might look an awful lot like what you saw.'

Daniel went pale. 'The vessels would have to be at least a quarter the size of our moon to be spotted from such a distance.' He turned Tory's suggestion over in his mind. 'But, yes, I suppose that could appear as I described.'

'That theory would seem to justify a conspiracy,' Brian agreed with his sister. 'Do you think it might be Maelgwn and Co, heading our way?'

Tory raised both brows, unable to say for sure.

The comment got Rhun thinking, however, and he looked to Daniel to quiz him further. 'This … body,' as he decided to call it in the absence of more information. 'Could it have come from the general region of the Sirius system?'

'I can't prove it for sure, but there are factors supporting this assumption. The constellation of Taurus, against which I first spotted the anomaly, appears close by Sirius in the sky. And, the fact is, the star clusters are over sixty light years apart. Sirius is much closer to us at eight light years away, than say … the star Aldebaran in the constellation of Taurus is sixty-eight light years away. Therefore, if one considers the ascent angle a space station might take to approach our galaxy from Sirius, there's actually more chance that it would come from that system as opposed to any other star cluster in the vicinity.'

Rhun clapped his hands together, pleased to hear this. 'The Dragon's on his way.'

'But what of the supernova Maelgwn said would coincide with his arrival?' Tory was not yet convinced.

Rhun shrugged. 'Well, it's over one light year to the Oort Cloud at the outer reaches of our solar system, so they still have quite a way to travel before reaching us. Father's prophecy may yet be fulfilled.'

One month later the prophecy did come to pass, although once again Daniel could offer no explanation for the occurrence.

What appeared to be a large supernova flare erupted in the vicinity of Sirius. Such a colossal stellar outburst was the result of the collapse of a massive star, much larger than our sun. Stars subject to this kind of behaviour were dubbed red super-giants; trouble was, there were no such stars in that region of space.

Daniel was the only one amongst his kin who seemed even mildly worried about the paradox. 'It just can't be,' he mumbled, as they all stood on the canyon ridge staring up at the newest, brightest light in the night sky.

'You keep saying that, and yet there it is.' Tory grinned broadly, knowing this was a sign that her reunion with Maelgwn was imminent.

'So what's the official word?' Brian looked at Noah, who was their propaganda hound.

'A supernova.' Noah stated the obvious. 'They're blaming an unknown super-giant in the deep reaches of space that must have remained hidden from us for all these years thanks to Sirius A's bright luminosity.'

'I don't think that's very likely.' Daniel sounded disappointed, as a reasonable theory would have been really friendly right now.

'Why?' Tory was interested to hear his view. 'What do you think it is?' She didn't really have to ask, for she knew his mind, but she wanted Daniel to feel confident in voicing his speculations.

He hesitated, thinking his hypothesis far too outlandish. 'Perhaps it is the first evidence of the eruption of a white hole?'

'You might not be too far wrong.' Rhun considered. 'My father never actually said it would be a supernova. We just assumed it would be from the phenomena he described.'

'Good point.' Tory realised he was right.

'Well, one thing's for sure …' Brian threw an arm over his son's shoulder. 'If this means what we think it means, it's a good omen.'

Over the next twenty-four hours, Daniel studied the progress of the eruption of light in the sky.

If this anomaly was truly a supernova flare, a gas and dust-filled cloud should have been zooming away from the imploded star at several kilometres per hour. Yet, as far as Daniel could see, the bright disturbance in the fabric of space appeared to be remaining perfectly constant. By the same token, if this was a white hole it should have been spewing forth cosmic matter, and this was not the case either. Round and round in his head the theories went, until he was left with only one.

'It has to be a wormhole.'

Closely allied to black holes and white holes, wormholes could best be described as tunnels through space, connecting one part of the universe to another, or connecting this universe with parallel universes and dimensions.

'Well,' Dan decided, after too many hours without rest, 'the only way I'm ever going to prove it is to find out where the wormhole leads. And I've got about two chances of doing that — zero and none.' He leant forward to rest his weary brow on the desk, dreaming of a spaceship with light speed capabilities. He drew a few deep breaths in an attempt to clear his muddled thoughts, and in so doing drifted off to sleep.

She was a beautiful, fair-skinned beauty, with eyes like emeralds, and long locks of flaming red hair. *It's time to wake up*, she whispered, her sweet smile enchanting him. *The wait is over.*

'Dan!' Noah came bursting into the room, and on finding the astronomer asleep at his desk made haste to wake him.

'Leave me be,' Daniel muttered, doing his best to slap Noah away without emerging from his dream. 'I'm far happier here.'

Noah wasn't listening to Dan's sleepy drivel. 'You're coming with me, my friend … sorry.' He grabbed hold of Daniel under the arms and hoisted him from his seat.

Dan was on his feet before he awoke fully, and was

none too pleased about his return to reality. 'Jesus, Purcell, couldn't it wait!'

'I don't believe so.' Noah had transported them to join the others on the canyon ridge.

All eyes were upturned to the night sky and everyone maintained a reverent silence, in awe of the wonders they were witnessing.

An enormous vortex spiralled above the Earth, out beyond the orbit of the moon. Its centre was expanding to form a huge glowing corridor through the fabric of space. This brilliant mass shot forth thousands of glowing balls of light, that proceeded to descend toward our planet.

'Well, now I know where the wormhole leads. I suppose it's safe to assume the premise is correct,' Daniel mumbled, even more in awe of the marvel than his crewmates were, as he truly understood how incredible it was. 'Einstein and Rosen were right.'

'Should we panic?' Noah prompted the expert for comment.

Daniel closed his jaw as he considered how to answer. 'The wormhole presents no real threat to us, as it neither sucks in nor exudes matter. It's like a tunnel through space that is constructed of antigravity, or so the theory goes. As for the lights it's spewing, I have no idea.' But then, recalling his dream, Daniel put forward the theory that perhaps they were some sort of craft, which glowed when emerging from light-speed?

'I'd say that's a damn fine theory,' Tory exclaimed. 'Now all we have to do is figure out if these are the good guys, or if it is they who are still making their way to us from the outer reaches of the solar system?'

'No,' Daniel ventured, at the risk of sounding like he knew what he was taking about. 'The wait is over. This is them.'

A faint rumble echoed across the landscape from the distant horizon, growing rapidly louder as something approached. Though it was still dark, the phenomena in the sky lit up the night far better than the brightest full moon and they could suddenly see what was coming.

As a wave of supersonic airforce fighters passed overhead, Tony got the feeling Daniel was right. Somewhere in this light wave of alien craft was her husband, and she didn't much like the reception the defence department had planned for him and his company.

When the thundering mass of aircraft had passed, Brian started firing orders. 'Floyd, Noah, Nick. Get down below and find out what the official word is. Cadfan, track down Taliesin or my father and see if they know what the hell is going on. Dan —'

'I know — telescope.' Dan vanished to do his father's bidding along with the others who had their instructions.

'Tory, Rhun and I shall keep watch out here. I want everybody else underground and out of sight until we know what's really going on. Jen,' Brian made one last request, 'round us up some binoculars and fetch me three Stormers, will you?'

'You got it!' She winked, fading from sight along with Rose, Tom and Patrick.

Brian looked to the heavens where the first wave of space lights had begun to enter the atmosphere. These had turned amber in colour, becoming balls of flame as they plummeted toward the Earth. 'At last, some action.'

'And that could come in a much sweeter form than you imagine.' Rhun raised his brow suggestively.

This certainly put a smile on Brian's face. 'We can only hope.'

The dawn saw the first of the glowing pods crash to earth not far from Watarrka, and several others followed it in close succession. Central Australia was not the only place the strange fiery pods had landed, however. Every nation in the world was being bombarded by the phenomenon.

'Let's get closer.' Tory willed herself to the old, abandoned ranger station on the outskirts of the canyon in the general direction of where the group of pods had gone down.

She arrived at her destination expecting to see some evidence of a crash site close by, but there was no smoke, no churned-up dirt, nothing?

'Don't do that!' Brian arrived on the scene, fuming. 'From now on you wait for us, understood?'

'What do you think I'm still doing here?' She raised her binoculars to scan the surrounding area.

'I'm serious, Tory. We don't know what we're dealing with yet, so please don't go charging off on your own.'

She wasn't listening. She was madly trying to zoom and focus the glasses on something she'd spied way off in the distance.

Rhun had arrived by this time, and noticing his mother's excitement he was curious. 'What is it?'

She gasped, too overwhelmed to speak right away. 'It's him.' She shoved the binoculars in her son's hand and took off toward the horizon as fast as her legs would carry her.

'Damn it, Tory,' Brian pursued her, again angered by her lack of caution. 'You don't know that for sure.'

'Yes I do!' she insisted, picking up speed to escape her brother. This attempt proved useless, and he tackled her to the ground moments later.

'Let me go.' She fought him off.

'Please, Tory, listen! You've waited an eternity for him to return, I know, but a few more minutes isn't going to kill you.'

Tory gave up her struggle, cursing Brian's good sense even though she knew he was right.

Rhun caught up to them before the eleven darkly-clad figures advancing across the plain got too close. Eight of the eleven were females, and having feasted his eyes already, Rhun passed the binoculars to his uncle. 'Take a look,' he prompted, with a devilish grin.

Brian discarded the glasses after only a moment's use. 'Naomi.' He'd spotted his love and was off across the dry, grassy plain to greet her.

'I guess that means it's safe now.' Tory commented sarcastically, rolling her eyes as she and Rhun pressed on.

The sun was higher in the sky now, and visibility was better. As Tory neared the line of advancing people, only some of whom she recognised, Maelgwn's dominating form stood out a mile.

'Tory!' he called to her, breaking into a run.

Just when she thought she could move no faster, the sound of his voice nearly caused her to fly. The next thing she knew, Tory was wrapped up in Maelgwn's arms mumbling his name over and over.

'I must be dreaming.'

'This is no dream,' he assured, giving her a kiss that was long overdue.

'Do you two need a private room or something?' One of Maelgwn's male associates jeered, coming to a stop beside them.

'Yes, please,' they both replied, parting for breath.

Then Tory realised it was Sir Rhys who addressed them, or rather, his perfect incarnation, Sir Robin of Loxley.

'Well, if you'll kindly tell me where I might find my other half,' Robin said, 'I'll gladly leave you to it.'

'I suppose we should help him out?' Maelgwn looked down upon his love, his smile as broad as could be.

'But what of your transport?' Tory quizzed. 'The Air Force is going to be combing this place before long. In fact, I'm surprised they're not here already.'

'They won't find anything, bar a few holes in the ground. I have my vehicle right here.' Maelgwn gestured to the rather complex-looking module he wore around his left wrist. Then, noting Tory's concern, he laughed. 'I haven't gone mad,' he assured her, as they began to walk after the others. 'Let us collect Nin Bau, and I shall demonstrate for you.'

'What do you want with Rose?' Tory wondered, jealous already.

'It is not I who wants her, but the Lord Marduk. It is my charge to collect her and take her to him.'

'And where might he be?'

'He's back at base,' Maelgwn announced casually. 'I thought that after we drop Nin Bau off, you might like to come back to my place … or is that being a bit presumptuous for a first date.'

'Hardly,' Tory quickly replied, thrilled at the prospect of going anywhere with him.

At the massive reunion, many inhabitants of Watarrka recognised their other half immediately, due to the dreams or past-life experiences they'd had during their time in exile. Others experienced an instant affinity with a total stranger.

Naomi's 'Chosen' incarnation looked more like her Atlantean self: dark eyes, long, dark curls and an olive complexion. She was the Middle Eastern Queen, Candace of Shamar, a wise and benevolent ruler who had been a contemporary of Alexander the Great. Even with his blond hair and blue eyes, she recognised Brian as the great warrior who had stolen her heart back in the third century BC, when he'd saved the life of her son. Brian found it hard to accept her claim that he was once the legendary King of Macedonia, for he had met Alexander's daughter, Neraida, and she had not seemed to identify him as her father.

'You did not part on the best of terms,' Candace told him. 'In fact, you banished her in a fit of rage when her lover, your cook, found the water of life you were seeking and gave it to Neraida instead. To punish her lover, Andreas, you tied a millstone around his neck and had him flung into the sea.'

'Oh,' Brian said, feeling a little guilty. 'Then I shall apologise.'

'That won't be necessary, because Andreas has been returned to her this day in the form of his perfect incarnation, King Cadwell of Gwynedd.'

They couldn't help but marvel at how intricately interwoven their lives had been throughout history. In one way or another, they had all assisted each other to greatness at some time; souls threading their way through the fabric of time until their turn for greatness came. Brian found it hard to believe that the Gods would choose his present incarnation over that of Alexander the Great. But when Candace pointed out how ruthless the great ruler had been when it came to achieving his desires, Brian began to understand why he might have been the preferred choice.

Daniel finally met the beautiful redhead of his dreams, whom he was bowled over to discover was the great Queen Cleopatra, who at once recognised him as her beloved, Mark Antony. As it turned out the classic film image of the great Queen was all wrong, for she was not an Egyptian, but a Greek.

The one woman amongst the newcomers whom Tory would have initially pegged as Cleopatra turned out to be Queen Hatshepsut, the first female to rule Egypt, in the year 1665 BC. She and Cadfan stood regarding each other fondly, as he knew her to be his beloved wife and Queen who had died giving birth to their son, Cadwallon.

510

Nicholas was completely unaware of who he was supposed to be looking for. Yet he had no complaints when the woman whose face had launched a thousand ships stepped forward to introduce herself as Helen of Sparta. Paris, she called him, the Trojan prince who had risked everything to have her.

As there were only three women among the ranks of those inhabiting Watarrka — Jenny, Rose and Tory who were all spoken for — Tory was wondering who the other male in Maelgwn's party had come in search of.

'We call him Season. His real name is hell to pronounce,' Maelgwn whispered to Tory confidentially. 'He ruled for a time in Memphis, around 3000 BC, and was hailed as a great and wise Pharaoh until he refused to marry, having fallen in love with another man. This so outraged the Gods of Enlil's flock, that they forced Season to witness the brutal murder of his lover before being stripped of his title and place in history. He was then banished into the desert to die like a dog. Your great-grandfather, Enki, seeing Season for the great and honest man he was, selected him as one of the Chosen, and promised him that there would come a time when his homosexuality would not be frowned upon.'

Tory realised that Season had come to claim Patrick, who was both excited and relieved to find his perfect other half was a male and not a female, as Patrick had feared.

Floyd found his Boadicea, and Rhun was reunited with Brigit's perfect incarnation, Sybil, the prophetess of Atlantis. Thais and his love recognised each other immediately, despite the fact that they were both in human form. She was a centaur, as was he, named Hero, whom Thais had not seen in over six thousand years.

The last member of Maelgwn's party was a beautiful Indian squaw. 'John …' she approached Noah shyly, 'it is I, Pocahontas, though you used to call me Rebecca. Do you remember?'

'I do,' he lied, so captivated by her beauty that he could not bring himself to disappoint her. *I must have been John Rolfe once,* he surmised on the quiet; Noah had recalled many of his past lives, but this had not been one of them.

Rebecca caught his mind, however, and thought his lie a sweet one. 'I remember every second of our time together. I could tell you about it, if you like.'

'I like,' he assured her, and they walked away to talk in private.

'Well,' concluded Maelgwn. 'I don't think that we'll be missed here this evening. Shall we away?'

'Please,' urged Rose, eager to join her lover in the heavens.

'So be it, then.' Maelgwn raised his left arm, aiming the module he wore at the pool before him, then clamped his right hand over the top and uttered the words: 'AN-ME-A-DU.'

The language he spoke was Atlantean, thus Tory understood the instruction to mean: Heavens – Flying ship – Water – Initiate. And from what happened next, she knew her translation to be correct.

A blue beam shot forth from the module and formed into a bright ball of light several feet away. Once the beam was spent, the ball of light expanded and began to assume a physical form.

'Oh, my lord,' Tory mumbled, as a large disk-shaped object, made of the strange black metal she had come to associate with Nefilim construction, took form. It was not a perfect disk shape, however, as two opposing sides of the craft curved slightly down and under.

'Wow.' Rhun was mind-blown. 'Total particle manipulation.'

'And this is only one of the various forms these craft can assume,' Maelgwn advised his son, 'depending upon the conditions one is dealing with.'

'What's the power source?' Rhun circled around the edge of the pool of water to view the ship from another angle.

'Simple crystal-generated energy blasters to get it airborne, then what you might know as an A-frame propulsion system kicks in.'

'Never heard of it.' Rhun pleaded ignorance.

'It's a form of magnetic propulsion, whereby magnetic rings are shot forth from of the front of the vessel. The ship, being made of a highly conductive metal, is pulled into the magnetic field. As the vessel moves forward, the magnetic energy is sucked back into the rear and recycled.'

'Incredible.' Rhun shook his head in amazement. 'What's the maximum speed?'

'Ah, I knew that would be the next question.' Maelgwn grinned. 'By your terms of measurement, about nine-hundred thousand kilometres a second, in free space.'

Rhun's eyes parted wide. 'But that's over three times the speed of light — nearly a parsec per second!'

'Very good. I'm glad to see they're teaching something down here. Ladies,' Maelgwn motioned Tory and Rose into the vessel, as a hatch on the side raised itself to grant entry.

The long, slender, inner body of the craft was designed to accommodate eight people, including the pilot and co-pilot. But the cockpit was not a mass of switches, buttons and flashing lights as were modern, Earth spacecraft. A large, round telekinetic plate was positioned beside the joystick that steered the craft, along with a couple of round plates that Tory assumed were screens for communication and tracking.

When Rose was comfortably strapped in, Maelgwn invited Tory to sit beside him in the co-pilot's seat. 'Word has it you've become a pretty good pilot yourself?'

Tory shrugged modestly, as this craft could hardly be compared to the archaic equipment she was used to operating.

'We'll have to get you onto a simulator,' Maelgwn suggested. 'I'm sure you'd be able to operate one of these with your eyes closed.'

As Tory planted her butt in the co-pilot's seat, the safety harness startled her by automatically locking her in. 'I don't think so,' she said warily.

'It's easier than it looks.' He grinned, settling into his seat. 'If you can think, you can fly.' Maelgwn placed his hand on the telekinetic control panel and, as the thrusters lifted them above the surface of the water, he guided them towards the opening in the roof of the cavern.

Rhun made a dash around the pools to the far end of the cavern to watch the craft depart. The rounded flanks of the transport folded underneath it to form a long cigar-shaped object. The thrusters cut out as the vessel was catapulted forward, and was gone in the blink of an eye.

'Hey,' Sybil called to Rhun. 'If that's what it takes to get your attention …' She held up her arm, exposing the craft module on her wrist.

'What a woman.' He smiled gleefully, making his way back to her.

Their craft was out beyond the stratosphere of Earth before Tory had fully realised they'd even taken off. There was no evidence of the massive forward thrust that was a feature of existing twenty-first century spacecraft. Tory could have been sipping a cup of tea during their ascent and not have spilt a single drop. There was no loss of gravity, either, and their flight was completely silent. 'Tell me …' she had a thought. 'Couldn't we have simply willed ourselves to your base craft?'

'Sure,' Maelgwn conceded, 'but this is more fun, and I get to show off.' He kept well clear of the space stations and satellites that were orbiting the planet. 'Cadwaladr's been busy, I see.'

'Oh, you bet he has,' Tory confirmed. 'But I'd say all the phenomena you've manifested over the past twenty-four hours has got him worried.'

'Don't count on it,' Maelgwn scoffed. 'He knows Shamash is on his way, although from our calculations we're maybe a week ahead of his fleet. A good thing, too, as it buys us some time.'

'Some time for what?'

'Oh no.' He avoided answering. 'That's business, and business can wait until tomorrow, hey?'

'Agreed.' Tory was all for that. Her gaze shifted back to the front window and she noted that they seemed to be heading for the wormhole. 'You're not taking us in there?'

'No, no.'

'Then where? I can't see any vessels out here. Certainly nothing big enough to be a space station.'

Maelgwn found her guesswork somewhat amusing. 'Do you think we'd leave the ATEN sitting out in the open for all to see?' ATEN translated into 'imperishable star' — Tory recognised the word from ancient Sumerian texts. 'Cloaking device?' she assumed.

'Correct.' Maelgwn placed his hand on the telekinetic control panel, whereby a headset lowered from the roof to encompass his eyes and forehead. *Dragon One requesting permission to dock, landing code, CX 509.*

Permission granted, Dragon One. Please proceed to Docking Bay Seven.

A ripple penetrated the space before them, and was seen to rip a hole in the fabric of the universe. As their craft proceeded through the illuminated tear, the massive body of the ATEN suddenly appeared before them.

'Holy shit.' Tory had not expected their destination to appear so large, so quickly.

'Relax. This is home,' Maelgwn advised. The headset retreated back into the roof from whence it came. He guided their craft around the huge bulk of the

ATEN and into a long, circular tunnel that became smaller and smaller until the craft finally docked comfortably within its circumference.

'Are you alright,' Maelgwn asked Tory, who seemed to have stopped breathing.

She let out a huge sigh of relief, realising the flight was over, when her seat harness suddenly retracted and startled her again.

Maelgwn laughed at this. 'You'll get used to it. Oh, speaking of scary surprises, this might be a good time to inform you both that Homo sapiens are not the only form of humans in existence.'

'What?' Tory frowned, not really getting his drift.

'Well, as we were fashioned from apes, other breeds of human have been fashioned from creatures who are better adapted to the different climates and terrains of other planets. Take Thais, for example, who was fashioned from a horse, a breed known as Homo gammurugu. You'll see what I mean.' He decided a picture was worth a thousands words. 'Just try not to stare. These people are my friends.'

'I'll try not to embarrass you too much.' Tory raised herself from her seat.

Maelgwn gave her a squeeze, not wanting her to get him wrong. 'That will never happen,' he told her. 'It's just that I have told everyone so much about you, my associates could seem a little overwhelming.'

'I understand.' She held his face a moment, thinking how handsome he was.

'A-hum!' Rose gave them a wave to get them moving.

25

BODY PARTS

When the hatch opened they were greeted by a stocky, round-faced lad with a great mane of long, curly auburn hair. 'Hey, boss.' He waved to Maelgwn, fleetingly admiring the females at his side. 'Good flight?'

'Not bad, thanks Remme,' Maelgwn answered, taking off his control module and handing it to the lad. 'The thrusters are still a bit sluggish, though.'

'Roger that, Commander.' He smiled broadly. 'I'll give 'em a service then, eh?' Remme watched Rose pass him by on her way out, and gave a low purring sound of approval.

It was not until Tory glanced over her shoulder at Remme that she noticed he was sporting a long, tan tail, with a furry tuft on the end that was twitching uncontrollably.

'Let me guess. Some sort of feline?' She whispered to Maelgwn once they were a safe distance away.

'Homo dullogu,' he enlightened her. 'Remme is very good natured, but his breed are often fairly short-tempered, especially the females.'

'I'll remember that,' Tory mumbled, her attention already diverted to a couple of men with huge brown and black wings. These two were fluttering around the top of another craft in the huge dock area, repairing it, presumably.

One of them, having spotted Maelgwn, came swooping over to address him, fluttering above them as he spoke. 'Greetings Dragon. Is this the little woman?'

'Yes, indeed it is. Tory, I'd like you to meet Leander.' Maelgwn did the honours. 'Leander, this is Tory.'

'Very nice,' said Leander, 'for a hairless ape, you understand.' He winked at Maelgwn, then looked back to Tory. 'I'm delighted to make your acquaintance.' He bowed his head, one hand over his heart in sincerity.

'Likewise,' said Tory, quite sure that Leander had meant no offence by his comment. It seemed to be more of a private joke between Maelgwn and himself. 'And may I say you are very fine for a nearly featherless bird —'

'Falcon,' Maelgwn whispered on the quiet.

'Falcon …' Tory was quick to correct her error.

'I'll bet you say that to all the Homo felemous,' Leander flirted.

'Oy, Leander,' his friend yelled from the vessel they were preparing. 'Do you want to stop socialising and help me fix this damn accelerator?'

'Gotta go.' He gave them a wave and flew back to work.

The three of them exited the dock area through a door that vanished upon their approach. It led into a series of corridors, where they met others of all the differing races Tory was becoming aware of. Maelgwn seemed to know just about everybody in this sector of the space station, and was obviously well liked and respected. There was one other breed, however, that had distinct differences to the rest. Maelgwn advised that these people were of the Homo delphinus variety. Bred from dolphins, they could be distinguished by their webbed feet and hands. They were extremely good natured and telepathic. Their skin was very smooth and had a bluish tinge about it. Naturally, they were excellent swimmers, and they had a blowhole on the crown of their heads, as dolphins did, for breathing underwater.

Maelgwn left Rose in the care of one of these people — Dylan. A personal servant to the Lord Marduk, Dylan had been sent to collect Rose and guide her to his Lord's Star Chamber.

The errand for his superior completed, Maelgwn's time was now his own. He turned to the stranger beside him, unsure of where to start with her. If he'd been able to calm himself, he might have been able to read Tory's thoughts. As it was, he was at the mercy of his instincts. 'So, what shall we do? I could show you around. Or if you're hungry, we could get something to eat.'

Tory looked down the wide, arched corridor that, consistent with everything else she'd seen, was a dark, moulded, metallic structure. There were long, clear sections inset along the walls, ceiling and floor that allowed a subtle light to illuminate the infrastructure.

'This is only the maintenance level of the ATEN,' Maelgwn advised. 'The rest of her is far more spectacular.'

This was a tough call in Tory's opinion. Should she go exploring an advanced alien civilisation, or get laid for the first time in forty years? 'Mmm. It all sounds wonderful, but I think I'd like to see your place first.' She raised her eyebrows and awaited his reaction.

'Really?' Maelgwn suppressed his enthusiasm. 'It's a bit of a hike from here. But, I could will us there … if you like?'

'Well, it does seem silly to walk all that way.' She played along, placing her hand in his.

Tory's eyes remained fixed on her lover's face. As the ethers of their passage departed, she inquired if Maelgwn lived alone.

'Yes I do, as it happens, because —'

A long and luscious kiss, that shocked Maelgwn slightly, interrupted his explanation. Still, he was only stunned that his aspirations were being fulfilled sooner than he'd hoped — or so he thought.

Tory let go of him just as abruptly as she'd taken hold. 'So, this is where you've been hanging out all this time?' She made polite conversation, as though her emotional outpouring had never taken place. She gazed about his chambers, seeing nothing of how aesthetically pleasing the design was, nor how amazing and functional the furnishings were. In her mind she was still hugged close to his body, reeling at his touch, his scent, his taste.

He took up her hand gently and tugged her back into his embrace. Maelgwn pressed her body to his, to let her know that she was not the only one who was eager. 'Time spent here is time spent missing you.'

'Not any more,' she smiled.

In that instant, the years of separation melted away and they allowed their long forbidden affection to flow freely and easily between each other.

'This is not how I planned it,' Maelgwn said, struggling to remove the skin-hugging jacket of his flight suit. Tory was making it twice as difficult for him as she caressed the smooth skin of his exposed torso with her fingers and her lips. 'I promised myself that I'd at least take you to dinner. You know, in a token stab at romance?'

'This is romantic,' she whispered, kissing his mouth to silence him.

Given leave, Maelgwn carried her over to his bed and laid her down. The lighting dimmed, and a haunting tune began to waft softly through the room. Beneath her body his bed felt as soft as air itself, yet it cushioned their weight as they quickly dispensed with the remainder of their clothes. Tory laid back to welcome Maelgwn's naked body to hers. It was then she noticed that the bed-head was a huge circular window. It curved over their heads following the shape of the external structure and gave views of the Earth, the Moon and the great expanse of space. She looked back at Maelgwn, who had not come upon her as expected. All she could make out was a dark silhouette, standing quietly in the shadows beyond the bed. 'Am I raising your expectations, Commander?' she asked playfully, the subtle movements of her body urging him forth.

In Tory's beauteous form, bathed by the blue light of the moon, Maelgwn saw both his greatest desire and greatest fear unfolding. The latter he'd been sure he could deny, but now that it came down to it, the horror recollections were flooding back.

'Maelgwn?' Tory queried his restraint.

'You'll have to go easy on me. It's been awhile.' Maelgwn bowed his head forward to smother his sudden feelings of hurt, guilt and loathing.

Though Tory could not see Maelgwn's expression underneath his long, straight hair, she sensed his dismay. She ignored her scattered emotions in an attempt to bethink the problem from him, but no images would come. Whatever it was that taunted him was being blocked out with all the might he could master. When he turned away from her, Tory knew there was something seriously wrong. He'd never been fearful, not like this. As she sat up, her mind turned to the one event that had happened during their separation that could have caused him so much damage. 'Do you want to tell me about Inanna, Maelgwn?' She nearly choked on the words, so afraid he was going to tell her that he was having an affair with that Goddess. His hesitancy to answer was even more alarming, so Tory thought she'd best put them both out of their misery. 'Are you in love with her?'

'No,' he stated, surely. 'I despise her more than any creature I have ever encountered, for she is by far the most wretched.'

'What did she do?' Tory leaned towards him in a desperate attempt to reach him, but he drew away beyond her reach. 'To hate someone with such intensity, is —'

'A drain on my energy. I know!' Maelgwn pulled on a loose-fitting pair of trousers and seated himself in a large hanging chair that faced the bed. 'I've had all manner of spiritual tutors in my head trying to put straight what Inanna messed up in there, and the truth is, telling you is the only thing that promises to be of any help whatsoever.'

'I'm here to help.' Tory pulled one of the bed covers around herself and awarded him her full attention, at which time he became warier.

'Even now I am wondering if it is really you I'm addressing, Tory.' he stated in all seriousness. 'Even though I came and got you myself, Inanna could have got to you first.'

'She tried —' Tory began.

But Maelgwn raised a hand to prevent her from trying to convince him. 'Please, I just need you to listen.' Tory nodded for him to continue, and he did so without delay. He'd dreaded this conversation for so long that all he wanted now was to get it over and done with before his fears drove him insane.

So she listened, with mounting horror, to how Inanna had tested out the stolen prototype of the NERGUZ on Maelgwn. Using the power of suggestion that the module gave her over her captive, she had instructed Maelgwn to see her as his beloved wife. She'd raped him several times before her desire for him to love her in her own form brought the affair to a grinding halt. No amount of seduction or torment could sway his resolve once he'd learned of the deceit. This infuriated the Goddess; if he didn't love her, then she would to see to it that he loved no one. Inanna used Tory's image when torturing Maelgwn and, due to the number of mindlessly violent acts he'd witnessed her commit, the Goddess had done her best to tarnish the memory of his wife forever.

When Maelgwn seemed finally out of words, Tory felt as though she'd been cursed; she had been! Now she understood why Maelgwn hadn't visited her more than once. The sight of her must have induced the most vivid memories of his harrowing ordeal. Tory swallowed back her tears, and slid off the bed to find her clothes.

'I knew she wasn't you, Tory, but still —'

'You couldn't have resisted her Maelgwn. I am well aware of how the NERGUZ works. Your entire being would have believed whatever she wanted you to believe. And now, without the module, you remember the truth of it, as if those decisions and thoughts had been your own.' It was a horrid form of torment. Tory paused from dressing, overcome by nausea and sadness. After all this time apart, the Gods had found a way to destroy even this moment for them. 'I am only sorry that I am unable to be of any comfort to you, as Inanna has obviously made me your worst nightmare.'

'None of this is your fault.' Maelgwn came near to her, though he paused short of touching her.

'Still,' Tory smiled meekly, having noticed his attempt at contact and his overpowering reluctance to make it, 'I blame myself anyway, for entrusting our lives to outside forces for so long.'

As she pulled on her trousers and fastened her belt, Tory had that going-into-combat look about her, and that was a worry. 'Tory. Please, don't do anything rash. Tell me what you're thinking. I really need to hear it.'

'I'm thinking … that I want to hate that bitch for what she has done to us.' Tory pulled on one of her boots and, with a mixture of determination and frustration, laced it up. 'But I also know that hate will not take away the doubts she has forced upon you, nor will it change the crux of the problem. Which is,' her head shot up, and her eyes were bulging from her burst of clarity, 'Dumuzi. Yes!' She was suddenly excited, drawn into the scenario unfolding in her mind. 'Remove the prime motivation, and the rules of this game will change.'

Dumuzi's disappearance had taken place the last time the Nefilim were frequenting the Earth. She knew Inanna believed Dumuzi had been dismembered and hidden by Marduk. 'Find Dumuzi and Inanna can have her lover back. This would, in theory, give her nothing more to war about. Plus, we could establish my grandfather's innocence in regard to Dumuzi's murder.' She looked back to Maelgwn to catch his response, and found him looking astounded, and quietly pleased.

'You asked me earlier why I needed to bide my time in this region of space before the arrival of Shamash's forces. It is because it has fallen to me to find Dumuzi and, as you say, prove the Lord Marduk's innocence.'

This was a stroke of luck by Tory's reckoning, as she wasn't going to have to con him into aiding her with the search. 'So Shamash has taken up his sister's cause, I assume, and is opposing my grandfather?'

'So he would like it to seem,' Maelgwn scoffed in frustration. 'In truth, it is Shamash who has the greatest motive for getting rid of Dumuzi. Before Inanna's marriage, Shamash had been his twin sister's regular lover and was most put out when she wed another.'

'I know,' she grinned, confident of gaining the upper hand. If she could endeavour to solve the bulk of the Nefilim's disputes, then perhaps the war at the prophesied Gathering might be avoided altogether. Clearly, they needed Dumuzi as bargaining power and Tory did not expect that obtaining him would be easy. Dumuzi's true attacker had kept his or her identity and the victim's location a secret for eons, and probably planned to keep it that way.

'I know what you're thinking, Tory, and I have to say I love you for it.' Maelgwn gripped hold of her hand and squeezed it tight.

'Well, it's clear that you will have trouble relaxing with me until this matter has been laid to rest and you know it cannot come back to haunt you.' She let go his hand to put on her other boot. 'I can see no point in sitting around here moping about it, so we may as well get on the case.'

Maelgwn watched as she finished preparing herself to depart, and her resolute manner was breaking his heart. She did not attempt to place blame, burst into hysterics, or begin plotting her revenge. Instead, she calmly went about doing whatever it took to right the situation; this was Tory, there was no doubt in his mind.

'You don't have to come with me,' she offered, noting Maelgwn hadn't budged. 'I can do this alone.'

'I vowed to myself that once we were reunited we would never be separated again.' Maelgwn gathered up his flight suit to get changed, and then paused to look at his wife. He was sorry now that he'd doubted and disappointed her. 'We don't have to leave right away.'

Though Tory noted that familiar glint in his eye, she knew that if she rushed him, it might disappear just as quickly. 'We have forever,' she smiled and shrugged, seeing this as a way to tease him out of his dilemma. 'Why rush?'

Half of Maelgwn appreciated her patience and understanding. The other half cursed that he'd denied himself the chance to love and trust her.

The ATEN, one-third the mass of Earth's moon, was one huge city. Long observation walkways connected the outer buildings to the inner structure.

Tory observed the various flying craft beyond the transparent domed ceiling of the observation bridge that they were crossing, when she spotted a male of the falcon breed. Unlike Leander, this Homo felemous was zooming along in an enclosed vessel and Tory had to wonder why he wasn't using his God-given attributes to transport himself. 'Do any of the other human races have the immortal gene?'

'No, Homo sapiens are pretty much unique in that sense. Enlil and his clan would never have known about us either, if Inanna hadn't captured me and discovered my everlasting capabilities. There are a few exceptions among the other races that your great-grandfather and his kin have set apart as Chosen, like Hero and Thais for example. Even so, those of the other breeds who live here on the ATEN have an extraordinarily long lifespan anyway, as they have no real concept of time.'

'So that's why there's such a big interest in this sector of space all of a sudden.' Tory was still dwelling on the first part of Maelgwn's reply to her question. 'The Nefilim are heading this way to see how out of control the immortal problem has become on Earth. And, in light of this new investigation, there's a chance that a tonne of dirt from the distant past could be dredged up in the process.'

'Indeed.' Maelgwn marvelled at her perceptiveness. 'But it was bound to happen, sooner or later. The prophecy of the Gathering, when the Gods would return to sit in judgment on mankind, was also inevitable.'

They entered a large multi-level structure. Maelgwn explained it to be the main technological centre of the ATEN. 'The Lord Gibal works out of here, and your grandfather advised that Gibal could head me in the right direction to begin the search for Dumuzi.'

'So, you finally put all Gibal's parts back together again.' Tory assumed this must have happened if the God was returned to his work.

'Not exactly …' Maelgwn paused in a quiet corner to explain. 'By the time I found the all-important head, we had no time to recover the parts still missing.'

'What?' Tory stepped away in horror. 'He's nothing more than a head!'

'We needed his mind to make the wormhole happen. It is a new and experimental technology, using antigravity, which he developed. If we'd mucked around finding his other parts first we would never have beat Shamash here. They were counting on Gibal's dismemberment to delay us longer than it did ... I got lucky. I found his head early in the search.'

'But you said he was working here?' Tory tried to refrain from being amused by the notion. 'How does Gibal function with just a head?'

'Ah?' Maelgwn continued down the corridor towards the double doors at the end, turning briefly to urge her to follow.

The doors vanished before them, and Maelgwn led Tory into a huge chamber containing technological equipment of mammoth proportions. The layout of the machinery was not in any way orderly to the untrained eye. In fact, it just looked like piles and piles of matted, twisted junk and wiring. But the apparatus had the familiar hum of processors at work. High above their heads, the arms of a huge metal spider reached down to tend the differing areas of circuitry in the room. A long, steel shaft extended down from the spider's belly to a platform. On the platform was a mound, on the mound, a head, and on the head was a helmet. The headgear encompassed the controller's eyes and connected him, via the long shaft, back up to the maintenance arms above.

'It is all psychokinetically controlled,' Maelgwn

whispered to his awed companion. 'Gibal sees all through his machines, just as he always has.'

'Greetings, Dragon.' A pleasant voice resounded round the room. 'Marduk said I could expect you. He failed to mention your beautiful companion, however.'

'I am Tory Alexander, your brother's grand-daughter, or Lamamu, as he insists on calling me.' She looked about her, unsure from which direction Gibal was viewing them.

'I see you from all angles,' he advised. 'I know why you have come, and as I now have a vested interest in your negotiations with Inanna, I shall tell you my theory as to what became of my baby brother.'

'Have no fear my Lord Gibal. I shall persuade Inanna to return your missing portions, whether or not your theory proves correct.'

'That's what I like about you, Dragon. Always straight to the point.'

Maelgwn bowed his head to accept the compliment, but said nothing more as he awaited Gibal's summation.

'It is my guess that Shamash's father, Narnar, may have aided his son with Dumuzi's disappearance. Narnar had already been banished to the Otherworld of your world's moon before Dumuzi mysteriously vanished. Therefore, Narnar had nothing to lose by aiding his son.'

But he might have had something to gain? Tory posed on the quiet, wondering what Shamash might have offered his father in return for storing Dumuzi's body. 'May I know why Narnar was banished?' she asked.

'It was discovered by his wife, Ningal, that Narnar had forced himself on many of her female staff. Rape is a most grievous offence by our laws, Lamamu, deserving the punishment of banishment or dismemberment.' Gibal sounded a tad bitter about the latter.

'Nice,' Tory commented. She could hardly wait to meet the fellow. 'So, Narnar is still to be found in the Otherworldly realms of the moon then?'

'Oh yes,' Gibal assured her. 'He is still brooding there, waiting for the time when Ningal will forgive, and return for him.'

'Is Ningal with you,' Tory excitedly entreated Maelgwn.

'Unfortunately, no, she is back on her home planet of Tarazean in the Sirius system,' he regretfully replied. 'She has not yet forgiven her husband it would seem. The Nefilim really know how to hold a grudge.'

'Especially the females,' added Gibal.

'So how do we find the entrance to Narnar's Otherworldly realm?' Tory was not too familiar with the moon's surface, so she had little chance of just willing herself there.

'On the moon there is a crater, in that crater a cave. Follow it.'

A red light flickered and then materialised as a small ball before them. Its abrupt appearance startled Tory, though Maelgwn didn't bat an eyelid. He stood observing the face of the rotating holographic moon, studying the craters until their proposed destination lit up in blue.

'I see,' Maelgwn acknowledged, spotting the hole in the crater wall inside the designated area.

'I have already programmed the coordinates into

your transport, Dragon. May the universe speed your quest and safe return to us.'

'Many thanks for your time, my Lord.' Maelgwn waved as he retreated to the door, and Tory followed his lead.

'Just let me know if I can be of any further assistance.' Gibal went back about his business.

Their transport awaited them at Maintenance Level Dock Seven, so Maelgwn got Tory geared up in a flight suit in the adjoining suiting station.

'What is this stuff. It feels kind of funky.' Tory had trouble adjusting to the feel of the fabric, which hugged and moved with her body like a second skin. It was made of a rubbery, leather substance, that allowed the body to breathe whilst keeping it just warm enough.

'It's living organic fibre,' Maelgwn began.

'It's growing on me?' Tory was horrified.

'It's protecting you, and it repairs itself.' He explained the nature of the invention. 'It expands and contracts with the prevailing conditions, acting like a protective outer layer. Likewise, the boots will protect your feet, and keep them at a pleasant temperature no matter what extremes you may be trudging through.'

By the time they were space-borne Tory was used to the suit and forgot about it. The scenery out here in the solar system was totally awe-inspiring, and she decided that she could really get used to this intergalactic lifestyle.

Their vessel steered well clear of the moon's populated areas, heading them into a vast, grey desert of craters. Here they descended and slowed as if they were to land. But their craft kept moving, or rather, creeping, towards a huge cavern that was situated at the base of one of the larger craters.

'You're taking the ship in there?' Tory squirmed in her seat.

'Sure,' Maelgwn acknowledged cheerfully, 'unless you'd rather get out and walk?'

After observing the great boulders strewn over the cavern floor, Tory frowned. 'I think I'll pass.'

At this point, they lost the natural sunlight. The pilot's headset automatically extended from the ceiling, and Maelgwn made himself comfortable in his seat to view the dark world outside.

'What do you see?' Tory was uncomfortable with flying into blackness. 'Hasn't this thing got lights?'

'Then the inferred vision wouldn't work, and everyone would see us coming,' he grinned, maintaining his visual advantage. 'O-oh.' He slammed his left hand onto the control plate, and clutched the joystick in his right fist. 'Brace yourself,' he warned, calmly.

'Do you want to be more specific?' Tory looked at the blackened windscreen in a useless attempt to be enlightened. That's when she noticed the craft begin to tilt. 'What are you doing? Whoa …' In the next instant she was upside down heading headlong into a downward spiral, and in a dark rocky cavern, she knew that wasn't good. 'Is this really necessary? Can't you stop it?'

Maelgwn let go of the controls altogether, his headset retracting, and still the swirling, diving motion of the craft continued. 'I'm not driving any more. It's a magnetic tracking system in the tunnel. It's pulling us along.'

'Hopefully not into a dead end?' Tory forced a smile and closed her eyes. She gulped down her fear, and her urge to be sick subsided. The ride seemed to be getting easier, and when their craft swerved out of the final bend the flaming torches of a great stone palace lit the way to Narnar.

It was a cold, bleak-looking structure — a ziggurat. The ancient dwelling would have appeared completely abandoned, if not for the torches burning brightly up either side of the entrance stairs.

Tory stood staring up at the palace, thinking it not too inviting with its stony gargoyles perched all over the place like a silent army ready to strike.

Maelgwn dispensed with their transport by aiming the module he was wearing at the craft. It decomposed, at his word, into light matter and was sucked back into the storage module. 'Come on.' He held a hand out to Tory, who took it gladly.

They strode up the stairs to the opening on the first level of the ziggurat. A long, wide stone passage led into the belly of the structure. Torches lined the walls to light their way. Between each torch was a pillar, and on each pillar was a gargoyle. These winged, spindly-limbed creatures struck a variety of poses, and were the very image of little devils, though they were as grey as the stone they were carved from.

'Narnar really has a thing for these little guys, hasn't he?' Tory observed the statues as she passed them by, feeling that they were observing her just as closely.

'What was that?' Tory paused to listen. 'I could have sworn I heard a whistle.' She placed both hands on her hips, accusingly, looking to the gargoyle she had just passed.

The sound of devilish laughter began to emanate from the carvings and echo round the chamber.

'You're brave,' the accused statue turned its head to address Maelgwn, 'bringing a woman down here.'

Suddenly all the creatures broke from their poses, and fell about laughing on their pedestals.

'In fact, I'd say you're brave coming down here — period!' The troublesome creature sprang onto Maelgwn's back, screaming with laughter as he yanked at his hair.

'Oy.' Tory drew the attention of the whole swarm when she dangled a ring on a chain in the attacking creature's face. These little fellows were of your basic variety of Earth elemental, which meant they had a real fetish for trinkets of precious metal.

'Ah!' The stony demon grabbed for the jewel.

'Not so fast!' Tory quickly withdrew the item. 'Take us to Narnar, and I shall give this to you as payment.'

All the little beasts screeched with laughter again.

'What if I just took it anyway?' The creature leant over Maelgwn's shoulder to call her bluff.

'What if I just wring your neck?' Maelgwn raked the critter off his back, but it had vanished before he got a chance to finish the job.

'Deal.' The demon reappeared between Maelgwn's shoulder blades, near startling the life out of him. 'I'll take you to Narnar. But I expect payment despite his reaction.' It vanished again before Maelgwn could hit it, and then materialised further down the passage. 'This way.' He flew off ahead, his buddies resuming their motionless forms.

The creature led them through a labyrinth of passages and stairs, until they came to a grand central chamber. A masked warrior sat playing cards with hordes of the stony, grey devils.

Their guide did an about-face, and demanded payment with a whistle and a click of his fingers.

Where have you been, Tobit? Narnar inquired of their guide.

'Wait.' Tory went after Tobit, having handed over the ring as promised. 'You were sent to get us?'

A devilish grin consumed the creature's face, but before he could nod, Narnar stood, enraged.

How dare you bring a female here! I have banned the foul creatures from this place.

Maelgwn restrained his wife, clamping a hand over her mouth to withhold her fiery protest. 'I do apologise, my Lord, I did not realise —'

It's too late now, Narnar interrupted him to announce. *You'll have to fight me for her.*

'Pardon me, my Lord, but I was under the impression you didn't want her here.'

I don't. If I win, I shall kill her.

The stony beasts all seemed to like that idea.

'Pardon again, my Lord, but she is immortal, you cannot kill her.'

There was an almighty gasp as all present drew back in reverence, and Narnar changed his tune.

You are Gods? Narnar assumed.

Maelgwn nodded, sensing it was the safest way to plead, when Tory elbowed him in the ribs and he was forced to free her.

'We have come in search of the Lord Dumuzi.' She strolled forward to confront the huge warrior. 'You can name your price if you know of his whereabouts?'

I don't like females of any breed! Narnar leaned forward to impress his words on Tory, his huge form towering over her.

'Ah …' Maelgwn intervened on cue, pulling Tory back out of the way. 'If it pleases my Lord, you may deal with me.'

In whose name do you seek Dumuzi? Narnar lowered himself back into his throne, as Tory held her tongue and remained in the background.

'The Lord Marduk wishes to prove his innocence in the affair of his brother's disappearance.' Maelgwn decided honesty was the best policy, despite the fact that Narnar belonged to the house of Enlil and was not of the Serpent's clan.

Does he now. Narnar gave half a laugh. *And it would serve that lying maggot, Shamash, right, if he did.*

'But Shamash is your son, Sire,' Maelgwn reminded him, just to see what kind of a reaction he'd get.

Not any more he isn't! The warrior was back on his feet and fuming. *He broke his vow to me!* Narnar brought his fist down on the card table, smashing it in two, whereby all his fellow players threw in their cards, disappointed.

'Perhaps I could succeed where Shamash has failed you?' Maelgwn's suggestion brought the God's flight of anger to an abrupt end. 'What is the vow of which you speak?'

All the creatures burst into giggles, which they immediately suppressed as Narnar took offence.

Silence! Begone, he ordered, and it was so. *Well*, he grumbled, once they were alone. *It is a matter of some delicacy.* Narnar motioned Maelgwn closer so he could privately speak of his dilemma, keeping a watchful eye on Tory all the while. She folded her arms, rolling her eyes at their boyish behaviour.

After a short time, Maelgwn stepped away from Narnar. 'Well, I have a little experience with this,' Maelgwn commented, trying not to look as affected by what he'd learnt as he obviously was.

That's females for you. Narnar's gaze was fixed on Tory, and she felt he was begging for a fight. *They're merciless enchantresses, every one of them.*

'Oh great.' She threw her hands in the air. That was exactly what Maelgwn didn't need to hear right now. But she paced out her frustration, and took the matter no further.

'So if I was to return your …' Maelgwn searched for a subtle word for it, 'property, are you in a position to hand over Dumuzi to me?'

Hands, legs, and the rest of his body parts. I will hand them over gladly for this item. His business done, Narnar returned to his throne. The card table righted itself and the cards fluttered up and into a neat pile, ready to play. *I hope Shamash rots in hell, just as I have.* Narnar leaned forward and dealt the cards, whereby his Otherworldly playing partners returned to the game.

Maelgwn backed out graciously, and made his way past Tory towards the door.

'You're going to take *his* word that he knows where Dumuzi is?' She ran to catch up with Maelgwn.

'What choice do we have?'

'But I don't understand. What's this item he wants?'

'I'll tell you once we're out of here.'

As it turned out, Narnar's lost property was his penis and matching genitalia; his wife had cut it off before his banishment and kept it as a memento.

'First Gibal's brain, now Narnar's genitals.' Tory couldn't resist the urge to laugh. 'Have you ever thought of taking headhunting up professionally?'

'Tory, please, it's no laughing matter,' Maelgwn struggled to keep a straight face. 'Especially when Ningal is back through the wormhole on Tarazean.'

'To the Sirius system, then,' Tory announced, as their craft came screaming out of the cavern to skim across the moon's surface.

'And don't spare the horses,' Maelgwn added, activating his headset to request that Gibal plot them a course.

26

UПİŤE

The churning clouds of dust and wind that constantly plagued the Middle East made for poor visibility.

Candace had been instructed by the Lord Marduk to investigate this region and report on any activity taking place there. Due to the annihilation of all life in the Middle East some seventeen years before, most at Watarrka fully expected her mission to be a non-eventful one.

To their surprise, they discovered that on the barren desert floor was a huge structure — the excavation went for miles.

'What the hell is that?' Rhun gaped at the massive dig from inside the control deck of the *Goddess*.

'It's a landing pad,' Season advised. 'It has been hidden on Earth since the Nefilim's departure.'

'Then it's just as we suspected,' Noah commented. 'The premature detonation of that bomb was no accident.'

'I'm going to take a closer look.' Rhun vanished. Brian, Candace, Robin and Boadicea went after him.

'What the hell.' Floyd decided to get involved in the heroics, not wanting to tarnish the brave image his new lady friend had of him.

Everyone else stayed put to man the *Goddess* and continue the air surveillance.

Rhun's party watched all the activity at the site from behind one of the huge mounds of earth that surrounded the dig.

'Jesus,' uttered Brian, 'looks like it only needs a bit of a polish, before it will be alright to go.'

'At least we know what's been keeping Doc amused all these years. I knew we should have been keeping an eye on him.' Rhun cursed under his breath.

'No, Rhun, this is good.' Candace whipped an ultra-thin viewing mechanism from her belt and placed it over her eyes. 'We want Shamash to come here and make himself at home.'

'We do?' This was news to Brian.

Candace nodded, though her viewing distracted her from explaining further. 'There's something going on down there.' She dispensed with her device, pulling a gun-like weapon from her thigh holster, the barrel pulsating with light once she'd activated it. 'It's Talynn.' She looked to Boadicea.

Boadicea immediately pulled out her weapon. 'Cover us,' she instructed Robin, following Candace over the dirt mound.

'What's happening? Who's Talynn?' Brian implored Robin, who had pulled out his weapon and nestled himself into a comfortable firing position.

Robin took the viewer from his belt and attached it to his gun. Its magnified sights helped him keep a close eye on his comrades. 'Talynn was one of the Dragon's original circle. A woman called Alma.'

'I remember her,' Rhun cut in.

Brian and Floyd were a little slower off the mark. They both had recollections of their lifetime in Gwynedd under the Dragon's rule, but only fragmentary.

'Sir Angus' wife,' Rhun prompted.

'Oh yeah.' Brian made the connection and nodded in accord. 'Blonde, blue eyed. Sweet little thing.'

'Whatever became of Angus?' Floyd wondered, having several recollections of the knight.

'He outlived you Tiernan, I mean Floyd,' Rhun shook his head. 'Boy, this is weird.'

'I know what you mean,' Robin agreed. 'I don't know by what name to call anyone.'

Rhun raised his binoculars to view the commotion. 'What are they doing, anyhow? It looks like they're hauling a body.'

'Ha — ha!'

Someone somersaulted over the earthen bank to stand before them, and all weapons turned his way.

'Greetings! You lot certainly took your time getting here.'

Rhun recognised this man as his son and father-in-law. Cadwell was the spitting image of Vortipor, High King of the Britons between Maelgwn's reign and Rhun's own. Which was not surprising, as Vortipor had been Cadwell's grandfather.

'What's wrong, little Dragon, has the past got your tongue? Do you not recognise your own son?' Cadwell teased with a laugh.

'Aye, all too well.' Rhun moved to shake his hand.

'This arsehole is your son?' Brian lowered his weapon. 'Well, I suppose that figures.'

Candace, Boadicea, Neraida, and Talynn dragged a fifth party over the earthen mound.

'Neraida. What are you doing here?' Brian recognised her at once.

'I live here,' she replied, as they lay their unconscious captive on the ground.

'And who might this be?' Brian referred to the body.

'He's my son.' Neraida bent down to check him over. 'I had to get him away from the Unken. I couldn't wait any longer.' She pulled out an ENZU-GUZ to disconnect him from the module's influence. These devices had been widely distributed to the underground tribes following its invention.

Brian crouched beside Neraida, recalling what Candace had said about his life as Alexander. 'I don't remember any of it,' he began, 'but if in some past life I caused you pain, I want to say that I'm very sorry.'

'It was a necessary phase of history, I see that now.' Neraida shrugged.

'Hey, why don't you apologise to me,' Cadwell invited Brian. 'I'm the one you tied to a millstone and threw in the sea.'

'Yeah, but you probably deserved it,' Brian jeered. He looked at the face of the unconscious man. 'It's Angus.' He nearly passed out from the shock.

Rhun, Floyd and Robin rushed over to check for themselves.

'So it is,' Robin confirmed with a light-hearted chuckle.

'I told you I'd find him.' Talynn winked back at Robin. 'Hell, it looks like I found everyone!' She saw so many familiar faces amidst this crowd, some of whom she had not seen in lifetimes.

Rhun backed away, seeing vivid images of his youth when all the original members of the Dragon's circle had last been gathered in one place. 'Masters of the Goddess, you are all here.'

'Yet the Dragon and our Sensei are still absent,' Talynn noted.

'They have another task to perform,' Candace advised. 'But, Goddess permitting, they will join us soon.'

Mongolia was graced by an unusual amount of sunshine this winter. The only bad news was the freezing gale force wind that blew across the barren landscape. Autumn and summer brought fierce thunder, lightning, heavy falls of snow, and hurricanes. In spring, storms rose out of the Gobi Desert and lasted for weeks at a time.

Doc had waited until late winter to make his trek into the Hentiy Mountains. His party flew into Ulaan Baatar, where they met up with an official escort who were to guide them on horseback to their destination. Doc did not need directions, however. He knew the terrain like the back of his hand. If he'd been able to pull off this quest alone, he would have popped in and out of Mongolia and bypassed the Government altogether. Unfortunately, he suspected he would need labour, which was why he decided to make his trip official. This meant dealing with the escort that the Mongolian government arranged to accompany them into the mountains, but better that than being caught illegally digging up a communist state.

The official escort was not the threatening force Doc had expected. The ICA team outnumbered the seven middle to old-aged herdsmen by two to one. These local men appeared surprisingly healthy and unaffected by the radiation sickness that plagued the rest of the world's population. These folk were so tanned and weather-worn from enduring the conditions of their harsh climate that their tough immune system was no doubt keeping them alive.

The same couldn't be said for Rhiannon, however. She hadn't been well for months. Aged forty-one, she still hadn't experienced physical death and therefore suffered the ailments of a mortal. Doc's doctors had detected the cancer that was slowly eating her brain when Rhiannon first fell ill. But Doc's relationship with his wife hadn't been the same since the Death Valley earthquake disaster. Shamash's constant lectures on how

Rhiannon would deceive Doc had succeeded in brainwashing him. Somehow Shamash managed to attribute every little misfortune to Rhiannon's scheming. The evidence became so overwhelming in the end, that Doc believed her treachery was real. So, her illness brought a timely opportunity to dispose of the problem; she knew far too much about his operations.

Through involving her in his affairs, Doc had also to a degree earned Rhiannon's trust. When Doc advised her that she was suffering from nothing more than a passing virus, she believed him. The disease had rendered her psychic abilities useless and the pain-killing drugs his doctors were pumping her full of kept her controllable and semi-delirious.

Doc had not told anyone what his little expedition into Mongolia was all about; he knew Rhiannon would be curious and insist on coming along.

It was true to say that Rhiannon had no idea of the agonies this journey would expose her to. All she knew was that Doc was up to something, and despite how she felt she had to go with him.

The still morning air at Ulaan Baatar was absolutely chilling, and though the sun shone brightly above, Rhiannon felt nothing of its warming effects.

The herdsmen who awaited them with horses took one look at Rhiannon and started waving their arms about in protest.

'What is it?' she inquired of Doc, who spoke the language like a local.

'They say you are too frail to ride alone.' He appeared to be disappointed. 'I've equipment that I have to carry with me, as do my men. I'm afraid you'll have to stay behind. You need to rest.'

'No,' she insisted stubbornly, nearly passing out where she stood. 'I shall pay one of the herdsmen to take me. Ask them to name a price.'

'You're being unreasonable —'

'Just do it!' she snapped.

'Okay.' Doc held both hands up in truce, struggling to keep the smile from his face as he turned to consult the herdsmen. He was enjoying toying with her and watching her suffer; it was karma, or as he saw it, self-defence.

It was one of the older herdsmen who stepped forward to accept the offer. He bargained a damn good price for the service too, demanding payment up front.

Fees settled and horses loaded, the party headed off across the barren grassy plains towards the Hentiy Mountains.

The old herdsman had seated Rhiannon in front of him on the horse so that she could lean back against him as they rode. She was thankful for the support, and the time to rest. Her medication made her so drowsy that she couldn't feel the thumping pain in her head, nor the biting cold wind. Her eyes were lulled closed with the gentle rocking motion of the horse, and it was only then that she noticed the sunlight on her face. *This is almost paradise*, she decided on the quiet, as their horse had fallen behind the rest of the party.

My dear girl, what has become of you?

It was Ray's voice Rhiannon heard in her head, and it brought tears to her eyes it was so clear. The drugs were obviously playing havoc with her imagination, and she refused to succumb.

What happened? he persisted. *What did he do to you?*

It's not what Doc did to me, Rhiannon answered in her mind, as her thoughts drifted back to the day Ray had been shot. *I just stood there and watched Doc murder you. At the time it meant nothing. It wasn't until the effects of the NERGUZ wore off that I realised you'd surely perished that day. I couldn't stop the contempt from growing inside me after that, or the guilt.*

No, you must let these feelings go. They are the root of your disease. The nightmare will be over soon, Ray told her. *Your kin are coming for you.*

Ray's words were comforting, however imaginary. So Rhiannon allowed his memory, and those of her family and friends, to take her far away from her bleak reality.

As a sigh of delight escaped his passenger's lips, the old herdsman looked down upon his charge and smiled too.

The spinning, surging motion of their craft being shot through a multi-coloured vortex in space at several times the speed of light, was a heart-stopping experience. Tory felt sure she didn't drawn breath for the entire duration of their ride through the wormhole, which could have been minutes, hours, or days — the event seemed endless at the time.

As they emerged out of the far side of the porthole, their craft righted itself and slowed down.

'That is such a rush!' Maelgwn let loose a howl of exhilaration. 'Are you still with me?'

'I … I, yes.'

Tory hazarded a laugh. Here she was in an entirely new solar system, one that revolved around twin suns. Tory could see these stars ahead, burning brightly in the distant space, one vastly outshining the other.

'You see that star over there.' Maelgwn drew her attention to the direction they'd just come from. 'That's Apsu, your sun. I can spot it easily, as I have looked for it often.'

'I have been wondering about this place where you have dwelt.' Tory turned back to look ahead. 'How long till we reach Tarazean?'

'As luck would have it, the planet's current position in orbit places her between us and her suns.' As Tory stared at him blankly, Maelgwn clarified. 'Shouldn't take more than a couple of Earth hours.'

'Is there a plan? I don't suppose you know this Ningal at all?'

'Not really.' Maelgwn shuddered to think what such a woman would be like. 'But considering she cut off her husband's private parts, I might let you do the talking this time.'

Their craft flew itself with little guidance needed. Tory and Maelgwn spent the next few hours discussing what their friends might be up to back on Earth. They told stories about their individual adventures during their separation. Both carefully avoided the subject of Maelgwn's capture, though they knew it was an underlying bone of contention.

By the time they were entering Tarazean's distinctly purple atmosphere, good conversation had swept away any care they might have had.

His face sore from laughter, Maelgwn took a few deep breaths. 'I've missed this,' he confessed, only realising how much as the words left his mouth. 'I see you now for the person you truly are, Tory Alexander. And just for the record ... if I were again given the chance to be intimate with you, I would not hesitate. I just had to be sure.'

Naturally, for Tory it was a major relief to hear him say so. 'How long have we got before we land?' she queried innocently.

Her question was answered as the pilot's headset extended from the roof. Maelgwn shrugged apologetically.

The misty, purple cloud cover cleared and the dusky sunset was alight with the most beautiful mauve hue. Night lighting lit up a spectacular city that was nestled in the side of a mountain with steep, rocky inclines towering around it on three sides.

'Gibal said Ningal would be expecting us,' Maelgwn informed Tory, heading them into the docking bay entrance beneath the city.

The Goddess was expecting them alright. There was a small army of officials waiting to greet them as they landed.

Tory was surprised to consider that her surroundings were not so unusual — for her first glimpse of an alien nation. These people seemed to have all the same creature comforts as humans did, and probably then some. In fact, Ningal's officials looked human.

'They are,' Maelgwn informed on the quiet. 'This is what became of the Mayan population.'

They were of similar build and features to the Indian peoples of Central America, though their skin was paler, perhaps due to the different climate of their adopted planet. Tory was not given the chance to have a proper look around, because they were immediately escorted to a large, metal plate in the docking station. Tory followed Maelgwn onto a designated section of the floor, whereupon it lit up and they were instantaneously transported to Ningal's quarters.

'So this is where Taliesin acquired his technology,' Tory commented upon arrival.

'What can I say. The Merlin has foresight.' Maelgwn spotted their hostess awaiting their attention at the far end of the chamber, and so headed that way.

High, smoked glass walls sloped and met in the centre of the ceiling, forty or so feet above them, forming a long triangular room with spectacular views. Outside, the cliff wall towered to the left of them and on the right, the twin suns set over the canyon. The floor was laid with large tiles, smooth as marble, but reflective and purple in colour. The chamber was sparsely furnished with a lounge here and there, a table, a work of art, or an unusual plant. Much like their hostess, the decor was breathtakingly simplistic.

Ningal was seven foot tall and as slender as a waif. Her short, black hair accentuated her milky-white skin, her pixie-like features, and her luscious, blue-painted lips. Her large almond shaped eyes of deep violet had whites that were so brilliant light appeared to beam from them. Her long, white dress hugged her slender shape and trailed off behind her.

I am told you have just come from visiting my husband? She directed the query at Tory.

But the shock of Ningal's surpassing beauty caused Maelgwn to speak out of turn, for he now believed he knew what she needed to hear. 'We have, Nin, and he misses —'

I asked Lamamu. She used Tory's Atlantean name, though Ningal had not learnt this via a formal introduction. *How is* dear *Narnar, in your opinion?*

'Well, Nin …' Tory considered her true impression, 'he's coming apart.' The Goddess began to chuckle at this, so Tory added, 'No pun intended.'

You may stay, she held her hands to her heart, delighted. *I have had quarters prepared for you, Dragon. You may retire to them for now.*

'As you wish, Nin.' Maelgwn was a little offended by her dismissal. 'But we are running on a rather tight schedule —'

I am fully aware of how much time you have. Ningal's eyes turned stormy, and then immediately calmed. *But as we are expecting a sandstorm, I am afraid you shall be my guest until at least tomorrow morning.*

'In that case,' Maelgwn bowed slightly in leaving, 'I hope to make your acquaintance again, sometime before then.'

Mmmm. Rather charming, really, Ningal commented, once Maelgwn had returned to the transporter plate and left. *It's a pity my venomous daughter got to him. She has a knack for ruining the very best in men.* Ningal shook her head and looked back to Tory. *And why have you not healed his pain, Lamamu?*

It took Tory a moment to find her voice. 'Sorry?'

He craves your love terribly. He needs you to soothe away the dreadful images that Inanna implanted in his mind.

Tory decided to go on the offensive herself. 'And what of your husband's pain, Ningal?' The Goddess looked set to fly into a rage, but Tory persisted to plea Narnar's case regardless. 'I feel sure that Narnar is not the same man you condemned ... but rather a faint, mad shadow of that warrior. If it was your desire to cut him down to size when you seized his manhood, then I would say you have well succeeded.'

He is mad, you say? Insane? Ningal inquired, sounding almost concerned.

'Your husband has been playing cards with stone deva gargoyles for thousands of years, without so much as being able to scratch his balls.' Tory held up both hands in supplication. 'How long do you think that kind of lifestyle can be healthy for him?'

A fair point, Ningal conceded.

'If you are not going to fetch him off that rock, then at least allow me to return his missing parts.'

Half a solution still leaves half the problem to fester. The dulcet tones of Keridwen's voice resounded round the massive chamber.

Tory and Ningal were stunned into silence by the unexpected interruption. They bowed their heads in reverence to the Goddess as she manifested before them in a blaze of misty light.

554

Keridwen had the same pixie-like features as her niece, but her long hair shimmered with silver and her presence exuded the life-force of an enlightened soul.

Ninharsag, I am deeply honoured by this visit. Ningal lifted her head, even more overwhelmed than Tory was to see the wise woman. *Is there something you require of me?*

Indeed, Ningal … it is time for Narnar to resume his rightful place in the Pantheon of Twelve. But his peers will only forgive him and welcome him home if you do. Therefore, I would ask you to accompany Lamamu to DUG-GA-E, to return what you took from Narnar. Sensing how unfair Ningal thought the request to be, Keridwen smiled. *I know you still love him, Ningal, and, furthermore, he still loves you. Why fear and delay the one and only act that can bring you true peace and happiness.*

Ningal looked down at the ground. She could not deny the truth of her aunt's claim. Despite her husband's faults, she missed him terribly. Lately, all her fond memories of Narnar had begun to replace the not-so-pleasant ones. The only reason Ningal had delayed his release was because of a fear that her husband would despise her for waiting so long. *You are right, Aunt. It is high time I faced my fear and forgave him.* Ningal looked to Keridwen, longing to believe her nightmare would come to a happy end. *But dare I believe that his time in isolation has changed Narnar's contempt of women so much that he will now treat me, and all women, with the respect he always should have afforded us?*

Tory was a little worried at this point, recalling how Narnar had reacted to her presence.

Ningal, my dear child. During Narnar's banishment he has realised the error of his ways, Keridwen assured her. *You are the only woman who ever truly held his favour, and by going with Lamamu and setting Narnar free, you will redeem his faith in women.*

Ningal ventured a smile, and nodded to confirm she would do as suggested.

Tory was pleased by Ningal's decision, but said nothing as Keridwen turned her large green-grey eyes Tory's way.

Lamamu, I wish to apologise for the trouble my kin have caused you, and I assure you that all shall be amended very soon.

Ningal's spirits were high and a generous mood overtook her. *I feel sure that I can assist Lamamu in amending some of the damage done her by my daughter.*

Tory moved to decline the offer, wary of pushing Maelgwn into an uncomfortable predicament. 'But you have both already been more than enough help to our cause, I —'

Do not fear, child, Keridwen interrupted, knowing Tory's mind. *You have been studying the ancient texts of your planet, so consider Ningal's acclaimed talents … she has experience and expertise in such matters.*

Ningal had been revered as the saviour Goddess of the soul, and had had a reputation for wisdom and grace. Tory thought that perhaps she *could* be of some aid. 'When you put it that way, it would be foolish not to accept.'

It is the very least we can do, Keridwen said.

Ah, Dragon. There you are. Ningal swept into the chamber where Maelgwn was pacing, and he ceased his frustrated movement.

'Yes, Nin.' He gave a slight bow. 'I am right here, where you put me.'

Could you find nothing to entertain you? Ningal completely ignored his sarcasm, and neared Maelgwn to place a hand upon his cheek.

Overwhelmed by her amorous mood, the warrior king was struck dumb.

Well then, we shall have to see if we cannot devise something for your amusement.

The next moment they were in a lush, forest garden, alive with colour and as tranquil as paradise. 'Where have you brought me?' Maelgwn became a mite uncomfortable — Ningal was Inanna's mother, after all.

These are my private gardens, she told him, her emphasis on the 'private'. *And they are yours to explore.*

That sultry tone in her voice was a worry — Maelgwn backed up a step. 'Where is my wife, Ningal?'

Oh, I am sure you will find her around here ... somewhere. The Goddess looked around, and then unexpectedly vanished.

'A-huh.' Maelgwn cocked an eye, sensing there was a game afoot.

The rooftop garden was a huge greenhouse that, at night, was internally and externally lit. Outside, the lights were much brighter to highlight the swirling purple sands that came with the raging desert storms that often plagued the city. Inside, the lighting was used to add atmosphere or to light a beautiful sculpture, the exquisite plants or the gushing fountains and waterfalls.

Maelgwn turned in circles, wondering which way to go, when music came wafting along to guide him. 'Albinoni,' he smiled, heading down the garden path in the direction from which the tune beckoned. It had been Tory who had first introduced him to the works of this early seventeenth century composer. This particular concerto for violin, when played allegro, was a joyous piece with a hint of mischief. The music spurred Maelgwn on; it stirred memories of striking clarity, of the life and times he and Tory had had together in Gwynedd. It was as if he had locked away the precious images for safe-keeping, and through music Tory had found the key to unlock that sacred place.

A pond, alight with numerous floating candles, brought the trail to an end. On the far bank Tory was seated amid a picnic dinner, wearing the dress she always wore in his dreams.

'It is a superb rendition of this piece,' he commented across the water to her.

'Why, thank you.' Tory stood and approached the water's edge. 'Ningal recorded it from my memory, upon which it is eternally etched.'

The Albinoni concerto ended abruptly and a soothing concerto played adagio replaced it.

'You see, my lover, I figured that your problem is not what you need to forget … but what you need to remember.'

'Aye, I do remember.' Maelgwn's eyes began to water, but he pulled his emotions into line before they got the better of him. 'So, tell me. Am I to swim across to you?'

'Chivalrous,' Tory judged, 'but unnecessary. You might prefer to take the maze.' She motioned to the large, thick patch of trimmed hedges that lined the pond at the far end.

'Not likely,' he announced, proceeding to strip down to his trousers. 'I could be lost in there for hours.'

'That's the spirit.' Tory cheered him on, unable to believe he'd chosen the quicker, though more inconvenient route; that had to say something about the way he felt.

Maelgwn pulled off his second boot, and dived out over the water. He never broke the surface, however, just vanished in mid-dive.

'Hey, that's cheating.' Tory turned to encounter him.

'I have dreamt of you in this dress, or rather in part thereof, more times than I care to recall.' Maelgwn slid his hands around her waist to pull her close.

Tory was a little thrown by this sudden eagerness. This kind of amorous behaviour was indicative of the Maelgwn she remembered, but with the way he'd been acting since they'd been reunited she had good reason to wonder if she wasn't being deceived by an impostor.

'I told you I would not hesitate.' He gently moved Tory backwards, against the soft, mossy surface of a nearby tree, and with a long, lingering kiss he put her doubts concerning their love to rest.

27

RAISING THE DEAD

The mountain Doc sought was Burqan Qaldun, although no one had called it by that name for centuries. This was the source of the three great rivers of the Kublia Khan: Orhon Gol, Tuul Gol and Herlen Gol. High in the mist-swathed hills of this place, an ancient tree marked the burial chamber of an old cohort of Cadwaladr's, named Temujin. No one but Doc knew that they had camped for the night just a few kilometres short of this burial ground. As far as the locals knew this was a surveying trip. They were completely unaware that come first light, their services would no longer be required.

Whatever the herdsmen were feeding Rhiannon, it was keeping her alive and kicking. This was fortunate from Doc's point of view. He had feared that his wife was so weak that she might die and assume her immortality before they arrived at their destination, which would make the task of her disposal far more difficult.

The old herdsman she'd hired to transport her was particularly attentive to her needs. Besides cooking for her and feeding her, he also made sure she was kept warm. He pitched and dismantled her tent as required. The old man brewed a tea-like substance especially for Rhiannon, which kept the nausea caused by her medication under control, and made for a much more pleasant trip for all concerned.

'Good value, these herdsmen,' Doc commented to Stanley, as they saddled up for the day.

'Yeah. It's a shame they wouldn't take the modules when we offered them,' Stanley added. 'Now we have to leave them behind, and the little buggers are damn useful when it comes to setting up camp.'

Once they were loaded up and ready to go, Doc had Stanley rally together their guides. The old herdsman lifted Rhiannon onto her mount before walking over to join the assembly. She watched as Doc addressed the locals, as he'd done every day before setting out.

But today, Stanley Brennon stood behind the herdsmen and blasted them all to unconsciousness in seconds with his treasured Stormer. 'No!' Rhiannon half climbed, half fell off the horse. 'What are you doing?' She stumbled over to fall at the side of the old herdsman. This man had made her feel better than she had in months, and the thought of pressing on without his aid was far too terrible.

'You'll just have to manage on your own.' Doc pulled her to her feet. 'We haven't got far to go.'

'But you said there was a storm coming. You can't just leave them here at the mercy of the elements!' Rhiannon pleaded, knowing he had every intention of doing just that. 'Leave me here with a tent and I'll take care of them.'

Doc and Stanley just laughed at this. 'You can't even take care of yourself,' Doc reasoned, mocking her.

'I'll manage.' Rhiannon glared at him, though her growing anger made her head throb.

Again the men laughed.

'She's really got a thing for the old bloke,' Stanley jeered.

'Well, I tell you what.' Doc put an arm around his wife's shoulder to suggest: 'We'll stick the old man in front of you in the saddle, and as long as you can hold him up, you can keep him. Fair enough?'

The hatred that burned in the pit of her stomach gave her the determination to accept his terms, despite the fact that she had needed the herdsman's help to keep *herself* in the saddle the day before. 'What about the others?' she queried.

'That's a bit adventurous.' Doc made light of her concern. 'I hardly think you'll be able to support all of them. Think of your poor horse?' He walked off, motioning for Stanley to load the old man up for her.

'Prick,' Rhiannon muttered under her breath. She collected the herdsman's bag containing his herbs and utensils before following Stanley back to the horse.

It may be that they rode only a few hours that

morning, but to Rhiannon it felt like days. The herdsman was a dead weight in her arms and her weakened back was aching from having to support him. *Come on, Ray.* She closed her eyes, in need of rest. *Speak to me now. Tell me how everything is going to be fine.*

He had spoken to her often during this journey, yet now, when she really needed to hear it, he did not speak.

By the time they finally stopped, Rhiannon just sat in the saddle. She was too exhausted to even dismount, and was trying to figure out how to unload the herdsman without killing him, when two of Doc's muscle men dragged both her burden and herself off the horse.

The rest of Doc's cronies had set to work digging at the side of a hilly mound. Rhiannon sat marvelling at the speed of their progress, when she spied her husband approaching.

'Your friend is still with us, I see.' Doc made reference to the herdsman, whose head was resting in Rhiannon's lap.

Rhiannon was tempted to say, 'no thanks to you', but refrained for fear Doc would take the old man's life out of spite. 'Are you going to tell me what we are digging for?'

'An old, old friend of mine,' Doc informed her, with a grin. 'Temujin was his name … though his people called him Khan the Mighty.'

'What!' Rhiannon was nearly sick. She didn't know what she'd been expecting him to say, but this certainly wasn't it. 'Are you telling me you knew Genghis Khan?'

'Pardon me, but I was the reason he believed in immortality,' Doc advised. 'Together we searched for the secret place of the three sacred fountains. Unfortunately, Temujin died before we found the elixir of everlasting life.' Doc shrugged. 'But now I have it, thanks to Shamash, so I am delivering it as vowed.'

If the subject didn't have the vital gene in his make up he could not return to life. Rhiannon knew this, but still felt she had to protest — just in case. 'You can't just raise him from the dead after eight hundred years! His soul has surely moved on elsewhere.'

'And what of Jennifer Pearce's soul? She was raised from the dead in this fashion, *after* I killed her.' Doc's smirk broadened as he perceived Rhiannon's dismay. 'How do I know about her resurrection?' He crouched beside his wife, to better perceive her rising dread. 'Well, honey, it's like this … you're not suffering from a virus, but rather a big, bad growth on your brain. This growth is playing havoc with your mind's functions and you're remembering things that you thought were long erased from your memory. For, as with a computer, data is never really erased from the mind. It just gets stored in an out-of-the-way place, waiting for some hacker to come dig it up. It was a nice try though,' he allowed in closing. 'You really had me fooled for a while there. A long while.'

By now, Rhiannon really felt like she'd had the shit kicked out of her. 'What else do you know?' She was almost too afraid to ask.

'Oh, lots of interesting things.' Doc took a long pause to consider which pieces of information would vex her the most. 'For example, I found out Ray Murdock was your lover … which did seem to explain why you've been pissed at me since the Death Valley disaster. It must have felt really shitty, just standing back and allowing me to fill your true love full of holes.'

'Shut up.' Rhiannon made a feeble attempt at hitting him. 'I am glad you know. Now I can tell you how every second I spend with you makes my skin crawl —'

'However, that's not the best thing I found out.' Doc spoke up over her outburst and ended it. 'I know where the base of your illusive kin is located.' He raised his eyebrows and nodded surely to confirm her horror. 'But before I can deal with them, I need a strategist, someone I can trust. And that's why I have come to fetch Temujin, as he was, after all, history's foremost conqueror.'

Rhiannon began shaking violently when she realised that the only way she could stop Doc was to kill herself. She grabbed for his gun, but in her weakened state her reach fell short of her hopes.

'No heroics, thank you.'

Rhiannon felt the familiar prick of a module being clapped around her wrist, at which time she knew it was all over.

'Stick around. The fun has only just began.' Doc left her to check on the progress of his excavation.

Rhiannon checked her pockets for the ENZU-GUZ as soon as Doc's back was turned, but between all her layers of clothing and her fragile state she could not locate it.

Within the hour Doc's workers pulled back the tombstone, and they all entered the underground passage that led to the burial chamber. Here was inscribed a curse on those who would disturb the resting place of the mighty Khan. Doc took this curse to mean the smell that got worse the further they proceeded into the crypt.

The great ruler had been buried in five coffins, one inside the other. The innermost one was made of pure gold; Doc knew this as he'd been at the burial ceremony. He also knew Temujin had been entombed with several slaves, horses, jewels and so forth. But, since it was only the ruler's body he'd come for, Doc left all else as it was.

As the workmen hauled the huge coffin out into the daylight, Rhiannon was seized by two of Doc's men and hauled towards the entrance of the tomb. Doc was insisting that she see the inner sanctum and, although she was just as insistent about not seeing it, when he ordered her inside Rhiannon could not refuse.

She edged down the passage, Doc pushing her onward, the smell of death wreaking havoc with her already sensitive stomach. Up ahead, a couple of torches had been lit, so when they entered the chamber all the beauty and the horror of the sacred burial place impacted on Rhiannon to its fullest extent.

Jewels and great treasure glistened around the rotten remains of men and horses, who had been buried alive with their leader.

'Okay, I've seen it. Can I go now?' she pleaded, quickly covering her nose and mouth once more.

'No.' He shoved her to the ground, and she sprawled in the space the huge coffin had once occupied. 'You get to stay. The module on your wrist will prevent you from willing yourself out of here and destroys all hope of your kindred ever finding you. And, just in case you're thinking you can cut your way out of this one ...' he held up the ENZU-GUZ that Ray had died to give her, 'you'd best think again.'

She was beyond words, beyond hope.

Rhiannon had nothing left to fight him with, no trick left up her sleeve.

'But just to show you there are no hard feelings, I won't leave you to rot alone.'

Stanley entered carrying the unconscious herdsman and dumped him on the ground beside Rhiannon.

'No, please, he'll surely die.' She begged them to reconsider.

'Well, it wasn't my idea! You're the one who insisted on bringing him with you.' Doc grinned and then followed Stanley out. 'Ciao bella, it's been fun.'

'This isn't goodbye, Cadwaladr, you scum sucking maggot!' Rhiannon yelled after him, though her fury only made her feel worse. 'I hate you,' she screamed with the last of her strength, as they sealed the tomb over. 'I've always hated you,' she mumbled, collapsing into an exhausted heap of tears.

Soon the torches would use up all the oxygen and burn themselves out. Rhiannon wondered if the dear old herdsman would have the chance to regain consciousness before they both died of asphyxiation. She would be born again, but the herdsman would not.

He would end up like the other poor bastards who had been entombed alive in this place, and then she would have to live with his death and his rotting corpse.

Upon leaving Tarazean, Tory and Maelgwn felt a lot better than they had when they'd arrived. Besides their renewed trust and zest for each other, they carried with them Narnar's private parts, the ransom the God had asked for Dumuzi's release.

This is like a bad dream, Ningal said, as she caught sight of Narnar's stone palace, for she remembered how her husband had implored her not to leave him there. *It does seem to me now that I must have been as heartless as he.*

'But we are going to change all that,' Tory assured her. 'Just by being here, you have already become part of the solution.'

How clever of you, Lamamu. I have, haven't I? The Goddess touched an escaped tear from her cheek. *It just hurts less when you're part of the problem.*

Tory shook her head to disagree. 'No. Fear, hate, pain, guilt, lust, excess, greed — they kill the emotions. You're numbed! So in reality, it only *seems* to hurt less.'

I knew that once, the Goddess announced, a mite ashamed of being lectured in the nature of spirituality by one who was not of her breed. *I knew it, I believed it, I lived it. But I have long forgotten the wisdom taught to me by my father. Since Enki vanished from our midst, I think we have all forgotten.* Ningal bowed her head in shame.

'What happened to him?' Tory was intrigued, Enki being her great-grandfather.

Ningal looked back at Tory, and with a casual shrug replied, *He became so enlightened that he evolved to a higher state of consciousness. As did Enlil, Ninlil, Ninki and Ninharsag.*

The last three Nefilim mentioned were females, who Tory felt confident comprised the triple goddess she had encountered on more than one occasion. She already knew Ninharsag was Keridwen, so the rest just stood to reason. 'So who is ruling the galaxies if all the responsible adults, so to speak, have moved on?'

The Pantheon of Twelve, of which I am a member, Ningal informed her, taking offence.

'Shamash and Inanna too, I suppose?' Tory got a nod for an answer. 'Marduk,' she went on.

'No, Marduk was banished, because of Dumuzi,' Maelgwn cut in. 'Since then, it has been discovered that your grandfather further offended the Pantheon by making love to a mortal woman, even though Enlil expressly forbade it.'

'Several women most likely,' Tory added, considering that all the immortal tribes had acquired the vital gene from someone.

But Maelgwn knew different. 'Marduk swears he only ever loved the one woman. It was just over several of her lifetimes.'

Well, I cannot see that his coupling with this woman is as great a crime as Enlil once decreed, Ningal reasoned. *Not if the likes of you and your husband are the result ... at least Marduk still has the capacity to truly love another.*

'That's a lovely thing to say, Ningal,' Tory told her.

'I would ask that you bear that view in mind at the Nefilim inquiry into these matters. Which is bound to be forthcoming,' Maelgwn added.

Fear not, Dragon. I predict Marduk's children shall fare well. If what you claim is true, it shall be my children who rue the day.

Tory and Maelgwn followed Ningal down the entrance hall on the first level of Narnar's ziggurat, for Ningal needed no guide to find her way to the main chamber.

'Just where do you think you're going?' Tobit appeared between Maelgwn's shoulder blades, but did not attack.

'I'm sorry,' Tory forced a grin, 'but I don't answer to lying, cheating scumbags like yourself.'

Ningal stopped and turned to address the little grey creature. *Give Lamamu back what is hers, or I shall reduce you to a one-fold elemental so fast it will make your head spin.*

Tobit appeared horrified, both by the Goddess and her threat. 'But if you take away my fire, I won't be any fun … I won't have any fun!'

Then do not abuse the privilege, Ningal advised.

The gargoyle's face drooped into a moping expression as he stroked the golden band that hung loosely around his scrawny neck.

We are waiting, the Goddess pushed.

Reluctantly, Tobit pulled the ring off through his neck and held it out to Tory.

And what do we say?

'Sorry,' Tobit sniffled, fit to cry. 'But when you held the jewel before my eyes, it made me crazy!'

'Apology accepted, Tobit,' Tory said cheerfully. 'You may keep the ring.'

'What?' His mood turned to elation, and tears of joy rather than sorrow filled his eyes. 'I don't understand.' He wiped the water from his face. 'What's happening to my face?'

That is water, Tobit, the seed of emotion, the Goddess granted. *Use it well, for it can help balance your hardworking earth side with your creative and often mischievous fire side.*

'I am three-fold!' Tobit felt very strange, having never really felt anything before.

'See, Tobit,' Tory nudged him. 'There are rewards to be had from doing the right thing, and that is always far more satisfying.'

Too confused and dumbfounded to comment, Tobit took flight over their heads. 'I must go and warn, I … I mean tell, my Lord of your arrival. Narnar will be pleased.' The beast tried to sound more confident than he was, crying and laughing uncontrollably as he made haste to Narnar.

Tobit ended a good hand of poker when he crashlanded in a heap in the middle of the table. 'My Lord, forgive me,' the deva sobbed, and then chuckled as he found his feet.

What the hell is wrong with you, Tobit? Narnar threw his cards on top of the beast in disgust.

'My Lord,' Tobit cowered, shaking like a leaf. 'The young Gods have returned with your …' he pointed coyly to his master's groin area.

571

Excellent! Narnar rose, grabbing Tobit and throwing him in the air.

When the creature had regained its equilibrium, he fluttered in mid-air beyond his master's reach. 'Ningal is with them.'

What! Narnar stood. *They would dare bring that creature here!*

'But my Lord,' Tobit appealed bravely. 'What if Ningal is coming to reinstate you? She does seem to have a rather giving spirit. Look at what she did to me!' Tobit motioned to his new-found tears. 'Ningal granted me my three-fold nature, just for being good!'

The other gargoyles gasped, the notion being inconceivable to them.

For being good, hey? Narnar rubbed the empty space between his legs. *I haven't tried that for awhile. I'm not sure I remember what that entails.*

'If I may say, sire, I believe the qualities you seek are love, honesty, respect, truthfulness, loyalty … that was a difficult one for you sire, if memory serves.'

Yes, thank you, Tobit, Narnar said irascibly.

'Now, sire, be nice,' Tobit warned as Ningal entered. 'Forgiving, warm, hospitable — you can do it.' The creature encouraged Narnar with a nod.

Ningal froze when she spotted the hooded figure of her husband in the midst of the accoutrements of his existence all these years. Her guilt consumed her. How was she to forgive Narnar, when she could not forgive herself?

'Allow me, Nin.' Maelgwn took possession of the metal canister that contained Narnar's organ. He then approached the God alone. 'My Lord Narnar,' Maelgwn bowed. 'I have succeeded in the task you set me I believe beyond your expectations. But, I would suggest that we retire to a more private place to conduct our business.'

Narnar looked to Ningal, who nodded to give Maelgwn the authority to speak on her behalf. *This way.* Narnar motioned Maelgwn to exit.

As the two men retired to another chamber, Ningal stood staring at the door they had passed through. *I had forgotten what it was to have a friend.*

'After last night, I believe Maelgwn feels he owes you a favour or two.' Tory placed an arm around the Goddess to reassure her.

The Goddess smiled at this, patting Tory's comforting arm affectionately. *The unconditional love you have for each other is an inspiration, Lamamu. I knew that feeling once, and with the grace of the Gods I will know it again.*

Maelgwn and Narnar returned to the chamber, only Narnar was not hooded any longer. His locks of blonde hair framed his smiling features, and his blue eyes beamed with delight. *Tobit shall show you to Dumuzi,* he instructed Maelgwn.

Tory wished Ningal well, before following Tobit and her husband from the room.

'Do you think it's safe to leave them alone together?' Tory queried her husband once they were well away.

Maelgwn raised his brow and with a broad grin announced, 'With what's at stake, I do believe they'll work it out.'

'Now for Dumuzi and Inanna.' Tory rubbed her hands together expectantly.

'You really haven't changed one bit.' Maelgwn halted to give Tory a squeeze of appreciation. 'Still, I would not be so eager if I were you.'

'And why not?'

'Because Dumuzi was the God of Fertility, and he hasn't fertilised anyone for thousands of years.' Maelgwn grinned at his wife's dismay.

'Perhaps I should wait here.' Tory pushed her rather amorous husband away.

'Only if I can too.' Maelgwn kissed her, drawing the rest of her close with ease.

That's it, do it, do it! The couple parted abruptly, looking to Tobit who was casually leaning against an archway support watching them.

Well, please don't stop my account.

The words did not come from Tobit, but he pointed upwards to the keystone of the arch where a head was embedded.

'My God!' Tory backed up a few steps, noticing the support arches had legs cemented into them. Two arms were embedded in the arch, and hands held up the keystone. 'Dumuzi?'

Oh yes, say it again, enchantress, this time with meaning, the head encouraged, blowing her kisses.

'Watch it,' Maelgwn warned, 'or you will remain as you are.'

You mean you've come to rescue me?

'That depends on how helpful you are prepared to be?' Maelgwn advised.

Oh anything, anything! Dumuzi insisted. *But who sent you? How did you get past Narnar?*

'Your brother Marduk sent me,' Maelgwn said no more, seeking an honest reaction.

Oh praise Anu. I knew Marduk could pressure Shamash into disclosing my location.

'I'm afraid Shamash has fooled everyone, Dumuzi, for it was Marduk who was accused of your murder and banished.'

What! But that's simply not true. Who accused him?

'Inanna, I'm afraid,' Maelgwn advised.

But, whatever put that notion into her head?

'Her former lover of course!' Tory couldn't believe how slow he was.

No, that can't be. Inanna said that she was through with her brother ... that she could not go back to him after me.

'Where is the rest of you?' Tory was curious.

'Behind those doors, yonder,' Tobit pointed. 'And I can help you with these bits of you like?'

'Yes, thank you, Tobit,' although Tory cringed at the thought, 'that would be most appreciated.'

Closing his eyes, the creature raised both claws towards the archway and the stonework vanished. The cold gray body parts fell to the ground, but Tobit caught the head on its way down.

Thanks. Dumuzi smiled at the creature.

'You're welcome,' Tobit told him, tucking the head underarm like a basketball, Dumuzi's nose to his armpit.

Oh no, please. When was the last time you had a wash? Dumuzi protested as he was carted off down the corridor.

'Arms or legs?' Maelgwn gave Tory first preference.

Screwing up her face, Tory reached for the arms.

'Legs it is then.' Maelgwn gathered the leftovers, and followed Tory and Tobit to the rest of the body.

They were down to the last few dregs of the oxygen inside the crypt. The torches died, leaving Rhiannon with vivid images of the bony remains that surrounded her. She huddled close to the one living thing in the tomb with her, the unconscious herder. He was struggling for air as she was. 'Thank you for your kindness,' she whispered, 'and forgive my selfish desires that brought you to this end.'

The herdsman's eyes opened as Rhiannon's closed.

It took a moment to orientate himself to the darkness.

'Rhiannon?' Cadwallon felt the dead weight against him and pulled off his gloves to search the features of the face, realising it was her. 'What is that smell?' Cadwallon resumed his normal appearance and attire. He retrieved a glow-light from the belt of his flying suit, giving it a shake, and the tiny tube lit up the entire crypt. 'Oh dear Goddess. How did we get here?' Cadwallon gathered Rhiannon in his arms to help facilitate her return to consciousness. She began drawing in breaths of stale air, and coughed them back out, her eyes opening wide. 'It's alright. Just don't draw breath. You don't have to any more.'

'Ray?' She urged him to kiss her without delay, and Cadwallon obliged. 'I have died and gone to heaven.' She fell back into his arms, but then, noticing the surroundings, was startled upright. 'No I haven't.'

Cadwallon shrugged apologetically.

'Then you can't be Ray?' Rhiannon was horrified that she'd just been so intimate with a total stranger, but then she couldn't deny that his kiss had kindled emotions in her she thought were long dead.

'Ray is a part of me, Rhiannon, for I am his Chosen incarnation.' He stood to introduce himself properly. 'My name is Cadwallon, and I am very pleased to meet you at last.'

'I'll bet you are,' she scoffed, trying to figure out where she'd heard that name before. 'Hold on. You're not Cadwallon as in Cadwaladr's father, Cadwallon?'

'The one and only,' he smiled, with a bow.

'Oh boy, that explains an awful lot.' Rhiannon bit her lip. 'Like Doc's resentment of Ray, for starters!' As her eyes wheeled about trying to process the information, Rhiannon noticed the herdsman was missing. 'Where's my guide?'

'I'm right here.' Cadwallon threw his arms wide.

'No. The local who has been tending me these past few days?' Rhiannon continued her gruelling search for him.

'Aye,' Cadwallon acknowledged surely. 'That was me.'

'That was you?' Rhiannon's attention shot back in his direction, her heart all a-flutter in her chest. 'So it was you who was bethinking me as we travelled.'

'It was not my intent to deceive you, I just —'

'No.' Rhiannon approached, not wanting him to get her wrong. 'The things you said were beautiful.' Upon nearing him she noticed how well-built Cadwallon was. This man was a warrior, like her brother.

'It is you who are beautiful,' he told her. 'You are every bit as brave and wonderful as you ever were.'

'Oh Goddess,' Rhiannon felt herself drowning in his eyes. 'Is it hot in here?' she inquired casually, fanning her face in the hope of composing herself.

'Of course.' Cadwallon held out his hands to her. 'Allow me to get you out of here. You can tell me the story of how we came to be in this wretched place at some later date.'

Rhiannon gladly took hold, closing her eyes to be transported somewhere else. It would be home, most likely; she must warm them of Doc's pending attack.

'Yes!' She opened her eyes to find herself alone in the crypt. 'Cadwallon?' She called meekly to him, fearful of waking the dead. 'Oh shit! The module must have prevented him from teleporting me.' She shrugged if off, thinking he would return at any moment. But as time dragged on, she recalled that Cadwallon had been unconscious for the last part of the trek, and the module would prevent him from willing himself back to her. 'Oh Goddess no,' Rhiannon uttered. 'Please let him find me.'

'Sorry about that.' Cadwallon reappeared, with Rhun. 'I got a bit caught up with your brother here.'

'Rhun.' Rhiannon rushed to his familiar embrace.

'Are you alright?' He checked her over, hugging her intermittently.

'I'm fine, really I am. But,' she turned back to Cadwallon, 'how did you locate me?'

'Are you kidding?' He glanced around. 'This place lingers in your memory.'

'Oh Rhun.' Rhiannon's mind skipped to more important matters. 'We must evacuate Watarrka at once. Doc knows of its existence and is planning an attack.'

'Whoa girl, slow down,' Rhun urged. 'We have already relocated.'

Rhiannon closed her eyes to say a quiet, thank you, whilst Rhun pulled an ENZU-GUZ from his pocket and cut her loose from the module's restraining device.

'Let's get you back to the *Goddess*, hey.' Rhun took one of her arms, and Cadwallon the other, and together they conveyed her back to base.

Five coffins made of various precious metals were laid out before Doc, one next to the other. The separation procedure had taken place in a long, wide gallery in the west wing of Doc's manor. He'd had the area cleared, to be alone with his colleague when he awoke. All the curtains had been drawn and candles lit the room. The smallest coffin, made of gold, was the only one still sealed.

'I have missed you, my friend.' Doc gazed at the ornately carved figure of Temujin resting peacefully on the lid. 'Through the ages, there are few people I have trusted so well as you.'

At Doc's willing it, the heavy gold doors of the coffin opened to expose the skeletal remains of the warrior, fully attired in battle dress.

'You boasted often that you were the son of a God.' Doc removed the stopper from the vial in his hand, as he positioned himself at the head of the casket.

'If your claim to divinity be true,
let you stand before me now,
the warrior, the friend, the brother,
that once I knew.'

Doc poured the elixir over the skull of Temujin, and held his breath. He really needed an ally now, someone he could trust beyond question.

'Temujin is not one of the Chosen — it is a waste of time trying to resurrect him.'

The comment startled Doc and he did a quick about-face to find a woman whom he knew not. And then, in the next instant, he thought he recognised her. He marvelled at her strange, black attire and all the gadgets and weapons she sported. 'How did you get in here?'

'You let me in,' she replied, taking a seat on a nearby table.

Doc noticed the symbol of the serpent on the shoulder of her suit. 'What can I do for you, I am in the middle of something here —'

'The base at Watarrka has been abandoned, Doc. If you were hoping your dead friend there was going to assist you to attack the serpent's clan, you're wasting your time. The only strategist you need the aid of right now, is me.'

'And why should I believe you?' She only smiled at the question and Doc worked at preventing his jaw from hitting the ground — the woman was beautiful. Tall and slender, she had pale, ivory skin that was in vast contrast to her long, brown locks and eyes of ebony. 'I know you, don't I?' His memory was doing overtime trying to place her.

She nodded in encouragement. 'Think harder, Caradoc.'

'Caradoc, eh.' Doc turned and walked away from her, searching his memories for the answer. 'Vanora.' He turned his eyes back in her direction. 'If I remember rightly, you left me to rot in your father's dungeon.'

'Well, I was possessed at the time,' she said defensively. 'But back in Atlantis I was your wife for hundreds of years and in Troy we were wed for near to sixty … are you going to let one bad lifetime spoil an almost perfect track record?'

'I don't believe I need anything from one who is in league with the Serpent's clan.'

'But you are one of us, Cadwaladr.'

'No! I have never been one of you!' He flew into a rage. 'I have always been on the outside, looking in.'

'And do you know why?' Vanora queried calmly, as if he were as relaxed as she.

'Because Taliesin locked me out!'

'No, my sweet. Shamash locked you out, and he locked you out on purpose. I have the proof.' She held up a headband.

'What is that?'

'It is a recording of the murder of your father, Cadwallon.'

'That does sound entertaining.' Doc grinned, but he was still wary of the unfamiliar device.

'There's nothing to penetrate the skin. It's perfectly harmless.' She held it out to him. 'Just put it on your head.'

He took the device in hand, but was still hesitant to wear it.

'Cadwaladr,' she implored him gently. 'All your life you've wanted someone to aid and guide you in times of crisis. Well, here I am. If it is allies and friends you seek, you have many. Don't allow Shamash to keep you locked out any longer. If you do, you could spend the rest of eternity regretting it. Shamash is going down, and your resolve in this instant will decide whether or not you are condemned with him.'

Doc gazed at Vanora as she assisted him to position the mechanism on his temples. 'Blind trust. This is a first for me,' he told her.

'Close your eyes.' She gently stroked his lids with her fingertips. 'And allow all to be made clear.'

When Doc had perceived the entire recording, tears were welling in his eyes. He removed the device, pressing his fingers hard into his tear ducts to stop the flow of emotion. 'My whole life has been a lie,' he realised. Cadwaladr had not felt the urge to weep since he was a small child, but his remorse and anger in that instant were so overwhelming that he was tempted to succumb to the pain he felt. 'Goddamn my ignorance!'

'It wasn't your fault,' Vanora placed a hand on his shoulder. 'The Dragon knows that.'

Doc shrugged off her touch; the very mention of his great forefather enraged him. He was so used to despising his kin, that now he didn't know what to feel. 'I have betrayed everyone! I have lied, I have schemed, I have *killed*, to avenge the wrong done me —'

Vanora made haste to grip both his hands, before he worked himself into a state. 'But still you were "Chosen", Cadwaladr.'

This realisation silenced him.

'There are no accidents in that regard.' Vanora's eyes were diverted to the coffin behind Doc, where the reconstituting remains of Temujin arose to a seated position. 'I stand corrected,' she uttered, aghast. 'This is unexpected.'

'No, it isn't. This man is one of the finest who ever lived. Some histories blackened his name and he and his conquests have been widely misunderstood.' Doc moved to greet the age-old warrior, who was once again in his prime. 'Temujin, old friend, I have returned for you as vowed.'

Doc had switched to the Khan's native tongue and Vanora understood it perfectly. All the Chosen were well practiced in telepathy.

Temujin leapt from his resting place, alarmed. His dark eyes darted about, assessing his situation. Suddenly he sprang into a triple backflip, before coming to rest a safe distance away from his company. 'Who are you?' He looked from Doc to Vanora and back again.

'Sorry, my fault.' Doc urged the warrior to stand easy, having realised his error.

The newly-revived twelfth century conqueror stared in amazement as Doc's pale blue eyes turned dark as night. His short, blond hair turned black and thickened as it grew to his waist. The soft features of his face hardened into those of Cadwaladr, and his body erupted with muscles that threatened to tear through Doc's comfortably fitting shirt.

The Khan relaxed as he recognised his host, and opened his arms wide. 'Cadwaladr, my brother.'

'Indeed,' he affirmed as he approached to embrace Temujin. 'Welcome, mighty Khan, to the twenty-first century.'

28

THE GATHERING

The *Goddess* was submerged at the bottom of the Persian Gulf when Tory and Maelgwn rejoined her. They had the reconstructed, washed and partly-clothed Dumuzi with them, who was still over-amorous, but under control.

Dumuzi had begun to radiate light as soon as his body had become whole. He was short for one of the Nefilim breed, being scarcely taller than Maelgwn. His glowing amber eyes gave him a devilish appearance, as did his straight, amber-brown hair that fell to a point in the middle of his forehead. When offered a flight suit to wear, the God would only succumb to wearing the bottom half. Dumuzi was not affected by temperature and liked to flaunt his tanned muscular body at all times. Clothes were against his religion.

'Look at all these beautiful women.' Dumuzi kissed the hand of every one he could. When he tried his charms on Boadicea, however, she socked him one in the eye.

Maelgwn was pleased to see Talynn had found Angus, whose perfect incarnation went by the name of Ethan. Still unconscious, they had tied Ethan in a chair just in case he came out of his coma swinging punches.

'Hello, father.' Rhiannon emerged from the crowd to meet the legendary Dragon she'd heard so much about.

Her appearance floored Maelgwn for only a second. 'Hello, Princess.' He drew her to his chest to hug her as Miles used to.

'It is you.' She squeezed him tight, moved to tears.

'Well, who were you expecting. Superman?' Maelgwn posed in jest, which made her smile.

As Tory watched her husband and her daughter become reacquainted, Rhun's arms enfolded her waist from behind and she glanced over her shoulder at him.

'How about that. The whole family together in the same place, at the same time.'

'It's a miracle to be sure.' Tory smiled, leaning back against her son to enjoy the moment.

'Oh, speaking of family …' Rhun thought he'd best keep her informed. 'No one has seen hide nor hair of Myrddin or Taliesin since the day the other half of our force arrived.'

'That's odd,' Tory mused. 'I was under the impression they would be here guiding us through this.'

'You don't think …' Brian had overheard the conversation. His voice trailed off as he shook his head in rejection of the idea.

'What?' Tory insisted.

'Do you think they had a perfect other half?'

'Aye, they do.' Maelgwn broke from the conversation he was having with Rhiannon. 'I know Taliesin's female half. Her name is Seshut. She has been an adviser and scribe to Marduk all through his exile. Myrddin's true love, however, has been trapped in a part of the Otherworld that has been shut off from this plane since before I was born. It was said that the window to that place would re-open at the time of the Gathering.'

'Avalon,' Tory surmised, thinking it all very romantic. 'Then the perfect incarnation of our mother must have been Vivien, the Lady of the Lake. No wonder we could never get Dad to leave England for any great length of time.'

'But he never mentioned any of this to us,' Brian protested. 'I was under the impression that merlins were beyond the need for earthly pleasures?'

This notion put a smile on the face of everyone within earshot, as all had been indulged of late.

'Their desire to seek each other is wholly spiritual, for until they are joined with their other half, they cannot evolve to a higher plane of consciousness.' Maelgwn found the notion beautiful and rather comforting.

Tory, however, was distinctly disenchanted. 'My father and Taliesin could be evolving from this existence as we speak?'

'Aye,' Maelgwn stated, grabbing hold of his wife to prevent her from dashing off in a flight of hysterics. 'This is a very special time for them, Tory. Don't spoil it by demanding goodbyes or explanations. If either of them wish to see you, they will come to you.'

Tory stood staring at Maelgwn like a scolded child, wondering whether to cry or rebel.

'We can pull this off on our own.' He placed a hand on each of her shoulders to emphasise the fact. 'You said it yourself, Tory. We don't need higher supervision any more.'

Tory nodded, agreeing to let the matter rest for now.

'Excuse I, Commander.'

'Vanora!' Tory gasped upon sighting her.

'Tory.' Vanora acknowledged her, before looking to Maelgwn to report. 'Cadwaladr is ready to talk. Our place or his?'

As the sound of his name almost incited a riot in the room, Maelgwn decided that Cadwaladr's place might be best.

'There's been a little unexpected development,' Vanora added. 'It would seem the Khan had the immortal gene in his make-up after all.'

Maelgwn raised both eyebrows, surprised. 'He must have had the immortal gene in his family line, but was bypassed as one of the Chosen at the time of his death. Not to worry. The elixir Doc has given him will grant him life for only so long as it suits Shamash's purposes.'

'Hey!' Brian alerted everyone to Ethan, who was sitting up in his chair, observing the scene before him with a blank look on his face.

588

'I seem to be having a flashback.' Ethan cracked a huge smile. Although his mother was of the middle eastern tribes, Ethan had more Anglo-Saxon in him. His father had been a knight in the Crusades — Neraida had recognised Ethan's father as one of her lost love's reincarnations. Ethan's skin was olive like his mother's, but fairer in colour. His trimmed-short hair was brown and his eyes were hazel-brown.

Neraida and Talynn rushed their patient, showering him with hugs and kisses.

'It's good to see you, man.' Brian held a hand out to shake Ethan's.

'Brockwell,' he mumbled and moved to take the hand of his old comrade, only to realise he was tied up. 'Um, I really don't think you people have anything to fear from me.'

'Sorry about that.' Talynn explained as Neraida cut her son's bonds: 'You got a bit out of hand when we tried to disconnect you from the module.'

'Aw ...' he grabbed hold of his head with both hands. 'Now I remember.'

'Take it easy, lad.' Cadfan came forward to lead Ethan off to a quiet room to recover his strength in peace.

But as they passed by Maelgwn on the way out, Ethan wavered. 'I know the inside of that base like the back of my hand. Don't be going in there without me.'

'You go and rest yourself. Shamash has yet to arrive and we have other matters to attend to. I promise I will seek your counsel if that need arises.' With a slap on the shoulder, Maelgwn sent Ethan to bed.

Everyone else gathered round Maelgwn and Tory to brainstorm the next step in Shamash's downfall.

All the same faces, and a few new ones, graced the circle. Many of them had only met in the last few days and yet a myriad of experiences bonded them together, so that no one was a stranger. These were history's finest warriors, scholars, strategists, technologists, healers — the list went on. If they couldn't pull this mission off successfully, then nobody could.

Maelgwn chose a token band of people to accompany him to a meeting with Cadwaladr. Not so many as to be intimidating, but a suitable force to deal with an ambush should that be Cadwaladr's intention. Except for Tory and Vanora, Maelgwn selected people who were emotionally detached from Cadwaladr: Robin, Boadicea, and Cadwell.

Vanora guided them to the hallway outside the conference room in Cadwaladr's mansion. She knocked and entered ahead of the others to announce their arrival.

Tory closed her eyes to prepare herself for confronting Cadwaladr again. *I saw enough good in this man once to ensure his soul was spared. Rejection is what Cadwaladr fears most ... don't feed his fear.*

The double doors parted before them. Cadwaladr stood at the far end of the conference table with a couple of bodyguards and Vanora at his side. 'You wished to see me, Dragon?'

As the party entered, Maelgwn couldn't help but stare at their host, who was the identical incarnate of his brother, Caradoc. He and Caradoc hadn't been friendly since they were teenagers, but Maelgwn strived to recall the times they'd been together before the war that changed them from kinsmen to enemies. 'I have come to ask you to unite with us against Shamash, Cadwaladr.'

Behind Maelgwn and his band the doors closed of their own accord.

'It seems we have come full circle, Maelgwn.' Cadwaladr had to smile at the irony of the situation in which he found himself. 'And, in light of the fact that the last time you gave me such an ultimatum I refused and lost badly ... I figure, it might be wise to cooperate this time.' Then Cadwaladr became more serious. 'It is clear from the evidence Vanora has presented to me that Shamash had planned my plight since before my father was even born. He has kept me in the dark my whole life. I'd like a shot at keeping him in the dark for at least a few days.'

'I would also request that you release all those you hold under the influence of the NERGUZ,' Maelgwn stated firmly.

'Apologies, Commander,' Vanora came forward to present Maelgwn with Doc's master control module. 'I meant to advise you — it has already been done. Shamash will arrive at his excavated landing base in the Middle East to find it devoid of occupants.'

This came as a shock to Maelgwn. He'd expected an argument at the very least.

'It's strange, isn't it, Dragon,' Cadwaladr commented. 'Endeavouring to trust someone you're used to despising. I know your doubt and hesitation. Believe me, I know it.'

There was a knock on the conference room doors and Stanley Brennon entered. He was surprised to find strangely-clad visitors therein, and was reluctant to speak in front of them. Instead, he walked all the way to the other end of the room to have a quiet whisper in Doc's ear.

'Well, then,' announced Cadwaladr. 'The moment of truth.'

'Shamash has arrived,' Maelgwn assumed.

'Soon. And he will expect me to be present. So what's the scam?'

Maelgwn closed the distance between himself and Cadwaladr. 'Did you tell Shamash of your intention to dispose of Rhiannon?'

'He wanted it,' Cadwaladr frowned. 'Maybe Utu even put me up to it. But, no, to the best of my knowledge I did not tell him of my intentions. I suspected for some time, though, that Utu was twisting my mind to suit his purpose. I needed someone I could trust, someone Utu was unaware of, who could monitor this for me … that is why I went in search of Temujin.' He motioned to his silent partner, now standing behind him. Temujin did not understand the language being spoken, but Cadwaladr would fill him on the outcome of the proceedings after the meeting had adjourned.

Maelgwn looked over the renowned conqueror of the orient who was observing him just as closely. His appearance was of a warrior to be reckoned with, and quite frankly, Maelgwn was relieved that the Khan was now on their side. 'Well, then,' he concluded, sensing Cadwaladr spoke the truth. 'It seems that you have ended up with more allies than you bargained for.'

Cadwaladr shook his head in bafflement. He just couldn't imagine fitting in with the Dragon's kin. 'Half of your flock would see me drawn and quartered.'

Maelgwn shrugged. 'Same old, same old, really,' he said. 'However, as of now you are under my protection. If anyone wants a piece of you, they'll answer to me.'

'And me.' Tory strode down to join them. 'If Shamash starts manipulating you and gains control of your domain here, we're all stuffed.'

'I can't say how much Shamash already knows about my operations here.' Cadwaladr wanted to make that clear. 'To keep things secret from Rhiannon, I allowed Utu to wash away aspects of our conversations, but then I could never really be sure he didn't do more than that.'

'Then, he most certainly did.' Maelgwn found himself feeling rather sympathetic.

'We must secure the fusion reactor in space and the facility at Farwell,' Tory suggested. 'If Shamash gains control of either of those, he can shut down the world power grid, or blow us all to kingdom come.'

'You know about that?' Cadwaladr was sure he'd kept the glitch under wraps.

'It was us who stole your hard-drive,' Tory explained apologetically.

'I knew it —' Cadwaladr began.

'Later people,' Maelgwn advised. 'We're a little pressed for time. Vanora — assume Rhiannon's form and accompany Doc to greet Shamash.' He looked at Cadwaladr. 'I leave Cadwell, Robin and Boadicea with you also. They can be disguised as your personal bodyguards. Shamash will get himself settled in before causing too much havoc, but should all not go well with his arrival, my people will get you to a safe place. Meanwhile, Tory and I will arrange for the defence of the power grid, and see if we can't round up an army for you, to replace the one you've lost ... save, having to explain to Shamash what happened to the immortals you have released from the influence of the NERGUZ. Sound good?' Everyone nodded in accord, except Cadwaladr.

'Just one thing.' He seemed reluctant to bring the point up. 'The module? If I am not seen wearing it, I can hardly claim to be controlling the masses. There is only one of its like on the planet.'

Though Maelgwn could see the sense of what he said, he also knew that many of the ICA's abductees would not yet have found their kin, or indeed their own mind. A split-second change of heart on Cadwaladr's behalf and he would be calling on all those that had not yet recovered from the module's influence to follow him.

'You're just going to have to trust me, I'm afraid,' Cadwaladr prompted.

Maelgwn looked to Tory, who, after a second's consideration, gave the nod.

The band was passed over, and Cadwaladr was dumbfounded by their resolute style. 'You always were too trusting, Maelgwn,' he said, his voice even hoarser than usual.

Maelgwn shook his head at this. 'I never lose, Cadwaladr, because I only ever back a sure thing.' With a confident grin, Maelgwn slapped his hands together to get everybody moving. 'Stay alert, people. At the first sign of trouble head back to the *Goddess*.'

The two huge cylindrical craft belonging to Shamash finally approached the Earth. One parked itself in orbit, amid the satellites and space stations, while the other proceeded toward the exposed runway in the Middle East.

Pictures of the alien craft were being beamed to Earth via satellite from the Brunanburh Space Station. This facility was now a permanent attachment of the fusion reactor that supplied power to the moon's bases as well as the Earth's. The Brunanburh was supplying the bulk of the information on the new arrivals because it was the closest space station to the visitors.

The crew members of the *Goddess* who were watching the broadcast were starting to get a little concerned. Maelgwn and his team were taking longer than expected.

Floyd was especially nervous. He'd only just found Boadicea and his fear of losing her made him braver than usual. 'I think we should go after them.' He attempted to distract everyone from the television.

'Dear Floyd.' Candace placed a hand on his shoulder sensing his personal dilemma. She couldn't help but smile at how little he knew about his love. 'I know Boadicea very well, and I assure you, the only reason we need go after her is if you wish to save her foe.'

595

'Yo, team.' Tory called everyone to attention.

When Floyd saw that only Maelgwn and Tory had returned, he panicked. 'Where's Boadicea?'

'I left her guarding Cadwaladr, with Vanora, Cadwell and Robin,' Maelgwn informed him.

'What!' Floyd couldn't believe his ears, and moved to confront the huge warrior.

'Now, Tiernan —'

'Floyd.' Tory corrected Maelgwn.

'Floyd,' he continued. 'We have no time to argue. I am told you are a code breaker.'

'Well, yes.' Floyd was overcome by the man's forthright manner and followed an overwhelming instinct to hear him out.

'Then I need you to accompany Rhun, Brian, Season, Candace and Sybil to Farwell.' Maelgwn turned his address to his son. 'Rally the local tribes if you have to, but you must secure the host station for the fusion grid.'

'Aye, aye, Commander.' Rhun grinned, happy with his mission and his team.

Maelgwn looked back to Floyd. 'I need you to override, and then rewrite code for, the security system of the host station and the reactor in space. Can you do that?'

Floyd's eyes boggled at the task. 'What kind of a time frame do I have?'

'Yesterday would be nice, but as soon as immortally possible will do.' Maelgwn gave the hacker a friendly slap on the shoulder, knowing he was asking the impossible of Floyd, but then, where this man was concerned, he was used to getting exactly that in the end.

'Gotcha,' Floyd replied, scratching his head as he considered what he'd need.

'Cadwallon.' Maelgwn motioned him closer. 'It was as Ray Murdock that you designed some of the systems for the fusion reactor.'

'Yes,' Cadwallon replied, anticipating his question. 'I still recall the layout of the Brunanburh and her fusion reactor's electronic monitoring system. What is it you wish me to do?'

'For the present, I just need you to go to the control room, secure it and await further orders.'

Rhiannon stepped forward to accompany Cadwallon. 'Well, as no-one knows that Doc has tried to knock me off, I guess I still have the authority to give orders up there if you have no other mission for me?'

'Good.' Maelgwn gave her the nod. 'You can also act as a messenger. At the first sign of trouble, report back here.' Rhiannon understood his meaning. She was not to wait for Cadwallon in such an event.

'Neraida.' Maelgwn turned to her at the last. 'Take Tom, Hero, Ethan and Talynn and rally as many of the clans as you can to go to the landing platform in the Middle East. Cadwaladr has released all those under the influence of the NERGUZ, so we need the numbers to replace them. Keep an eye on Boadicea and the others, and do not attack unless Cadwaladr or myself order you to do so. You are supposed to be under his influence, so do not blow his cover unnecessarily.'

'I understand,' Neraida advised. 'But are you sure we can trust him?'

'If there is one thing I know about Cadwaladr, it's that he gives his complete devotion to whatever cause he is fighting for. Now that his gripe is with Shamash, he shall not betray his allies.'

Neraida nodded to confirm she would respect his judgement.

'The object of this mission is to defend,' Maelgwn raised his voice for all to hear, 'but mainly to stall. Narnar and Ningal of the Nefilim are rallying the Pantheon of Twelve to apprehend Shamash. We need only keep him occupied until his peers arrive.'

The whole room gave a cheer at this, as salvation was in sight.

'I want one person from each mission's team to check in here at hourly intervals. Should anyone fail to make this contact, we shall assume the worst and plan accordingly. The rest of you are to stay here and keep the lines of communication flowing. Tory and I are off to take Dumuzi to Inanna to sway her to our cause. Any questions?'

'Ah, just one.' Patrick pointed to a bright ball of glowing blue light that was heading toward the large observation porthole of their submersible's control deck. 'What is that?'

The ball passed straight through the glass, homing in on Tory and disappearing into her forehead. When she had absorbed the message, she opened her eyes and looked at Brian. 'It's Dad, Brian. He wants to see us.'

'Now!' He snarled, exasperated. He was preparing to leave for Farwell.

Tory nodded, looking at Maelgwn to seek his leave.

Maelgwn sighed heavily. 'If Myrddin is asking to see you both, it must be important. You go. I shall take Dumuzi to Inanna. Brian, you can rejoin the others at Farwell when you're through.'

'Oh shit!' Brian threw his backpack on the ground, annoyed.

Tory took hold of Maelgwn's hand, knowing how he feared confronting his torturer again. 'Please, wait for me. I want to come with you.'

He raised his brow, wishing it could be so. 'Circumstance decrees I must face her alone, so let's not argue.'

'He shall not be *alone*.' Dumuzi came forward to hasten the proceedings. 'I shall be with him. And as he is my saviour, I can assure you, Nin, he shall not be harmed.' The God kissed Tory's hand, and then turned abruptly to Maelgwn. 'Can we go now?'

'In a minute.' Tory urged Dumuzi aside. She wanted to kiss her husband.

'Well, you don't have to rub salt into the wounds.' Dumuzi folded his arms, impatiently gazing upon the lovers' rapture.

'Come on.' Brian held out his hand to urge Tory along. 'There's a mission at hand. Let's not miss the *whole* thing.'

'I'll join you as soon as I can,' Tory vowed as she parted from Maelgwn.

Brian gripped his sister's hand and they were gone.

When the ethers of their flight dispersed, Tory and Brian found themselves high on a hill overlooking a parched, abandoned countryside.

Tory didn't recognise the landscape at first. It was reminiscent of the Australian outback, though not as red in colour. When Tory turned to confront the Glastonbury Tor, she realised exactly where they were. 'Oh dear Goddess! This is Britain?'

'Looks like the solar radiation has hit here hard.' Brian shook his head in despair, before the thought of his mission urged him to wonder: 'So, where the hell is our father?'

Tory shrugged as she wandered over to the ruins of the tower to have a look there. 'You willed us to him, I gather?'

'Of course.' Brian followed her inside, and was disappointed to find the place abandoned. 'Has he no idea what's going on in the world? I mean, if Dad *must* pull us out of the battle of the millennium to have a family chat, you think he'd do us the common courtesy of at least being here.'

Tory, not as impatient as her brother, could sense her father's presence. When she also sensed her mother, it took her by surprise and she gasped.

'Have you got something?' Brian approached her. She turned to face the entrance, her violet eyes wide with wonder.

'Something is happening,' she replied, eyeing the inner walls of the tower.

Brian followed her line of sight to discover bizarre shadows running round the inner stonework. The reflected images took a semi-human form and the sound of childlike laughter accompanied their frenzied movements. Through the great archway that led outside a body of mist was seen to enter, yet the day had been fine and clear only moments before. 'This is no time for Otherworldly archaeology, Tory?'

'This is not my doing.' She spied a familiar figure emerging from the mist and moved toward it. 'Mother?' Tory stopped short, realising she was addressing nothing more than a ghost.

The last time Brian had seen his mother was at her funeral, so he found her manifestation a little off-putting.

Helen Alexander had died in the Heathrow plane disaster of 2007, along with the rest of the orchestra she had been on tour with at the time. Brian hadn't shed many tears at the funeral. His mother had become a stranger to him when she divorced their father to marry a younger man. Not that they had been especially close before his parents separated; Helen was a harpist and was always on tour with one orchestra or another.

Oh Brian, his mother entreated him. *That was several lifetimes ago for me, and I believe I paid dearly for my mistakes. Life without your father took a distinctly downward spiral.*

'But what has happened to you?' Tory referred to her mother's lack of physical form. 'I was under the impression you were one of the Chosen, and therefore immortal.'

I am, child, and have been for a long, long time. She smiled. *So long, in fact, that it is time for me to move on in my journey. The molecules of my body have risen to a faster vibratory rate to attune to a higher plane of awareness. My physical body has given way to an etheric one and soon I will vanish from this earthly existence altogether.*

'After you and father merge back into one being, and ascend, as it were?' Tory couldn't help but be upset that she was about to lose her parents to totality.

You are not losing us, Tory, we are simply assuming a different form, a higher function, that is all. She looked to Brian, who didn't seem to know what to make of their dialogue.

In truth, Brian hardly recognised his mother with her long, flaming-red hair and a figure that rivalled his sister's. She was not a warrior like Tory; she appeared to be more like a Celtic princess.

She was amused by his assessment. *That is not so far from the truth, you know. I am known by the name of Vivian these days.* She encouraged Brian to approach. *Please, let me look at you both. It has been forever since I have seen you.*

Brian did as she bid, but only to bombard her with questions. 'Where are we? Where is Dad? I *am* supposed to be on a mission in New Mexico right now, and —'

Yes, Brian, we know all about it, she assured him. *You shall find your father yonder, discussing exactly that with Taliesin.* She calmly motioned to the arched exit, out in the mist.

'Thank you.' Brian was mildly appeased. 'And may I say that besides being see-through, you are looking mighty fine, mother.' He gave her a wink as he headed off to find his father.

'Taliesin is here, too?'

Vivian raised her brow and nodded to give Tory leave to follow her brother outside.

'Now this is more like it,' Brian announced, whipping an apple from a nearby tree and shining it on his shirt as he admired the view.

Mists drifted over a lush, green landscape, littered with abundant orchards, gardens, forests and rolling green fields.

'No.' Tory snatched the apple from him before he bit into it. 'You'll get trapped here. Don't drink anything, either.'

A whistle drew their attention to Myrddin, who beckoned them to join him on the nearby hillside.

Taliesin was with him, and standing between the two High Merlins was a beautiful lady, whom Tory assumed was Seshut — scribe to the Lord Marduk. As she drew near, Tory recognised Seshut as the Azorean beauty Teo had married. Of course! She should have guessed Taliesin's perfect other half would be this woman. After all, Teo had also wed the same girl back in his days as an Atlantean prince.

'Well, now I've seen everything,' Tory announced as she came to stand before the three etheric beings, and though she tried to hide her fear of loss the tears welled all the same.

You know why we have summoned you? Taliesin asked her.

'Yes.' Tory bit her lip to stop it quivering. 'You're leaving us to it.'

Now please don't be like that. Taliesin felt her sorrow. *You have known ever since you joined the ranks of the Chosen that this event was forthcoming. Your training is complete, Tory. It is time for me to hand over the guardianship of mankind's destiny, just as Keridwen handed it to me all those eons ago.*

'I beg your pardon?' Tory backed up a few steps. 'I just thought you wanted to say goodbye.'

Well, that too, Taliesin conceded fondly. *But first, I have a graduation present for you. Hold out your hand.*

'We really don't have time for this,' Brian said impatiently.

Hush, lad, Myrddin scolded. *This is very important. Just bear witness. That's what you're here for.*

Overwhelmed, though curious, Tory did as requested. An orichalchum pendant on a long, matching band materialised in her palm. It featured a ball that connected to a small three-sided pyramid, the pinnacle of which pointed down. 'It is beautiful.' She placed the chain over her head and admired the Egyptian hieroglyph depicted on each side of the object.

Beautiful! Taliesin scoffed at her understatement. *This is the* Tablet of Destinies, *the most powerful tool of divination in the known universe. It was given to me by Keridwen to guide my way and now it shall guide yours. That is her wish.*

Tory had read of the Tablet of Destinies when searching through ancient Egyptian texts for information about her grandfather. 'But the Egyptians claimed that the crone gave this pendant into the keeping of Thoth.'

Yes, that was the name I was known by at that time, he announced casually, though Tory was bowled over by his statement.

'I really don't think I can accept this. What if I lose it, or it is stolen? I can't be responsible —' Taliesin just shook his head calmly, so Tory didn't bother finishing her protest.

Brian. Would you try and snatch the item in question from your sister.

'Sure.' He reached for it, but his fingers passed right through the metal. 'Huh?'

It is attuned to Tory's personal sonic. No one else can touch it, or read it, including myself.'

'So, how do I make it work?'

The pyramid is magnetised, so it easily detaches from its setting. Taliesin nodded for her to give it a try.

Sure enough, the tool came away from the chain. Seeing the Eye of Ra on the base of the treasure, Tory placed it against her third eye.

Excellent, her father stated proudly.

As the trinket began to glow and expand, Brian became more interested. 'Wicked. What is it doing?'

Suddenly, the pyramid leapt away from Tory's forehead and began unfolding before her eyes to form a flat triangle containing four smaller triangles therein. In all four fragments of the tablet Tory saw a different image. 'Awesome, what does it all mean?'

In the centre you see your concern, the Merlin advised.

The picture Tory saw in this portion was that of planet Earth. 'Okay, that makes sense.'

'What does?' Brian gazed at the huge triangle that hovered before his sister like a monitor, yet that was all he saw.

Bottom left, Taliesin continued, *you shall find the best-case scenario of your intent.*

Tory saw a beautiful civilisation like Atlantis. 'Could such a heavenly place still exist in the Middle Kingdoms of this day and age?'

The Tablet never lies, the Merlin told her. *Now look to the bottom right, to see the worst that could result from your present intent.*

Tory frowned at what she perceived. 'Now it has lost me I'm afraid.'

'Why?' Brian was dying to know what she saw that he could not.

'It's nothing.' She shrugged. 'There's nothing there. Just empty space — as in the cosmos.'

Top segment, you shall find the result should no action be taken. Taliesin raised a brow, eager to hear her impression.

Tory gazed at the segment a moment, at first perplexed and then terrified. 'No,' she cried, backing into Brian in her attempt to draw away from the tablet.

'Jesus, Tory, what is it?'

She gripped hold of Brian, trying to recover from the shock of what she'd learnt. 'Shamash means to destroy us all.'

29

THE GREAT
CRACKER

The Brunanburh Space Station had a crew of twelve, who were into the second month of a six-month tour. These six men and six women had been working overtime since the arrival of the alien craft. They had continued transmitting updated pictures, and details of the vessel's movements, even after they had lost all their audio feeds to mission control at Farwell.

When Cadwallon and Rhiannon arrived in the control room, there were only two crew members present, and both were so absorbed in their work they didn't see their visitors materialise. Cadwallon recognised one of the men as Commander Philip

Merchant, who had headed Ray Murdock's tour in the Brunanburh. 'Merchant, you old space junkie. Don't you have a home?'

Both men dropped everything when they saw the outsiders. Nobody should be able to get in or out of the space station without them knowing about it. If some of their systems hadn't been down, they would have been forced to assume it was an act of God.

'Ray Murdock. Am I ever glad to see you.' The commander drifted over to shake Ray's hand. 'How the hell did you get here, son?'

'Classified,' Rhiannon announced.

The commander suddenly saw who Ray's companion was, and became more formal. 'Mrs Alexander! I am sorry. I barely recognised you.'

'No need to apologise, Commander,' Rhiannon assured him, launching herself through zero gravity in the direction of the control deck. Here she could view the monitor that displayed pictures of the huge vessel outside, as seen through the lenses of exterior cameras. 'My husband has instructed that we sit this one out with you. Will this inconvenience your routine in any way?'

'There's nothing routine about this tour lately. The more the merrier,' the Commander replied without reservation. 'I don't suppose you know what has happened to our audio-visual feeds? Are any of our pictures getting through?'

'They are reading you clear as a bell down there,' Cadwallon advised, having seen the pictures himself. 'The problem must be at this end ... I'll take a look at it for you.'

Philip smiled, weary-eyed from no sleep. 'Christ it's good to see you, Ray.' He'd never known anyone with as much technological expertise as Ray Murdock, and during an event of this magnitude it was comforting to know that the man who had designed many of the space station's systems was along for the ride. 'Come on, I'll get us some coffee. And when I say coffee, I mean it in the broadest possible sense, you understand.'

'Fear not, I've suffered worse.' Cadwallon motioned him to lead the way.

Cadwaladr could almost hear all the phones ringing back at the ICA. The Agency had taken over the investigation into all the strange space phenomena that had been taking place in recent weeks. The vortex had proven harmless and a source of much astrological excitement. Not a trace of debris had been found from all the fiery lights that had plummeted to earth. There had been a few isolated reports of visitors from outer space and their vanishing craft, but these had been easily dismissed and the whole incident written off as a freak space anomaly.

These two huge alien craft were not going to be so easy to explain, however. Shamash had said he would be discreet about his arrival, but maybe the sight of the vortex had led him to assume this was no longer necessary. Or perhaps the God had entirely different reasons for making his presence known.

From the ground, the shape of the vessel could only be defined by the bright, billowing clouds encasing its bulk as it ploughed down through the atmosphere.

609

Cadwaladr's team had so far been unable to power up the control room of the complex they'd unearthed in the Middle East, yet suddenly, the whole structure was fully operational.

The pairs of towers that lined each side of the long runway lit up, shooting several bands of green laser light between them to form a series of nets.

The entire site must be activated by the approaching craft, Cadwaladr concluded on the quiet, gazing at the light show that stretched out before him for miles. But the multitude of warriors who formed neat lines on the landing pad diverted the diplomat's attention. Doc presumed them to be the stand-in army Maelgwn had promised. They were all wearing Unken attire and NERGUZ modules, though they were not the same fighters Doc had recently freed. *Who are all these people? I had no idea Maelgwn still had so much influence here on Earth.*

'They are your kindred … and just like you, they are Chosen.' Vanora enlightened him, obviously following his every thought.

'Damn it!' Cadwaladr turned to her. 'How am I too hide my intentions from Shamash if I can't even shield my thoughts from you?'

'Just concentrate on your original plan, and all shall be well.' Vanora told him. 'The four of us surrounding you will act as an additional psychic field. You have nothing to worry about.'

Temujin stared at the awe-inspiring spectacle taking place around him. How much the world had changed in his absence. He moved away from Cadwaladr, so that he did not seem to be a bodyguard. Back in the days when he had ruled most of the known world Cadwaladr had watched his back. Now Temujin felt it was his place to return the favour.

The cloud cover began to disperse from the narrow length of the vessel approaching the illuminated runway ploughing through the first rows of the glowing green web. Each laser barrier the vessel encountered slowed it down until it hovered to a graceful stop in front of the main complex where Cadwaladr and his army awaited.

Hidden in the midst of the hundreds of troops, Maelgwn's additional force assessed the situation.

'That is not a transport, it's an entire city,' Neraida uttered as she witnessed Shamash's legions being beamed forth from the belly of the obstruction. His warriors were a wild array of differing human breeds, and they appeared to be armed to the hilt.

Talynn was closely scrutinising the weaponry they carried. The troops were not armed with sonic pulse blasters like the ones she and her friends carried. These guns were unlike anything she'd ever seen. 'What do you think they are?' Hero whispered to her. 'Some sort of molecule converter?'

Talynn folded her arms, concerned. 'Whatever their function, they are illegal issue. Shamash couldn't have cleared the design with the Pantheon — or I would know about it.'

Since being plucked out of ancient Gaul by the Nefilim, Talynn had carved herself an illustrious career as an industrial spy for Marduk. There wasn't much in the way of technological research and development that she wasn't aware of.

'Get close to Cadwaladr,' Talynn advised the others in her party. 'Shamash is sure to move inside before getting down to business, and we must keep Vanora and the others covered.'

Ethan grabbed hold of Talynn's arm as she moved to sneak off. 'Where are you going?'

'To see if I can't get my hands on one of those weapons.'

'Lead the way then.' Ethan let her go.

She rolled her eyes, not wanting to argue or otherwise draw undue attention to them. 'No. I work better alone.'

'Really.' This was news to Ethan. 'I seem to recall we were a team once, a great team.'

'Not now, children.' Neraida urged them along. 'Just do it and meet us inside.'

Neraida kept low and headed off towards the complex, Hero and Thais hot on her heels.

Inanna had no desire to accompany the landing party her brother sent to deal with the abominations of this planet. She wasn't in the mood for retribution, possessed as she was by a deep melancholy. She wondered why she'd allowed Shamash to persuade her into returning to this godforsaken place, as she observed the planet through the large windows of her chamber. *A paradise lost*, she mused. The greatest and only happiness she'd ever known had been here. But Gaia had also been the stage on which her lover's undoing had unfolded. *I searched for you, Dumuzi, and although I never found you, I avenged your unfair sentence … I am still avenging it.*

You have been seriously mislead, I fear, Dumuzi replied.

His words struck the fear of the Goddess into Inanna's heart. She turned, unable to believe it was her lover — even when she saw him with her own two eyes.

What trickery is this, Dragon. She spotted Maelgwn beside the illusion of her husband, and her vindictive mood was rekindled. *Come to seek your revenge, have you?*

At her words, Dumuzi's playful, lighthearted demeanour departed, for he saw how his wife had tormented his saviour. Maelgwn had done well to keep his torture a secret. Dumuzi turned and bowed to him to thank him for his discretion. *You are an honourable man, Dragon. I feel my wife does not deserve the respect you award her.*

Then the God turned his woeful face to Inanna. She humbled herself as she realised this was no deception; her own spiteful thoughts had just condemned her in her lover's eyes.

I can hardly believe how wretched time has made you, Inanna. Marduk warned me of how easily you could be so inclined.

Inanna drew herself up into a righteous stance. *Marduk drove me to this madness. He was against our union from the very beginning —*

My brother may have arrested and punished me for my offence, Dumuzi spoke up. *But it was not he who*

613

dismembered my body and set it in stone to rot for all eternity. It was Shamash.

The claim was earth-shattering for Inanna. Shamash was her twin, her brother, her closest confidant. *He could never have sustained such a lie all this time ... not with me!*

'Both your parents are willing to testify to the contrary,' Maelgwn told her. 'I am sorry, Nin, but it is the truth.'

As the implications of this revelation rebounded through time in her memory, remorse flooded in and she had to be seated. *Oh, dear Goddess, what have I done?* A multitude of emotions matted themselves around and into her heart, expanding and exploding. *There is so much to amend. I do not know where to start.*

'In the name of Marduk, I am at your disposal, Inanna,' Maelgwn advised. 'My lord understands that you have been as much a victim in this affair as he.'

Although Maelgwn spoke for his lord, Inanna knew that deep down these sentiments were more his own. She looked at him unable to comprehend how after all she had put him through he could stand there before her willing to help her out of the hole she had dug for herself. *You make it painfully clear, Maelgwn of Gwynedd, who the superior race really is.*

'Superiority is an ego-based delusion,' Maelgwn advised her. 'Love, however, is a life-giving force. You were a Goddess of Love once, Inanna. You have just forgotten how.'

The Goddess was near to suffocating from suppressing her emotions. She could not speak, she was so moved.

I have not forgotten. Dumuzi neared and knelt before her, clutching Inanna's hands in his own. *We have both been foolish, Inanna. … always wanting what we could not have. But, during all that time without you, I realised that all I ever really wanted was to make you happy.*

And I, you, she wept openly. *But I have done dreadful things in your absence, shameful things that —*

Shh, Dumuzi urged her, placing a finger to her lips. *There is nothing that has been done, that cannot be undone. Help us bring my rightful assassin to justice and clear my brother's good name. In so doing we shall save the Dragon's kin and then maybe, just maybe, we shall find it within ourselves to forgive each other and start over.*

Yes. Inanna pledged herself to their cause. *I'd like that very much.* She leaned forward to kiss Dumuzi, but suddenly drew back. *The Great Cracker,* she gasped, turning to Maelgwn. *Shamash has developed a new weapon that was specifically designed with the Chosen in mind. Yet it could just as easily destroy my kind as yours.*

'What manner of weapon is it?' Maelgwn inquired.

It is a double-action, hand-held weapon. Equipped with heat-seeking pellets that will turn a living target to stone on impact. This molecular blast is followed by a pulse laser bullet that shatters one's petrified victim into innumerable pieces.

The Cracker … I remember this, Dumuzi added. *Production of that weapon was banned by Enlil before the plans ever made it off the drawing board.*

Well, each member of my brother's force is equipped with this weapon, Inanna continued. *But an even greater threat is mounted inside the belly of the ship, for Shamash had a much larger prototype made. The Great Cracker he calls it, and it is very true to its name. I have seen its destructive force demonstrated on a planet not much smaller than this one … complete annihilation was the result.*

'Once the weapon has taken its ultimate toll, can the process be reversed?'

The molecular process, yes, but once phase two has been initiated, there is no reversing the outcome.

Maelgwn's mind went into overtime. He had people all over the place and he needed to warn them all.

Meanwhile, Inanna materialised several of the weapons that had been dubbed 'the Cracker'; half of these she handed to Dumuzi and the rest to Maelgwn. *Calm yourself, Dragon*, Inanna said, her tone stressing the importance of the pending announcement. *There is one more thing you must know.*

Rhun's team had materialised inside the control room of the main facility at Farwell to find one of Shamash's task forces waiting in ambush and were forced to fall back to the outside of the complex. The majority of the locals they'd recruited were turned to stone, along with Season, Sybil and Floyd. A couple of the local Indian lads had managed to grab Rhun and Candace and transport them outside the site's perimeters before they got hit.

'Jesus Christ, what the hell happened?' Rhun demanded an answer from Candace, insane with worry for his lover and comrades.

'I don't know,' she snapped back at him, still recovering from the shock herself. 'It is a new weapon. I've never seen it before.'

'Well, that's just great!'

Brian arrived on the scene to see Rhun toss his weapon on the ground in a fury. His eyes quickly darted around and, spying Candace close by, Brian breathed a sigh of relief. 'Thank god you're alright.' He moved to embrace her.

But Candace avoided his affection. She was still too disturbed by what had happened. 'Many of us are not.' Her focus rested on Rhun, who was so caught up in remorse he hadn't even noticed Brian arrive. 'What have you learnt?'

It's alright everybody, you can relax, I'm here, Dumuzi announced, handing out the weapons in his possession.

Rhun came bounding over to grab one and inspected it. 'Where did you get these?'

Compliments of your father, he advised. *Now, listen carefully.*

Dumuzi demonstrated how to activate the weapon while explaining how and what it fired. Rhun and the others listened impatiently to the information Dumuzi had acquired from his wife. They were eager to get back inside the complex before Shamash's force decided to finish off their team mates, shut off the power to the grid, or start blowing up energy plants at random.

Are we clear? Dumuzi finished, and everyone nodded in accord. *Then what do you say we secure this facility?*

They all activated their weapons and vanished.

Maelgwn arrived at the landing strip in the Middle East to find the battle over. The entrance to the underground complex was sealed and the spaceship hovered silently in its dock, not a guard to be seen. The army Neraida had rallied had become one with the landscape, the figures of petrified rock were scattered all over the runway and beyond. Maelgwn wondered at Shamash's restraint, for none of the victims had been finished off. Perhaps the God planned to collect them all like trophies when he was done. Or he might have spared them to use as bargaining power, should it come to that. Whatever his reasons, Shamash obviously hadn't planned on his foe getting their hands on his new power tool.

'Dear Goddess!'

Maelgwn looked across to find Tory grief stricken staring at the scene before her.

'I am too late,' she uttered.

'Though it would seem so, that is fortunately not the case.'

Tory was startled when Maelgwn spoke. 'Oh, thank God.' She flung her arms about his neck. 'I thought one of these statues was you.'

'I'm fine,' he assured her with a kiss and a pat on the back. 'Here …' Maelgwn placed a Cracker in her hands. His eyes became fixed on something yonder. 'I do believe I recognise that hunk of rock.'

Ethan and Talynn had been frozen together in an embrace, like a beautiful piece of sculpture. Maelgwn set his weapon into reverse and the burst it fired evaporated the stone. The couple fell to the ground shivering with cold and shock.

It took Ethan and Talynn a little while to recover their sensibilities, and Maelgwn started wondering if he and Tory should perhaps proceed without them.

'I'm okay,' Ethan assured him, having given his head a good shake, 'I'm only seeing double now.'

'Good man.' Maelgwn tossed him one of the weapons that had put him under. 'Now, you said you knew the inside of this base fairly well?'

Ethan nodded, torn between answering the question and checking out the weapon.

'I need a quiet area,' Maelgwn advised, 'where we won't be spotted on arrival. Preferably, this area should be situated not too far from the main chamber.'

'Yes.' Ethan finally snapped back to reality. 'There are a couple of antechambers that lead off the end of the main chamber to its mezzanine level. They offer partial seclusion.'

'Perfect,' Maelgwn decreed. 'Guide us there.'

Shamash stood in front of the monitors and controls that gave command of the entire fusion grid, limbering up his fingers to begin his reign of destruction.

Like his father and his grandfather before him, Shamash hated Homo sapiens, mortal or otherwise. Some of the human breeds he could abide, as they made obedient labourers or slaves or fighters. But Homo sapiens had never been very good in a subordinate role. The Nefilim had tried to wipe the rebellious breed from existence many times in the past, but the Serpent and his clan always managed to save a few. And Homo sapiens had, unfortunately, always proved to be reliable breeders. Their numbers had increased to outrageous proportions. Their technology, although primitive, was developing in leaps and bounds, and now that Marduk had started blasting wormholes between galaxies, humans were sure to start spreading themselves throughout the known universe. Shamash thought it better to be rid of them now, while they were still confined to this little, out-of-the-way solar system. His new weapon would see to their total annihilation fairly efficiently, but there was no fun to be had in destroying them all in the blink of an eye.

He would start with the seven main power stations, then move on to the sub-stations. Once all the power feeds were destroyed the Biodomes that were the last havens for the mortal beings of this planet would become giant tombs. Without power the air filtration system failed, and so did the exit doors and transport system. This would surely throw the creatures into a frenzied panic. They would kill and maim each other in an attempt to escape their fate, and such mayhem promised to be a good evening's entertainment.

Africa sounds like a good place to start. Marduk always liked it there. Shamash looked to the keypad, and it automatically began typing his instructions into the computer. Thanks to Cadwaladr, he knew the entire security system inside and out. He was about halfway through the initiation process when a great chill spread over him. It started at his legs and crept toward his thighs and torso.

Long time no see, Dumuzi said to his victim, who turned to face him. Shamash's movement was confined by the stone possessing his body. Dumuzi waited for the pellet to complete the transformation to solid rock before blasting his target away completely.

'Holy smoke!' Rhun came racing in from the

corridor, where he and the others had finished incapacitating the rest of the enemy task force. He fanned the flying soot away from himself to observe the pile of rubble left behind in the star warrior's wake. 'How are we going to bring Shamash to trial now?'

That was not Shamash, Dumuzi informed him. *That was a clone.*

'I beg yours?'

Shamash has made two clones of himself, and because they have no soul, he is free to occupy any one of them at will. Both are completely like-minded and know all that he knows. They think as he thinks. We shall have to destroy the other clone to trap Shamash and bring him to trial. Your father has gone after the second clone in the Middle East, and Inanna has gone after the original. A NERGUZ module will keep him out of trouble until the rest of the Pantheon arrive.

'Well, in that case, that's one down, two to go,' Rhun announced cheerfully, brushing the dust off the controller's chair. 'We'd best get Floyd onto changing the security programs before Shamash attempts to assume control of the grid again.' Rhun gave a loud whistle to call for order and get them organised.

The mezzanine level of the main chamber was, like the rest of the ancient landing complex, lit up like a Christmas tree. Obviously Shamash still had no idea that there were Earthlings roaming free with full recall of the layout of his base, for guards had yet to be posted on the upper level.

Upon materialising in the stairwell, Maelgwn, Tory,

Ethan and Talynn were surprised to find Temujin observing the scene unfolding in the chamber below.

On recognising an ally Maelgwn lowered his weapon, motioning for the others to do likewise. Once they had relaxed, Temujin did likewise, nodding to let them know he was pleased to have aid.

They could not see Shamash. From this position Cadwaladr had centre stage.

Ethan nearly had a fit when he spied his mother and the others encased in stone, but Talynn managed to smother his protest before he voiced it. 'Cadwaladr has betrayed us,' he whispered as Talynn set him free.

'Shh,' Maelgwn and Temujin cautioned as one. They wanted to hear what was transpiring between the diplomat and the God.

So, concluded Shamash, *are you still of the mind to aid the Serpent's clan? Think carefully now. The God nodded to the guard alongside him.*

The centaur raised his weapon, and picking one of the stone figures at random he blasted it to dust. The unfortunate victim was Stanley Brennon. The assassin could not have made a more vexing choice where Cadwaladr was concerned.

This situation unfolding below was most confusing. How, with so many of the Serpent's clan to aid Cadwaladr's psychic defenses had Shamash managed to perceive his intent? Or was Cadwaladr so accomplished at thought control that he had managed to deceive Maelgwn to betray the Serpent's clan voluntarily? Either way, there were several dozen troops surrounding Doc and his frozen security team, Maelgwn didn't like their chances of taking out Shamash's soldiers without risk of their own team being finished off in the process.

'We need a distraction.' Maelgwn looked to find Temujin had already disappeared.

'I have some explosives that might do the trick.' Talynn took Ethan's hand. 'We'll be right back,' she assured as they both vanished.

When Cadwaladr turned back to confront Shamash, the wrath of God was in his eyes. 'You have made my life a misery, Utu. Before I was even born you had seen to it that I would be an outcast.'

Is that what they told you?

'That is what I know!' Cadwaladr roared over Shamash's mocking laughter. 'I've dedicated eleven hundred years of my life to avenging a lie!'

'Not yet, Cadwaladr. Hold off,' mumbled Maelgwn. 'Just a few more minutes and we'll have our distraction.'

You made all your own choices, infidel, Shamash reminded his accomplice. He glanced at the armed centaur beside him who turned his weapon on Cadwaladr.

'Based on *your* deception.' As Doc raised his finger to point at the God, a Stormer slipped down his sleeve into his hand. Ironically, Stanley had insisted Doc carry the weapon as additional protection when confronting Shamash this day. They'd never tested the Stormer's kill function on a living target before, though on inanimate objects it had proven to have explosive potential.

But before Shamash's guard or Cadwaladr could fire, Temujin leap out of the rafters and knocked the centaur out cold. In an amazing display of martial arts fighting skill, the ancient warrior took out several of Shamash's guards before he was turned to stone and blasted to dust.

Talynn and Ethan surprised the guards that were posted inside the locked entrance doors of Shamash's unearthed base.

'Good work, you're a crack shot,' Talynn commented to Ethan, as she bent down to transport two of the unconscious guards to a safe distance.

'You could have given me a little more warning.' Ethan grabbed hold of the remaining two guards by the feet, and willed himself after Talynn.

They returned to the locked entrance doors, where Talynn detached a small metallic ball from her belt and began frantically unscrewing the top half of it.

'Get back to Maelgwn, and I'll finish here,' Talynn instructed as the top of the metallic ball in her hand came away to expose the tiny detonator. Talynn glanced up to find Ethan still observing her, and so stressed the urgency. 'Go man go, you've got five seconds.' Once the device was activated, the explosive casing was magnetised. Talynn simply attached it to the metal wall and willed herself after Ethan. 'Four, three, two ...'

'Damn you to hell, Shamash!' cried Cadwaladr, and at his silent command, a laser bullet shot forth into the God's body and exploded his form into a million flaming pieces.

'Oh shit.' Tory jumped into action, racing out along the mezzanine level blasting every warrior in sight. Maelgwn joined her, and in the confusion Cadwaladr

624

managed to slide for cover behind a huge marble support arch. He set the Stormer back to stun and began blasting away at the guards.

Shamash's forces were thrown into further confusion when an explosion was heard elsewhere on the base. Many of the troopers fled the chamber in fear of their lives. Between Cadwaladr's ground assault and Maelgwn's and Tory's overhead advantage, they managed to take out the few die-hard guards who remained.

'Nice work.' Maelgwn congratulated his great-great-great-grandson on his marksmanship, after he and Tory leapt down to ground level.

'I thought you weren't going to make it,' Cadwaladr replied, unable to prevent his mouth curving into a smile — the legend lived up to his reputation, after all.

'Oh, we're full of surprises.' Tory turned and blasted Vanora back into a human state.

As Cadwaladr was unaware of the Cracker's reverse function, his spirits suddenly soared. He had not failed his new allies after all. 'I am fast learning to love this family,' he commented to Tory as he knelt beside Vanora to aid her return to the land of the living. 'But what of Stanley and Temujin?'

'I am sorry, Cadwaladr,' Tory placed a hand on his shoulder, 'but their fate cannot be reversed.'

The huge figure of a man hung his head a moment to mourn the death of his two dearest friends. 'Well, at least Shamash has paid for their loss. My apologies for the mess.' Cadwaladr raised his eyes to speak with Maelgwn, swallowing back his emotions. 'I know you wanted to bring Shamash to trial ... but I had no idea if you knew what we were up against. I thought it best not to run the risk of him escaping.'

'Well, you *have* narrowed his chances considerably,' Maelgwn said, in all seriousness.

Cadwaladr thought him joking until informed that he had destroyed a clone. 'You are kidding me?' He simply refused to accept it.

'I kid you not. If that had been the real Shamash he would have reconstituted by this.'

Cadwaladr looked over the scattered remains, realising Maelgwn was quite right. 'So where is the double-crossing maggot?'

'Give the others a few moments to come round, and I'll enlighten you,' Maelgwn advised, while Tory went about restoring the rest of their team.

Shamash had a master control room overlooking the main bridge of his spacecraft, situated out beyond the Earth's atmosphere. It was here, where he was seated comfortably in his large, hovering seat amid his controls and communicators that Inanna sought him.

The lighting in the chamber was dim, but by all appearances her brother was alone in the large control room. She drifted over to Shamash, waving around a NERGUZ band that she toyed with in her fingers.

Shamash, my darling heart. I've been thinking about these NERGUZ modules. She slid up close to him on his righthand side. *And I've had a revelation.*

Save it, he advised her. *I am a little preoccupied at present.*

So I see. Inanna smiled when her brother's attention

did not waver from the monitors inside his headset. Slowly she slid the hand holding the module along Shamash's arm towards his hand. *This cannot wait.* She locked the module round his wrist and activated it with a word. *Now, brother dear, you will answer to me for your treachery.* She withdrew from him, hitting the plate that retracted his headset. *Did you dismember Dumuzi?*

Yes. Shamash emerged from the shadows at the back of the chamber, holding a cracker in his hands. *I hated sharing you with him then, and I will not share you with him now!*

As he advanced towards her, Inanna backed up. *There must have been three clones,* she concluded, realising her brother now held the upper hand.

I know Dumuzi has pulled himself together, Shamash told her. *He destroyed one of my clones with my own weapon!* He waved the Cracker about. *How did he get hold of the Cracker, Inanna?*

Dumuzi lives? she gasped, attempting to fake her way out.

Whore! he cried, whacking her across the jaw with the butt of the weapon. *How much have you told them?*

Inanna turned and spat the blood that filled her mouth into her brother's face. *Take me apart piece by piece. I still won't tell you.* She grabbed for his weapon as he attempted to wipe the blood from his eyes. In the ensuing scuffle, it fired, and Inanna froze.

The Brunanburh had re-established verbal contact with Mission Control at Farwell, and Cadwallon was overseeing Floyd as he altered the security codes for the station. Cadwallon was on his third container of coffee that he didn't really want to drink. He was amusing himself by allowing droplets to escape from the straw and then catching them in his mouth once they'd risen to the right height. He did this without really being aware that he was.

Commander Merchant chanced to look across and catch what he was doing. 'Murdock, I've told you a million times — don't do that. If any of that liquid gets in the instrumentation we'll be up shit creek.'

'Sorry, boss.' Cadwallon smiled when he recalled this had been one of Ray's common practises. 'I guess old habits die hard.'

'Greetings, Godbusters. It is I, Cadwaladr, with a handy, helpful mission update.'

'Mr Alexander,' Commander Merchant jumped to attention, again wondering at the completely unannounced arrival.

'You no good son-of-a-bitch,' Rhiannon sprang from her seat and launched herself at him. 'You left me to rot in that hole, *you* arsehole!' Rhiannon made it look like she was going to kick him, but she punched Cadwaladr in the nose instead. Zero gravity lessened the impact of the blow, though she still managed to break his nose, momentarily.

'No!' cried Merchant. 'don't let any of the blood escape.'

'Good idea,' Rhiannon realised, grabbing hold of her husband's nose and squeezing it tightly. 'Let's suffocate him.'

'Hi, honey,' he humoured her, figuring he *did* deserve it. 'Though I would dearly love for you to beat me around like this for all eternity, I have a rather urgent directive from your father.'

'But her father is dead?' commented Merchant, stating a well-known fact.

Everybody looked to the Commander, speechless for a second.

'You really don't want to go there, Commander,' Cadwallon recommended.

'Hello, father.' Cadwaladr gave Cadwallon a nod as he covered his healing nose with a handkerchief from his pocket.

'Hey?' Merchant was wondering if everyone else had gone nuts, or was it just him?

Cadwaladr, being in no way inclined to explain, blasted the Commander with his Stormer. He then turned and took out the other crew member working quietly in the corner.

'Jesus, Doc.' Rhiannon hit him again. 'The situation is under control. They work for us, remember?'

'Don't make me knock you out, too,' Cadwaladr threatened.

'Over my dead body,' Cadwallon came forward to make his presence felt. 'What does Maelgwn want of us?'

'We are to plot the coordinates of Shamash's vessel, and aim the fusion beam at her belly.'

'To what end?' Rhiannon was wary. It sounded like a revenge scheme Cadwaladr would hatch himself.

'That fusion bean is designed to hit conductor rods that are vast distances away. At this close range, it could do some serious damage to Shamash's vessel.' Cadwallon stared at his son, accusingly.

'I'm just telling you what Maelgwn told me. He said that you,' Cadwaladr referred to Cadwallon, 'ought to be able to do this, with some help from … Floyd?' Cadwaladr recalled the name, then shrugged to imply he didn't know if the message would mean anything to them.

Rhiannon moved to the headset to speak with the said fellow. 'Brunanburh to Mission Control. Have you been advised of a new directive?' She listened as Floyd said that Boadicea had just arrived there with the same instruction Cadwaladr had just given her. 'Well then, I guess we turn this baby around.' Rhiannon held out the headset to Cadwallon.

By the time Shamash gave the order to finish off the army of immortal warriors that he had turned to stone upon his arrival in the Middle East, Maelgwn's people had surrounded the transporter beam that operated from the belly of the docked ship.

Maelgwn, Tory, Ethan, Talynn, Neraida, Hero, Cadwell and Thais, turned several waves of Shamash's troops to stone before the invaders ceased their fruitless attempts to retake the runway.

The rocket ship's thrusters burst into life and the runway lit up. As the huge vessel moved off, the small rebel band gave a triumphant cheer.

'Well, that was easy,' Ethan commented to Maelgwn as they began freeing their comrades from the stone they were trapped by.

Maelgwn was still wary; 'We'd best get these people conscious and under cover in a hurry.' He looked over at the collapsed entrance to the landing base that

Talynn had demolished with an explosion. 'We'd best get Shamash's men dug out of there. They are not immortals, and will surely suffocate before too long.'

Ethan gave Maelgwn a wave to say he'd get right on it.

'Hey, Grandpa.' Cadwell wandered over in a rather concerned state. 'It just occurred to me that they might be of the mind to launch an aerial attack … it's not like Shamash to retreat that quickly.'

Maelgwn looked to the horizon to see the ship leave the landing pad. 'Indeed they might.' His gut instinct told him Cadwell was right. 'I want everybody who has a craft in the air now. Everyone else is to get to shelter. Neraida …' Maelgwn waved her over. 'Get to your communications room, and rally any of the Chosen who have fighter aircraft. Tell them the war of the sovereign is here and now.'

'Maelgwn.' Tory approached him cautiously, knowing he was not going to like what she was about to suggest. 'If Shamash has just given the final attack order, Inanna could not have gained control over him.'

What's that you say? Dumuzi arrived just in time to catch the end of the comment.

Tory put him off a second, staying focused on her husband. 'You must stay and fight. I, however, do not have a craft, and I am not going to sit this out in a shelter.'

'And you are not going after Shamash, Tory. Forget it! If Inanna couldn't subdue him —'

I shall go, Dumuzi cut in.

'And I shall go with you.' Tory took up his hand and was gone before Maelgwn could argue.

'No, stop —' Maelgwn decided to save his breath, though he had a sudden urge to hit something.

'Commander,' Vanora called to him as she climbed into her craft. 'The fight is up there, but if you don't move your arse it is going to be down here.'

It was not easy to put his fears aside, but what choice did he have?

Once he had activated his craft, Maelgwn climbed inside and took the pilot's seat. As he breathed deeply in an attempt to ease his worry, the voice of his old mentor was heard to say:

> Heed the call to battle, Dragon,
> the time of the Gathering
> is upon you.
>
> Sons of Bedi arise, and reclaim
> thy rightful inheritance.
> The Chosen, by the power of air
> will fulfil my age old vow ...
>
> I saw Maelgwn battling,
> the host acclaimed him.
> To him they gave their blessing,
> to regain his Eden lost.

Maelgwn closed his eyes, comforted to know Taliesin was still with them. *Keep Tory safe*, he requested quietly, as he fired up his craft.

Haven't I always, the Merlin replied.

30

RETURN TO EDEN

Cadwaladr, Cadwallon and Rhiannon watched in horror as Shamash's vessel lowered its primary weapon.

'He *is* going to use it. We have to destroy him now!' Cadwaladr appealed, but Cadwallon refused.

'Not until Maelgwn gives the word.'

'And what if he's tied up right now?' Cadwaladr persisted.

'Cadwallon's right,' Rhiannon had her say. 'We don't know who might be on Shamash's craft.'

'Oh, well there's a surprise, you agreeing with him.' Cadwaladr was enraged by their complicity.

Rhiannon rolled her eyes, and was about to get into an argument, when she thought of a more constructive form of criticism that might serve her better.

'Cadwaladr, think. You're the brilliant criminal mind. There must be something else we can do?'

Cadwaladr took another look at the weapon. Now that it was fully extended from the ship he noted the single metal arm that secured it to the vessel.

'We'll just blast it off,' he announced.

Cadwallon gave half a laugh at the suggestion. 'That's a damn small target. What if we miss?'

'It's no smaller than the host station conductor rods on the moon and Earth that we align the beam to hit every day.' Rhiannon seconded the idea.

'You're both insane.'

'Aw,' Cadwaladr waved his father off, 'you always were a wimp. Come on.' He motioned Rhiannon to follow him. 'We'll use the targeter in the fusion station.'

'Hey, I wasn't the one who lost half of Britain.' Cadwallon raised himself into the air to follow them to the reactor control room.

'No, you just conveniently died in the middle of a war, and left me to deal with it.'

'Truce, guys!' Rhiannon urged strongly. 'Armageddon. Remember that?' She propelled herself along in front of them, motioning them after her.

Dumuzi and Tory found Inanna petrified in rock. Beside her sat Shamash in a hovering, control chair. In one hand he held a Cracker, which was aimed at his sister's frozen form. The God's other hand rested comfortably on a telekinetic control panel on the arm of his chair.

Lamamu, Shamash pronounced upon sighting her. *My sister's earthly counterpart, who, like Inanna, is as beautiful as she is dangerous. And my brother-outlaw.* His delight changed to boredom as he looked to Dumuzi. *Disappear, lover boy, or your wife is dust.*

Dumuzi faltered, having made an unspoken promise to Maelgwn to stay with Tory.

Do it now, Shamash ordered, digging the weapon's head into his sister's belly.

Dumuzi turned to Tory, torn between loyalties.

'Go,' she bade him.

Forgive me. He faded from her sight.

'So, I get to stay do I?' Tory had her weapon aimed at Shamash. If he decided to shoot her, he'd be stone before he could finish her off.

I find a victory is not the same without some poor victim to share it with.

'Your morbid humour will be your undoing, Shamash. Give me one good reason why I shouldn't turn you to stone right now?'

You are at an impasse, I'm afraid, he explained. *Your battle and your little planet are lost without me.*

'Yeah, that's what you think.' Tory made a habit of never believing anything she was told. 'Call off your fighters, or you're stoned.'

Make me, he dared her. *But I must warn you ... I have set the Great Cracker on its own time schedule and it will fire unless I override the order.*

'How much time do we have?' Tory questioned down the barrel of her weapon.

More than a second, less than a day. He smiled, admiring her form. *You know, some of you Earthlings really aren't that badly put together. If you are as smart as*

635

you are valorous, I'm sure you could figure out a way to extract from me the information you seek.

Tory smiled, though on the inside she was fuming. 'We'll figure it out without you,' she assured him, taking aim.

Now all you have to do is figure out how to shoot both of us at once.

A chill crept over Tory, and she sensed a presence behind her.

Dumuzi appeared in the co-pilot's seat of Maelgwn's vessel. The sky was filled with fighter craft engaged in battle, and although Dumuzi could see that the Dragon had his hands full he also felt he had a right to know what had happened.

Ah, Commander?

Maelgwn peeped beneath his headset only long enough to make out who addressed him. 'Dumuzi! What are you doing here?'

Shamash persuaded me leave.

'You left Tory alone with him?' Maelgwn grabbed for the God to extract an explanation.

I had no choice. He has turned Inanna to stone, and was threatening to finish her. Watch out! Dumuzi warned of an oncoming craft, which Maelgwn promptly avoided. *Drive, man, drive. That's why you have controls.*

'Well, you're disturbing me!' Maelgwn endeavoured to steer them away from the heavy fighting.

Hold on. Dumuzi noted another incoming wave of craft. *They are the fighter craft of Horus, Ningal and her brother Nergal.*

'Nergal, the head of the Pantheon is here?' Maelgwn wanted to confirm this before he got too excited.

Yes, the markings are unmistakable. Dumuzi gave a cheer, as the reinforcements began taking out Shamash's fighters.

'And not before time.' Maelgwn aligned his ship with an oncoming enemy fighter. He retrieved his Cracker and gripped Dumuzi's wrist, willing them to Tory.

You're a maniac, Dragon! Dumuzi watched with horror as the approaching fighter ploughed into the ethers and vanished in a blaze of light.

It was not like Tory to give up without a fight. She kicked out behind her, knocking Shamash's weapon from his hands, but he grabbed for her weapon. As she struggled to keep her Cracker from Shamash the clone that was still seated in the control chair attempted to get a clean shot at her.

Well, Shamash prompted his double. *What are you waiting for? Shoot!*

A pellet came speeding past Shamash's body to plant itself in the clone's third eye. The God witnessed himself freeze, before turning to confront Maelgwn's fist.

Shamash went flying backwards, to land in a heap on the ground. When he recovered from the blow, he glanced up to discover three Crackers were aimed at him. He chuckled as he raised himself, pressing a pendant on his chest.

An alarm sounded. All the doors in the room were flung open and a mass of soldiers entered.

A bunch of outlaws are not going to seize me on my own ship!

Perhaps not, but I certainly can.

This was the voice of Nergal, supreme ruler of the Pantheon, and Shamash trembled at Nergal's intonation.

All Shamash's soldiers knelt in reverence to their high lord's presence. Maelgwn and Dumuzi bowed, but Tory remained as she was.

Nergal was tall and slender and light radiated from him — especially from his large, violet eyes. As with his sister, Ningal, his hair was dark and cut short to accentuate his angel-like features. His fine robes were adorned with jewels. Here was a very imposing figure of a God, despite his youthful appearance.

Shamash looked towards Nergal to also see his reunited parents and most of the Pantheon. Before he recovered from the shock, Nergal's warriors had slapped restraining bands on Shamash's wrists to prevent him from disappearing.

'He has the Great Cracker on a detonator. We must get him to cancel the instruction before it destroys what is left of our planet.' Tory strode into the middle of the gathering of Gods to demand justice.

Well, Shamash. Nergal ordered him to act.

I am sorry, but I had my clone wipe that information from my memory, he advised in a vague, indifferent manner.

'I am going to tear you apart myself.' Tory took a swing at him, but Maelgwn and Dumuzi prevented an incident.

This is the woman who taught you how to love again? Nergal questioned his sister, as he watched the two men struggle to restrain her. *I pictured her differently,* he confessed.

'Well, I am sorry, your worshipfulness,' Tory composed herself, 'but don't you think we should do something?'

Oh, besides rumble, you mean? Nergal queried. *Yes, quite. I suggest we get Gibal onto it.*

When the ship suddenly rocked and a great boom was heard, Tory feared that the Great Cracker had fired.

A single soldier entered the master control room, surprised to discover what had befallen there.

Yes what is it? Nergal insisted he speak up.

'My lord Nergal.' He bowed deeply, sounding a little hesitant to voice his news. 'My lord Shamash, we have just lost our primary weapon.'

Lost it, Shamash was furious. *How?*

'I am sorry, Lord,' the soldier advised, 'but it has been shot off.'

Tory and Maelgwn looked at each other, puzzled. 'Cadwaladr,' they resolved at once, releasing an almighty cry of victory as they launched themselves into each other's arms.

Nergal set the trial hearing for the following morning, Middle Eastern time. The Pantheon would hear everyone's grievances in the main chamber of the landing base there, once Nergal's forces had cleared the passageway. He asked that all the Chosen attend, and the banished Marduk, also.

Meanwhile, Cadwaladr got in touch with the United Nations and the US President, Hagar, who had been kept in the dark about the entire affair. The dogfight that had taken place just beyond the atmosphere of the planet had been witnessed firsthand by no one, as all satellites in the area had been destroyed. The demolished equipment was blamed on all the freak space anomalies that had occurred of late. The Brunanburh Space Station had been the closest to the action, but when Shamash had invaded Mission Control at Farwell, those visual feeds had also been lost. So, as all the alien aircraft were now cloaked, Doc explained the whole incident as an elaborate hacker fraud. Several individuals had besieged the main fusion station at Farwell. After playing havoc with the security codes, they managed to pass on their footage of the phony alien invasion to the media. Having come through all the right channels this footage would, to all appearances, have come from the Brunanburh's cameras.

Doc assured the United Nations that no such threat had ever really existed, and if any satellite or moon base data indicated differently, they could safely assume the aforementioned hackers had also screwed with their systems. Cadwaladr wasn't really surprised when the authorities bought his story. Why wouldn't they? A simple rational explanation sure beat the hell out of believing the world was under alien attack. Doc advised that his people had the culprits in custody, and a full confession would be forthcoming. With that, the affair was all but forgotten by mainstream Earth society.

The enormous audience chamber at the landing base in the Middle East was filled to the rafters both on the ground and at mezzanine level. As the Dragon and his kin were so intimately involved in the proceedings, they were assembled directly in front of the full Pantheon of Gods.

Tory spied an old acquaintance of hers standing amongst those Gods gathered before them. He was Shu Micah, the High Magi of the Orders of Passage, whom she had met in Atlantis. At that time, he had told her that they would meet again at the time of the Gathering, and he acknowledged Tory's presence with a polite nod.

Noah was feeling particularly honoured to be the only reporter present, and busied himself capturing the event on his motion CD camera.

The first item on the agenda was the pardon of the Lord Marduk in the Dumuzi affair. But when invited to resume his rightful place in the Pantheon, at Nergal's side, Marduk refrained.

Though it would be my greatest honour and joy to do so, Nergal, if my chosen concubine cannot be at my side, he motioned to Rose, who appeared rather tiny beside him, *then, regrettably, I shall be forced to decline.*

'Are you crazy?' Rose gasped, looking to her masked lover and shaking her head to urge him to retract the ultimatum.

But Marduk only looked back at Nergal, whose sister was having a quite word in his ear.

Yes, quite, Nergal nodded, looking back at his breathless audience. *Considering how many children you*

641

two have obviously had, we have decided to make an exception to the law in your case. Putting this family through a separation would be hell. You shall wed immediately following these proceedings. Nergal smiled as the entire room cheered the ruling.

Marduk removed the helmet-like mask from his head, casting it aside to pick up his soon-to-be wife and kiss her. His long, dark hair and dark eyes were akin to the Dragon's clan, whom he had fathered.

Narnar was reinstated to the Pantheon, and Shamash was charged with Dumuzi's disappearance, Cadwallon's murder, Cadwaladr's misspent years, and a good part of the Earth's destruction. Utu-Shamash was therefore sentenced to his father's cold Otherworldly prison on the moon, until such time as Narnar and Dumuzi saw fit to release him. Inanna was absolved of her part in the affair, though she was to give up her place in the Pantheon in favour of her husband, Dumuzi. Inanna was more than grateful to accept this as her punishment, and promised to return the rest of the Lord Gibal's body parts to him.

As for Cadwaladr, Nergal decreed that for his crimes against humanity Cadwaladr would answer to his own kind and left Maelgwn to nominate his fate.

'I believe Cadwaladr has suffered enough for one lifetime,' Maelgwn advised. 'Due to the part he played in Shamash's downfall, I am willing to grant him a full pardon for his crimes. Provided, of course, that he strives to amend the damage he has done to the Earth and her occupants.'

Vanora and Cadwaladr were well pleased to hear

this. Cadwaladr turned to Maelgwn and held out his hand to him. 'I have never in my life been grateful for anything, but I am most obliged for this.'

'Friends then,' Maelgwn suggested.

'Brothers,' Cadwaladr assured him.

Well then, Nergal announced, *all is well that ends well*.

'My Lord, I beg to differ.' Tory spoke up, for she had Taliesin in her mind urging her to do so.

All those speeches you've been serving me over the ages about how unjust the Gods have been? This might be a good time to get that off your chest, the Merlin advised.

'Tory?' Maelgwn objected quietly. 'We've done well. Don't push it.'

'Done well?' Tory scoffed, 'I hardly think so.' She scaled some of the steps that led to the stage, to where she could address all the Chosen. 'What we've done is solved all the Nefilim's problems and disputes. All through history we've dug their mines, fought their wars, and suffered their wrath and superstitions. And now that they have finally sorted everything out, and can live happily ever after, we are left with an exhausted, dying planet, with air not fit to breathe, water too filthy to drink, and land not fit to produce or mine.'

There's always one in every crowd, Nergal commented to Horus beside him. *And of course, it's the little prima donna who will not even bow before ME, supreme ruler of the heavens*.

'I will bow before you, Sir, when I see your judgments are just, and worthy of respect.'

643

Maelgwn very much wanted to cut in at this point, knowing how powerful the being she addressed truly was. An evil entity like Shamash didn't cower before Nergal for no good reason. But Tory had a beef that she would voice no matter what anybody thought, including himself, so why fight the inevitable?

Ah, you almost make it sound like a challenge, Lamamu. Nergal smiled, thinking her very clever.

'If you find it challenging to be just, I suppose it is,' she told him surely.

Nergal was amused by this woman's whole demeanor. She was forthright, witty and fearless — much like himself. *Am I then to assume that you hold us to blame for your misguided ways and the degenerated state of your home planet?*

'Well, as far as I know, Lord, apes are not prone to killing one another for enjoyment, or destroying their natural environment. The same could not be said of the Nefilim, however.'

Nergal considered this a justified statement. *Monkey see, monkey do, you think? Well, you could be quite right.*

Tory allowed the condescending remark to pass, only because he was agreeing with her.

But you all know better now, is that it? You think the human race would have done a much better job of it if we'd only left you alone? Goddess, I've heard this before.

Tory turned to the rest of the gathering to seek their opinion, which, of course, was unanimous.

Right then. I have the very thing to resolve this dispute once and for all. Nergal seemed rather pleased by the response and stood to announce his proposal. *We have just discovered a small planet in a galaxy not too far from here that is very similar to this planet ten thousand years ago. We have already introduced various forms of flora and fauna, most of which you would be familiar with.*

'Pardon me.' Tory had to cut to the chase. 'Are you offering us our own planet?'

Well, it would be on a trial basis, of say … How long ago, in Gaia orbits, since we first got here? he questioned his associates.

'Four hundred and fifty thousand years ago, give or take a couple thousand years.' Noah spoke up as the Nefilim appeared unable to answer.

Then we shall give you as many orbits to prove your boast, Nergal decided. *If, as you say, you make a better go of it without us, then we will talk ownership.*

Tory didn't have to turn around to learn the rest of the room's thoughts on the matter. Their elation was deafening. Maelgwn grabbed hold of her, excited beyond belief about the deal she'd struck.

Nergal's warriors called the room back to attention and Nergal continued: *You who are the Chosen of the great Enki, and his son, Marduk. I believe you have earned the right to make a new start. The rest of mankind will be left alone henceforth by the Nefilim, to make the most of this world they, at least in part, helped to create. Who knows, maybe the old Gaia will come good after all. Collect your things — size is no object — and return here at dusk for departure. The planet for which you are bound is Kila, which, literally, means 'Gaia's double'. This is the word and the will of the Pantheon of Twelve.*

'So be it!' the room responded.

Tory bowed deeply to Nergal. 'Your decisions are just,' she told him.

It is a relief to hear you say so, Lamamu. Nergal was in good spirits. *I thought you were going to start a rebellion there for a moment.*

'As long as you stick to your end of the bargain, Lord,' she announced in a cheeky fashion, 'you need have no fear of that.'

Although Tory was excited about settling a new planet, she was also the keeper of the Tablet of Destinies, and was therefore bound to consider the fate of the world she would have to leave behind.

Ningal had said she would speak with Gaia's elementals, and urge them to return to this time to assist with the planet's re-growth. As Cadwaladr would be staying, Ningal instructed him in the art of fairy sight. If he played his cards right, he would have many willing helpers to aid him with the restoration of Gaia's natural beauty and health.

Vanora had elected to stay with Cadwaladr, to help repair the wrongs they'd both done the planet at one stage of history or another. Together, these two soul-minds had ultimately been responsible for the sinking of Atlantis and the near ruination of the Dragon's empire in the Dark Ages. Added to Cadwaladr's current crimes against humanity and nature, the pair certainly had much amending to do.

As head of the ICA, Cadwaladr's task was well within his means. The question was, could he be trusted to properly tend and protect the tarnished jewel left in his care? Did he possess the conviction and vision to transform the world's greed into awareness?

Alone in her cabin, Tory consulted the sacred divining tool on the matter. Her head was telling her to stay behind; but that was fear, fear of trusting Cadwaladr. Her heart was urging her to go, as it had been she who had struck the deal with Nergal, and she could hardly see to living up to her end of the bargain if she stayed here.

'But Gaia and her people must be protected too.' Tory closed her eyes, and placed the eye of Ra against her forehead. 'Could Cadwaladr be the one?'

His first ten years with the ICA indicated that he was capable of coordinating world solutions and cooperation. But his last ten years as Cadwaladr, King of Gwynedd, exemplified the barbaric lengths the demi-god could resort to if so inclined.

The small trinket against her forehead expanded and unfolded as it positioned itself before Tory, where she could view it's advice clearly.

In its central triangle she saw Gaia — the cause of her concern. In the triangle pertaining to the best outcome, Tory saw the people of the Earth emerging from their Biodomes into a vast, thriving wilderness outside. In the triangle that divulged the worst outcome she saw the same vision. Tears welled as she viewed the crowning triangle that foretold of what would happen if Cadwaladr was not entrusted with this charge; the planet seen here appeared a dry and wasted place.

'He will succeed.'

With her words, all four sections of the Tablet were suddenly filled with a glowing green presence that radiated light from its core.

Gaia's destiny and your own lie along a different path now, Lamamu.

The three voices of the Triple Goddess — the maiden, the warrioress and the wise woman — were comforting her. *As a protector of humankind, realise that they are far more widespread in the universe than just this small pocket of civilisation. Take our Ark and present it to Cadwaladr, for it will allow you to guide and advise him from your new home on Kila. The Tablet of Destinies will enable you to follow Gaia's progress. This is the will of the Great Houses, Lamamu.*

The glowing green presence burst forth from the tablet, bathing Tory in it's lustre as the loving, calming, empowering energy of the divine quickened her entire being and magnified her senses.

When the powerful life-force retreated, it left Tory revitalized and pulsating with awareness. She realised that Cadwaladr needed love, reassurance, acceptance and forgiveness the same as anyone. With the emotional void in his life filled, he would find the divine in himself, just as the rest of his kindred had.

Go in peace to your new life, knowing that you leave Gaia in the very best of hands. For, more so than anyone, Cadwaladr knows what must be done to solve Gaia's problems and who must be influenced to enable her to heal.

'I see the truth of it,' Tory conceded, her heart and her head at peace with each other. 'As you wish it, great mother, so shall it be.'

Fortunately, the home of Tory's kindred was fully mobile already; the *Goddess* would serve as a marvellous temporary home for them on Kila until they built more permanent dwellings. But theirs was not the only such vehicle to appear out of nowhere. Many other tribes had managed to keep similar observation craft a secret from earthly civilization.

Tory, Brian, Maelgwn and Rhun visited Myrddin's cave at Dinas Emrys to retrieve the remaining twelve wonders of Britain to take with them to their new home. Taliesin and Myrddin had made a gift of the thirteenth treasure, the Chariot, to Noah — their merlin-in-training. They also retrieved the Ark to present to Cadwaladr, as the Goddess had instructed. Tory had half expected to see her parents at the cave, since their goodbye had been cut short by Shamash's devastating arrival. But the cavern of treasures was quiet and empty. Not even Tobias, Myrddin's owl friend, frequented the cave any longer. Once they had collected the twelve treasures and the Ark the cave was devoid of any evidence of the great Merlin's existence.

Alone in his office at the ICA complex in Biodome, London, Cadwaladr gazed out his window over the hustle and bustle of people going about their daily routine. For them, today was just another day in a week like any other. The affairs of interstellar importance that had transpired this fortnight past had been completely life transforming for him, and yet to the remaining population of the planet, it had been just another news story — a hoax to capture the imagination or ignore.

'Ah ... what's up, Doc?' Tory employed her very best Bugs Bunny impersonation to advise Cadwaladr of her presence. He projected the appearance of Doc today — blonde, blue-eyed, slick and businesslike.

He smiled, surprised by her visit, but he did not turn from his view to address her. 'Have you come to lecture me before your departure, Goddess?'

'Hardly. You've done well, Cadwaladr. I am here to reward you.'

He turned and saw an ornate golden treasure that must have materialised with Tory and wondered at its purpose.

'It's a gift,' she caught his mind, 'from the Goddess.'

Cadwaladr cocked an eye; perhaps it was some sort of entrapment device, or a spellcaster.

'It's the Ark ... it was in my father's safekeeping, and now it is in yours.'

The gesture completely overwhelmed Cadwaladr. It was a great honour to be entrusted with such a treasure.

'It has many functions,' Tory informed the dumbfounded recipient. 'It can enable you to speak and visit with us on Kila —'

'You don't trust me.' He assumed the worst reason for being granted such a treasure.

'On the contrary.' She held out her hand to him.

Cadwaladr had to smile at his own apprehension. 'I don't understand.'

'It's very simple, Cadwaladr ... you just take my hand.' She beckoned with her fingers for him to comply.

'But why? To what end?'

Tory rolled her eyes, not really surprised that he still considered her to be a threat. 'I'm just going to show you a safe place to store this. You have nothing to fear.'

The smile on his face broadened, as he transformed into the warrior he truly was. 'Down through the ages I have feared no one. I'm not about to start now,' he assured her, slapping his hand into hers and gripping it tight.

Cadwaladr found himself in a huge cathedral-like room, filled to the rafters with exquisite art, artefacts and furnishings, all of which he could well appreciate being a collector himself. The main feature of the chamber was a huge stone that was inset into the centre of the floor, upon which was carved a Celtic cross.

'This was Taliesin's Otherworldly abode.' Tory found her companion's thunderstruck expression most amusing. 'He has no use of it any longer, but I thought it might suit your purposes well.'

Cadwaladr gulped back the emotion that welled in him — having finally been made privy to the secret place where all his forefather's had been instructed in the greater mysteries. 'I heard the legends about this place when I was a boy in Gwynedd ... but I never imagined that I would ever see it.'

'Taliesin would want you and your descendants to continue to make use of the facilities here. Beyond those doors,' she referred to the double doors at one of the chamber, 'is a whole world of discovery ... all the knowledge that was wrongfully denied you.'

Cadwaladr looked from the doors back to Tory. Such an act of trust confounded all reason. 'After everything I've said and done, you would entrust me with such a place?'

Tory smiled and gave a nod. 'It is the will of the Great Houses, Cadwaladr, that I welcome you home.' With this, Tory approached the huge, dark warrior and embraced him.

Cadwaladr held back a moment. He was so used to her as the enemy, he was startled by the fact that she obviously bore him no malice. 'Tory Alexander, your compassion is a wonder to me.' He let go of his hatred and hugged her back.

'If there's one thing I hate, it's hate. There's no one happier than I that we got to the bottom of all the deception and misunderstanding.' Tory pulled away from Cadwaladr to find him blinking the tears from his eyes.

'I thought I had forgotten how to cry.' He wiped the water from his face, forcing a smile.

'And love, and trust,' Tory added. 'But now you remember, and shall never again forget.'

He nodded in agreement, looking around his new home base. 'On that you have my word.'

'That's all the assurance I need.' Tory placed a hand on his shoulder, and stared up into his dark eyes. 'The Goddess is with you, Cadwaladr. Always was, always will be.'

The statement stirred something deep inside the warrior and he sank to his knees before Tory. 'I am her humble servant.'

'The divine is within you, Cadwaladr.' She crouched down, to avoid his adoration. 'Serve it and the Goddess will be appeased.'

'I am proud of my family,' he advised with absolute conviction, 'and they will be proud of me.'

'You do us proud already, Cadwaladr.'

Tory placed the palm of her hand over his cheek and he leant into her touch, closing his eyes to be relieved by the calming energy it extended him. The guilt and hatred that had possessed his soul for so long seemed to flow from his body with his tears.

But Tory felt more than this. The loneliness the man had endured in twelve hundred years of life and the accumulated bitterness of his abandonment were so all-encompassing that the mother in her was compelled to comfort the child in him. 'Your isolation is at an end.' She hugged him to her. 'You shall never be forced to stand alone again, I swear it.'

'Forgive me.' He'd curled up in a foetal position in Tory's lap and he openly wept.

'All is forgotten … you have only to forgive yourself.' She stroked his hair, and cradled him as he let his pain go.

Cadwaladr was going to be alright.

Back in the Middle East most of the Chosen had already boarded Nergal's huge vessel, but Maelgwn was still on the runway, pacing to and fro. 'What is taking her so long?' His eyes scanned the vast wasteland around him.

'Are you waiting for someone?'

Maelgwn swung round, relieved. 'I was worried. Does all go well with Cadwaladr?'

'All does.' Tory smiled, then, looking around the landing strip, her good spirits dampened. 'He has a huge task ahead of him, I fear. But his hunger for the battle is fueled as always, so he ought to do well, Whether he can induce mankind to come to the party remains to be seen. If Gaia is to heal, it will require the awareness and care of every living soul, not just the crusaders.'

Maelgwn raised his brow, not overly concerned. 'Well, if history proves one thing, it's that Homo sapiens always shine in crisis situations.'

'Well, they'd better,' considered Tory, 'before Gaia is so fed up that she completely rids herself of the torment.'

'It won't come to that ... we shall aid them from Kila.' Maelgwn tried to perk up her spirits.

He knew Tory would miss Gaia for awhile, just as he had, but the universe was an amazing place and there were ever-expanding parts of it to discover and explore. If he could just get Tory on their transport and out of here, he felt sure she would love life outside of this star system.

'Stop worrying,' he encouraged. 'Where's your sense of adventure?' But Tory continued turning in circles, observing the landscape with a rather solemn look on her face.

'My father has never been very sentimental,' she said, suppressing her disappointment down deep to prevent any tears, 'but I really thought that Taliesin would show up to say well done, good-bye ... or something.'

'Why would he think to say goodbye, when he hasn't left.' Maelgwn placed a hand on her shoulder to get her full attention. 'Stop looking outward, Tory. The Merlin is inside now.'

She sniffled. 'It was he who urged me to confront Nergal this morning.'

'And that is just the first of many such urges, I am sure.' He squeezed her shoulders and turned her around. 'Like, right now, I feel certain he is urging us to board this craft.'

Tory submitted with a smile, but then turned back abruptly to wave farewell to the planet of her birth. 'So long Gaia. Ours has been a grand adventure. May the Goddess protect and guide you, for all time.' She bowed, as she would have to her Sensei.

Well done, good-bye … or something.

Tory straightened up at the sound of Taliesin's voice, and could not stop her tears flowing when he was nowhere to be seen.

Gaia has been a truly grand adventure. But a whole new adventure awaits us on Kila. You are beholden to none, Tory Alexander, and a master of your own reality. You must make something of this new-found freedom. So let us go, before you get left behind.

Tory breathed a deep sigh of relief, and with a deciding nod, she took up her husband's hand and made a dash for the transporter beam.

On the first night of their voyage to Kila, the Dragon's kin were to be entertained with a preview of Noah's long-awaited novel.

They gathered in the *Goddess'* rec room for the event, and proved a rowdy bunch to settle down by the time the storyteller finally got up his nerve.

'Before I begin, I wish to dedicate this work to Tory Alexander, my inspiration and saviour.' Noah spurred a round of applause and whistles from the crowd.

'You saved yourself,' Tory corrected. 'All I did was give you a job.'

'You did a lot more than that,' he insisted, but moved on. 'I would also like to dedicate this story to you, the characters, without whom this whole tale would obviously not have been possible.'

His audience outdid themselves with recognition on that score, but fell silent as the lights dimmed.

All that could be seen was Noah's face, illuminated by the light projecting off his computer screen and a candle that sat beside it on the bench. His first words were not read, however. Instead, Noah addressed his audience directly.

'The tale of the origins of the Chosen is as complex and baffling as time itself. For they were the legends and heroes of myth made manifest, and were, among men, righteous kings and philosophers, seers, healers, astronomers, and orators wise. The beginning of the Dragon's line of these immortal warriors can be traced back to one afternoon in Oxfordshire, England. The day of the summer solstice in nineteen ninety three ...'

He looked to his computer and began to read. 'As evening cast its shadow across the horizon ...'

BIBLIOGRAPHY

Ash, David A., *The Vortex*, Golden Path Spiritual Developement Association, Devon, 1991

Ballard, Robert D., *Explorations*, Weidenfeld & Nicolson, London, 1995

Berlitz, Charles, *Doomsday 1999 AD*, Souvenir Press, London, 1981

Bletzer, June G., *Encyclopedic Psychic Dictionary*, Donning Co, Virginia, 1986

Davies, Paul, *About Time*, Simon & Schuster, USA, 1995

Devereux, Paul, *Secrets of Ancient and Sacred Places*, Blandford Press, London, 1992

Devereux, Paul, *Earth Lights Revelation*, Blandford Press, London, 1989

Frederic, Louis, *Dictionary of the Martial Arts*, Athlone Press, France, 1991

Hope, Murry, *Ancient Egypt — The Sirius Connection*, Element Books, Shaftesbury, 1994

Hope, Murry, *Time — The Ultimate Energy*, Element Books, Shaftesbury, 1991

Kerrod, Robin, *The Star Guide*, RD Press, Australia, 1993

Lorie, Peter, *Revelation*, Labyrinth Publishing, UK 1995

Mallove/Matloff, *The Starflight Handbook*, John Wiley & Sons Inc., USA, 1989

Moore, Patrick, *Guinness Book of Astronomy*, Guinness Publishing, U.K., 1995

Plato [Desmond Lee (trans)], *Timaeus and Critias*, Penguin Books, London, 1977

Sitchin, Zecharia, *Stairway to Heaven*, Avon Books, N.Y., 1983

Sitchin, Zecharia, *The 12th Planet*, Avon Books, N.Y., 1976

Sitchin, Zecharia, *The Wars of Gods and Men*, Avon Books, N.Y,. 1985